Michael Morley grew up in and around Manchester. He has written several bestsellers including *Spider* and *Viper* alongside a stellar career in TV production. He has been behind some of the hardest-hitting crime shows on British television including *Murder in Mind, The Hunt for Baby Abbie* and *A Shred of Evidence.* These shows have not only broken boundaries but have also won him awards from both the Royal Television Society and the British Medical Association.

He has three sons and now lives in the Peak District with his family, eleven ducks, a few squirrels, a flock of Canada geese and a fat heron.

Interact with Michael through:
www.michaelmorley.com
Facebook.com/MichaelMorleyAuthor
@spreeauthor
@spreebook
www.spreeincidentroom.com

DROITWICH

MICHAEL MORLEY

SPREE

headline

First published as an ebook serialization in 2013 by
HEADLINE PUBLISHING GROUP

First published in paperback in 2014 by
HEADLINE PUBLISHING GROUP

1

Cataloguing in Publication Data is available from the British Library

ISBN 978 1 4722 1047 0

Typeset in Palatino Light by Palimpsest Book Production Limited,
Falkirk, Stirlingshire

Printed and bound in Great Britain by
Clays Ltd, St Ives plc

Headline's policy is to use papers that are natural, renewable
and recyclable products and made from wood grown in
sustainable forests. The logging and manufacturing
processes are expected to conform to the environmental
regulations of the country of origin.

HEADLINE PUBLISHING GROUP
An Hachette UK Company
338 Euston Road
London NW1 3BH

www.headline.co.uk
www.hachette.co.uk

Acknowledgements

Spree is the thriller that it is because of two very special people, my agent Luigi Bonomi and my editor Vicki Mellor. The best ideas in the book are pretty much all theirs – I just listened and typed. Many thanks to them and to their teams, especially Alison and Ajda at LBA. At Headline my gratitude goes to Emily Griffin and Darcy Nicholson who helped carry the editorial load, Jo Liddiard and Beau Merchant for their fabulous work on Twitter, Facebook and the wonderful www.spreeincidentroom.com site. *Spree* wouldn't have got there without Ant Simnica and Siobhan Hooper, wouldn't have sold without Frances Doyle and Katie Day and wouldn't have been noticed without Caitlin Raynor. Thanks too to 'Scary Jack', Michelle and co. at Everett, Baldwin and Barclay. Finally, thank you Donna, Billy, Elliott and Damian – you make it all worthwhile.

Chapter 1

Psychological profiler Dr Angie Holmes was sprinting.
Not jogging.

Not running.

Flat-out sprinting.

The kind of bust-your-lungs, sweat-yourself-ugly exertion that only happened when she needed to exorcise the ugliest of demons.

The former Californian track star was twenty-eight, but when she was mad or stressed, the years rolled back and she ran like she was seventeen.

Today she was fired up enough to smash a personal best.

Two things were driving her crazy.

First off, the man in her life, FBI Special Supervisory Agent Jake Mottram, had left a message on her phone saying he loved her. In itself, not a bad thing. Except he only said *those words* at a time like this. As he strapped on a Kevlar vest and went gun-to-gun with a Spree.

Sprees were the worst.

A special breed of killer who appeared out of the blue and slaughtered indiscriminately. No rhyme or reason. And since Sandy Hook, Santa Monica and the other public shootings, Jake had been the man in charge of catching the worst of the worst.

The Bureau set up the SKU, the Spree Killer Unit, under direct orders from the White House. Since then, it seemed like Jake worked at least a case a month.

1

Angie broke her stride and put her hands to the back of her head. A bunch of shoulder-length auburn hair had flopped out of its tie band. She fumbled it back in and regained her rhythm. Stretched tense muscles. Stepped up the pace. Felt her heart hammer against her ribs.

All was becoming good.

Adrenaline masked the worry.

She glanced at her wrist as the white line slid towards her Nikes. Five twenty.

Damn.

She could go faster. Faster meant more pain in the body and less in the head. It was a good trade.

Angie breathed deeply. Filled her lungs. Lengthened her stride.

Jake should take a desk job.

The thought came up like a hurdle. He was ten years older than her; the right age for his ass to polish an office chair.

He'd be safe.

She'd stop worrying. They could settle down. Not that he'd ever mentioned doing that. Three years together and not one hint of the M word. In fact, not even the E word. But no worries, they were solid. Of that, she was sure.

Thinking about him threw up a picture of the Spree he was hunting. Corrie Chandler. Former soldier. Former security guard. More bull than man. Now out of work and out of his mind.

A bad combination.

One day after he got laid off, his drunk of a wife walked out on him.

Corrie walked after her.

Shot her in the back.

Pumped a hole through the head of a neighbor stood gawping while gardening the patch of dirt that divided their homes.

Then Corrie got in his old Jeep and disappeared.

After twelve hours of eluding the LAPD, he'd been found by Jake and his team. Hence why Angie was wearing out the track of her local club.

The lap line came into view. She checked her wrist again.

Five zero five.

Christ, she was feeling old. She should be able to bust that five-minute mark. And Jake sure as hell should know it was time he quit the fieldwork and drove a desk. That way he could look after her.

Her and the baby she'd just found out she was carrying.

That was the second thing she was worrying about. That and the fact she hadn't yet found the right moment to tell him.

Chapter 2

Griffith Park, LA

I t looked like a convention of hard asses. Top marksmen from the LAPD and FBI gathered outside the gates of one of America's biggest urban parks. All getting their respective shit together.

Gun checks. Body armor checks. Comms checks.

Check, check, check.

That was what these guys did in the down time. The nervous, laugh-too-loudly time. The last guaranteed moments of your lifetime before stepping into the cross hairs of a crazy with a gun.

Up in the cornflower blue Californian sky, two helicopters hummed and circled like mating dragonflies. Beneath them, staring out at three thousand acres of forests, lawns and trails were the operational heads of SWAT and SKU.

Thirty-eight-year-old FBI Special Agent Jake Mottram stood six five and two hundred pounds. Connor Pryce, the thirty-two-year-old, newly appointed LAPD commander, was seven inches shorter and fifty pounds lighter. Little and large, both licensed to end their mutual problem with deadly force.

As a former soldier, Mottram knew only too well the value of studying the terrain as closely as the psychology of the enemy inhabiting it. He and Pryce had halted their squads at the edge of the Ferndell side of Griffith; a Jurassic Park patch of dense greenery with towering trees and jungle-thick foliage.

The FBI man used field glasses to stare through the gnarled

oaks and leafy undergrowth at a famous building way off in the distance.

The place Corrie Chandler had holed up.

He let the glasses fall from his pale blue eyes and thump on their strings against his broad chest. 'Seems ironic.'

'What does?' Pryce felt edgy and had started to pace.

'Us, observing an observatory.' He pointed into the distance. 'Mr Crazy over there is most probably staring right back at us through a free-standing scope, or even that big Zeiss thing that can watch fleas crap on Mars.'

The cop didn't answer. He was worrying about the press and how they'd crucify him if this didn't end quickly and without any more loss of innocent life.

Jake was relaxed but focused. Totally at home in an environment where shots were likely to be fired at him. He looked around and took in the beauty of the park. 'I came here some time back with my girlfriend. We did all the tourist shit. Used scopes to find the Hollywood sign. Rode white horses down a wooded trail.' He turned to the smaller man. 'You ever been inside the Observatory?'

Pryce had found a thumbnail to chew. 'No. Saw it in *Terminator Salvation*. I think it was even in *The Simpsons*.'

'Man, I love that show. I remember now, they called it the Springfield. I can picture parts of the layout but not all of it. I've got one of our techies pulling together film clips to add to the schematics so everyone knows the place inside out before we go in there.'

Pryce had gotten to worrying about the Spree's background. 'Chandler was military, right?'

'Right.'

'Was he a marksman?'

'No. Just a grunt. But he was in a top outfit.'

'Which?'

'Tenth Mountain.'

'That infantry?'

'And some. As well as mountains, they're specialists in Arctic survival. Real tough mothers. You can lock these guys naked in an ice box and they'll ask you for sunscreen.'

5

Pryce arched an eyebrow. 'Great.'

Jake studied the cop. He was too uptight for a guy of his rank. 'Did you come up through SWAT or through admin?'

'SWAT.' Pryce brushed off the insinuation. He took a second and then decided to come clean. 'Only arrived a year ago, though. I'm what I believe the squad call the "smart" guy.'

Jake laughed. He knew what the phrase meant. Pryce was a desk-jockey. University-educated and fast-tracked to senior command. During an armed raid, he would be the last in and first out. Five years from now, if he lived that long, he'd probably be in the running for chief.

A young agent appeared at their sides. Jenny Dickson blanked the cop and spoke to her boss. 'We've got feeds from the mini-drones, sir. Looks like at least five dead on the observation terrace.'

'Fuck!' Pryce put his hands to his temples as though an explosion had gone off.

Jake's voice stayed measured. 'Were the fatalities in the east or west of the building, Jenny?'

'The east, sir. And we think there's a further fatality just by the entrance for wheelchairs, at the back of the Planetarium.'

He raised his field glasses and studied the white building in the distance. The sun was high and would be casting long shadows for at least another two hours. This was no time to be running an assault. 'We got any eyes and ears in there yet?'

'Ears, yes. We've got dishes up all points of the compass. Our only eyes are the drones.'

Pryce consoled himself out loud. 'At least we got the public clear.'

'Only coz he let us,' added Jake. 'I guess he emptied his anger when he let off that magazine out on the terrace. It gave everyone else a chance to run.'

Pryce squinted up into the sky. 'That a news copter up there?'

Jake swung the glasses to the blue. 'Yeah. Fox's eye in the sky.' He dropped them to his chest again. 'Jenny, get someone to tell the station to shift that bird before I ask the military to do it for them. Have our press people tell the channel heads I don't want pictures of us on screen. Anyone blows you off on that, tell them I said they best book themselves a hospital bed.'

'Sir.'The young agent scurried back to the truck.

Pryce's cellphone rang. He patted down the jacket of his blue suit until he found it. 'Hello?'

Jake watched him again. He was sweating and it wasn't down to the heat of the day. Only time and experience would take nerves like that away. He remembered the first time he'd shot someone. It had been in Afghanistan. A sniper covering a strip of road that wasn't worth jack shit to anyone had killed two members of a three-man unit patrolling it. Jake had been the third. He'd spent the next four hours in the baking sun hunting down that asshole. Then, when he got the jump and it came to pulling the trigger, he'd hesitated. Only for a split second. But long enough for his enemy to spot him and almost get a shot away.

Jake Mottram never flinched again.

By the time he left the army, he'd killed thirty-two people in five different locations.

Pryce finished his call and slid the phone back in his jacket. There was a smile on his face. 'Chandler's made contact. He's on a line from inside the Griffith.'

Chapter 3

LA Athletic Club, LA

Angie showered and toweled dry. She slipped on her brown skirt suit and mentally reran her 'routine' appointment that morning with Bureau doctor Suzie Janner.

The profiler had completed her annual physical and had mentioned – more in passing than anything – that she'd been 'feeling out of sorts'.

Doctors being doctors, Suzie inevitably ran a list of questions about stress, diet and alcohol.

Then she got to pregnancy.

'Pregnancy?' Angie had almost laughed her ass off. 'There's more chance of Jake being pregnant than me. I've been on the pill since I was fifteen and never missed taking one.'

'No contraceptive – except abstinence – is *one hundred* percent effective.' She handed over a testing kit. 'Now go pee.'

Ten minutes and a whole seismic shift in the world later, Angie returned with a blue stick and accepted she was 'with child'.

Fortunately, Suzie Janner was more than her doctor. She was seven years older than Angie but they were friends. Members of the same female business groups. They'd even co-written papers together. In short, she knew her well enough to ask the big question: 'How do you feel about the news?'

Angie stared into space, as though the answer was an elusive star lost in a cloudy night sky.

'Angie?'

'I don't know. I really don't know.' She'd finally looked at her friend. 'Is that pathetic? I mean, what do people usually say?'

'Usually?' Suzie had smiled reassuringly. 'There's no such thing as usually. If the pregnancy hasn't been planned, then the reaction is often the same as yours.'

Angie nodded sadly. 'I feel bad.'

'Bad *how*? Sick bad?'

'No. Screwed up in my head bad. *Guilty* bad.'

'Guilty?'

'Yeah. Not getting pregnant is kind of thought of as the woman's job . . .'

Suzie shot her a stern look of disapproval.

'And I feel bad about feeling confused. I mean, I should either be overjoyed, right? Or –' she struggled to complete her thought – 'or I guess we should be talking termination.'

'We shouldn't be talking anything. Not yet. You should just be absorbing the news. Getting used to it. Thinking about what it means to you – not only in the next months and years, but for the rest of your lifetime.'

'You mean I should think like a psychologist not a shell-shocked lunatic?'

Suzie laughed. 'Something like that. There's really no mad rush. Take your time. Get used to the idea *then* decide. You're what – twenty-seven?'

'Twenty-eight. Twenty-nine in a month.'

'Still young. You ever thought about being a mother? Just before thirty is a good age.'

'Hell, no!' Angie responded more strongly than she'd meant to. Of course she'd thought about it. But not long enough to get used to the idea. 'Suzie, you know my background.' She slid her gaze to the thick file on the desk. 'It's all in those notes. Parenthood is *not* something I was cut out for.'

'That's nonsense. You're the shrink, not me. You know that having an abusive father doesn't mean you're going to be abusive yourself. You're not some poor, weak-willed waif, caught in a deprived and unbreakable circle. You're one tough lady who's kicked ass all her life.'

9

'I know all that. It's just that, being a mom –' saying the words out loud shocked Angie – '*being a mom* will open doors to rooms I had shut. Locked and nailed up for good. Living through a new childhood might make me live through my own, and I don't want that.'

'Motherhood might be the greatest thing that ever happened to you. It was for me.'

'Was it?' She sounded skeptical.

'Absolutely.' She eyed a silver-framed photo of a gap-toothed blonde girl on her desk. 'I'd die for Bethan. She's just everything.' She enjoyed the thought of her daughter before she moved on. 'You won't have to give anything up, Angie. You've got a great career – *and* a great guy from what I hear. Now, if you want it, you can be a great mom as well.' She smiled warmly. 'Most people would say that's game, set and match. But listen, it's really all down to what *you* want. Don't let me, Jake or anyone pressure you.'

'Jeez, I haven't even got round to thinking about Jake.'

'How do you imagine he'll take it?'

She widened her eyes and shrugged. 'God knows. He's as much a screw-up as I am. No parents. Orphanage and army raised – and you know what that means.'

'Emotionally locked in.'

'Hard as marble, stubborn as a mule.'

Suzie felt obliged to bring some balance. 'He's also a war veteran. Purple heart hero. Decorated by the freakin' President. I mean, what kid wouldn't want him as Pop and you as Mom?'

Angie scratched at her neck until she felt raw. A nervous habit since childhood. 'Do you have to tell McDonald about this?'

Suzie looked sympathetic. 'I can't keep it out of the report, and the Assistant Director is certain to read it. But I *can* hold back the file for a few days.' She tipped her head to a mountain of paperwork. 'It needn't get put through until all that's cleared.'

'Thanks.'

The physician sensed it was time to change the subject. She picked up the results of the medical. 'Aside from the pregnancy, you're in great shape. Bloods are good. Heart and lungs of a teenager. Protein count and cholesterol better than fine. You get a clean bill of health from me, Doctor Holmes.'

'Thank you, Doctor Janner.' Angie stood and pinned on a smile. 'Anything I *can't* do, given the *development*?'

'*Development*?' The word made her smile. She pulled a stack of leaflets out of a tray. 'Read and digest. Main thing is don't smoke and you don't, so no problem there. Oh, and cut out the alcohol. All of it.'

'Shit.'

Suzie hiked an eyebrow. 'Yeah, that one hurt me too.'

Angie took the leaflets and slid them into her purse. 'Can I run?'

'No problem. Watch the weights, though. Technically, even that's okay at this stage. I just suggest you be sensible.'

'Sensible would have been not getting banged up.' She glanced at her watch and then looked up with bravery in her eyes. 'I'm gonna go tell Jake straight away.'

'Best of luck.'

All that had been some hours back.

Only Jake hadn't been around to tell.

His cell had been turned off.

Never a good sign.

When she'd called his unit they'd told her exactly where he was and she'd felt sick to the pit of her stomach.

A Spree.

The thought had made her dizzy. For an hour, she'd sat and watched the news in her office, and then she'd headed to the track.

Only it hadn't made things better like it normally did.

And now she was at her wits' end.

Angie Holmes, seven weeks pregnant, stared at herself in the locker room mirror. She smoothed her skirt and turned sideward on.

There was nothing to see.

But she felt something. Not a stirring inside her body, but something in her soul. Something she'd never felt before.

Chapter 4

Griffith Park, LA

'I'm going to kill every motherfucking one of you.' Corrie Chandler
screamed the threat down the phone. He stood, shaking, inside an
office in the Observatory. Blue veins on his neck twitched like baby
snakes. 'I mean it, man, I'm gonna take down any cocksucking one of
you who tries to come in here.'

Jake listened impassively on a speakerphone in the armored
command truck. He didn't interrupt. Didn't hang up. Nor did he try
to reason with Chandler or talk him down.

'You listening to me, cop? I am *not* fooling.'

'I'm not a *cop*.' Jake calmly stressed the last three letters, just enough
to separate himself from the perceived 'enemy'. 'I'm ex-army, Corrie,
just like you are.'

'Then you're friggin' *nothing*. Coz that's what I am.' There was a
whole book of grievance bound in those few words. 'That's how this
freakin' country sees me.'

'Not true, buddy. Not those who served. They *get* you. They understand every blunderfuck moment you're living through.' He stopped
and waited for a rant.

It didn't come.

It meant Jake had his attention. There might yet be a way to end
this without more bloodshed. He shut his eyes and pictured the scene.
'I'm thinking, Corrie, that right now you've got the phone trapped
between your ear and neck and you're wondering how the fuck you

ended up in this shit. My bet is there's a weapon cradled in your hands and the safety's off. You're probably pressed tight to a wall, squinting out the window, getting twitchy every time the light changes or a bird flies by.' He stopped again. Waited for a contradiction that didn't come, then added, 'They're gonna come for you, Corrie. Hell, you know that. You're high up, looking down on everyone, like King Gun on a hill. But you know the routine, don't you, buddy? Snipers rule the day. Commandos rule the night. Come the blackness they'll slither in there and bring you down.'

Jake let the words sink in and listened hard.

Through the black silence of cyberspace, Chandler's shallow breaths broke cover. They came out one by one. Surrendered all his hopes.

'How long did you serve, Corrie?'

The breaths ran back and hid. Made space for an easy answer. It came in a sad and reflective voice. 'Three years, one month, two days.'

'Notes I've got said you were Tenth Mountain. Man, that's a hell of a unit.'

'Sure is. Had some good brothers there. Some bad sonsofbitches too. And you?'

'Marines then MARSOC, best part of a decade.'

Chandler blew out a long sigh of admiration. 'Brother, you must have faced some motherfucking times in special ops command.'

Jake laughed. 'I did, but sometimes it seems a whole world tougher out here than it was in service. You know what I mean?'

There was a pause, then came the answer, creaking with pain and emotion. 'Yeah, I sure do, man. However Fucked Up Beyond All Recognition it was in there, it's doubly FUBAR out here.'

The chat was easy now. Two vets at a bar downing beers. Buddies in the making. 'So why'd you quit, Corrie? You were doing damned good with a bang stick in your hand.'

A pained laugh rolled down the line.

'I pulled your sheets,' added Jake. 'You were A-okay, man. I would have been more than proud to have served with you.'

'I quit because of a whole lot of shit, but mostly coz the woman I loved asked me. Said she *missed* me.' He put on a sarcastic emphasis.

'Wanted me *home*. Anyways, I came out and me and Carlyann got married. Took a job working security. Working freaking *see-cure-it-eey*.'

'No shame in that, my friend. I've done a shift or ten myself.'

'That's what I kept telling myself. Said at least it was a job. Something to build on. Only nothing got built. Just the opposite. Everything fell apart and turned to shit.'

Pryce passed Jake a note. It read: WE'VE TRACED THE ROOM HE'S IN. KEEP HIM TALKING. I'LL GET MEN BLIND SIDE.

Jake nodded.

Chandler was still venting about the bad old days. 'Carlyann – she started wanting more. Had some fancy friends with good jobs. Said I should work hard – like her sister's husband Ralph. *Fucking Ralph*. You know what Ralph does for a living? I'll tell you. He's a *proctologist*. You know what that is? A frigging ass doctor.' Chandler laughed. The kind of laugh that was only an octave away from an hysterical cry. 'Then I get laid off. Chopped like liver. Guess how the bastards done it?' Anger started to boil in his voice again. 'I'll tell you. They sent me a text. You believe that?'

Jake actually couldn't. 'No, man, I can't.'

'A freaking text. Then the bitch walked out. One-time "love of my life" said she was gonna find herself "a real man". One who could *provide* for her.' He waited for Jake to coax out more of his vitriol.

The FBI man stayed silent.

'You still listenin'?'

'I feel for you, Corrie. More bad luck in a couple of years than most folk get in a lifetime.' Jake let silence lap down the line, then made his play. 'You want me to come and get you out of there? No other fuckers. Just me.'

Jake listened for the shallow breaths.

None came.

'Corrie?'

'I'm *thinking on things*.'

Jake knew he couldn't let the guy dwell on it. Crazy minds quickly went back to crazy thoughts. 'I got to press you, man. Your war's over. Best I can do is come in and walk you out of there without anyone else getting hurt.'

The silence fattened out. Bloated so much it seemed like it'd burst.

'Come on, Corrie, it's decision time. You don't want SWAT on you. That's no way for grunts like you and me to sign off. No dignity. No courage. And here's the rub, some of those guys you might shoot are ex-army too. Done their time like us. A few of them are even moonlighting security jobs to make ends meet.'

'I don't want to kill no one else.' There was remorse in the voice. The adrenaline had worn off. He was starting to think straight.

'That's good, Corrie. I'm glad you said that.'

Jake's big fear was that Chandler's mood could swing like a teeter-totter. Tilt one way and he'll kill himself. Tilt to the other and he'll go out all guns blazing. Somehow he had to keep him stable. 'Give me a couple of minutes, then I'm going to come in the front door, Corrie. It'll be just me. There'll be no gun in my hand and I'm hoping none in yours.'

Chapter 5

FBI Field Office, LA

Angie took her worries and confusion back to her desk. She sat in a trance opposite her long-suffering research assistant, a gorgeous geek she'd picked as an intern back at Quantico. Now she and 'Chips' were more like brother and sister than colleagues.

The smart young man had been christened Oscar Edgar Chipstone. But, to his great relief, no one had called him that since kindergarten. Not even his mom and pop, the misguided English teachers who'd thought Oscar – as in Wilde – and Edgar – as in Poe – were cool names to give a kid in a roughneck neighborhood full of Duanes and Kurts.

The tall, thin, lank-haired twenty-four-year-old was pre-destined to *earn* the Chips moniker because of his passion for computing and all things technological.

He was dressed today in the blue jeans and the matching sneakers he always wore. The only thing that visibly changed with Chips was his T-shirts. He had a vast closet of plain Ts, all bearing different slogans he'd made up. Angie's favorite this week had been IS GOD A CHICKEN OR AN EGG?

'You okay, Doc?' He looked at her in a way that said he knew she wasn't.

As the words fogged across the room, she realized she'd been staring absent-mindedly his way. 'Yeah, I'm good.'

'You worrying about Agent Mottram?'

'Guess so. How about you go buy us espresso and ice cream?' It was her panacea for all ills. She pulled her purse from beneath the desk. 'As bitter and sweet as you can get.'

He dragged his FBI sweatshirt off the back of the chair. 'Whatcha want, chocolate brownie, tutti frutti, minty chip?'

She handed over a twenty. 'Sounds good.'

'Which?

'The lot. I'm comfort eating.'

'Gotcha.' He squeezed out a wink and vamoosed.

Angie turned to the work on her desk and tried to forget everything else. A few days back she'd been called by cops in West LA about a serial rape. They'd finally got round to sending the papers they'd promised.

The file was phonebook thick. Four women, all Caucasian, all over sixty-five, raped in or near their homes. The work of a true sicko. One she feared would end up as a killer.

The MO had been so similar the cops hadn't needed a profiler to tell them it was a Serial. The UNSUB always attacked the women from behind – their dresses or tops were pulled over their heads – then he bundled them to the floor and attacked them. According to the medical reports, there'd been no penile penetration. They'd been violated with a pointed stave of rough wood approximately two inches square and at least a foot long. The docs had settled on the dimensions by combining six inches' worth of internal injuries with the fact that if the average man gripped a piece of wood the width of his hand it would take up at least five inches.

Angie's expertise was in profiling serial sexual offenders and she always went about it in a highly methodical way. While cops searched first for forensics, she was more interested in signature actions and MO.

MO she defined as 'learned behavior' – what the offender knew he *had* to do to commit the crime. Signature was not what had been practical and necessary, but what he'd *wanted* to do to satisfy himself. It gave away his personality and clues to his identity.

In this case, the *signature* was not the wood but the penetrative use of the stave. It hinted at possible impotence, sexual inexperience, and most of all a wild anger towards women.

17

The TV in her office was still tuned to a news channel but muted. Every minute or two, Angie glanced at the screen, feeding her anxiety.

A caption crawled across the bottom of frame.

BREAKING NEWS.

She thumbed up the sound.

A young woman with dark hair and a pretty pixie-face was at Griffith Park. The dome of the Observatory jutted above her left shoulder. On the other side flashed the word LIVE. She wore a red jacket and vanilla shirt that Angie reckoned should have been buttoned up some more. Another caption slapped on-screen and named her as SOFIE SANDHOLT. She took a cue in her ear-piece and started a piece-to-camera.'There's been a dramatic development in the hunt for spree killer Corrie Chandler, who yesterday shot dead his wife Carlyann, their seventy-year-old neighbor Russell Rayner, and then earlier today fired shots in the Griffith Park Observatory building behind me – the place where he has been cornered by law-enforcement.'

A photograph of Jake hit the screen.

Angie felt her nerves prickle.

'Special Agent Mottram, the head of the FBI's Spree Killer Unit, has been drafted into the hunt to bring it to an early conclusion. The former purple heart war hero has been working closely with the LAPD's newly appointed SWAT commander, Connor Thomas Pryce.'

Up came video of the blue-suited cop arriving in a black and white cruiser earlier that day. He looked lean and slick. *Too* slick for Angie's liking.

'Pryce and his team are widely regarded as the finest special weapons and tactical firearms unit in the country. Minutes ago he spoke exclusively to me.'

Angie shook her head and wondered what Miss Pixie Face had promised in return for the scoop.

The cop came back on-screen, dressed in combat blacks, stood by the open door of an ops truck. Monitor screens flashed in the darkness of the vehicle as he looked beyond the reporter and straight into the camera.'I am confident that this terrible incident will soon be resolved and then we will have the time to pay our proper respects to the families who have lost loved ones today – my heart goes out to them and I know they'll be in all our prayers tonight.'

Sofie had a question, and a good one too. 'Can you confirm reports that Mr Chandler discharged a firearm inside the Observatory and took at least one more life?'

Pryce didn't flinch. 'I *can* confirm that a weapon was fired by Mr Chandler. According to witnesses, at least one person was hit as crowds fled the building. I *can't* confirm the state of the victim or whether there have been any fatalities inside the building. You must understand, even if there have been, we will want to try to identify those people and contact their relatives before we talk publicly to you or anyone else about it.'

'I *do* understand that and I'm sure everyone watching does. Commander, can you give the people of LA any more of an idea of how and when this incident will be resolved?'

'Quickly – and I hope, peacefully. I've just authorized an initiative which I am certain will close this sorry chapter in our city's history. Now if you'll excuse me, I have to go.'

Pryce peeled away and the reporter did her best not to look too smug as she launched into another direct piece-to-camera. 'Well, I recorded that interview just ten minutes ago and since then there has been the significant movement SWAT team leader Pryce promised. Our eye-in-the-sky copter has just picked up these dramatic pictures.'

Aerial footage hit the screen along with a burst of copter noise.

The images were shaky but still clear enough to cause Angie to go slack-jawed.

She closed her eyes and wished she was mistaken about what she'd just seen.

One thing was for sure, this siege wasn't likely to end without violence.

Chapter 6

Griffith Park, LA

The California sun stayed mercifully hidden behind a mess of scrambled cloud as Jake Mottram started his long, solitary trudge towards the Observatory perched high on a hill.

Eyes straight ahead, he kept a soldierly watch on the row of main level windows. Somewhere behind the shimmering black panes, Corrie Chandler was looking back at him – down the barrel of a gun.

The SKU boss had started his approach from way, way back. He wanted to make sure he could be *seen* to be alone and unthreatening. He guessed Chandler would pick him up as he rounded the Astronomer's Monument and hit the path that led to what locals called the Solar System Lawn.

As he closed on the north doors, Jake struck up more of a march than a walk. It was important Chandler saw a fellow soldier proudly and bravely coming to meet him, not an armed cop sneaking slowly his way.

He kept a steady pace. Didn't break rhythm. Not even when a copter stupidly circled lower than it had been cleared to. His arms stayed straight and swung high, while his hands remained open-fingered and clearly weapon-free.

Path dust kicked over the bottom of his black boots and combat pants. There was no weapon tucked into the back of his belt. But down the right sleeve of his black tunic was a throwing knife that could be in his hand and through Chandler's chest within a second.

A Kevlar vest covered Jake's upper torso, but he wore no helmet and no shades. His eyes were going to be key weapons in this skirmish and he didn't want them holstered.

The grounds had been cleared by the cops and there was a strange emptiness in the air. Flocks of birds pecked opportunistically on the strangely deserted lawns and pathways as they devoured scraps dropped by tourists.

Wings clattered as they rose to escape Jake's advancing feet.

His eyes fell on the steps in front of him. From this point, he was only seconds away from entering the Observatory.

The internal plans he'd studied flashed into his mind. He remembered briefly where he'd stood with Angie when they'd visited. The quality of the light, the height of the ceilings, the width of the corridors. With each stride he mentally visited an extra square yard of the Observatory.

Dark clouds ominously snuffed out the last light of the sun as Jake climbed the steps.

Somewhere on the other side of the thick stone walls, Chandler would be sliding away from his window. Deciding whether he was ready to surrender or not.

The big north doors were unlocked.

He pushed them open and shouted, 'Corrie, it's Jake Mottram. I'm alone – like I said I'd be. I'm *coming in*, to help you.'

The entrance hall was cold and eerily quiet for a public building. Up ahead was the gently swaying Foucault Pendulum, a mesmerizing two-hundred-and-forty-pound sphere of brass on a cable forty feet long swinging in a constant direction while the earth turned beneath it.

To the left was the deserted ticket office.

To the right an unmanned information desk.

Jake heard the squish of his rubber soles on the hard floor as he rounded the Pendulum.

On the vaulted ceiling was the Observatory's greatest treasure: the Hugo Ballin Murals. Images of classical celestial mythology hovered over him. Powerful gods tracked his every move.

Jake had almost forgotten how damned big this place was. The space made him a sitting duck for any half-decent shot, and Corrie Chandler was dangerously more than half-decent.

He found the stairs to the lower level.

As he descended, his hearing heightened and his footsteps lightened. He looked for shadows on the wall as he spidered down the steps.

Pryce's team had traced the call to an admin office at the bottom of the stairwell, close to a corridor exhibition called the Cosmic Connection. It was likely he was still there. From Jake's experience, once Sprees made contact, they more or less settled where they were. It was a stage known as 'the root before the shoot'.

The FBI man reached the bottom of the staircase, stopped and rubbed an itch on his right arm. At least that's what it looked like. He lifted the knife from its Velcro strap and felt cold steel against warm flesh. He palmed the blade as he raised his hands above his head and shouted again. 'I'm coming for you, Corrie. I'm unarmed and my hands are high.'

Jake took the steps two at a time. Measured, not fast, just like his heartbeat.

At the bottom, he turned and called down the cool, shadowy corridor. 'Where are you, buddy? Tell me where you are so I can help you finish this up.'

A shadow drifted on the floor.

'I'm here, motherfucker!'

A weapon cocked.

'Right behind you.'

Chapter 7

FBI Field Office, LA

The tub of ice cream had melted into cold slop.

Angie had spent the last ten minutes glued to the live news bulletin and hadn't had a spoonful.

Jake was walking up to the Griffith.

On his own.

The word *'idiot'* popped from her mouth. 'What in God's name do you think you're doing?'

She already knew the answer. He was trying to save the Spree and had figured the best way to do it was unarmed and on his own. *Psychologically* it made sense, but not emotionally. *Emotionally*, his selfless act was breaking her heart.

Chips put a spare chair close to the TV. 'If you're going to worry, you may as well sit down and do it.'

'Thanks.' She eased herself down, her eyes never leaving the screen. Pixie-faced Sofie was jabbering excitedly over the footage, but Angie wasn't listening. She was studying the body language of the father of her unborn child. Watching him control his nerves. Suppress his fears.

As Jake entered the building, the TV news anchor unnecessarily stressed the drama of the development, then crassly announced a commercial break.

Chips put his hands on Angie's shoulders and offered words of factual reassurance. 'Statistically, Special Agent Mottram has the most successful and injury-free clean-up rate in the Bureau. Case by case, there have been almost twenty percent fewer injuries on those *he* has worked than any other field agent—'

'Shut up.'

'Sorry.' He took his hands away and cleared the tub of melted ice cream from her desk. 'You want me to try to refreeze this?'

'No, thanks.' She realized he was being sweet but would only fuss unless she distracted him. 'I'm sorry I snapped. It'd be good if you got crime stats on the areas where the old women were attacked. We still have a case of our own to work.'

'Sure.'

'And split them out – violent, non-violent, burglary, theft, and all types of sexual.'

'I'm on it.' He headed to the galley kitchen at the bottom of the corridor to dump the trash and grab some bottled waters.

The commercials finished.

The news restarted with a shot of the middle-aged anchor recapping the day's events.

Angie shifted in her seat.

The anchor handed back to the live outside broadcast.

She could tell from the look on Pixie's face that serious shit was going down.

The reporter glanced nervously around; her eyes more off-camera than on.

Angie read the signals.

There'd been a death.

She was sure of it.

Chapter 8

Griffith Park, LA

Jake kept his hands high and turned slowly.

Chandler was five yards away. A Remington pump action shone in the space between them.

The cops had missed it.

Their intel had said that the former soldier had only two registered weapons, both Glocks. There had been no mention of a blast-a-hole-in-your-gut shotgun.

The SKU man stared at the barrel of the 870. It was spirit-level straight and still as a statue. Not a twitch of nerves.

He slid his gaze up to Chandler's face. It was scarlet. Flushed with blood. He guessed the dude's heart was beating double quick. The old soldier was out on the edge but still holding his shit together.

Just.

'I'm Jake.' He spoke casually, as non-threatening as someone his size could manage. 'We talked on the phone.' He nodded to the gun. 'You have to let me help you.'

Sweat popped on Chandler's forehead. 'An' what if I don't want helpin'?'

Jake took a gamble. Sneaked a pace towards him, hands still surrender high and behind his head. 'Then one of us is going to die.'

'Don't take another fucking step!'

The barrel shook now. Wavered like a sapling in a storm. He was only a twitch away from snagging the trigger.

'Corrie—'

'Stay the fuck away from me, man!'

Five yards separated them. A good distance for a knife. Jake looked into Chandler's eyes. Pupils were blown big. The brows above them were pitched high. His sweat-beaded forehead was corrugated with stress.

Chandler swallowed a lump in his throat. He knew the ball was in his court. 'Turn around. Face the other way and kneel down.'

'That's not going to happen, soldier.' Jake's eyes were battlefield cold. 'You want to shoot me, you look me in the face and do it.' He gently slid his left hand from behind his head and held it out, open-palmed. 'It's time for you to give me your weapon, Corrie.'

The sweat beaded some more and rolled from forehead to cheek.

'Give me the gun, Corrie.' He could see Chandler was stuck in a mental no man's land. He didn't want to be in this mess.

'Come on, buddy,' Jake said it in as friendly a way as he could, 'we're all done here. It's over now.'

Down the corridor came a dull thump.

Chandler's head swiveled.

They both knew what it was.

Cops.

They'd come through a window.

The Spree lumbered out of limbo. There was no way back. The only option was to scatter lead.

Thuff!

Jake's knife hit Chandler in the face.

Three inches of blade spiked his nose and stuck in skull bone.

Chandler screamed and fired wildly at the ceiling.

Plaster fell like rain as Jake dropped his left shoulder and threw a high kick at Chandler's Remington.

The shotgun clattered against a wall.

Chandler was spurting blood through clasped hands and groaning in agony.

Jake grabbed him by the throat. 'It's okay, soldier. Go easy.' He hooked a heel behind the wounded man's legs and guided him to the floor.

The first SWAT figure appeared. He was in full combat gear, face masked, assault rifle sweeping left and right.

Jake knelt on Chandler's chest, pulled the knife out and stepped away. He wiped blood from the blade and glared at the armed cop.

It was Pryce.

He'd gloried up and come in front of queue.

The FBI man shook his head. 'You fucking idiot.'

The cop looked confused. More black figures materialized.

'I had him under control, this could have ended easy.' Jake decided to go before he really lost his temper. 'Fix Chandler's bleeds and get him out of here.' He punched a finger on Pryce's visor glass. 'And you'd best stay the fuck away from me until I've found the gift of forgiveness.'

Chapter 9

FBI Field Office, LA

The TV in Angie's office showed footage from a news copter filming with a long lens. It wasn't billed as 'live' but she could see it was only minutes old.

Black figures with SWAT emblazoned on their backs roped their way down onto the center of the observation terrace where she'd once walked. No sooner had their feet found the deck than they split in opposite directions and took up positions by windows.

There was the muffled bang of a shotgun being fired.

Angie found she'd put her hand to her mouth in shock.

The TV pictures cut to a bland, high shot of the Observatory and surrounding gardens.

Angie guessed the copter pilot had suddenly been ordered out of restricted airspace.

A single shot.

Jake had been unarmed.

That meant he must be the target.

SWAT breached the building.

She was aware of Chips moving closer. Getting ready to console her.

The aerial was followed by cutaways of cops and agents at command trucks.

'He'll be okay.' Chips squeezed her shoulders from behind.

Angie said nothing.

Sofie the Pixie came back in vision, looking startled. She jabbed a finger in her ear and listened to her studio director as she spoke. 'I am being told that the images you just saw effectively signaled the end for spree killer Corrie Chandler. A few moments ago, SWAT leader Connor Pryce got his man. But not without bloodshed.'

Angie felt a stab in her heart.

'LAPD SWAT entered the building just as Chandler discharged a weapon at FBI Agent Jake Mottram.'

'Sweet Jesus.' Angie felt her legs shake.

New footage hit the screen.

Shaky exteriors shot high and wide from the copter.

The reporter strung her voice under the unfolding action. 'What you are seeing here is Agent Mottram, one of the heroes of the hour, returning to the operations cordon.'

Angie almost collapsed from the release of tension.

'While he escaped uninjured, former soldier Corrie Chandler clearly did not. He is now being brought out of the Observatory on a medic's trolley. This is Sofie Sandholt, live – thank goodness – from Griffith Park.'

'I told you not to worry,' said Chips triumphantly.

Angie grabbed her cellphone. She speed-dialed Jake's number.

It was engaged.

She hung up and hoped.

It rang in her hand. Caller display said it was him. She almost hit the wrong button keying it through. 'H'lo – are you okay?'

He sounded relaxed. Like his car might have blown a tire and he was waiting for the repair crew. 'Yeah, I'm *fine*. Not a scratch. Cops made it a bit gnarlier than it should have been, but everything's cool now.'

'*Cool?* What you did was mad, Jake. I get the reason why, but it was crazy.'

'The whole job's crazy, honey. That's why I do it. I just didn't want to see another screwed-up army guy coming out in a police body bag.' He knew how to curtail her lecture. 'Hey, you fancy going somewhere special – *really special* – tonight?'

She knew he was unwinding in his own way. Coming down from

all the immense tension and fear in his highly controlled and emotionally tight manner. 'Why wouldn't I? *Really special* is something always worth fancying.'

Chips was earwigging and gave her an approving glance.

'I need to go out,' Jake added. 'Celebrate the good luck of being alive and in one happy, healthy piece. I've been taking things like that too much for granted.'

Angie thought about giving him a psychological explanation for why being close to death had made him feel more alive, but skipped it. 'We are both lucky. Much luckier than we often realize.'

'I'm gonna wrap things up here, then I'll come back and change. What time d'you think you'll be free?'

She looked at the stack of case papers and decided she'd have to take some home with her. 'Seven-thirty, eight.'

'You got it.'

Angie stared at the dead phone. She'd wanted to add 'I love you' but hadn't. Like a lot of things, it had gone unsaid.

She put the receiver down and for the first time noticed the slogan on Chips's T-shirt. It said SPEAK NOW, OR FOREVER HOLD YOUR PEACE.

Chapter 10

Santa Monica, LA

Jake booked a late table at Veros.

It had two Michelin stars and was the kind of joint they'd never normally visit on their paychecks.

It was quintessentially French, with wainscoted walls, starched white cloths and gleaming silver. A single rose held center stage on every candlelit table, and classical music played at just the right level to fill dead air but not intrude unless you wanted to listen.

They were shown to a place at the window. One with a view of the bay and a sunset that made the sky look like it was lit by pink and purple neons.

Thierry, the maître d', let them settle. He gave them the cards and a warm smile. 'The patron, Monsieur Veros, recognized you and asked me to send his regards.' He turned sideward to reveal a dark-suited, dapper man in his mid-sixties sat at a single table in the corner. He nodded in their direction.

Jake and Angie nodded back.

Thierry continued, 'It would be the delight of the house if you would be so kind as to dine at our expense tonight.' He floated a hand across the menus he'd just placed on the table. 'Whatever you like. Please do not spare any extravagance. There will be no check for you.'

He drifted away before they could argue.

Jake grabbed the menu, like a kid finding a gift on a day that wasn't a birthday or Christmas. 'How kind is that?'

31

Angie coolly flipped open the card. The generosity was a distraction from the big news she'd planned to break. She examined the nine-course menu découverte and couldn't help but splutter when she saw the price. 'Six hundred dollars! My God, did you know these prices before you booked?'

He laughed at her. 'No. I was planning not to look until after we'd eaten.' He opened the wine list and sighed. 'Do you think he really meant we can order *anything*?'

'That's what the man said.' Her smile slipped as she realized he was going to order wine and she wouldn't be able to drink it, then he'd ask why she was abstaining and she'd be stuck for words.

Jake's head stayed buried in the list. 'Man, there's champagne on here for ten thousand bucks a bottle. Jeez, the house fizz is two hundred bucks.' He dropped the card on the table and seemed to have been exhausted by the prices. 'We'll have that. I'm sure it's amazing.' He looked across the immaculate linen and saw something was troubling her. Years together had taught him that a look like that usually meant he had screwed up somewhere.

The penny dropped.

He hadn't asked about her day. Her case. Her work.

Everything had been about him. Given the kind of freaks she chased, her afternoon had probably been almost as bad as his.

'Hey, I'm sorry.' The look on his face backed him up. 'Sprees get me hyped up and very self-focused. I should have asked earlier. What was your day like, what have you been working on?' Then he remembered what she'd said when they'd parted that morning and he felt a cold jolt of worry. 'Hell, you had a physical today – are you all right?'

The sommelier arrived before she could answer.

'Have you decided on the wine, sir? Or can I be of assistance?'

Jake turned his head to a smart young man in black dinner suit and bow tie. 'Just the house champagne and some still water, please.'

'Thank you, sir.' He took the list back and slid elegantly away.

Jake waited until he was out of sight and leaned across the table. 'Is there something wrong, Ang?'

The moment had gone.

She couldn't tell him.

Not here. Not now.

She'd hoped they'd have a lovely meal and then right at the end she'd find the perfect moment to tell him. 'No, nothing's wrong. I'm fine. I passed the physical, no problem.' She carried on talking just in case the secret came out. 'Suzie Janner said I was as fit as a teenager. She told me I –'

Her silence worried him. 'What?'

'She told me I was fine.' Angie smiled away the stumble. 'Let's choose the food. We can talk when we've decided what we're going to eat.'

He knew he was being scammed but couldn't figure out why. 'Sure, let's do that.'

She tried to lose herself in the menu. If the food lived up to the descriptions then it was going to be astonishing. After an agony of indecision she settled on *Terrine de betteraves, burrata, sorbet au raifort* – a terrine of baby beets, burrata and horseradish sorbet – followed by *Filet de saumon, pomme et jus de verveine* – salmon with apple and lemon verbena. 'What you gonna have, Jake?'

The lack of any response made her look up.

He was staring at her.

Oddly.

'What's wrong?'

'Nothing.'

She checked the top of her sleeveless black dress to see if she'd popped a button. 'What is it, what are you looking at?'

'You. You and how beautiful you are.'

She felt relieved. And pleased. Jake didn't often say things like that. He was a locked-up guy. Awkward when it came to talking about his feelings or trying to pay a compliment. Which made it all the sweeter when he managed the odd romantic line or two.

'As I walked up those steps at the Griffith, all I could think of was you.' He felt far away. Back in the park, treading the path with the flocks of pecking birds scattering from his feet and the sun sinking behind the blackening clouds. 'I almost turned around, Angie, and went back to the holding cordon . . .' He dried up mid-sentence.

She waited but the rest didn't come. 'Why?' She tried not to sound like a therapist.

He shrugged his big shoulders. 'I guess I felt selfish.' He knew she needed some more explanation. 'I just couldn't bear the thought that I might never see you again.'

She huffed out a laugh. 'That's not you being selfish – you know what *that* is.' Her eyes teased him. Prompted him to come right out and say it.

But he couldn't.

Not face to face.

Over the phone was okay – more than okay. But not in person. He'd never said such a thing to anyone else in his life and couldn't yet say it in person.

Jake reached across the table and took her hands.

Angie looked up and caught his eye. 'It's okay to say it, Jake. You won't fall apart if you do.'

He felt as though he might. He looked away. Down at the tablecloth.

She waited until his head rose. His eyes were shiny. The tough guy the world knew looked ridiculously soft and vulnerable.

She waited.

And waited.

Finally, the words came out. Warm and uncertain, like they'd just been born. 'I love you, Angie Holmes.'

He watched her tear-up and something inside him broke. Something that had been there since his days in the orphanage. Since he'd worked out that if you didn't allow anyone close, you didn't hurt when they weren't around any more.

Glassy-eyed, she looked at him.

This was big stuff.

A breakthrough.

His opening up, his first face-to-face declaration of love flooded her with emotion. 'Oh my stupid, gorgeous giant of a man, I love you so much as well.'

In the heat of the moment, all her professional caution and well-rehearsed pre-dinner thinking went out the window. 'I'm pregnant, Jake.'

Tears hit her cheeks.

'I'm going to have our baby.'

Chapter 11

Time seemed to stand still.

Angie's news somehow robbed Jake of the power of speech.

Worse still, in that truly pregnant pause, he already knew he was handling things badly.

Before he'd even shifted uncomfortably at the table or asked the dumbass question, 'Are you sure?' he knew he'd blown it.

'Yes, I'm sure.'

He decoded her three-word answer. '*Yes*' was said with sharpness and annoyance at being asked to give confirmation. '*I'm sure*' came out like a rebuke. Neither part of the sentence gave him the clues he was after. He had no choice but to ask another question: 'How?'

'How?' She frowned at him. 'I think you know how.'

'What I mean is, I thought you were on the pill?'

'Yes, I was. I am. I even took one first thing this morning. Seems the dose of food poisoning I had when we were on holiday killed the effectiveness.'

He resisted swearing, and instead managed, 'Are you *pleased*?'

Angie sat back in her chair and gripped the edge of the faultless table. 'Am *I* pleased? What do you think, Jake?'

He felt like he'd walked on a landmine and heard it click beneath his feet. Another wrong move would be fatal.

'Come on,' she said impatiently. 'I deserve a little more from you than *questions*. My life's just been turned upside-frigging-down, and all you can do is interview me.'

Suddenly he felt vulnerable. 'Hey, don't bark at me.'

'*Bark* at you?' She flushed with anger. 'Since when did I become a dog?'

'I'm sorry.' He stretched a hand apologetically.

She left him hanging. '*Your* turn to answer the questions, Jake. Tell me, how do you *feel*?'

He was lost.

Feel was such a complex word.

'I don't know. I really don't know.'

His voice creaked with hopelessness and she felt guilty for being so savage with him. She'd mistaken his tenderness as an open door to his heart. It hadn't been. It had just been a crack in his defensive wall. A tiny slit through which she glimpsed all that was lovely and warm about him. Now he was just as lost as she'd been earlier when Suzie Janner had told her the test results.

Jake sensed she was softening and made a tentative step towards appeasement. 'I just need some time to take it in, Ang. It's all a bit of a shock.'

'Good shock or bad shock?'

He wished he'd kept his mouth shut. 'Please – just give me some time to get my head around this.'

'You're diverting, Jake.' She couldn't help herself. 'Good shock or bad shock?'

'Maybe both.'

'Which did you feel first?'

Feel. There was that word again.

'Bad. I felt bad shock first.'

She tried not to be judgmental. At least, she tried not to show the judgment she'd come to.

Angie took the lovely white napkin off her knee and placed it on the table. 'Do you mind if we just go? I've kinda lost my appetite.'

Chapter 12

Mar Vista, LA

E ight hours later, Jake woke in a dead man sprawl, face down and naked, both arms flopped lifelessly across the mattress.

He reached out for Angie.

Wanted to pull her close to him. Smell her hair. Feel her snuggle up against his hungry body. They'd make love. Sleepy sex. Slowly, to stretch their muscles. Then, when their bodies were flooded with blood and passion, they'd all but wreck the room with their desperation for each other.

Only she wasn't there.

And neither was he.

He wasn't in her bed, like he had been for the past months.

He was back at his own place.

That's how bad last night had got.

Awkward dinner – or *non-dinner* to be more precise – followed by a near silent drive back. Then Angie rounded it all off by saying, 'Maybe you should go back to your place? Use the space to "get your head around this", as you so eloquently put it.'

So he'd slept alone. With a little help from a bottle of Jack and the kind of cable movie that would send anyone to sleep.

The clock on the nightstand said 07:30. He slapped the top before the alarm went off and reached for the TV remote.

SpongeBob was sitting his driving test. Charlie Sheen was young and squeaky clean. A woman on QVC was selling steam cleaners.

He found a news channel and heard that Chandler had been charged with the murders of his wife and neighbor before being sent to County and put on suicide watch. The former soldier had refused the offer of an attorney and said he planned to represent himself.

He turned the TV off and tried to grab another five minutes' shut-eye.

The baby.

Boom, there it was, front of mind.

He was barely awake and the elephant was back in the room, busting holes in his brain.

Baby.

Was it *really* a problem?

He knew guys who were desperate to get their ladies in the family way. They'd trade their house and car to be a father.

Dad. Pop. Pa.

Small names with big impact.

How do you feel?

The words twisted like a knife in his gut.

Jake pulled the quilt up over his head and tried to think of his favorite baseball game. Tried to remember the score. The team. The last man in.

Yesterday had been a shitter.

He wasn't anywhere near ready to get up and face today.

Chapter 13

Angie had worked most of the night.
She'd gone over all the police files from the first rape to the last. Once she'd gained an oversight she made columns of psychological notes about victim selection, crime scene geography and case linkage.

What she hadn't managed to finish she'd taken to the office with her, along with a full-fat cappuccino and the largest double choc muffin she could buy.

Screw the calories.

Angie was exhausted and her spirit so low she needed all the caffeine and carbohydrates she could get.

While her computer warmed up she read the notes that Chips had left. The guy had clearly stayed late and done a lot of work. The sexual attacks were spread across four neighborhoods of LA – Inglewood, Hawthorne, Lynwood and Huntington Park. Chips had pulled all the crime stats and ranked the areas according to the number of murders, rapes, robberies, assaults, burglaries, thefts, motor thefts and arsons. He'd compared them to each other then to the average crime rate in California and the US average.

For the past three years all the areas had recorded higher than average annual crime. That came as no surprise to Angie, who had grown up just a few miles east of Lynwood.

Inglewood had the dubious distinction of being top of Chips's offender table, with twenty homicides a year and almost forty rapes.

Huntington Park came bottom with four rapes and six homicides. There wasn't much between Hawthorne and Lynwood.

The one thing that caught the profiler's eye was the fact that hate crimes across all four hoods were way lower than Californian and US averages. She put this down to the high settlement of ethnic minorities in these poorer areas and the strength of black gangs. Not many white boys went into South Los Angeles shouting racist crap and spoiling for a fight. She was intrigued, though, because the serial offender she was hunting was undoubtedly full of hate for one particular minority – all the poor women attacked had been white and seniors. She made a note to herself to have the police prioritize a search for black-on-white sexual offenders.

From the photographs and case notes Angie had studied most of the night before, she'd learned that all the victims had been kicked and punched after the sexual violations had been completed. They'd sustained multiple injuries to the back of the head, the side of the ribcage and back of the legs.

The shape of the bruising had made it possible to work out the angle of attack and determine that the offender favored both his left hand and left foot. Left-handers were a rare breed, amounting to less than ten percent of society. It was an observation Angie suspected might prove crucial if the cops pulled in suspects.

The attacks told her something else as well.

The UNSUB was a coward.

He didn't even have the balls to go face to face with an elderly woman.

Angie's preliminary profile already had him marked down as young, sexually immature, not in any adult relationship, sulky, introverted and hypersensitive to criticism. He was also likely to be physically weak and consider himself inadequate.

The attacks were gradually getting more violent. Angie took this as a sign of two things. Firstly, the UNSUB was starting to feel confident about spending time with his victim and as a result was less anxious about getting caught. Secondly, he needed to vent more rage in order to feel satiated.

Both thoughts made her feel sick.

Not just mentally sick. Physically revolted as well.

She put her half-eaten muffin and coffee to one side. No way could she finish it. In fact, she had to take a second or two to stop herself from hurling.

The baby.

Could it really be making her feel ill?

Morning sickness?

'Jeez.' Angie dismissed the thought. At least tried to. Another hit of coffee to put it to the test.

Thirty seconds later, she rushed to the washroom.

Chapter 14

The morning news was full of the Corrie Chandler story.

Jake caught soundbites on the TV as he dressed for work in plain black pants and a matching black shirt that he wore tieless with the sleeves rolled up.

He drank tap water and slugged black coffee. There was nothing else in his apartment fit for consumption. A carton of milk had bloated ominously and a cooler of crisp vegetables was now a tray of toxic mush.

He and Angie had hooked up three years back and for the past twelve months he'd barely used his place. She'd even suggested he got rid of it and shifted the other half of his meager closet to her apartment, but that had never happened. At first, the very thought of co-habiting had scared the living crapola out of him. Given that Angie wasn't the kind of woman to ask twice it never came up again.

Baby.

He caught himself picturing a child crawling the floor in a yellow romper suit. Podgy, dimpled hands. Head all bald and wobbly. A toothless grin.

'Shit!'

Jake shut the front door and went down the stairs two at a time.

He didn't want to be a father.

Absolutely not.

He'd grown up as an orphan. Hadn't known his parents. Didn't want to. He needed no one. Depended upon no one. Certainly didn't want anyone depending upon him.

Especially a baby.

The rising sun was soft and mellow as he started his old car, a classic '58 Custom Royal Lancer. It was the limited edition Swept Wing with a pimped V8 that would leave dirt on the hood and windshield of any boy racer's 911.

The big old engine growled like a lion on testosterone shots. He roared from the curb but resisted turning on the radio.

More than anything, Jake needed to think. Figure things out.

There was no doubt in his mind that Angie had screwed up his life philosophy. Things now were so different to how they'd been when they'd first hooked up.

Their relationship had started as fun. Great sex. Fabulous company. A non-judgmental equal who'd understood him from day one.

They'd connected from the off, probably because he'd felt she was just as messed up as he was. Her baggage of a broken home, an abusive father and an alcoholic mother matched his crappy orphanages, useless social workers and thousands of other kids who wanted to fight him every day just because he was different.

They were a good fit.

Their first year together had been a fierce personal tussle. Headily competitive. Black run skiing, base jumping, free diving. And fucking. Fucking like the world was going to finish before they did.

Year two was when it went weird.

He felt unbalanced when she wasn't with him. Like he'd lost a limb in combat and was still reaching for something that should always be there.

She phoned him less and he called her more.

They would tell each other things. Stuff neither of them had told anyone else. They'd lay down their vulnerabilities like they were playing cards. He'd talk about the people he'd killed in battle and how he sometimes saw them in his dreams and woke sweating. She'd talk about her father, what he'd done to her, and how her mother had looked the other way.

It got so they didn't need the dating glue of places to go or things to do. Just being together was enough.

Then year three rolled up under their feet.

Just like year two but even weirder.

Nicely weirder.

He'd relaxed. Felt attached. Protective as well as passionate.

She'd started holding his hand, putting her head on his shoulder, linking arms.

And it was okay.

Even in public, it was okay.

And now . . .

Now he'd been exiled. For the first time during their spell together. And it was crap.

Worse than crap. It was unbearable.

Jake was done with thinking. He'd fix things when he got to work. He'd go see Angie and tell her exactly how he *felt*.

Chapter 15

S ERIAL RAPE. OFFENDER PROFILE. PRELIMINARY DRAFT.

1. Male.
2. 15–35.
3. Single.
4. Immature.
5. Introverted.
6. Volatile.
7. Possibly has explosive personality disorder.
8. Left-handed.
9. Not currently in a relationship.
10. Poorly educated.
11. Maybe has learning difficulties – dyslexia, attention deficit disorder, etc.
12. Unemployed.
13. Likely to have been dismissed from manual jobs because he has trouble accepting authority.
14. Possible record as a juvenile offender (most likely petty theft or handling).
15. May have small circle of male friends, not a gang member.
16. Could still live with parent(s) or friends. Doesn't own accommodation of his own.
17. Does not own a vehicle.

18. Lives within a ten-mile radius of first victim.
19. May have been a victim of hate crime or wrongly accused of hate crime.
20. . . .

Angie Holmes stood back from the large evidence board and reviewed her preliminary profile.

Some of the assumptions were obvious. Others weren't. They all came from a mix of statistical, psychological and geographical profiling techniques that had been perfected by the FBI over almost half a century of behavioral science practices.

Inevitably, she'd have to explain her reasoning to the cops. They always wanted to know the thinking behind the thinking. She'd explain that studies of sex offenders showed they mostly struck in areas that they knew. First offences generally took place in these comfort zones; areas where they believed they could get away with their crime and then quickly return to the cover of their homes. The more offences they committed, the further away from their abode they tended to commit them. She'd add that the cowardice of the attacks suggested someone without physical stature or sexual experience, so she'd set the age range at 15–35. If the cops pushed her on this she'd consider narrowing it to 15–25. Left-handed kids in poor areas tended to struggle in school. On top of that, sexual violence on the level in this case looked like a clear articulation of anger. She'd explain how offenders who physically articulated anger were usually compensating for their inability to do so through oral or written means.

Then there were the poverty and education issues. Contributing factor one: uneducated kids who struggled to express themselves usually drifted into minimum-wage jobs and the 'supervision' of poor-quality managers all too ready to sack them at the first sign of trouble. Contributing factor two: out-of-work youngsters with little education, zero income and no strong parental role models would almost inevitably turn to crime. At first, it might just be stealing food or fencing stolen goods, but once caught, their offending would escalate.

Angie knew the cops wouldn't need telling that not every juvenile offender got caught, so there was also a good chance the UNSUB they were hunting had been smart and lucky enough to have stayed out of the system.

What puzzled her most of all, though, was his choice of victims – female and old. Add to that the extreme violence and mutilation of their genitalia and you had the reason why Angie still hadn't filled in the twentieth point of her profile.

His race.

She was uncertain whether he was black or white. And given the race cauldron that had bubbled up post Trayvon Martin and George Zimmerman, she knew she had to be certain.

Chips arrived while she was still making up her mind. 'Breakfast's here!'

Angie turned around from the evidence board and saw he was carrying coffee and muffins. 'Oh God, I'm sorry, I should have rung you – I came in early and brought my own.'

'No worries.' He hid his disappointment and placed a cardboard cup marked Colombian Roast on her desk. 'Just in case you crave more caffeine.'

She smiled and then felt sick again.

Chips put the disposable tray and muffin bag on his desk and nodded to the board. 'Were the notes I left any good?'

'Better than good. They were excellent. When you've finished your food, can you pull together a list of everyone in all four areas who has been involved in hate crimes over the past two years?'

'Hate crimes?' He turned his computer on and rummaged in the muffin bag for his Triple Choc Daystarter.

'Please. And break them down by sex, age, ethnicity and religion. I don't think we're looking for your "normal" sexual offender. I think our UNSUB comes from the violent, angry end of the spectrum rather than the sexual power or sadistic end.'

'I'll get on it as soon as this old steam box is up and running and me and this sweet chocolate floozy have had our moment.' He bit into the glazed top of the muffin.

'That's disgusting,' she said jokingly. 'And petty theft. Go back five to seven on that one.'

He nodded full-mouthed, his lips peppered with black crumbs.

Angie's desk phone rang. She picked it up and grabbed a pen to make notes. 'Doctor Holmes.'

'Hi, this is Cal O'Brien. I'm the officer in charge on the Serial we sent you. Do you have time to talk?'

'We're still working the profile.' She gestured to Chips to hurry up. 'I should have a preliminary for you in a couple of hours.'

'Any chance you could drop whatever you're doing and meet me at a crime scene in Compton?'

Angie glanced at the map on the wall next to the evidence board. 'We don't have a crime scene in Compton.'

'We do now. An old woman, a widow living alone, was attacked in the early hours of this morning. Violated the same way as the others, so we're sure it's our guy.'

The profiler resisted lecturing him on the dangers of being 'sure' so early. She scribbled with her pen to get the ink flowing. 'I'll come straight away. What's the address?'

'She lives on East Kay, but meet me at the corner with Long Beach and I'll sign you through the cordon. Could you be there in half an hour?'

'Not unless I fly. Traffic's bad all down to the I-10 at the moment. Make it forty-five. How's the victim?'

'Not good. She's in ICU. Cracked ribs, broken nose and lost three pints of blood. Given she's eighty in two days' time, that's a big list of injuries to get over.'

'Poor woman. You said broken nose – was that from a fall?'

'No. The UNSUB hit her in the face with the baton he uses for the violations. I know what you're thinking – he normally only comes at them from behind.'

'Yep, that's what I'm thinking.'

'When you get here I'll tell you more. His MO is similar but different. Our sicko has a new prop. One that opens up a whole extra dimension to his offending behavior.'

Chapter 16

SKU Offices, LA

Jake had hoped to sneak into work. Get his paperwork done. Scoot over to Angie's unit and begin some serious bridge building.

It wasn't to be.

His entry was greeted with embarrassing applause. It spread from the gunned-up hard asses in Kevlar tux to the short-skirted secretaries who gave him doe-eyed looks as he passed by.

Ruis Costas, Jake's number two, was just back from holiday. Freshly tanned and full of energy, he couldn't wait to give his boss a vice-like handshake and hero hug. 'I saw the news footage at the airport. Man, that Corrie Chandler's one lucky fucker.'

'Come into my palace and let's catch up.' Jake gestured to a tiny glass booth that housed a single desk and an old filing cabinet. Once they were alone, he opened up. 'The cops *so* nearly blew it.' He wrapped his jacket round the back of his chair and sat. 'Do you know a guy called Connor Pryce?'

Costas took the seat opposite. And shut the door. 'Yeah, I do. Friend on the force said he worked Fraud with him. Said he was a proper hotshot. Great brain but by all accounts an *ambitious* sonofabitch. Smart money is on him making chief within five.'

'Only place he'll *make* is ER if he ever screws me over again.'

'What did he do?'

'What *didn't* he do? Mr Future Chief let a news copter fly into the restricted space when I was walking up to the Observatory. Then, when

I'm inside with Chandler and have just talked him down to a puppy whimper, Pryce comes banging down the corridor in his combats like a Hummer running on busted rims.'

Costas laughed.

'Not funny. I had to knife Chandler to stop him spraying me with a Remington.'

'That'll explain why Dixon was down here just before you came in.'

'Tell me you're jerking my string?'

'Afraid not.'

Jake pictured the section chief getting all hot under the collar and not understanding how everything could have been so much worse. 'I best go up and get my ass kicked then.' He got to his feet and almost turned the tiny desk over in the process. 'If I don't come back then all this is yours.'

'Gee, thanks boss, it's so much more than I deserve.'

They squeezed out of the office and went their separate ways.

Jake took two corridors to Crawford Dixon's corner office, a slab of real estate five times the size of his box, with rubber plants standing either side of his door. The chief's secretary was on the phone at her desk and mouthed for him to go on through.

He knocked, opened the door and stuck his head inside. 'Morning. I'm told you were looking for me.'

Dixon was hunched over a stack of paperwork pounding an oversized calculator. Bespectacled, mid-fifties, silver-haired and trim, he was dressed in white shirtsleeves and a tight black tie. 'Come right in.' He didn't look up. 'I'm just arm wrestling the budget and need to total this mother.'

'Rather you than me, sir.'

He totaled a column and looked up with a smile. 'One day, Jake, as you ascend the greasy pole of further promotion, you'll have to do more than just stick in your figures for SKU and complain about the raw deal you get back.'

'I'm praying that's some way off, sir.'

Dixon took off his glasses. 'I just wanted to congratulate you on yesterday. I had the mayor on the phone first thing. He'd been expecting a bloodbath out at the Observatory and was relieved it ended without any further body bags being paraded on the news.'

'We got lucky.'

'No, you handled it well. I received a note from Chief Rawlings at the LAPD. He said Pryce had written you up as a star. Also went on record to say he would most probably have had to kill Chandler if you hadn't dropped him with the knife.'

Jake bit back the lines of criticism that came to mind.

Dixon knew what he'd been thinking. 'Let it go. Pryce knows he fucked up, rushing in there, Jake. This is his way of making good. It keeps the saints from Internal Affairs off your back.'

'I understand. I'll call him.'

The section chief rose from behind his desk and extended his hand.

Jake took it and Dixon shook hard. 'What you did yesterday made me proud to be your boss. It took courage. The American people feel better – safer – when guys like you do things like that. Just be careful that those big balls of yours don't block your eyesight and you make the wrong call.'

Jake smiled and reclaimed his hand. 'I'll try to keep my balls out the way, sir.'

Chapter 17

Compton, LA

Angie swung her Toyota off North Long Beach Boulevard onto East Kay and spotted a worried-looking man pacing the sidewalk some twenty yards ahead on her right.

She'd never met Callum O'Brien, but everything about him said he was a cop working a difficult case: the crinkled brow; the cigarette he was lighting from the one he hadn't yet finished; the crumpled suit and thatch of hair he'd forgotten to comb. They were all indicators of a rape investigator lost in the puzzles and horrors of his work.

She parked the Avensis and called as she walked back. 'Lieutenant?'

'That's me.' He extinguished the cigarette with a rub of his fingers and slid it into his jacket pocket.

'Angie Holmes,' she said up close.

'Thanks for coming.' He pointed across and down the road. 'The victim is a Mrs Lindsey Knapp. Her house is on that side, about a quarter mile away. You want to ride or walk?'

'Walk's good. I'd like to get a feel for the area.'

He set off at a casual pace and took out his smartphone. 'Hang on and I'll pull up a Google map, so you can see approach roads as we talk.' His nicotine-stained fingers stubbed the device and Angie smelled years of tobacco on the blue wool of his jacket as she leaned close to see the display.

'This is us; we're heading towards Van Ness. As you can see, the

UNSUB could've come south down Long Beach like you did and turned into Kay, or caught an earlier right into East Peck and then worked his way through the back streets on foot.'

Angie ran a manicured nail over his screen. 'Or driven down to Van Ness, dropped his wheels there and come back.'

'Guess so.' O'Brien added another option. 'Could also have parked up on Rosecrans and walked through.'

Angie lifted her eyes from the phone and took in the roughness of the street. 'No disrespect to our lady, but she's not a celebrity and this ain't Bel Air.'

'Meaning?'

'Meaning, our UNSUB had to know this hood. He knew Mrs Knapp lived alone. Knew where to park and walk from.'

'You're figuring pre-meditated victim selection?'

'I think so. And given all that knowledge, it would mean he'd be relaxed and blend in. The steps we're making now are in his comfort zone. So if the UNSUB had wheels, he left them somewhere nearby that he was sure he'd be safe walking back to.'

The cop thrust the phone at her again. 'Okay, look at this on satellite feed. East Kay is bottom of frame; the grey building to the right is a big thrift store. He could easily have parked there and walked through an alley.'

Angie shrugged. 'It's possible, but unlikely. Those kinda stores have more surveillance cameras than the CIA. Local guy would know that. Kid brought up on the streets would be totally aware of where each and every security lens was.'

He put the phone away. 'Sometimes you get lucky. I'll still check it out.'

'You do that.' She didn't think it'd pay off and O'Brien didn't look like the type of guy who got lucky very often.

They walked in silence and Angie mulled things over. For sure, they were in the run-down end of a better part of the hood. Two parallel lines of cheap and neat detached homes were set back behind metal fences and rubbed out patches of fried grass. Some folks had painted and fixed up, others had just let *run-down* slide irretrievably towards *broken-down*. The one thing they had in common was barred windows.

There wasn't a glint of glass without anti-burglary bars. A certain sign that fear came with the darkness.

Behind the visible housing were dozens of other identical boxes, stacked in as tight and deep as developers had been allowed. Litter clogged storm drains and a heap of broken windshield glass sparkled in the gutter like someone had dropped a sack of diamonds.

Angie saw crime scene tape fluttering up ahead and got the heightened sensation she was walking *exactly* the same route the attacker had done.

She glanced back across the blacktop. There was no street lighting here. The homes immediately opposite were unoccupied. Trees on the sidewalk obscured the views from those further up and down the block. She imagined herself as the offender. If she tucked in closer to the garden fences, she'd be invisible once the sun had gone down.

O'Brien badged a uniform standing duty by the gate and signed his access log. He held up the tape for Angie to duck under but she wasn't ready. She was still taking in the victim's small detached home.

It was made from clapboard that had, once upon a long time ago, been painted a cute apple white and maybe looked something close to welcoming. Hot summers had bleached away the color and exposed the board. The roof looked short of a tile or two. A postage-stamp lawn was dominated by a big old beech. It had sucked the life out of the ground around it and stretched up high and proud above the little house. Right now, the tree was dripping a big pool of shade, but late at night it would provide a black wall of solid cover for any scumbag wanting to steal his way to the house. A low-level, rusted metal front fence was interrupted by an unlocked gate that might as well not have been there. Angie guessed that the best it had ever managed was to stop kids running across the lawn. There were no burglar alarms, sensors or cameras on the property. Anyone living here was a sitting duck for the criminally minded.

She dipped beneath the tape and followed O'Brien down a concrete path broken by weeds and tree roots.

He held the door and she walked inside.

It smelled of cats and dust. Fouled kitty litter and an overflowing kitchen bin regurgitating left-overs. Years of wet laundry had caused black damp to climb a wall by the back door.

Away from the stench Angie picked up the scents of Mrs Knapp's life. A cheap perfume that no doubt she'd been making last as long as possible because she couldn't afford a fresh bottle. Out-of-date potpourri, frazzled up in a dish on a small replica table by the gas fire, most likely where she sat and watched TV with a blanket over her knees in winter. It was way past its best but still gave off hits of jasmine and cedar. Angie envisioned Mrs Knapp being loath to throw it away. She seemed to have a love for nature. A vase by the window contained withered flowers and water gone green. The blooms had never been anything special, just carnations; they came cheap and lasted a long time.

Angie bit back the sadness and asked O'Brien the big question: 'How did the attack go down?'

He picked a photo frame off an old sideboard. 'This is Lindsey Knapp.' He handed it over. 'The guy in the shot with her is her late husband Gerry; he died five years back. It was taken at Disney in Anaheim. He had cancer and wanted to go there once more before he died.'

She looked at the shot. It was one of the auto prints you get when you go on a ride. By the startled looks on their faces, it had been snapped halfway through a run on a scary rollercoaster. Gerry had chemo baldness and his face was already skeletal thin. Lindsey had white, cotton-candy hair, young blue eyes and a happy mouth. Angie saw no signs of lipstick or make-up.

O'Brien got around to the unsentimental part of his story. 'Mrs K. had been watching the tube and dozed off. Something woke her. Maybe the UNSUB breaking in, maybe noise on the TV.'

Angie looked around. 'How'd he break in?'

'Bedroom window had warped last summer. She'd never got it fixed. He could've come through there. Or he simply could've opened the back door – she hadn't locked it.'

Angie shook her head. It was a practice more common among the elderly who lost keys or simply liked to wander in and out of the yard and have a breeze brighten up their homes.

'Anyway,' continued the cop, 'she opens her eyes and there he is – stood bold as brass right in front of her.'

She remembered his comment on the phone about the frontal attack. 'Wait a minute. In front of her? This doesn't sound like our guy.'

'He was masked.' O'Brien took a beat. 'Scumbag was wearing a black ski mask but he wanted her to see what was on it.'

'Which was?'

'RAPIST. Across the front of it in big, white capitals.'

Chapter 18

SKU Offices, LA

Ruis Costas had that look on his face.

The kind that told Jake he wasn't going to get the time to sneak off and make his peace with Angie.

The big slab of Hispanic muscle squeezed into his boss's tiny office. 'We've got a really bad one. SWAT is on the way to Strawberry Fields, a family fruit farm out at Moorpark. A shooter's been picking off a class of ten-year-old kids out in the crop fields. Just learning how many are injured or dead.'

The rest of the briefing came as they headed for the garage.

The location was almost an hour away and the FBI helicopter was already in use.

They climbed into a Fed Ford, a 4×4, with roof lights, gun kit and medi-packs in the back. Ruis was still talking as he started her up. 'Ventura County Sheriff's Office and the Highway Patrol are both based in the same building, just a spit from the crime scene, but they have no specialist marksmen and there are none at Thousand Oaks.'

'What about Simi Valley?'

'Same story. They've got Patrol, Traffic and Dispatch, not much else.'

Jake pulled out his cellphone and dialed the number Pryce had given him yesterday.

The LAPD man picked up instantly. 'H'lo?'

'Connor, it's Jake Mottram – you on your way to Moorpark?'

'Five minutes off. I just got coptered to a nearby field, we're grid searching for the UNSUB.'

'D'you already know how things went down out there?'

'Not in detail. There's still a cloud of panic over the place.' He sounded close to breathless as he hurried away from the chopper.'Two teachers and one kid dead. Another teacher and two more children wounded. No one's seen the shooter, just who he hit.'

Jake had lots of questions but they'd have to wait.'Catch you at the scene. Hey, before I forget, thanks for the report you filed. My boss says you've kept Internal Affairs off my back.'

'You're welcome. Thanks for the slack you cut me. It's appreciated.'

Jake dropped the call.

Ruis gave him a knowing look.'He cover your ass on his screw-up?'

'Yeah, he did.'

'Smart move.'

A silver Merc slid out slow in front of them.

Ruis flicked on the lights and sirens. The driver in front swerved out of shock then pulled to one side and let them pass.

The road stayed a maze of stopped and crawling vehicles, right the way down to the I-405, then they got to open up the Explorer's three-and-a-half-liter engine for almost thirty miles.

Fast road ran out as they exited Ronald Reagan Freeway and turned into Los Angeles Avenue.'We've only about a mile to go.' Ruis wished he hadn't spoken as they hit a crawl.

Jake's phone rang. He expected Pryce.

It was Angie.

He hit the red button and killed it. This wasn't the time to get distracted.

Baby.

Just the sight of her name on his cellphone had thrown a grenade across the floor of his mind.

Ruis noticed his tension.'You okay?'

'Just some personal stuff.'

He knew better than to ask and concentrated on driving.

Finally, they saw ambulances parked up ahead. Back doors were wide open and steps down. Roof lights flashing. Paramedics in body armor stood waiting for clearance from SWAT to go into the fields. Down the road, another ambulance did a J-turn and whooped its sirens. Jake guessed it was leaving with the injured that Pryce had mentioned. They were lucky to have got away from the shooter.

He stepped from the Ford and almost got clipped by a white Lexus – a hybrid that ran on batteries and moved quieter than a Ninja. At the wheel was Shelley Davies, the ME. She waved an apology. Jake looked back to see what else was on the road. Fifty yards away, the county coroner's blacked out van was pulling in, trying to keep a discreet distance. It coughed fumes and came to a halt.

Everyone was here now.

The Circus of Death had come to town.

Chapter 19

Compton, LA

Angie called Jake as she left O'Brien and walked back to her Toyota. Being inside Lindsey Knapp's house had left her flat. She needed to hear his voice and fix a time for them to get together and talk.

It rang unanswered.

She left a message asking if he was okay and saying she'd missed him this morning.

That was her olive branch.

If he had any sense, he'd grab it while he still could, because she sure as hell wasn't going to go chasing him.

There was no doubt in Angie's mind that regardless of how rough on him she might have been in the restaurant, he had to man up and come to her with a mature response to the news she'd given him.

The traffic back to the FBI offices proved even worse than it had been coming out to the crime scene. The fender-to-fender crawl gave her time to run the case back and forth. O'Brien had said the UNSUB had just stood there in his RAPIST mask. When Mrs Knapp freaked, he beat on her while she was still in her seat. He pulled her out of it by the ankles and she cracked the back of her head on the floor. She started shouting, so he hit her and then wrapped tape around her face. He flipped her, taped her hands, then violated her with his trademark stave of wood.

Angie figured a lot of things had changed since his first attack almost a year ago. Back then, he'd attacked a woman in her back yard when she'd gone to put trash in a can. It had been crude and nasty but nowhere near as prolonged and brutal as anything endured by future victims. There'd been no tape, just a hand over her mouth. No mask. The stave of wood had been the only thing he'd gone prepared with. That and the pre-determination to attack an elderly white woman when she least expected it.

The latest assault had been similar but horribly different.

He'd come with a rape kit. Tape. His 'souvenir' weapon. No doubt a bag of some kind to conceal everything in. He'd confronted the victim wearing a mask and had almost certainly got a thrill from facing her and seeing her fear.

That was the bit that worried Angie the most.

The thrill.

He had progressed from isolated, vented anger to working out how to become instantly empowered and – she guessed – probably sexually aroused by the attack.

The next assault was bound to be worse.

He was evolving as a predator. Changing from the crime being principally a rushed and frenzied attack to slower, prolonged and even more sadistic acts. He was certain to continue his metamorphosis and add layers of torture and suffering. There was a good chance he'd even try penile penetration. And if that went wrong – as it very well might – then the inevitable would happen.

He'd kill.

Of that, Angie had no doubt.

Half a mile from her office, she pulled into the lot of a small mall and went to the florist she regularly used. She bought a large bouquet of pink lilies for Lindsey Knapp and paid extra to make sure they arrived at her hospital bed before closing time.

Chapter 20

Moorpark, Ventura County, LA

J ake slipped on shades to shield his eyes from the blazing sun and scanned the flat and wide-open countryside. All around him was farming land. So many fields, crammed with so many vegetables that he felt like a Borrower who'd fallen into a grocery basket.

He tightened the straps on his Kevlar vest and checked the weapon on his belt. As he did so, he walked to where the cops, sheriffs and SWAT were gathered. There was no need for him to reach for a shield; he could hear them talking about him and the events at the Observatory as he approached.

Pryce was in his combat blacks and looked relaxed, giving orders and sorting out a bewildered group of uniforms. Yesterday's business with Chandler had already rubbed some of the green off him.

The LAPD man broke from his conversation when he saw Jake and headed over. 'Seems summertime is a busy time for Sprees.' He stuck out his hand. 'How you doing?'

Jake realized it was a wipe-the-slate-clean gesture and took it warmly. 'I'm good. Picture any clearer now than when we spoke on the phone?'

'Not a whole lot. Two of the wounded pupils limped out the strawberry field, bleeding like crazy. They'd both taken single shots. One to the leg, one in an arm.'

'Lucky kids,' added the FBI man.

'Yeah. I'm sure they don't feel that way at the moment.'

'They will when they see the names of the dead in the newspapers.'

Pryce pointed across the fields. 'There's an injured teacher still out there. One of the staff said the guy was hit in the back as he was trying to get everyone inside.' The cop squinted into the heat haze. 'I suspect when we get to him we'll find he's paralyzed.'

Jake tried to be optimistic. 'Might just be muscular spasm. Nerve damage. Shock.'

He wondered about the shots. None of them were to the head. Made him think the shooter wasn't professionally trained. He'd probably lain in wait, sized up his first hits, then when everyone had scattered he'd lacked the skill to kill anyone else.

A helicopter buzzed by and sounded like a distant chainsaw. Jake knew the crew would be using telescoping lenses and thermal cameras to get a fix on the gunman. Even if the punk hid under crops or in an outbuilding, his body heat would be picked up.

Pryce guessed the question the SKU leader was about to ask. 'Dragnet's pitched good and tight. There's no way the crazy can get to a major road, let alone back to the freeway. The one thing there's no shortage of out here is highway patrolmen and sheriffs, and they all know the terrain like the backs of their hands.'

Jake hoped he was right. But something inside him told him things were going wrong. Maybe mistakes had already been made.

Footsteps made them turn.

Behind them was the ME. Shelley Davies cracked a smile. She was in her late forties, early fifties, but still a looker. A Californian Carla Bruni was how Jake had heard Angie describe her and there was little arguing with it.

Shelley was already in her whites and rubber boots. She'd have gloved-up as well, only in this heat she knew her hands would be puddling in sweat within minutes. 'Been out here with my kids,' she said by way of a hello. 'They did summer camp here some years back. Had a whale of a time and picked enough fruits to feed us through to fall.' She put a steel case down in the sun and straightened up, stretching cricks out of her back in the same movement. 'Gentlemen, can one of you show me to my work?'

'Afraid not, ma'am,' said Pryce. 'We still don't have a fix on the position of the shooter.'

She nodded understandingly. Looked wistfully out to the fields of ripening strawberries. 'Shame a place as sweet and innocent as this will always be remembered for the bitterness of today.'

Chapter 21

I t was almost an hour before SWAT completed the sweep and were confident the area was safe enough to send the help in.

The good news was that the injured got treated. The downside was that the gunman had slipped through at least the first security cordon.

Paramedics found local teacher Jon Stenson lying face down in the shattered green plants and churned brown soil of the strawberry fields. The back of the forty-year-old's balding skull had been burned red raw by the uncaring midday sun. The bleed hadn't been as bad as it could have been and there was still enough of a pulse to give them hope.

As they fitted drip lines and called in the air ambulance, Jake walked the scene and tried to figure out where the shooter had made his nest.

He started by standing near the three corpses being attended to by the ME and her two assistants. The bodies were clustered together. A slim brunette in her late thirties had been hit in the heart. Jake guessed this had been the gunman's first shot. He'd taken his time and gotten himself absolutely ready before squeezing the trigger and starting the carnage.

A few yards away lay the body of a tall, dark-haired man. He'd taken it in the gut and from the pooling had bled out quickly.

Jake looked again at the cluster of bodies and surmised the shooter had lacked the expertise to hit two hearts in a row. At least he wasn't ex-military. That was a small consolation. A couple of strides from the male teacher lay the corpse of a young girl in a yellow and white summer dress. She was half-covered by the green leaves of strawberry plants. Jake looked back and imagined the male teacher had probably grabbed her hand and started running. He'd gone down shot. She'd hesitated out of shock, run a pace or two, then been hit.

Flies buzzed and settled in the dead youngster's long blonde hair and he had to walk round to see where the round had entered.

It was in the neck. Just above a gold necklace that bore the name Amy.

Jake tried not to think of her parents. Blocked out a surprising thought of how he'd feel if someone had done this to his child.

Child.

He forced himself to concentrate. If all three victims had been standing up, the shots would have been on the same level, meaning the shooter had probably been lying down and would have had to make a small right to left pan as he picked off his victims.

A picture was forming in Jake's mind, but before he let it fully develop he wanted to examine the last person to be shot, the injured teacher who'd taken the bullet in the back.

Marks in the soil told him Deputy Head Jon Stenson had been hit a few yards back from where he was now being treated by the paramedics. It was clear he'd been running down a gap between two thick fruit rows. Abandoned baskets showed where the kids had been harvesting when hell broke out. Small footprints in the soft soil spread in all directions.

Jake followed the bigger prints and could see the teacher's right leg had been extended when the round had torn into his spine. It was bad luck. An inch lower and the bullet would have hit a thick leather belt and maybe done less damage.

The scuff marks on the ground showed Stenson had stumbled and twisted his left foot. His survival instinct had kicked in and he'd managed one more stride before his strength had given out, then he'd gone down on his knees and planted his face in the dirt. Four small rake marks in the earth showed where he'd clawed with his right hand and tried to raise himself up.

Round about then, the deputy head would have realized his legs weren't doing anything. Jake figured he had either decided to play dead in the hope of not being finished off by the gunman, or he'd simply passed out.

He followed the line of Stenson's run and added it to the movements of the blonde girl and the other teachers. A hundred yards beyond where he stood, the land rose up into a tall and wide ribbon of long-established evergreens that ran along the edge of the property. From what he could see, it stretched for maybe half a mile or more in each direction. The map he'd glanced at on the way over showed open fields beyond, some containing broken-down outbuildings, and then there was scrub and the Moorpark freeway. The police copter had already swept the area and found no one, but Jake was certain this would have been the Spree's route out. From there he would either escape completely or find a place to kill himself.

Pryce came into view and headed over.

Jake wandered towards him and they met just past the medics.

The SWAT leader had something in the palm of his hand. 'Just dug this from outta a fence near where one of the injured kids was.'

Jake looked at the chewed-up slug and shook his head in dismay. 'Point two two three Remington. I'll bet my ass it's from an AR-15.'

The two men knew they were thinking the same thing. This was the rifle Adam Lanza had used to slaughter twenty-six innocents at Sandy Hook. As soon as Obama said that he wanted the weapon banned, it sold like hotcakes and quickly became America's most wanted gun.

Pryce bagged the slug and put it in his pocket. 'What kinda distance would you say the 15 was accurate to?'

Jake looked off to the ribbon of woodland. 'Three times from here to where those trees are, which I'm certain is the spot the Spree fired from.'

'I've got men heading over.'

'You'll find flattened grass where he was lying. Get them to go careful. Guy lying in the grass for a long time gets to spitting, might even take a leak just a couple of steps from his gun. Have them snip the surrounding grass and bag it. The spit or piss might give us DNA.'

Pryce nodded.

Jake was still staring into the distance. 'Men I served with could snick an apple off a tree at five hundred yards with a rifle like that. Six if the scope was good enough and the wind was light.'

'I'm thinking our UNSUB got so close it's a sign he's no pro.'

'Then you're thinking right.'

Pryce took a punt. 'Which means the killer might have had a rush of blood and come out here to settle a grudge. Maybe he got sacked by the farm and wanted to bring them bad publicity.'

'Maybe.' Jake wasn't yet concerned about the *why* of the matter. He was more interested in the *where*.

Where had the sonofabitch come from?

Where was he hiding out?

Where was he going to strike next?

The incessant chatter of rotor blades pulled his attention skyward. A big bug of an air ambulance circled and sniffed out a place to land. It made Jake wonder why the LAPD copter had missed the Spree. The thermal cameras should have picked him up. He and Pryce shouldn't be here, they ought to be chasing the crazy across a field, eating up the ground around him, running him into a dead end.

But they weren't.

The UNSUB had vanished. He could feel it. The scumbag had run long and far. He'd been smart enough to get out fast and was now free to kill another day.

Chapter 22

FBI Field Office, LA

C hips was out for the afternoon, so Angie had the office to herself.
He'd left the stats breakdown she'd asked for, detailing all the hate
crimes that had taken place in the areas where the elderly women
had been assaulted.

And he'd left her something else as well.

A brown paper bag containing a salmon and cream cheese bagel.
Plus a note that read: 'In case you came back late and forgot to pick
up lunch. See you later. X'

His kindness made her smile. He was a sweet guy. Maybe too sweet
for the FBI. Chips had chosen to work in one of the few organizations
in LA where being gay wasn't something you spoke openly about,
and Angie figured she was the only person he'd confided in. Not that
you had to be a genius to deduce his sexuality. About once a week,
his daily T-shirt slogan would be something like THINK PINK or TWO
PAIRS BEATS A STRAIGHT.

She made coffee to go with the bagel and in the process reminded
herself she could no longer stomach milk. Which in turn triggered
thoughts of the child growing inside her and how she was prevaricating
over what to do about the pregnancy. Work was a great distraction,
but this wasn't like any personal problem she'd faced before and it
was never really out of her mind.

For a moment she considered calling Suzie Janner, but figured with
her being a mom herself, she was almost certain to try to talk her into

the marvels of motherhood. Instead, she went online to seek some clarity.

Big mistake.

Having typed in the word PREGNANT she was instantly bombarded by a plethora of sites selling everything from diaper packs to breast pumps. She adjusted the keywords to JUST PREGNANT and a new but equally commercial slate of sites came up.

Angie worked her way through her bagel and bullshit adverts aimed at exploiting first, second and third trimesters. She avoided suggestions on how to calculate the due date, choose a pre-natal caregiver or pick a power diet for the next nine months. A sneak at pregnancy fashion left her horrified but the final insult was a pop-up that would help her choose the baby's name.

The one thing she certainly wasn't going to do was pick the child's name. That would be the point of no return. All her psychological training told her that putting a name to a pregnancy made termination a thousand times more difficult.

Lily if it was a girl.

She put her head in her hands and screwed her eyes shut.

Where the hell had that thought come from?

The damned name had zipped below her radar like a Stealth bomber.

Then she remembered.

She'd had a ragdoll called Lily. Big blue eyes and a half-moon smile. Black wool ponytails that got sucked and a red and white checked dress. She'd literally loved Lily to bits. Her arms and legs split so many times Angie developed sewing skills a theater nurse would have been proud of.

She snapped out of her melancholic reminiscences by typing three words in the search box: ABORTION CLINICS LA.

What followed made difficult reading.

First came the commercial onslaught of people vying for her 'business', then an oily slick of slogans to pull her in. Most managed to use the same phrases – Your Life. Your Decision – Make the Smart Choice – Forget don't Regret.

A click or two later, she found a community site run by women who'd had abortions in the LA area and had left comments and ratings.

One was so full of praise she made it sound like a trip to a spa. Angie suspected it had been written by one of the clinic owners. Another left her speechless. A woman complained that because she'd had very little money she'd been forced to use an unlicensed clinic. The whole affair had been agony. Only when she was recovering did she discover they did liposuctions during the day, and in the evenings just switched nozzles for the abortions.

Angie felt a wave of revulsion wash through her.

She dealt with death on a daily basis but none of the traumas of her work had prepared her for a situation like this.

Blood pounded in her temples. Anger rose inside her. She had to pant to let go of the building tension. Angie was on auto-pilot now. It was the mode she'd often gone into when she was a kid. It was how she'd gathered her mental strength when her father came in drunk or angry and started throwing his weight and fists around. It was her defence mechanism. Her way of pulling down the shutters and squaring up to whatever stood in her way.

She dialed Suzie Janner.

She was ready to tell her she'd made up her mind. She knew what she wanted. What she had to do.

Chapter 23

A low evening sun had drizzled gold on the strawberry fields by the time Jake and Ruis decided to call it quits and head back to the Explorer.

Pryce had pulled out an hour earlier. He'd left a SWAT team to work the wider fields with deputies from the sheriff's department but by now, everyone believed the shooter was gone.

The next twenty-four hours would be critical.

They'd be spent interviewing the traumatized kids and teachers, scrapping around for a description of the UNSUB, canvassing locals about whether they'd seen anyone or anything unusual, running door to door inquiries and weapon checks, processing forensics and hoping there were prints on the slug Pryce found in the fence. Most of all, they would be spent praying for a break.

You needed more than luck when you were hunting a Spree.

One thing was for sure: sooner or later, they always surfaced and came back crazier than ever.

The men banged their boots against the tires then climbed into the Ford. Ruis kicked off the inevitable back-to-the-office discussion about the case. 'What d'you reckon happened out there? The cops messed up and he slipped through their lines? Or you think he's still holed up close by and playing Mr Normal in some unsuspecting family?'

'Maybe the latter. If the UNSUB's local, he could have dropped the gun into a shit pit and run home before the first cops even got there.'

Ruis drove with one hand on the wheel and searched the center console. He found a pack of gum and offered Jake a stick of melon and cranberry.

'No thanks.'

He took one himself then shared some of his thoughts. 'I've been thinking about what you said about the shooter being an amateur.'

'And?'

'And what if it's a kid? A teenager with a grudge against the folks who run Strawberry Fields Farm. He grabs his old man's rifle and goes out on a revenge mission because they sacked him, or maybe just refused him a job.'

Jake wasn't convinced. 'Pryce said the farm manager claimed they haven't sacked anyone for years.'

'They'll certainly have turned down people for jobs though,' added Ruis. 'And with Sprees, rejection is often the straw that breaks the camel's back.'

'I *hate* camels.' Jake pulled a face. 'Reminds me too much of Afghanistan.'

'They fight them like dogs, don't they?'

'They do. Both the Turks and the Afghans love camel fighting. Thousands of people turn up for the big bouts and there's a massive amount of illegal betting on it. I tell you, man, it's brutal. The owners whip all sense out of the big dumb lumps and make them butt and crash into each other until one drops dead.'

'And this is a country we sought to liberate?'

'Hey, don't start me on that topic.'

They made small talk all the way back to the office. Ruis promised to put in the case report while Jake headed over to Angie's office. He took a deep breath as he walked the corridor. Light spilled from her room and he could hear the TV playing.

He rapped on the door and walked in.

She was sat at her desk, a cup of coffee held in both hands, staring out of the window.

'Hi.'

She looked shocked to see him. 'Hi to you too. You been on this kiddy shooting?'

'Uh-huh.' He took a chair and swung it round so he leaned over the back as he sat. 'Spree's gone to ground but I suspect not for long. How are you?'

'Ha.' She looked back out the window to Wilshire. 'How am I? I guess I'm kinda screwed up.' She popped the cap off a bottle of water and swigged. 'Thought you might have rung.'

'I was with people all day and didn't have a chance. I came straight over as soon as I got free.'

She nodded. He could have made time. They both knew it. 'You managed to think a little?'

'I've done nothing but.' He blew out a deep sigh. 'To be honest with you, Ang, I don't see myself as a dad. I'd never thought about it until yesterday and now I have, well, I just don't think parenting is a mission for me.'

'A mission?'

He hated it when she repeated words like that. 'Bad phrase, maybe. I'm sorry. Listen, you wanted to know how I *feel*. Well, I feel the baby's a bad idea. We were good how we were. How we *are*. Doesn't make sense to change things.'

Angie sat in silence.

She had to go over everything he'd just said. Discover whether deep down she felt the same. Before he'd come over she'd rung Suzie Janner, but the doctor had been out. If she'd been in Angie would have confessed that she was leaning towards keeping the baby and wanted some advice.

Jake got up and wandered round her side of the desk. He squatted so he was at her eye level. 'I love you, Angie Holmes. I really do. And I don't want *this* – or anything for that matter – to come between us.'

She knew what it cost him to say that. Twice in twenty-four hours and no phone to hide behind or threat to his life to prompt it. In other circumstances, she'd have seen his words and openness as big progress in their relationship.

He took her hand and tried to leave her in no doubt about his feelings. 'I've never felt like I do with you with any other woman. I want what we've got to last but I just don't see a kid helping out on that score.'

She couldn't stop herself pulling away from him. 'And what if I told you that I wanted the baby?'

'What?'

'I'm not repeating myself, Jake. You heard me clearly enough.'

He didn't know what to say.

'I've been thinking about it. For and against.' She found herself smiling at her clunky way of summing up her feelings. 'And the more I think, the more I'm for.'

He shook his head. 'Have you forgotten how fucked up your childhood was – to say nothing about mine?'

'I've tried to. I try to forget it every day.' She narrowed her eyes at him. 'D'you know what? I actually thought because of all that shit, we might make great parents. We might be able to finally bury our own ghosts and rise above all that psychological baggage. Stupid me. What a dumbass.' Anger fizzed in her blood. 'Crazy bitch that I am, I'd talked myself into thinking that maybe this was a *good* thing for us. Admittedly, a hell of a surprise, but a good thing.' She laughed sarcastically. 'Get this – in my madness, I thought it might *complete* us.'

'Complete us?' His eyes widened in shock. 'Well, I felt pretty damned complete before this shitstorm broke over our heads. Turn back the clock a couple of days, Angie. Remember how it was. Then you try to tell me that we felt incomplete.'

She glared at him. He'd touched a nerve and they both knew it.

'Well, things aren't as they were. They're as they are. So what happens now, Jake? You want to break up? Because I sure as hell don't need another part-time parent in my life.' She struggled – not for words, but for the restraint not to let them out.

Her desk phone rang.

'Take it,' he snapped. 'I'll wait.' He backed away and stood around the other side of the desk.

Angie picked up the phone. 'Holmes.'

It was O'Brien. 'Bad news, Doc. Lindsey Knapp died ten minutes ago. Our rapist just became a killer.'

Chapter 24

California

Shooter woke with his brain buzzing.

His mind zinged with static from yesterday's murders.

The thrill of the kill still pumped in his heart. He'd slept well. The best rest he'd ever had. Now he was relaxed. Satiated. Like he'd made love all night then slept all day.

But it had been *better* than sex.

Less effort. More pleasurable. Less physical. More spiritual.

And another thing – any dumb fuck can have sex.

Few can do what he did.

Take a life.

Lives to be precise.

The media had announced that there'd been three deaths. Two teachers and a child. Others injured.

Shame.

He'd aimed to kill the running man, the balding teacher with the tires of belly fat, but had pulled his shot at the last minute. It had been the excitement. Distractions. Inexperience.

Next time he would do better.

Better and better.

Until he achieved what he wanted.

Perfection.

Murder, thought Shooter, is like art. You have to suffer for it. Work hard. Stamp your mark. Not mind that some assholes won't recognize the beauty of what you create. You have to have a plan and a structure. Something important to say. But you must be able to improvise as well. That's where the flair is.

Shooter shut his eyes and drifted back to the scene.

The shade had felt cool after the long walk in the sun, his throat dry from the dusty tracks he'd worked his way down. The woods smelled of Douglas fir and wild garlic. He'd settled in the long grass between trunks of evergreens and trained his telescoping sight on the strawberry fields.

He'd controlled his breathing. Learned to be patient. Caught himself listening to the rustle of birds in the dense green canopy of branches and leaves. He'd focused. Cut everything out. In his hands he'd felt the cool metal of the AR-15. Panned the rifle left and right. Taken practice shots like a golfer swinging a club.

Then came that wonderful thump of rifle stock against shoulder. Like an arm punch from a friend. And that delicious crack as the cartridge exploded and the slug smacked the air.

Shooter relived it all in slow motion. Birds screamed and scattered in the faultless blue sky. A hundred yards away the first of the pickers went down.

His pick of the pickers.

The memory made him smile. Those kids around the female teacher had sniggered at first. They'd thought Miss had slipped, looked stupid, spilled her basket of berries. Gotten strawberries all over her face and hands. Something to smirk about for the rest of the year.

Then they'd seen the red spurting from her back and chest and the little fuckers had screamed holes in the clouds.

Shooter stretched out on his rough bed and remembered his second shot.

He'd stayed calm and taken it well. The young male teacher had been staring in horror at his colleague when he'd squeezed the trigger and dropped him in the dirt.

Then there'd been panic. Screams he could hear from all the way across the fields. People running everywhere. Through the chaos, he'd killed the girl in the bright dress and injured the fat boys and the baldy teacher. It hadn't been good. Not how he'd wanted. Not clean. Not accurate enough. He'd lost his calmness. It had been like their panic had infected him. He'd snatched the shots. Swung the rifle like he'd been swatting flies. It had been bad.

Next time he'd do better.

Much better.

Shooter counted his blessings. He'd gotten away. The cops had been even less effective than he'd expected.

Looking back, he could see that crazy fuck at the Observatory had done him a favor. He'd figured chasing dumbasses like Corrie would drain the LAPD and FBI of their best men. Tire them out. Make them slow to respond.

He'd been right.

The first law enforcement teams to get to the Strawberry Fields slaughter had been the hick-town sheriffs and the leather-clad motorcycle riders of the Californian Highway Patrol. He'd watched them later on the TV news, with their puffed-out chests and heavy gun belts. An S&M drag show. What a joke. They hadn't an investigator's brain between them.

Shooter had slipped away before they'd even got there, let alone closed down the area.

He'd been back in his bolt hole, sipping soda and watching events on the news long before SWAT had rolled into town with their armored meat wagons and big egos.

He got out of bed and smiled. Today was a new day. He was a different person.

He was famous.

Chapter 25

LAPD HQ, LA

Serial rape-homicide.

Every cop in the world knows SRH is almost always the trump card in the grand game of winning all the resources needed for an investigation.

The only thing that beats it is child murder.

Once Lindsey Knapp died, Lieutenant Cal O'Brien found his penny-pinching chief more than willing to staff up his investigation to the level he'd asked for several months back.

As a result, psychological profiler Angie Holmes found herself at LAPD HQ, stood at the front of an incident room full of cops, presenting her insight into the offender who'd raped five times and killed once.

All those gathered across the four rows of chairs had been copied her preliminary profile. They'd been warned in writing that it was a filtering device for investigators who had possible suspects in mind. It wasn't a magical divining tool that would pull offenders out of the ground.

'What you have got –' Angie told the room – 'is a psychological profile, not a *psychic* one. It's based on best guesses, formulated off the back of half a century of compiled statistics and operational experience, but they are still guesses. So, please do not exclude lines of inquiry, or suspects, solely on the grounds of the assumptions I've made. Use the profile to prioritize. Look first for people and things matching my outlines, but do *not* exclude anything that you *would* have investigated if you'd not had this profile.'

Once she'd finished, she turned to the task O'Brien had given her of providing them with a better understanding of the *nature* of the UNSUB. 'Can you dim the lights please?'

A hand hit a bank of switches at the back of the room. Dust floated in a shaft of white projector light.

Angie looked across the pensive audience and began, 'Rapists fall into four principal categories. Every half decade or so it's fashionable to change these names, but I work on FBI diagnostics that existed way before any of us were born.' She pulled up the first slide.

TYPES OF RAPIST

1. Power Reassurance.
2. Power Assertive.
3. Anger Retaliatory.
4. Anger Excitation.

'Type one is by nature a sneak and weakling. He usually lives in the same area as the victims he attacks. He may have snooped on them. Once this type of offender has begun his criminality he will feel the *need* to regularly offend.' She took a pause to make sure they were all paying attention. 'The perp you are chasing started as a Power Reassurance rapist, but as you'll see, he has a dangerous mix of other categories as well.' She walked into the light of the projector and tapped the screen. 'Type Three – Anger Retaliatory – he's loaded with badness from here too.' Angie changed slides.

ANGER RETALIATORY

1. Attack duration is short.
2. Attack is extremely violent.
3. Violence is used before, during and after rape.
4. His main goal is to vent his cumulative aggression.

'Make no mistake,' she continued, 'the death of Lindsey Knapp will not have frightened or deterred him. To the contrary. He will have found it deeply satisfying.' She drifted even closer to the dropdown screen and tapped the fourth point. 'He vents his anger by making the victim represent what he's angry about. Remember this when you are interviewing suspects. He may be furious with a boss, a relative, a co-worker or a symbol of authority, but he cannot attack *that* particular individual. He can't do it because he has a reliance on them or he knows he would be immediately arrested as a suspect. So instead, he selects victims who symbolize them.'

A hand went up in the shadows. A young female detective with auburn hair managed to catch Angie's eye. 'Doctor Holmes, do you know who our elderly victims represent to the offender?'

'It's a good question but I'm going to partly duck it because I want to validate a few things and it's important you find the answer yourself.'

She saw Cal O'Brien scowling as she pulled up a third slide. 'This is the Anger Excitation Rapist. The next stage of our perp's evolution.'

ANGER EXCITATION (aka SADISTIC)

1. Rapes become planned in exacting detail.
2. Attack time is prolonged.
3. Victim count quickly rises.
4. Most likely of all rapists to kill victims.

'Until Lindsey Knapp's death, the offender hadn't thought of killing. But now that has happened, he has a taste for it. He will relive that attack in his mind and from this moment on he will build death into his fantasies.'

Angie looked across the rows of homicide detectives and continued. 'The more experienced among you will know that our UNSUB is what we call a *mixed* offender. Some of his behavior is organized and pre-meditated, some made up as he goes along. In truth, he's always had some of the latent characteristics of an Anger Excitation Rapist. What's happening now is that they have surfaced and will become increasingly dominant. My prediction is that he's enjoying the afterglow that comes with killing and not getting caught. Once that's worn off, he'll feel the need to strike again. And when he does, it will be more brutal, prolonged and awful than anything we have witnessed to date. You are no longer hunting a rapist. You're hunting a fledgling sadist, potentially the worst of all serial killers.'

Chapter 26

California

The place Shooter lived was special.

It had an invisibility shield.

At least, that's how he liked to think of it.

It was so run-down, so dead beat and bottom-of-pile that people drifted by every day and didn't so much as give it a second glance.

It was a lot like him.

Unnoticed. Full of secrets. Brimming with potential.

It was a big space and he'd been surprised to get it as cheaply as he had. Seemed that times were so tough, you could land a real bargain these days.

He'd spent months converting the inside of the abandoned building, creating a beehive of new, small rooms, some no bigger than a prison cell. Each had to be designed to fulfill its own specific purpose and fit perfectly into his grand plan. A high-tech alarm system with remotely controlled security cameras gave him a three-hundred-and-sixty-degree view of anyone approaching from road or sidewalk. The feeds went through to a secure room where Shooter ate and slept.

The outside was deliberately derelict. A spread of blacktop once white-lined with parking bays for staff, deliveries and outlet shoppers was potholed and covered in thick weeds and junk.

Beneath the trash, the old shopping trolleys and cardboard boxes, a small ring of fresh tarmac flowed like lumpy treacle around the circumference of the stand-alone building. If anyone found it, they'd presume the drains had been fixed or some cables laid.

They'd be wrong.

At strategic points, Shooter had planted homemade explosives and remote detonators, each wired to the windowless, central control room where he now paced the floor.

He had a lot on his mind.

Not yesterday's kill. That was merely a peep through the curtains onto the stage that awaited him.

Today was going to be the big day.

The biggest of his unnoticed life.

Chapter 27

Men's Central Jail, Downtown, LA

Jake's heart sank as he parked about a mile from the Hall of Justice, northeast of Union Station, and headed towards one of the biggest jail complexes in the world.

MCJ was built to hold around three thousand inmates but the country's hunger to jail offenders meant that these days some five thousand offenders were kept there.

The institution's primary purpose was to contain high-security and pre-trial inmates. Together with the Transportation Bureau, the Inmate Reception Center, the Twin Towers Correctional Facility and the Central Jail Arraignment Courts, it made up what was known as the Central Regional Justice Center and covered more than a million and a half square feet.

Jake reckoned that over the last few years he'd walked close to every inch of the place.

When he'd first joined the FBI, he'd been assigned to an academic research team that ran a project there. Their task was to interview offenders on their backgrounds and crimes. It involved a month of intensive visiting, getting to know inmates, breaking down barriers, winning their confidence and learning not just about what they did and why, but also how they felt before, during and after their crimes.

Jake had picked up a lot. It seemed to him that many young men from disadvantaged backgrounds had been shaped by prison in much the same way he'd been shaped by the army. It was their only anchor in a life full of storms. For some, the damp-free bed and regular meals were a better option than a life out on the streets with no job, no friends and no TV.

The SKU leader had never imagined coming back here. Nor had he wanted to.

He stopped on the steps and rang Angie. He'd put it off as long as he could. Now he was going crazy.

She picked up sharply. 'H'lo.'

'Hi, it's dumbass here – remember me?'

'Oh yeah, I do. Big hunk of a guy, great brain too – just a shame it doesn't always get used properly.'

'That's me, Doctor Holmes. Where are you?'

'LAPD. In the restroom actually and just about to leave.'

She sounded mellow enough for him to take his best shot. 'Can we meet and talk?'

'Yeah, we can. We need to. You wanna grab lunch?'

'I do, I'm starving and I'm desperate to see you, but I can't. I'm about to go in the slammer and will be at least an hour.'

'Pity.'

'I'll be back around two-thirty. We could go to the coffee shop. Hey, I really want to sort this, Ang.'

'I know you do. Me too. Call me when you're in.'

He hung up. Allowed himself a smile and a final breath of fresh air before plunging inside and getting hit by *the smell*.

Eau de Jail-ogne.

The Essence of Incarceration.

An unmistakable and unique odor, drawn from buildings where the windows were never flung wide open. It came from furtive sex, gassy foods, acidic disinfectants, blocked latrines, mountains of filthy washing – and fear. The stench of fear floated down every landing. You could smell it on the rival gangs, on the segregated sex offenders – most of all, on the jailers.

Memories flooded back as Jake walked the transfer bridge and entered the ten special-security acres that hosted the two high-rise inmate-housing blocks known as the Twin Towers. He waited, as he'd done many times, for new guards to take him to the five-story Medical Services Building and the room where the prisoner was waiting.

Corrie Chandler.

The man who had so nearly killed him was in a burned orange prison uniform with a plain white T. His wrists and ankles were manacled, the top chains looped through a hole in a metal desk bolted to the floor of the holding cell.

The face that Jake had knifed bore blossoms of black bruises and enough plaster to wrap a mummy.

'Hello soldier.' Chandler's voice was nasal and slow, a result of the long sedation while trauma surgeons staunched blood and splinted broken bone. 'I didn't think you'd come.'

The FBI man said nothing. He took the empty seat and nodded to the two guards. They slipped out and locked the door. Deadbolts clunked top, bottom and center.

Jake looked at the prisoner and pictured him killing his wife and neighbor in a rage that had started with rejection and finished in their confrontation at the Griffith Observatory.

'What do you want, Corrie? Why'd you ask for me to come out here?'

Chandler nodded. He hadn't expected to be cut any courtesies. 'What'll happen to my stuff?'

Jake's eyes narrowed. 'What do you mean?'

'House an' car. Personal belongings an' things?'

'Didn't your attorney tell you all that?'

'Didn't ask for no attorney. I used my call getting you. I told them I don't need no representation. I know what I've done and I ain't going to start denying it.'

Jake tried to explain. 'The State is going to seize whatever you had. They'll try you and then after you're sentenced everything you owned will be sold off to settle compensation claims filed by relatives of your wife and the old man you killed.'

'I'm *sorry* about them.' He lowered his head in shame. 'Both of them should still be alive and it's me who should be dead.' He rattled the chains falling from his wrists and seemed unable to look up.

'Remind me, what was your wife's name, Corrie?'

He struggled to speak. 'Carlyann.'

Jake had a question. Probably the same one most of America wanted to ask. 'I'm just wondering what might have happened if you hadn't had a loaded gun in the house when Carlyann told you she was leaving.'

Chandler finally looked up. 'I was so mad right then, I'd have probably hit her.' He thought on it some more. 'Maybe not enough to kill her. But I might have punched her or choked her or something bad.'

There was no need to ask about the neighbor. He'd just been in the wrong place at the wrong time. If Chandler hadn't had a gun, he'd still be tending his garden.

Jake sat patiently. He knew there was more to come.

Finally, the prisoner got round to it. 'When you was in the army, did you have a stash? You know, a fuck-off fund. Dough you kept hid in case shit hit the fan and you just had to get out of town?'

'Yeah, I did. Not much of one, but there was a little put aside.'

Chandler seemed pleased by the answer. 'I got one. Also not so big but I got one.'

'Then you best tell the cops. They'll be all over your bankbooks and property. Better to tell them now and save everyone a lot of time and trouble.'

'What? And have some dirty lieutenant stick it in his own pocket?' He laughed off the idea. 'I want to tell you, not no cops. It's a thousand dollars, that's all. But it's my thousand dollars and I don't want it going to some A-hole that my wife might have been banging behind my back.'

'What do you want to do with it?'

'The old man next door has a son. Give it to him. He's called Jacob. Can you give it to him and say I'm sorry?'

'To do what with, Corrie? To bury his father? Somehow I don't think he's going to appreciate the gesture. Tell the cops, or write the son yourself and tell him.' He looked to the door. 'Listen, I've got things to do. If that's it, I need to blow.'

Corrie put his hand to his face and bit on a thumbnail.

Jake sensed there was something else. The real reason for asking him to come by.

'I keep seeing them.' He stared straight at the FBI man. 'The fuckers I killed.'

'Show some respect – they were your wife and neighbor.'

'No. Not them. The others.' He dipped his head again.

'What others, Corrie?' Jake stretched a big hand across the table and pushed his shoulder. 'Sit up and tell me. That's why you called me here.'

'They're all lying there, face down, hands behind their backs and – and then . . .' Chandler swallowed hard. Sweat glistened on his forehead. He wiped it with the back of his orange sleeve. 'I was in eastern Afghanistan, Nuristan province.'

'Go on.'

'Our combat outpost had been attacked by the Taliban. We'd been caught badly. Insurgents hit us from all sides. Pounded us for six hours. It was fucking medieval, man. They hit us with mortars, rockets, snipers. Went down like the bastards had been planning it for weeks.'

'I remember it. Stuff got posted on YouTube. Big shitstorm about how we got caught napping.'

Chandler nodded. 'Too fucking true. We took it so bad we ran out of blood for transfusions. Donations were going on during the shooting. No fucking aerial backup.'

'Why?'

'Fighting elsewhere. Fighting *everyfuckingwhere*.'

Jake nodded. He'd been in the same kinds of scrapes.

'By the time an Apache flew by, we'd got more than forty casualties and ten dead.' He took a beat. 'Some were real close friends.'

'I'm sorry.' And Jake was. He'd seen post-traumatic stress disorder many times and it was always different. Some soldiers fell apart after their first kill. Others never got over the trauma of seeing friends die. 'I don't want to seem unsympathetic, but if you're going to play the PTSD card in court, you need to call a shrink and a lawyer, not me.' He put his hands on the table and started to leave.

'It's not that.' There was urgency in Chandler's voice. He had to get something off his chest. 'It wasn't the attacks on us that I wanted to tell you about. It was the payback.'

Jake sat back and settled to listen.

'A couple of days after the Taliban hit us, we got word on some of the ringleaders and hard asses who'd escaped. Four units went out on a sweep. I was in one.' He stopped and mopped another outbreak of sweat. 'I was in a four-man. Got split up and hung out just with the sergeant. We came across six insurgents. They were shit scared. Dropped their guns and grabbed the sky. No fight in them.' His face screwed up and he punched the metal table top. 'Damn!'

Jake let the rage go without comment. He guessed what was coming but hoped he was wrong.

'We shot them.' Chandler nursed his smashed knuckles. 'Just opened up and killed them all.'

'You were told to – or you just did it?'

'He shot the first three.'

'The sergeant?'

Chandler nodded. 'He turned to me and said, "Now you."'

Jake had to hear it. 'So you did.'

'Yeah, I did.' His eyes said he was back at the scene. Seeing the fear. Hearing the noise. Seeing the blood.

'And afterward? What did you do?'

'Nothing.' He looked alarmed. 'We didn't take no trophies if that's what you mean. We buried them in the dirt. Literally covered it all up.'

'Well,' said Jake, 'now you've uncovered them, Corrie.'

'I know. And 'fore you say it, I know what a load of trouble it means. Both to me – and you.'

'I don't think you do,' answered Jake. 'In fact, I don't think you have any idea what problems this is going to cause.'

Chapter 28

'Spare me a minute in my office?'

Angie was halfway down the corridor, heading for the elevator, when she heard O'Brien's voice. She knew what he wanted. The mention of race in the case conference would have spooked him. She turned and smiled. 'Lead the way.'

It was a short walk. He pushed open a scuffed door to reveal a tiny, dark room that smelled of cigarettes and sweat.

The lieutenant closed the door behind him. 'What the hell was that curveball about a "racial component"?'

'It was exactly what it sounded like – I think race might be a central driver with the UNSUB but I need to validate.'

'No,' he said firmly. 'You don't. You don't need to *validate* or *insinuate* or do anything that injects the word race into a case on my desk, with my name on it.' He glowered at her. 'Do I make myself clear?'

She met his anger with her own. 'Totally. You're a fully paid-up member of the cover-your-ass club, even if it means people out there die because you're afraid of the truth.'

O'Brien took a deep breath and tried to keep his temper.

Angie took advantage of his silence. 'Let's get some things straight, lieutenant. First off, I don't work for you and I don't take orders from you. Second – and here's the big one – if I believe that race *was* a motive in this case, then this investigation, that includes your people, my people and the elderly women of LA who are watching the media and living in fear of this scumbag, are all going to get told.'

'That's a big *if*.'

'All *ifs* are big.'

'Yeah, but that one's Trayvon Martin, George Zimmerman big.'

She laughed at him. 'I wondered how long it would be before you threw that up.'

He paced and hung his head in frustration. Finally, he turned and faced her again. 'Are you really ready to have the media writing headlines about us hunting a "Rape Racist"?'

'A what?'

'You heard me.'

Angie felt enraged. 'You think the word "rape" gets more frightening if you tag the word "racist" next to it?' She laughed mockingly. 'Believe me, you wouldn't if you were a woman.'

'It sure as hell doesn't make it any *less* frightening. And it could get some hate groups spooked into vigilante nonsense. Cut me some slack here, doctor. Give me twenty-four hours before you start elaborating to anyone on this *possible* race MO.'

She stared through him while she thought it over. She needed at least that time to convince herself that she was totally right. 'One more day, then that's it.'

'Agreed.' He forced a smile. '*Thank you*.'

Angie poker-faced him. 'After that, we need to start talking about it – even if it's in a very closed group.' She picked up her purse and was about to head out.

'Hang on. Can I run something past you before you go? It'll only take a minute.'

She dropped the purse along with a look that said she was clean out of patience. 'You've got five.'

'Thanks. We received an anonymous call late last night. Came in after Twitter and the TV stations started carrying the news about Lindsey Knapp's death. It was a woman's voice, young by the sound of it, made from a public booth in Lynwood.'

'She put the finger on someone?'

'Trent Bensimon. Local boy made bad. Done time in Juvie for inde-cent exposure and assaults on middle-aged women.'

'Define middle-aged.'

'Fifty-five.'

'How old was Bensimon back then?'

'Fifteen.'

A forty-year age gap fitted her profile. 'And now?'

'Twenty-two.' O'Brien could see that he had her interest. 'Single child. Lives rough. We've got a CI says he's been known to make cash running eight balls on a Bloods' corner.'

Angie knew an eight ball was street slang for an eighth of an ounce. 'He a black kid?'

'Wishes he was. He's whiter than white but talks like a rapper.'

She shook her head.

O'Brien smiled. 'You said not to discount suspects just because they don't tick all your boxes.'

'I *did* say that, you're right. Have you got his sheet?'

'Better. I just had word that we've got him. At least we will have in a few minutes' time. You want to sit in on the interview?'

'Not really.'

'Will you?'

She gave a slight nod. 'I have to make a call.' She went for the cellphone in her purse and stepped outside. There was no way she was going to make coffee with Jake at two-thirty.

She got his voicemail and left a message. 'Hey, I'm sorry, I can't get back from the LAPD for the time we said. They've got a suspect on the way to the station and I want to sit in on the interview. Listen, I'm not stiffing you on purpose. I really want us to try to talk again. How about we go for sushi after work? Or pizza, if you prefer?' She hated pizza but would eat glass and hot coal if it could fix things between them.

O'Brien appeared as she was talking: 'Bensimon's being brought in downstairs. They're gonna take him through to an interview room.'

She finished up with Jake and hoped to hell that this interview didn't take all day.

94

Chapter 29

SKU Offices, LA

Jake took Corrie Chandler's war story back to his boss.

Crawford Dixon sat in his big leather chair in his big corner office and wished this shit wasn't being brought to him. It was the kind of crap that stuck and stunk for the rest of your career. He listened intently to the account, then asked, 'Do you believe him?'

Jake's reply came without hesitation. 'I do.'

His boss gave him grounds for doubt. 'He could just be roasting the old chestnut of post-traumatic stress, preparing the ground for an insanity plea.'

'I thought of that. And by the way, I think he might well have *good* grounds for an insanity plea.'

'Hey, don't go all bleeding heart liberal on me.'

'Moral lines get blurred on the battlefield, sir. Right and wrong wear identical camouflage. The only thing for sure is that guilt over a kill is your worst enemy. It brutalizes you by day and stays so close it bunks with you at night.'

'I know. I served, remember?'

'No disrespect meant.'

'None taken. We all have ghosts of guilt chasing us. Every cop that's shot a gangbanger in an alley or a stickup guy in a 7-Eleven has night sweats; it goes with the territory.'

'I was just trying to say, I—'

'Then don't. Don't say it. Because this statement of Chandler's is a clusterfuck of a bomb and you've just pulled the pin.'

'I know.'

'Do you? Do you really? Let me tell you something. Everyone's going to catch shrapnel from this – State Department, Defense, White House, Army and probably us.' He made it personal. '*You* in particular.' Dixon took off his glasses and put them on his desk. He rubbed tired eyes and replaced the spectacles. 'I'm sorry, Jake. You've done the right thing. You bring your cross to me. I carry it to the director's desk and eventually the press finds someone to nail to it.'

'Chandler will name the sergeant if we want. He opened up to me because we shared that moment at Griffith.'

'How *lovely* for you both. I'm gonna take this upstairs and then I'll get back to you.'

Jake got to his feet. 'I'll send you a write-up this afternoon.' He headed for the door.

'Make it vague.'

He turned. 'How so?'

'Don't be too specific. Prison log will show you went to see Chandler so we can't say this never happened. At this stage, it's best if your report to me just says that he *intimated* there might have been a military atrocity that he took part in under instruction from a senior officer. Nothing more.'

'I'm not comfortable with that, sir.'

'Then get comfortable with it. And if you can't, then forget the whole damned thing.'

There was no point arguing. Jake nodded and left.

The ass-covering had already started.

One thing for sure, there was too much detail in Chandler's account for it just to be a shot at a lighter sentence.

Part way back to his office he turned his cellphone off silent and saw Angie's missed call. He picked up the voicemail and swore.

Chapter 30

Trent Bensimon was all attitude.

He was dressed top-to-toe in baggy blacks, a hoody pulled over his shaved head and oversized shades. Cheap gold chains dangled from a neck tattooed with a dotted line and the invitation: CUT HERE.

Bensimon rocked on the back legs of his chair and chewed gum loudly. O'Brien and a female cop called Vanessa Gutierrez threw questions at him.

'I tol' ya twice, I was wit' ma bitch. You do ya job an' check her, dog. I 'ang out dat pussy all nite.'

Angie watched from behind mirrored glass and felt for the young female detective.

'We *are* checking.' O'Brien leaned across the table. 'This *lady* you say you were with, Nina Mahoney, how old is she?'

He laughed. Let all four legs of the chair come back to rest on the floor and matched the cop's lean. 'You knows ma type, dog. I likes pussy bin around sum, pussy wot holds me like a velvet hand.' He squeezed his fingers sleazily and nodded to the female cop. 'Not like ya skinny young bitch here.'

'Watch your mouth,' said O'Brien.

The kid smiled wide and rocked back on his chair again. 'Nina's *fifty*. The big Five O. I gave her somethin' special for her birthday las' week. You know what I mean, dog?'

The cop didn't respond, except to bore a hole in his face with his eyes.

Bensimon realized he was on thin ice. 'Lissen, this *a-nony-mouse* call you got. I say it's from a bitch called Tracy Durrell. Me and hers had a beef. You follow?'

'About what?' asked Gutierrez.

He ignored her.

'Explain,' snapped O'Brien.

'She's fuckin' bizzo, dog.' He jabbed a finger to his temple. 'She's jealous 'bout Nina. Bitch wants me hanging outta her instead. Said she's gonna split us up. Dog, she's always shakin' her big ass at me,' he grabbed his crotch, 'jus' beggin' for bone.'

Angie had seen enough. She called O'Brien's cell. Watched him through the glass as it buzzed in his pocket and he reached for it.

'I need to step out of the room and check on your alibi, Trent.'

'Take your time, dog.'

'And *I* need to step outside and vomit.' Gutierrez got up and followed her boss. No way was she going to trust herself alone with that animal. Another word and she'd kill him.

Angie met them both in the corridor. 'His alibi *will* check out. Even if it doesn't, he's not your man.' She could see they needed an explanation. 'He's attracted to older women because he doesn't fear that they'll make him feel sexually inadequate. He's either a psychologically damaged premature ejaculator or, *more likely*, has an exceptionally small penis. Single older women understand his inadequacies. They will tolerate them because of the ego-lifting benefits that come from being with a young man.'

'He's no man,' said Gutierrez.

'Agreed, but he's no rapist either.'

The female cop looked disappointed. Nothing would have delighted her more than locking him up. 'How can you be so sure?'

Angie didn't mention that she was becoming convinced the offender was black. 'He's mouthing off all the time. Sex and talking about sex turns him on. That's not our UNSUB. Our scum isn't triggered by sexual urges; he's set off by hate, by rage and resentment. That waste of skin and words in there couldn't beat an egg let alone a human being.'

Almost on cue, a chubby detective appeared in the corridor. He was breathless from a run down stairs. Sweat stained his blue shirt and a sheet of paper fluttered in his fist. 'She vouches for him, boss. Nina Mahoney says he's been staying at her house every night for the past month, never missed an hour between nightfall and sunrise.'

'Fuck.' O'Brien looked like he wanted to punch a hole in the wall. 'Get corroboration. She might be lying.'

'She's not,' said Angie. 'I've gotta leave.' She turned to Gutierrez. 'While you're giving the boy in there the news that he's free to go, hold your little finger up like this and waggle it in his face. He'll know that you're onto his secret. Believe me, you'll ruin his fun for at least a few months.'

Chapter 31

California

The Strawberry Fields Massacre, as everyone was already calling it, was trending on Twitter. It was the most talked about subject on radio shows coast-to-coast and the lead story in all the national newspapers.

To Shooter, fame was sweet. He sucked up whatever he could find about himself.

A large selection of print coverage was laid out on his floor, including a detailed selection of head and shoulder photographs of the dead and injured.

He sat with his scissors and meticulously cut out the pictures. First those of Mrs Gina Page: 'a teacher of English and charity worker.' He put her photos in one pile and then snipped out those of Mr Zachary Borowitz, a teacher of mathematics and PE. Shooter had hated both subjects. Math was for the soulless, PE for the brainless.

The victim that had gotten the most coverage was Amy Cassidy: 'just ten years old and all her life before her.' Shooter caught himself saying, 'Boo hoo hoo,' and then he clipped the shots of her. Amy with her dog Zippy. Amy in school uniform. Amy winning a beauty pageant. There was no end of shots of Amy. He couldn't wait to see all the cry babies at her funeral.

He sat for a moment and played Happy Families by putting pictures of Zach, Gina and Amy together. Maybe they really were together in the afterworld, and the bizarre thought made him wonder if their families would like that idea or hate it?

He looked at a photograph of the teacher's husband, Andy; he was a truck driver and ten years older than her. Andy was a bull of a man, with rounded shoulders from leaning over a wheel and a barreled stomach filled with too many fried dinners. He'd hate the notion of Gina being with Zach. You could just tell he would.

The papers showed Zach was married to a pretty blonde called Ellen who ran an animal shelter. They'd only tied the knot a year ago, and from the wedding picture Shooter was looking at, he figured she was the free-thinking kind of woman who wouldn't begrudge her dead husband a little afterlife hanky-panky.

He took the photos and pinned them in the very top corner of a huge corkboard that covered an entire wall of a room he'd christened Death Row. The name seemed apposite for a lot of reasons. This was the place where he could see his community gather and grow. Kill by kill it would get larger and more meaningful.

Before he left the room, he looked at a side wall and a single picture he'd placed in the middle of it. To Shooter, it said more than the proverbial thousand words. It made sense of it all.

Of the murders that had happened.

Of the ones still to be committed.

Chapter 32

SKU Offices, LA

B ack in the office, Jake and Ruis rang Pryce on a conference line to compare notes on yesterday's incident.

The SWAT leader kicked off. 'We did a fingertip search of the woods and you were right, that's where our gunman had set himself up. By the way, I'm here with Bobby Mankoff, my new number two, he's going to fill you in.'

'Hi Bobby.' Jake knew him of old. A stocky New Yorker with a heavyweight's build. He guessed Pryce had decided to have him promoted so he could keep people in line. 'Missed you at the Observatory, where were you hiding?'

'Other side of the freakin' country with the in-laws, that's where.'

'Tough luck, Bobby. What you got for us?'

'A whole bunch of photographs taken out at the strawberry scene – I'll mail them to you shortly. You'll see flattened grass on high ground about a hundred yards from the kill zone and only a few yards back into the woods. The space the UNSUB had gotten himself into had no trees blocking his line of fire, just firs to the right and left giving him shade and cover.'

Ruis jumped in. 'Are there lots of clearings like that, or would he have had to know those woods to find that spot?'

'We asked ourselves the same question,' answered Mankoff. 'From what I saw, there were three or four areas along the tree line that would have given you as good a sight of the field. In fact, two would have been better.'

Jake threw in the obvious question. 'Bobby, any idea why he picked that spot?'

Pryce chipped back the reply. 'We think it's because of the exit route. Being higher up the hill gave him a more covered and quicker escape through the copse. Seems the back of the woods gets used for dirt bikes. We found a lot of tire tracks down there and that got us to thinking the perp made his shots, ran to a bike and then was outta there before we even got a copter up.'

'It figures,' said Jake. 'I was wondering why the thermal cameras might have missed him if he'd been hiding out. Looks like we got the answer.'

Pryce added some bad news. 'Before you ask, there are no traffic cameras around the link roads near the strawberry fields.'

'Course not. Why would we get so lucky.'

'Good news is there are plenty on the interstate heading into LA. We've got traffic cops pulling footage from anything with a lens to see if we can spot our Spree.'

'We're not holding our breath on that one,' said Mankoff dryly. 'Good news is that Forensics done some great work out at the scene.'

Pryce filled in the detail. 'Check this: from where the perp had laid out they located the depressions he'd left in the earth with his elbows, knees and the tips of his toes. Then they ran thermal scans over that precise area and from that heat map they were able to plot the outline of his body.'

'Impressive,' said Jake. 'How'd he measure up?'

'Not so tall. They set him between five nine and five eleven. The margin of error is down to what kind of soles he might have had on his boots.'

'Depressions give a clue to his weight?'

'The ground was too hard for them to stick their necks out on that.'

Aside from height, it didn't seem to Jake that they had a lot to go on. 'Connor, did you get someone to clip grass and take soil samples in case he'd taken a leak or anything?'

'Yeah, we did. Sheriff's Department swept up every bit of surrounding litter too, just in case the UNSUB snacked while waiting out there. I'll let you know when the DNA profiles get run through databases.' Pryce had something on his mind that he wanted an opinion on before they all hung up. 'From a SWAT point of view, we're done now. But I'm real uncomfortable just leaving this with deputies out in the sticks. What's your reading, guys? You think this worm is going to come out of his hole anytime soon?'

'Bet your ass on it,' said Jake. 'If he was a Serial then we'd be in trouble. Sprees are predictable but Serials are tricky fucks and can keep you waiting for months or years. Not the good old Spree though. Mark my words, he'll be back at it before the end of the week.'

Chapter 33

A ngie spent the afternoon working her profile and imagining how the rapist might develop.

She knew that from a perp's point of view a rape scene is a classroom. It's where he got to learn. Where he experimented and developed his techniques and confidence.

What scared the hell out of her was that she was sure he now realized he could spend much longer with his victims than he had.

And, even worse, he could kill and get away with it.

Angie was acutely aware that the UNSUB was preying on the most vulnerable group in society. Aside from their physical frailty, women in their seventies and eighties tended to live alone and go long periods without any contact from friends, neighbors or relatives. Certainly no one checked them from bedtime to breakfast, and none of the victims had money to fit their homes with security systems and panic buttons.

For now, her psych profile was the best thing the cops had to guide them. The UNSUB had never spoken to the victims and only Lindsey Knapp had seen him. Her death-bed description had been of a man of average height and build with a ski mask over his face and black leather gloves on his hands.

It was next to useless.

After the first assault, he'd bound and gagged his victim with heavy-duty tape. Two attacks in, he'd gotten inventive and used strands of tape like a sticky brush post assault to pat the women down and make sure he hadn't left any fibers or skin cells stuck to their clothing. Angie took this not only as a sign that he was becoming more forensically aware, but also that he may have made mistakes in the first attack. The tape had been manufactured by Scotch, not Duck, and was their most common silver-grey brand, sold worldwide in units of millions. Analysts were working on tracing the batches of powdered aluminum pigment used in manufacture, in the hope that it might lead them to sales distribution outlets. At best it would give them a haystack not a needle.

Her desk phone rang.

'Angie Holmes.'

'Hi, it's Suzie. I'm in the building, you got time for a coffee?'

She had but wasn't sure she wanted to have the conversation that Suzie would inevitably initiate.

'No worries if you're busy,' added the doctor intuitively. 'I just wanted to check you were okay.'

'I'm fine, thanks.' Angie gave in. 'Come on up, I could do with a break.' She put the phone down and shifted a pile of files off the spare seat at her desk. The room wasn't big enough for any soft seating. With Chips's expansive workstation and burgeoning computer equipment it was getting to the stage where she couldn't swing a mouse, let alone a cat.

Suzie rapped on the door before she let herself in. 'Hiya. Those lifts get worse, you could wait a year for one to come.'

The two women embraced.

'You really want coffee?' asked Angie.

'Naah.' She smiled, draping her purse over the back of the chair and taking a seat. 'I just want to know you're okay.'

Angie nodded, pulled her chair out and sat to one side so she wasn't behind the desk, but next to her friend. 'I think I'm getting to okay. Let's say, I can at least see where okay is.'

'That's a big improvement on when you were in my office.'

'Yeah, I know.'

'I'm not going to ask you if you've made a decision, I—'

'I have.'

Suzie read her face. The nervous smile said she was going to be a mom. 'You sure?'

Her eyes lit up. 'Yeah. It's taking some getting used to, but I'm sure. It feels right.'

'How right?'

'It's hard to say.' She took a breath and then tried to describe her feelings. 'It's like there's a river of decision flowing within me and the tide and force is in the direction of keeping the baby and seeing it all through.'

Suzie frowned a little. 'That's called being swept along by events.'

'I know,' she smiled wider now, 'I did psychology, remember?'

Suzie put up an apologetic hand.

'It's more than momentum. Going against the flow feels increasingly the wrong thing to do.'

Suzie allowed herself to relax a little. She'd guessed the wrong way. Had expected her friend to be set on termination. 'And Jake? How did that go?'

She rolled her eyes. 'Badly.'

'He's still a long way back from okay?'

'Uh-huh. A whole world away. He doesn't want me to have it.'

'I'm sorry. You think he'll come round?'

'I'm hoping.'

'And if not?'

'Then I choose the baby. No question about it.'

Suzie pulled her purse off the chair. 'Then I can stop worrying about you.' She got to her feet. 'Come see me tomorrow and we'll talk about health care and the little matter of telling your boss. If you make it for twelve, I'll buy you lunch.'

'You've got a deal.' She walked her to the door. 'Thanks for coming by.'

'You're welcome. I look forward to seeing you and your instinctive river tomorrow.'

Chapter 34

SKU Offices, LA

I t was the kind of call Jake knew he shouldn't make.

But he made it anyway.

He had a buddy who worked in Army Intelligence, a good friend who came from his old neighborhood. They'd played in the same football team. Fought in the same regiment. Even dated some of the same women.

'Lamotta.' The one word answer came from an African American with a right fist like a sledgehammer and the heart of a teenage girl.

'Joe, it's Jake Mottram. How you doing, man?'

Lamotta laughed like he'd slurped balloon gas. 'I'm doing *gooooood*, man.' He checked a calendar on his wall. 'Far as I see, there ain't no anniversaries coming up, so I'm figuring you've got bad news or you're after something.'

'Man, you Intelligence guys are so smart.'

'Which is it, Jake? I got to go find my funeral duds again?'

'No, no one died, Joe. It's a favor that I need.'

'A *favor*? You think you still got favors in the bank? After how fucked up you left me at that party in New York? Brother, it was like a scene from *The Hangover*.'

'Can you ring me back?'

'Fuck.' The comment had taken the wind out of Lamotta's sails. It meant there was bad news coming and Jake wanted to share it on a non-traceable line, a pay-as-you-go burner that all Special Services guys kept if they needed to call each other. 'Yeah, I can do that. Give me five. I need some fresh air.'

'You got it.' He dropped his desk phone and took out his own untraceable.

Couple of minutes later he was still looking at it when it buzzed. 'Hi.'

'Hi yourself. It's a beautiful day here in Washington, tell me you ain't gonna ruin it.'

'I can't promise.'

'*Sh*-it.'

'So here it is. I took down a Spree by the name of Corrie Chandler, ex-Tenth Mountain.'

'Saw it on the news.'

'What you didn't see is this morning I visited him in lockup and he told me a tale to chill your blood.'

'Which was?'

'He and his superior officer illegally executed some insurgents during Operation Enduring Freedom.'

'Oh fuck.'

'Yeah, I know.'

'Don't do this, man. Really. If you lift the rocks off anything to do with that campaign, then all hell's creatures are bound to come crawling out.'

'I have to, Joe. Can you have a sneak around for me?'

'No.'

'Chandler said the shit went down in Nuristan province.'

'I said no.'

'Emotions were high, a lot of their buddies had been killed and injured—'

'Jake, no! *If* this happened – and note that I said *if* – then it went down more than a decade ago. What the fuck's he doing bringing this up now?'

'Chandler killed his wife and a neighbor. Now he's banged up with nothing to lose so I figure he wants to confess all his sins and find some absolution.'

Lamotta laughed. 'Then it's bull. He wants to snag an insanity plea. He's using you, man.'

MICHAEL MORLEY

'I don't think so. I'm pretty certain the war fucked him up, Joe. There's no denying it does that, right?'

Lamotta blew out an exasperated sigh. The day had been going so well. His daughter had a sleepover tonight, he'd planned to finish early and take her to her friend's, then he and his wife were heading for an evening of serious loving. 'Have you taken this upstairs?'

Jake looked at the half-finished report on his desk. 'Only verbally. I haven't put in the paperwork.'

'Then don't. I'm guessing your boss will want to park a tank over it. I can be that tank, man. Say you ran some checks with a buddy and got zip.'

'And Chandler? What do I do about a guy who might have lived a different life if he hadn't got screwed up in some godforsaken part of Afghanistan?'

There was a long, dry silence.

Jake broke it. 'I just want to know if there's any truth in it, Joe. You don't need to go on record, don't need to do anything about exposing it, I just need to know.'

The silence lasted even longer this time.

It was Lamotta's turn to break it. 'You're gonna owe me, man. Owe me forever. I'll see what I can do.'

110

Chapter 35

California

The piece of paper in Shooter's hand had been thrown away. Discarded by someone he'd never met.

It had been mailed to that person's house, they'd read it, made a note about it and then tossed it.

The entire floor of the room he was stood in was covered in trash that people had jettisoned. Snippets of their lives. Clippings of their hair and nails. Tissues kissed with lipstick. Cotton wool pads, daubed with make-up and cleansers.

It wasn't all in one big mound. He had organized it into distinct piles and labeled each one.

Shooter had been collecting trash for a long time. He called it his 'life collage'. There was something fascinating about how close he could get to people through what they no longer wanted. He could work out their diets, their medical problems and their love lives. Most interesting of all, he could even work out when they were going to die.

Shooter folded the piece of paper and put it in the back pocket of his pants. It made him feel connected to the fool who'd thrown it away. Linked by his secret knowledge.

He used a tissue to pick up another note.

One he'd written for the police. Something to get their *juices* flowing.

He checked monitors, set alarms and slipped out of the shadowy safety of his sanctuary into the blazing sunlight.

Temperatures were pushing ninety. Everyone on the street was dressed casual and wearing factor 20 and fake designer shades. He checked the brands bobbing by. Oakley, Ray-Ban, Prada, Polaroid and his favorite – Police. He passed the journey thinking about the people behind the tints and what might be on their minds.

Some had their ears plugged, blotting music, others looked brain-dead. Stoned. Hung over. Just stupid. None seemed anything special.

Unlike him.

He doubted they had secrets that stretched beyond stealing sweets as a kid or fucking someone they shouldn't have.

They were the 'unfamous'.

People who would pass through life without leaving their mark. They were bit part actors on his stage, fit for screaming and freaking out, but nothing else.

Shooter rode the escalator from the sidewalk to the first level of the mall. It was good to be out of the heat. He put his hand in the black canvas sports bag slung over his shoulder and felt the cool metal lying in there.

The escalator evened out.

He stepped off and felt like he'd done when he'd been settled in the woods and watched the kids and teachers in the strawberry fields.

Things were coming together.

Impetus was building.

He paused in front of a store window and took a breath to compose himself. He had learned from yesterday. Don't rush. Don't make mistakes. Not out here in the open, in the midst of the crowd.

Shooter adjusted a white Lakers cap over his fuzz of tight, black hair. It had to be perfectly straight.

Dead straight.

Just below the purple writing and curve of the yellow basketball logo, he'd painstakingly fitted a pair of miniature 3D lenses. They were linked to a digital recorder resting next to the gun in the bag.

Slowly, he stepped away from his reflection. Walked the final fifty yards to the kill zone. Time speeded up. Nerves kicked in. Frames of focus dropped as his heartbeat quickened.

He slowed his breathing again. Told himself that in a moment he would feel better. All that welled-up pain and rage would be gone. Purged. Leeched away in a healing splash of blood.

He halted outside Bloomingdale's, dipped his hand in the sports bag and slipped off the safety.

Twenty yards to go.

The shiny, reflective glass of the swanky store window mirrored a thin, nondescript black kid in Police shades.

A kid about to become the most talked about person on the planet.

Not that you'd think it to look at him.

He'd dressed down in white, unlaced trainers, low-hanging baggy black shorts, that tricksy white Lakers cap and a white Nike T, with its big iconic tick symbolizing their 'Just Do It' attitude.

Cool.

And the coolness grew with every step.

Beats of heavy music struck up in his brain. A steady bass boomed. Kept rhythm with his pulse. Inside the sports bag, he fingered the curled trigger of the MAC-10. Stroked it gently. Feathered it.

No need to lift it out. No point drawing attention to himself unnecessarily early. Mr MAC was nocturnal, worked best in the dark.

His left hand dug into his pocket and found a Kleenex. Inside it, the fingerprint-free note that he planned to leave.

One word that told them why. It'd drive them crazy.

Up ahead was a sign: JUDY-JU'S GLASSES. He checked his watch. It was time.

Chicken time. No going back time. Killing time.

Chapter 36

The door was open, so Jake stuck his head through the crack.
Angie was sitting at her desk, long hair dangling like curtains, covering whatever paperwork she was bent over.

He missed feeling the brush of her locks on his face when she lay on top of him, when she teased him or when she rested there, all her energy spent and her face flushed from lovemaking. He missed the way she enchanted him with her soft brown eyes, made him feel like no other woman had ever done.

He just plain missed her.

'Hi.' He stepped inside, his heart over-revving. 'I got your message.'

She looked up from the victim statements. Pulled herself from a world of hurt. 'Hi, I didn't hear you come in.'

'Hope not. All my Ninja training would've been wasted.'

She smiled. 'I'm sorry I had to cancel.'

'Don't worry, I understand. How'd it go?' He perched on the edge of her desk.

She had to lean back to look up at him. 'Struck out. They're back at square one.'

'You'll get your guy – you always do.'

'Do I?'

He could tell she was tired. 'You look stressed. Is that because of me or the case?'

'Bit of both. I didn't sleep well last night.' She gave him an intimate look. 'Maybe I missed you being there.'

'I certainly missed being there.' He bent closer. Felt energy spark between them. 'You think we can wind back the clock? Maybe have that big conversation all over again, minus the shock?'

'Yeah, we can do that.' She teased him. 'But not now. Not until *after*.'

'After?' He played dumb.

She gave him no answer. Just a look that hit his heart like a shot of adrenaline.

Jake put his hand to her face and kissed her. Light and gentle, but enough to cause an explosion.

She pressed her lips hard to his. Let him know of her need. Matched his want with her own. No one had ever made her feel like Jake did. No one ever would.

They broke.

Both looked emotional. Aroused yet almost tearful. If they'd been alone at home they'd have been naked by now, shutting off their brains and leaving their bodies to find the common ground and peace they so desperately craved.

The clock over Angie's door said it was just after five. 'You know, I could just grab a whole load of stuff off my desk and we could get outta here.'

'What about your work?'

She started packing. 'I'll deal with it later.'

His eyes lifted. '*Later*? Is that before or after *after*.'

'Oh, after. *Long* after.'

Chapter 37

Sun Western Mall, LA

Shooter turned into Judy-Ju's.

He saw fifteen, maybe twenty people spread across the open-plan floor. Mainly couples. All browsing. Trying on designer frames. Posing in front of angled mirrors. Wondering if glasses could really be worth more than two hundred bucks.

He wanted twelve bodies. Just twelve. No more. No less.

A dozen dead.

An old black woman came into view. She was speaking too loud at the counter.

Shooter watched. The store girl raised her voice. The senior fumbled at a hearing aid. 'I'm sorry, honey, I wasn't switched on.'

'Take a seat,' said the girl. 'The optometrist will see you in a moment.'

Shooter's heart cramped. He stepped forward. The old woman saw him. Looked at him with her head tilted inquisitively. Her face asked what he wanted, why he was staring at her?

He watched her eyes as he squeezed the trigger of the hidden gun. The MAC kicked harder than he'd expected.

Bullets spluttered from the sports bag. Blood and brain spattered the wall behind the woman's head. It covered the ceiling, the mirrors and displays of glasses. She still seemed to be staring at him. Blood sprayed like he'd punctured a hosepipe and she was falling from the chair, eyes still open.

The 'unfamous' were slow to pick up their cues. They only screamed when she hit the floor, when the side of her skull cracked against the polished tiles.

Something detonated inside Shooter. An emotional bomb blast. A nuclear surge of euphoria and power.

He squeezed and sprayed.

This was infinitely more thrilling than yesterday. The closeness to the bodies added an extra frisson. The gun was somehow alive in his hands, like a powerful squirming snake spitting death. Men, women, children, black, white, old and young all fell victim to its venom.

Bodies on bodies.

Living and dead heaped together, a stack of human Jenga.

It was hard to count.

Difficult to be sure.

Twelve dead. No more, no less. It had to be twelve.

He checked them off in his head. Counted like it was a nursery rhyme.

One dead. Two dead. Three dead. Four.

Five dead. Six dead. Seven dead. More.

He sank bullets into their bodies to make sure there was no mistake, no repeat of the disappointment with the baldy teacher in the strawberry fields.

He sank the rounds deep. Like seeds. Lead flowers to grow in their backs and chests.

Bouquets for their graves.

Eight dead. Nine dead.

The screaming was different now. Soft moaning from the corners of the store. As though he was underwater and it was all happening up above him.

Ten dead.

He walked in their blood and checked again.

Ten.

His trainers daubed a fresco of red swirls and prints on the cream floor. He turned his head left to right so the Lakercams got a good shot of it all. Added a flourish with his foot.

A white kid, half his age, dashed for the exit.

A three-round burst cut him down. Shattered the boy's knees. Opened his stomach. Split his head.

Eleven.

One more. He needed only one more.

People were screaming louder, some crying, sobbing as he moved among them swinging his shoulder bag, his bag of death. Most had scurried to the corners of the store. Frightened mice, frantic for a hole to squeeze through.

He wanted to kill them all. The urge was there to wipe them all out. Exterminate them.

But that would make him as insignificant as the red-misters, the heat-of-the-momenters, the ones who killed without reason.

He wasn't like them. He had reason. Very good reason.

Twelve was what he wanted. No more. No less.

A man in his thirties, crouched over his toddler and wife, let out a roar of anger and charged him.

Shooter's burst of gunfire ran up his body. Sliced his thigh. Cut through his stomach. Cracked ribs. Burst his big, brave heart.

Twelve.

That was it. He was done.

He took his finger off the trigger. His hand felt hot. Burning like he'd dipped it in a volcano.

He turned from the carnage and dropped the note. It fluttered and flopped in a pool of blood.

That should get their attention.

Make them sit up and take notice.

Chapter 38

FBI Field Office, LA

Jake's phone rang as soon as he and Angie stepped out of the elevator. She gave him a look that said she'd rather he didn't answer it.

'I've got to.'

'I know.'

'Mottram.'

'Jake, it's Ruis. Shit's hitting the fan at the Sun Western mall. Some lunatic's opened fire on a load of shoppers.'

'I'm on my way to you.' He killed the phone and turned to Angie. 'Sounds like a Spree, I've gotta go.'

'Be careful.'

'I will.' He kissed her again. A peck this time. Nothing long or passionate but a connection every bit as meaningful as the one in the office.

Jake didn't wait for the elevator. He banged open the door to the stairs and took them two at a time all the way to the twelfth floor.

SKU was already snagging kit and buckling up. Ruis had mall security on speakerphone. There were screams in the background and it sounded like the gates of hell had bust open. He finished the call and updated his boss. 'It's bedlam over there. Cops are on their way. Meantime, the mall uniforms are shitting enough bricks to build a pyramid.'

'Evac has to be priority. The sooner the LAPD take over the better. With that kind of panic going on people can get crushed to death.'

Jake checked his own men. Most were still arriving. Just dressing was an operation in itself. They started with fatigues made from flame-resistant Nomex fiber, leather-palmed flight gloves that gave weapons an extra grip, heavy-duty kneepads and reinforced utility boots. Then came the military-issue gas mask with special air filters to cope with all manner of toxic attacks. The facial fitting had a drink tube so rehydration could take place without removal, and a voice box amplifier for communication with the two-channel radio package made up of an ear-piece, microphone and shoulder-mounted transmitter. Extra protection came courtesy of Kevlar chest, back and pelvic pads. Helmets and no-mist goggles, strong enough to withstand blasts and flying debris, completed the wrap.

Jake turned back to Ruis. 'Once they're togged, split them into four units of four and get them gridded around the mall. You take north and west; I'll go south and east. I'll call Pryce on the way over. I expect he'll set a central command vehicle out on the Avenue of the Stars and shut off traffic from there all along Santa Monica Boulevard.'

'Firepower?'

'Usual stuff for close quarters, but bring extra flashbangs and tear gas. We best prepare for a lock-down too. If the shooter gets himself in a store with a hostage then we're gonna need the whole caboodle – battering rams, bolt cutters, a Hallagan breach bar and shotguns with breaching rounds.'

Jake left him to get on. He grabbed his own sidearms: an M1911 semi-automatic pistol identical to the one he'd been issued with in the Marine Corps and a back-up Glock. For good measure, he collected his personalized Heckler and Koch MP5 sub-machine gun. It had been fitted with a tritium-illuminated front sight post and a stainless steel sound suppressor for use with quieter subsonic ammo.

'Listen up,' the SKU leader shouted across the room. 'Agent Costas is going to call your teams. I know many of you worked long and hard yesterday, way into the night, and I guess some of you were just clocking off shift, so I apologize for that. But make no mistake about this – I do *not* want anyone starting this new operation if you're anything less than razor-sharp ready. If you are exhausted and not fit to work then tell me now. There's no shame in that. Go home, get some sleep. If you're yawning and slow on this op then you'll be risking a colleague's life and that's unacceptable. Any questions?'

A chorus of 'No, sir' hit his ears.

'Anyone too tired to go hunt this motherfucking Spree?'

The chorus sang the same refrain. 'No, sir!'

'Good. Ruis, get the show on the road.'

Chapter 39

Angie grabbed black coffee from the corridor pantry and returned to the case files on her desk.

Her head was all mixed up.

She and Jake had been building bridges. Now he was back on the streets trying to get close enough to kill or be killed. It made her think he'd been right after all. Perhaps his whole life did make him completely unsuitable to be a father.

She'd hoped for just the opposite. Convinced herself having a kid might actually stop him taking risks.

Chips breezed in, oblivious to her personal drama. 'Never again.' He threw down his shoulder bag. 'I promise you, boss, I'm gonna resign rather than sit through another four hours about ethnic diversity and responsibility.'

She ignored his rant. 'You hear about the shootings?'

'No.'

'A Spree at Sun Western mall.'

'Oh my God.'

'Can you hack into their CCTV system?'

'Sure.' Chips sat down. 'But we don't need to hack.' He spoke as he picked up the phone and turned on his desktop PC. 'LAPD have all mall feeds linked to their central ops control. I can get a patch through to my monitor.'

'Thanks.'

As Chips dialed, the office door opened.

Angie's heart sank.

It was her boss, Assistant Director Sandra McDonald. Or 'Ronald' as Chips referred to her. The assistant director was forty-five, single and cut a trim figure in her trademark black business suit and platinum blond bob cut. She had the kind of cold and acerbic manner that always brushed Angie the wrong way.

'How's everything going with the rape-homicide?'

Angie suspected she'd heard about the difference of opinion on what should and shouldn't be revealed to the investigation team. 'We're making progress. I think the base of the profile is solid enough to help focus the team in the right direction.'

'I hear you and Lieutenant O'Brien aren't the best of friends.'

'Do we have to be?'

'No. But don't bring shit to my stoop. Do you understand?'

Angie bit her tongue. 'Entirely.'

'I'm seeing the director in the morning. Anything I should know about before I go in there?'

Angie nodded to the files she'd put back on her desk. 'I'll send you a full briefing before I turn in tonight. Feel free to call me if something's not clear.'

'You can bank on it.' McDonald left without a goodbye.

Chips looked up from his computer. 'You and Ronald are not exactly BFFs, are you?'

'Not exactly.'

'Why doesn't she like you?'

'We had a beef at a VICAP conference. It was before I even came here. It ended in her getting overruled by her section chief – which, I might add, he should have done privately. Anyway, McDonald never forgave me.'

'So why did she hire you?'

'She didn't. I was already in post before she was promoted here to AD.'

'Ah, I see.' He checked his computer. 'Feed's just coming up.'

Angie left her desk and pulled a chair alongside his.

The pictures hitting the monitor were in black and white from four separate cameras. They were displayed on the screen in quarter-frame feeds. Three showed people running everywhere. The fourth was fixed on a store. There was no movement here. Just too many bodies to count.

Chips glanced at his boss. 'That's a mess. A very *dangerous* mess.'

'I know.' Her voice was slow and sad. 'What the hell possessed someone to do that?'

They both looked back at the feed from the opticians. It was taken from a camera on the other side of the mall and the security operator had zoomed in as close as he could. Corpses were sprawled everywhere. Angie could see hands stretched out for loved ones and the bodies of men covering their partners in the hope of saving them. The lack of color made the black pools glistening on the floor all the more shocking. Angie noted the continued absence of cops or even security.

The reason lay in the adjoining feed.

The mall was consumed by madness. Crowds rushed everywhere. There were crushes and fights, bottlenecks and battles. Several old folk got pushed to the ground. Baby buggies were toppled. It was everyone for themselves. Survival of the fittest.

The way Angie saw it, the crush to get away could easily claim more lives than the UNSUB.

One of the bottom cameras showed the parking lot. The scene was terrifying. Shoppers and cars raced for the same exits. Metal hit metal. Bodies fell beneath wheels. Drivers broke down pay barriers. Many deserted their vehicles and fled on foot. Motorcycles slalomed through the mayhem.

The last remaining camera was an external one. It showed the first of the ambulances had arrived but no one was going inside. Not until the police escorts and sharpshooters were in place. The emergency teams realized there was every chance the scumbag with the gun might be lying in wait, more than happy to make them his next target.

Angie took out her phone and typed a text message to Jake. It said simply, TAKE CARE. I LOVE U. X

Chapter 40

Sun Western Mall, LA

Jake and Ruis had their teams in place.

Jake had settled one of his on Constellation Boulevard and the other in the middle of the landscaped lawns that languished between the giant glass and steel skyscrapers on the Avenue of the Stars. Ruis fixed units on Santa Monica Boulevard and Century Park West.

LAPD cars were already strung up and down the block like queuing taxis. Foot patrols were still fighting to shut down the roads while simultaneously guiding traffic out of the mall and away from the scene.

As Jake had guessed, Pryce had placed his command vehicle east of the mall and was prowling the back of it, giving instructions on a radio. The LAPD man was stood next to a clip-on whiteboard already marked with a zonal plan of where the attack had taken place and where the mall exits were.

'We're going to have to stop meeting like this,' said Jake as he approached.

'Couldn't agree more.' Pryce hung up the phone just as a blonde woman in SWAT fatigues came out the side of the vehicle looking for him.

'We've got security video of the shooter.'

The two men followed her up metal steps into the truck. One wall was racked with tech equipment, including a monitor and a playback machine. She waited until they were both in a position to watch and then she hit play. 'This is where it starts from. I've got the mall camera operators chasing other feeds to see where the Spree went afterward.'

'Right now, *afterward* is all that matters,' said Jake.

'I'm on it.' She grabbed a phone while they watched the video.

The screen showed a mix of people coming and going – young and old, smart and casual. In the midst, slowing down by Bloomingdale's window and incongruously browsing a collection of summer dresses, was a young African American male. He was dressed in white sneakers, baggy black shorts, white Lakers cap and white T-shirt. A black sports bag was slung low over his shoulder.

As the youth hitched it up and walked on, Jake had no doubts about what lay inside.

The cameras switched a couple of times as the young man made his way along to Judy-Ju's. He seemed to pause again just before he went inside and disappeared from view.

Then people started running out.

The camera angle switched again. The back of the UNSUB was visible. He was swinging the sports bag and chopping people down like it was a chainsaw. Jake saw a kid go down and a middle-aged man get cut to pieces.

'Cold-hearted bastard,' said Pryce.

'Where the fuck were security?' asked Jake.

'Probably keeping the hell away.'

The camera showed the gunman turn and leave. Not the way he'd come. In the opposite direction.

'Is that it?' Pryce looked at the blonde.

She cupped the phone she was on. 'I'm trying for more.'

The SWAT commander shook his head in disgust and left the truck.

Jake followed him down the steps.

'I've got men over that side of the building,' said Pryce. 'They're trying to clear shoppers. Once we have that mall level emptied, I'm going to send units in from the ground and roof and sweep the place clean.'

'He may have got into the crush of people and be gone by then.'
Jake unbuckled his Kevlar pads. 'Either that or taken a hostage.'

Pryce watched him start to strip. 'What are you doing?'

'I'm going in. If he can mix with the crowds, then so can I.'

Chapter 41

S KU always came prepared, and that included carrying street clothes in the command truck.

Time was bleeding out. Jake grabbed a white T-shirt and a denim jacket fitted with a buttonhole video camera.

Ruis Costas would be able to follow a live feed from it, just as he would from a helmet camera worn by his team.

Pryce briefed SWAT to get Jake up onto the roof and down through a works access on the east side.

The entry was locked from the inside. An officer opened it with a sledgehammer.

Jake slipped in.

It was dark and cool in the roof space. Thick with dust and covered in spider webs. He was still a level above the top floor of the mall, crawling through a vast snake pit of service cables and pipes. Muffled noises came from the floor beneath him. He used a compact Maglite to find his way across the floor to the exit.

Jake unfastened a service flap and stuck his head through the gap.

The bright light of the mall made him blink. He could see that this part of the shopping complex had been emptied. Shutters were down on some stores but not others. There were a dozen doorways in which the UNSUB could be lurking. Jake turned around and dropped through the gap.

His feet tingled on impact. Instinctively he checked his gun. It was still there – not dislodged and left in the roof space.

He moved briskly down the mall.

A noise stopped him. He heard metal on tiles.

Something had toppled over in the empty clothes shop he'd just passed. Jake put his back to the wall and peered sideways through the window.

The store was moodily lit. It had been fitted out to look like a garage and body shop. The hood of a car was embedded in one wall and the back of a Harley in another. Oil drums and a fake petrol pump interrupted hanging rails of grunge clothes. Jackets, jeans and Ts were spread over workbenches marked SALE and NEW ARRIVALS.

Jake went in gun first.

Everything was still, except for a rack of shirts to his right. The cuffs on the red check lumberjack XLs swayed then stopped.

Someone was behind them.

'FBI! Come out from behind the shirts. I'm armed and *will* fire.'

A metal bar smashed across the middle of Jake's back.

The impact threw him forward. He wheeled to his left and saw a bearded black man in his late twenties swinging hard with what looked to be the top rail of a clothes display. Jake resisted the urge to shoot him and stepped into the blow. The metal slapped his left shoulder. A split second later, Jake's right fist broke the man's jaw and filled his mouth with blood and broken teeth. He threw a follow-up gut punch and watched the guy sink to his knees. This was no Spree. It was a looter. One of two opportunist scumbags who'd hoped to grab what they could while others were running for their lives.

The second thief broke for the door.

Jake took a couple of steps, stuck out a boot and tripped him. The looter crashed face first into a workbench and squealed like a pig. Jake could see wads of dollar bills stuffed in his side and back pockets.

Jake grabbed both injured men and dragged them across the floor to the car display. First, he snagged their wrists together with plastic cuffs and then fastened their other hands to the fender.

Security could sweep up the dirt bags.

He had something more urgent to deal with.

Chapter 42

SWAT leader Connor Pryce had been stood with Ruis watching the action on Jake's jacket cam. He instantly dispatched two three-man units to sweep up the grunge store looters and search for more.

Ruis's men were now on Jake's tail and SWAT units were also inside the opposite end of the mall, systematically clearing and searching the lower floors.

A few minutes later, the parking lot and a route to the bodies in the opticians had been secured and declared safe.

Pryce spoke into his radio. 'Clear to let the paramedics in. Just make sure they don't stray from your sides.' He finished on the radio and turned to Ruis. 'Sun Western staff have set up a makeshift hospital in one of the work canteens. They've been doing a good job. Head of Security, Wayne Patterson, is an ex-cop so he's been able to help a little with the crowd control.'

Fire bells went off and almost bust their eardrums.

'I thought we'd killed the alarms.' Ruis had a finger in one ear.

'We had. They keep accidentally resetting. Probably, someone went out through an exit door.'

Ruis hoped it wasn't the UNSUB. 'Your team got any footage of where the shooter went after he exited the store?'

'Not yet,' said Pryce. 'Turns out these cameras have blind spots. Lots of them. The tech running the mall video system says the black guy with the sports bag turned the corner when he left the optician's place, went into a big sports store and then disappeared.'

'*Disappeared*? How the fuck can he have disappeared?'

Pryce stayed cool. 'He says it could be the camera angle, or the perp could have ducked low and come out in the body of the crowd. Flanked on both sides by throngs of people pushing like crazy, there's every chance he wouldn't have been seen.'

'Jesus.'

'Either that or he could have gone through the store and out another door, which is what we're looking for now.'

'Double Jesus.'

'We've made prints from the video footage and distributed to all patrol cars within the LAPD area. If he's slipped the mall, he won't get far.'

'Man, don't even think like that.' Ruis blew out an exasperated breath. 'Yesterday we lost the UNSUB out at Strawberry Fields; today we lose a nutcase in one of the biggest malls in the world. Believe me, that's not good. If he gets out of here untouched, we won't. Our bosses are going to skin us and drag our bloody corpses all the way to Washington.'

Chapter 43

News copters filled the fading light of the evening sky. Camera crews crowded the sidewalks. Most of the world was watching.

Jake desperately wanted to give them some good news at the end of a very bad day.

But it wasn't to be.

Come nine p.m. the LAPD pulled SWAT out of the mall.

Pryce knew what was coming just from the look on the SKU leader's face. 'Before you start, you need to know I'm just as unhappy about this as you are. I—'

'You're not even close to how I feel, buddy.' Jake jabbed a finger in the cop's chest. 'What the fuck are you doing pulling your teams out?'

'I don't have to explain myself to you.'

'You do while I still have men risking their lives to find this sonofabitch.'

'I'm following orders and sticking to budgets, that's what I'm doing.'

'You really are a useless fuck, aren't you?' Jake stepped so close they bumped shoulders.

Pryce backed away. 'Your UNSUB's gone. We both know that. There's no point staying here and wasting more manpower and money.'

'If he *is* gone then that's on you too. You should have already been in the damned mall before I even got here.' Jake slapped Pryce's chest. 'That's what this body armor and your balls are for. You do have balls, don't you?'

'It would have been reckless to have gone in. Given that the shooting had stopped by the time we arrived, the correct tactic was to proceed with caution and not further endanger life.'

'Correct tactic? Buddy, you've got to forget the textbooks, or at least find some better ones. At the Observatory you went in too quick. Today you stood off and went in too late. Jeez, in a world where timing is everything, you keep scoring zero.'

Pryce finally stopped defending himself. He stood in silence and hoped Jake's ranting was over.

It wasn't.

'He got *a-fucking-way*. You know what that means, don't you?'

'I do. It means we get a chance to use our intelligence, track him down and arrest him without having a gunfight in a shopping mall.'

'Sure. It either means that, or it could mean he pops up again out of nowhere and kills a whole bunch more people. Me – my money's on the latter.'

'Jake.'

'Hey, don't you fucking dare "Jake" me. Three categories of people get to use my first name. Those who pay me. Those I call friends. And those I respect. You don't qualify on any level.' He turned and headed to the SKU van.

'So where is he, Mr Bright Guy?' Pryce hollered after him. 'You're the hotshot hero with all the answers. Give me his location and I'll go lock him up myself.'

Jake wheeled round. His eyes were full of fury. He marched back and took camp deep in Pryce's personal space. For a second he said nothing. He just stood there. Eyeball to eyeball, he gave him the kind of military stare a drill sergeant burned into a raw recruit. When Jake spoke, it was soft and slow. Little more than a whisper. 'Way I remember things, the so-called rules of cooperation, SKU is required to support local SWAT, *but* – and this is a *but* as big as Kim Kardashian's – we have the power to take over the investigation if we feel it's in the immediate public interest for us to do so. So as soon as I get back to my office and file my report, consider that *immediacy* exercised. From now on, we run this show. No more SWAT. No more you. No more fuck-ups.' He slapped his hand so hard on Pryce's chest it sent the cop staggering backward.

Jake was still fuming as he walked away. Still seething as he briefed Ruis and the rest of his squad on what was going to happen and what he wanted them to do. As they set about their tasks he called Dixon and fessed up to his undiplomatic moment with Pryce.

'You want control, you've got it,' said his boss. 'But before I make the big calls, tell me one more time, Jake. Is this really how you want to play things? Because believe me, a request like this is going to turn our lives into the season finale of *Game of Thrones*.'

Chapter 44

Douglas Park, Santa Monica, LA

Angie had just got out of the shower when the doorbell rang. She pulled on her white toweling robe and went to the videophone on the wall. Jake was stood outside the apartment block, looking dead beat. He had a key but apparently hadn't been comfortable about using it.

She felt sad that such distance was growing between them.

For three years they'd been gradually getting closer, and then in two days they'd gone back to bell ringing and waiting to be asked in.

'Let yourself in,' she shouted through the intercom. It would have been easier for her to buzz him through but there was a point to be made.

She watched the door and waited for it to open.

He looked awful. His shoulders were hunched and his eyes showed all the strain of the day.

'I hope you don't mind me coming by.' He shut the door behind him.

'Don't be stupid. I want you here.'

'That's great, because you have no idea how much I want to be here.' He moved towards her. 'I need you, Angie. I need you tonight and I can't imagine my life without you in it.'

She closed the last of the distance between them. 'Nor can I.'

She kissed him. Lightly at first. A deliberate echo of their moment in the office.

The touch of her wet hair on his face sent shivers of pleasure through his tensed body.

Angie put her hands around his broad neck and squeezed close.

The smell of fresh oils and scents on her soft, warm skin overwhelmed him. His hands found the belt of the robe and unfastened it.

She kept her mouth to his and felt his hands find her breasts.

Jake slipped a hand around her waist and let his fingers glide over her buttocks.

Angie grabbed his wrists and pulled his hands away. 'Take me to bed and remind me of what I've been missing.'

Chapter 45

California

For the past hour, Shooter had sat silently in the darkness of his sanctuary.

He'd come in, stripped to his boxers and sunk cross-legged into the silence of a soundproofed room.

Eyes closed, his brain burst with colors and noises, sensory fireworks in his endless internal blackness. On the big screen behind shuttered lids, highlights of the momentous movie he'd just starred in played in fast cuts, like a Hollywood trailer.

SCENE ONE: Hero walks into mall off the street.

SCENE TWO: Unsuspecting shoppers gather in store. Cue laughter, joking, and idiots squandering their last moments of life.

SCENE THREE: Close-up of hero's face. Determined look. Shifts bag on shoulder. Camera tilts down to show outline of deadly weapon. Shot widens and hero strides like a crusading knight towards the battlefield.

SCENE FOUR: Hero enters shop. Hidden gun spits death. Enemy scatters but realizes there's no escape. Hero hunts them down.

SCENE FIVE: Close-up of old woman's face, cheek pressed to cold floor. Blood dribbles from corner of her mouth.

SCENE SIX: Hero vanishes into the sunset.

Shooter loved Hollywood endings.

All the anxiety he'd felt while leaving the mall had gone, but he knew the next forty-eight hours would be critical. Cops always made the most effort in the first two days. Clues were hottest. People's memories clearest.

Minds fogged over and trails went cold after the first forty-eight hours.

He sat in meditative silence and enjoyed the cool, damp darkness. His grey shadowy outline was statue-still but his brain was buzzing, checking he'd done everything correctly.

He'd never produced the machine pistol and he was sure the bag had caught all the cartridges.

Nevertheless, from the bullets in the bodies, the CSIs would know he'd used a MAC-10. It didn't matter. He hadn't touched the rounds without wearing gloves. They wouldn't find his prints or DNA on there.

In a service elevator, he'd pulled on the heavily stained painter's overalls he'd packed in the sports bag and placed beneath the weapon. He'd turned the bag inside out so it had become a workman's grey holdall with handles rather than a bag with a shoulder strap. He'd stuffed the camera cap in there. Taken out a couple of old paintbrushes he'd brought along and carried them in his hand as he'd walked away from the mall into the street.

From the opposite side of Santa Monica Boulevard, Shooter had watched as shrill alarms cut the soft summer air and triggered bedlam. He'd drifted away before the streets began to fill up and the cops even got there.

He presumed that round about now they would be focusing on the CCTV footage of him approaching and leaving the kill zone.

Idiots.

He'd seen the cameras on the escalators and all along the marbled shopping avenues. They were sunk high in the ceilings and set snug against the walls. He'd seen them and given them their fill. Full body shots. Head and shoulders. A feast of angles to gorge themselves on.

Shooter guessed they'd already copied the security tapes, printed off blow-ups of him and sent them to every police patrol and media outlet in the country.

That was fine. It would do them no good. He gazed across the darkened room at the shadowy heap of clothes he'd taken off on an area of plastic sheeting by the door. Garments he would never wear again. Items he would burn in a few minutes, along with the height lifts in the oversized sneakers, the reversible canvas bag and the fake hair he'd sewn into the edge of his cap.

He thought about the LAPD's stupidity as he headed into the tiny shower cubicle in an adjoining room and began washing. He had to be at work soon and Shooter always liked to look smart for work.

As he scrubbed the blood spatter from under his fingernails, he remembered an old saying. Cleanliness is next to godliness.

He was still laughing when he got out and toweled dry.

Chapter 46

Douglas Park, Santa Monica, LA

The alarm went off at six-thirty.

Jake hit it before it could wake Angie.

She didn't even murmur.

He creaked his way to the bathroom and took a leak. When he returned she was still lying in the same position, arms up like she was diving, head tilted left. He sat on the bed and moved a strand of hair so he could see the full beauty of her face.

They'd work things out.

What they had was so precious, they had to find a way through it all.

He picked up his phone from the nightstand, switched it off mute and saw a missed call. He swore softly and walked back to the bathroom to listen to the message.

It was from Connor Pryce.

'It's ten p.m., so you don't have to call me back unless you want to. I just learned you spoke to your boss and he spoke to my boss and as you know there's now this joint case conference planned at our place in the morning. Congratulations, you're gonna get the control you wanted. Best of luck to you. FYI, we're both gonna catch some heat for not playing nicely, so thanks for that. Anyway, if you want to swing by my office beforehand I'll have coffee brewing. We have to work together, so I'm reaching out here, trying to fix things. Goodnight.'

Jake killed the call and put the phone down. Pryce sure was smooth. He ran the shower and stepped in.

Maybe he had been rough on the cop. One thing for sure, they did have to work together. Even if it was only to minimize the heat from their brass.

The cubicle door slid open.

Angie slipped in.

'Morning.' Her voice was husky and drowsy. She stuck her head under the waterfall jet, tilted it back and leaned against him. 'I'm exhausted, wash me.'

'Oh, I so wish I had time to do that.' He lifted strands of wet hair from her face and kissed her neck. 'I was going to bring you breakfast before I left.'

'I've gotta get up anyway. May as well have you *help* me start the day.' She turned and pressed against him.

Jake let out a soft moan as she swayed against him.

His soapy hands slipped around her waist and his fingers slid down the insides of her thighs. He kissed her and whispered, 'I've got a case conference to go to.'

'Sure you have,' she said softly. 'But you've got other places to go first.'

Her mouth found his and stopped him saying anything else.

Chapter 47

California

The early morning sun was low but already hot when Shooter finished his overnight shift.

He loved this slice of day.

The world was off-balance.

Anyone out and about this early wasn't part of the norm. Night workers and early-shift workers, they were like him. They didn't feel right during the day. They were night people. They sucked energy from the darkness and lived on its vibe. They were at the edge of society.

The edge of life.

There was a bus that ran close to his place, and Lopez, one of his co-workers, went his way, but he always walked. The distance from work to bed gave him the chance to exercise his thoughts. Today, he dragged them along the sidewalk like a pack of twelve snapping dogs.

One for each of the people he'd killed.

He owned them all now. Kept them on choker chains in his mind.

Shooter entered the four square miles of Downtown that was officially known as Central City East, not that anyone in LA called it that. To the locals it was Skid Row. Home to the homeless. This was the patch of dirt that Tinseltown swept under Hollywood's red carpet, jumped on and hoped no one would notice. It was where the down-and-outs, drunks, druggies, no-marks and no-hopers settled.

All five thousand of them.

He picked his way past the pitched tents and the lines of dossers in sleeping bags. They looked like multi-colored earthworms. He felt for all of them. A life with no purpose was a terrible thing. He'd been there. He understood.

Shooter looked back along the street. It was impossible to see where blown trash ended and human life began. Every few days the cops moved people on and pretended to clean up. They would tear down the tents in the morning, but by nightfall, when the cruisers were busy chasing down the gang boys and the stick-up merchants, canvas city got pitched again, more often than not in exactly the same place.

The rising sun flared on the roof of the old factory that had become Shooter's sanctuary. He deactivated the alarms and let himself in to the shade and cool.

From the moment the door clicked behind him, everything was a ritual. There were rooms for work clothes and work activity. And rooms for his mission. His killings. He was careful things didn't overlap. Contamination could be disastrous.

He shed his overalls and walked into the first of what used to be workers' restrooms.

Shooter showered, dried himself and walked barefoot to his main living and sleeping space. He grabbed two remote controls, lay down on a mattress, then powered up a digital recorder-player and the flat screen monitor chained above his head.

He turned out the lights and watched the massive screen fizz grey and black. Finally, it burst into full color. Shooter picked up his 3D glasses and stared at the covert pictures taken from the tiny mini-cams on the Lakers cap.

The background of the mall was flat and dull, but there hanging down in the dusty space above him was Bloomingdale's window and a wonderful reflection of himself.

Shooter reached out and touched his own hand. He caressed the sports bag dangling from his shoulder. Marveled as it swayed with the weight of the hidden gun.

His eyes were tired and he could feel the leaden lids shutting down but he was determined to stay awake. He had to see the killings in all their glory.

Then and only then would he surrender to sleep.

Chapter 48

Jake had to bust the speed limit to make the case conference. Fortunately, the night before he'd entrusted Ruis with all the prep and had checked in with him on the car phone while driving over.

As he slid into his seat he saw Connor Pryce and realized the cop thought he'd snubbed his offer of coffee. The doors closed and Crawford Dixon shot him a look that said he didn't appreciate the late arrival.

Twenty seats had been filled with a mixture of senior LAPD and FBI personnel. In front of the early risers were briefing packs containing a factual summary of the crime, close-ups of the victims, and a layout of the mall marked with the kill sites.

LA's chief of police, John Rawlings, stood in front of a giant pull-down projector screen. He was a fifty-two-year-old boulder of a man, wrapped in a corporate black suit that no longer fastened because he'd spent too long driving desks and lunching politicians. His tabloid claim to fame was that when he found his teenage son smoking pot he hauled him down to the local precinct and had him charged.

'You all look *dreadful.*' He boomed to get their attention. 'There are clearly no beauty pageant winners here this morning.' Like any good comic, he waited for the laughs. 'That's because, like me, you should still be in bed, stoking up on some shut-eye.' He paced as he talked. 'This meeting shouldn't even be taking place. But it is.' He changed his tone and got to his point. 'And it is, because yesterday and the day before, in two entirely unconnected cases, the finest men and women of the FBI and LAPD screwed up. Out at Strawberry Fields, a scumbag with a gun shot teachers and children and got away. God bless the Sheriff's Department for now wanting to take that one on their slate and we wish them the best of luck with it. We, meanwhile, have to cope with an even more headline-grabbing clusterfuck. A lone gunman slipped through our fingers after he shot more than a dozen people in a city center mall. Not one of our proudest moments.' He took another couple of steps. 'There's no point playing the blame game on this one. Not now. But there will be a time when we need to.' He gestured towards the FBI contingent seated to his left. 'In the wake of events, it's been *mutually* decided that the FBI's Spree Killer Unit will from here on in take operational lead on this inquiry. It's what I want. It's what the mayor wants and what the Bureau wants. But to be clear, that doesn't mean the LAPD doesn't pull its weight or have its say. We're in this together. We solve it together and we do it quickly.'

The chief turned to Jake. 'Special Agent Mottram, the floor is yours. I look forward to talking to you afterward.'

'Thank you, sir.' He eased himself out of his seat and walked to the side of the screen. 'Dim the lights and play the first slide, please.'

A giant male figure slapped up against the white dropdown. 'Twenty-four hours ago, no one would have looked twice at this young guy in the baseball cap. Now he is the most talked about person in the whole goddamned state. Late yesterday afternoon he entered the Sun Western mall, shot dead twelve people, injured seven more. Then he pretty much vanished. Change the slide, please.'

A hazy post-shooting shot came up. It was grainy and hard to make out. Someone had blown it up and now each pixel looked the size of a baseball.

'We lost him on security cameras because of the density of the crowd but my colleague Ruis Costas found this – it's the Spree's reflection in a storefront window as he entered a service elevator, which he rode to a lower floor. And before you ask, the answer is "no" – there *was not* a working camera in the elevator, nor apparently on the floor where he came out.'

Sighs filled the dark room.

'Yeah, I feel the same way. Now, you can deduce all you like from those facts. Either he got lucky or he bust the cameras in preparation for his actions. It's one of many things we have to find out.'

The FBI man walked forward and the projector light caught him, casting a huge shadow on the screen. 'After this briefing, we'll issue you all with crime scene videos made by our forensic photographer, but right now I want you to watch the Spree in action.' He nodded towards the back of the room. 'Please play the footage.'

The edit that came up was a hasty hack-together of mainly high and wide shots, showing the now familiar sight of the young black guy coming off an escalator on the first level of the mall.

Jake's eyes strayed from the watching audience to the sports bag and more particularly what lay inside it. He was wondering where the guy had got such a powerful weapon and where he might have practiced firing it. He pointed to the screen. 'Take a long look at the UNSUB's clothes and work out why he chose that particular ensemble for his big day. The whole outfit is black and white except for the cap, which has got the yellow and purple Lakers name and logo on it. Why wear anything as distinctive as that? Is he "staging" us – deliberately drawing our attention to something that has no relevance in order to confuse the investigation? Is it to make us think he's a Lakers fan? Or is this his lucky cap and part of a crazy fantasy that's been building in his head? Whatever the reason, this piece of merchandising is key to our investigation. When was it bought? Who sold it? Was it from a franchise with security cameras?' He watched their faces fall. 'I know – all this is needle-in-a-haystack stuff, a *massive* haystack. But if we find the cap, or even where it came from, then, ladies and gentlemen, you can rest assured we'll find our Spree.'

Chapter 49

FBI Field Office, LA

There had been lots of things Angie had wanted to say to Jake but hadn't.

Not all of them related to the baby.

The profiler's specialty was 'Serials' not 'Sprees', and her instinct was not to stick her nose into his work. So she'd bitten her tongue. Hadn't mentioned the bad feeling she'd been developing.

The kind her instincts told her not to ignore.

And with every silent hour, it had gotten worse. Which was why she found herself rapping nervously on her boss's door.

'Come in.'

Sandra McDonald was dressed in what Angie called her uniform. A black business suit with white blouse and red shoes.

The AD was behind her desk. Small black glasses perched on her nose. A stack of reports spread in front of her. She looked up quizzically. 'Do we have something in the diary?'

'No, we don't. I came on the off-chance.'

She took an educated guess. 'Something personal?'

'Something personal and something professional.'

McDonald glanced at her watch. 'Can you cover both in less than ten minutes? Otherwise we can meet at the end of the day.'

'I can be quick.'

'Then take a seat.'

Angie slid into the chair on the other side of the glass desk and came straight out with it. 'I'm pregnant.'

'Oh.'

She read the shock on her boss's face. It was genuine. She was really surprised and that meant Suzie Janner had been as good as her word and said nothing. 'I've only just found out, so I thought I'd tell you early so you could detail cover.'

'Thanks.' She took off the glasses and put two and two together. 'Did the news come up at your medical?'

'Uh-huh.'

'I see. How far gone are you?'

'Seven weeks.'

'Was it planned?'

Angie hesitated. It wasn't an unreasonable question, but she didn't want to answer it. 'With respect, that's none of your business.'

'I'll take that as a no.'

'Take it how you like. You're the first person I've told apart from the father and I'd like this to stay confidential until I say otherwise.'

'As you wish.' Her cool tone frosted further. 'I won't mention it to anyone I don't have to. Now, you said there was something professional. I suppose you mean the serial rape case and Lieutenant O'Brien.'

'No, actually I don't.'

'Then what?'

'I'd like to provide consultancy on the Sun Western mall killings.'

She frowned. 'SKU already have a psychologist, and it's a Spree not a Serial so somewhat out of your remit.'

'I know. But given the scale of the offence, I think it would be helpful if I were involved.'

'Why?'

'It feels wrong. Coming right off the back of the Strawberry Fields Massacre, there may be elements to this case that don't fit a regular Spree investigation.'

McDonald pulled a sour face. 'Are you saying they're linked? The killing of schoolteachers and kids in a field out in the country and the brazen slaughter of shoppers in a city center mall?'

'There's a chance—'

'Is there? From what I've heard, the Moorpark massacre was with an entirely different kind of rifle, used on entirely different victims in an entirely different geographic setting.'

'Both shooters got away.'

'Ah, that's your link?' The AD shook her head scornfully. 'It's surely not news to you that we often have two or more Sprees on the go at the same time?'

'Of course not.'

McDonald gave her a dismissive glance. 'As you are aware, Angela, Sprees aren't my area of expertise – or yours for that matter – but I know many of them get away for the first twenty-four hours. Often the first forty-eight, or seventy-two. They shoot, run and hide. Then they get caught, or they die.'

'I'm sorry, I'm missing your point.'

'Then let me finish and I'll make it. If this current UNSUB's killings stretched in time beyond, say, a week, then maybe there'd be a need to look at your so-called link.'

'A lot of people could die in a week.'

McDonald was out of patience. She studied Angie quizzically. 'Are you glory hunting, doctor? Trying to hitch your star to the hottest case just so you'll get noticed?'

'That's as ridiculous as it is insulting.'

'As is your request for involvement. SKU already has perfectly good psychological support. They don't need you.'

'I'd like you to reconsider.'

'Tell me, is this your idea or Special Agent Mottram's?'

'Jake doesn't know I'm here and we haven't discussed the case.'

'Then he needn't know and you needn't discuss it.' She put her glasses back on. 'Request reconsidered and once more denied. I'm outta time now and you need to concentrate on clearing up that rape-homicide on your desk.' She smiled falsely and added, 'Thank you for informing me about your pregnancy. Please close the door on your way out.'

Chapter 50

LAPD HQ, LA

The last place Jake wanted to be was in the soft seat area of the chief of police's office, flanked by his boss Crawford Dixon and SWAT's Connor Pryce.

Soft seats always equaled hard talk.

The chief's secretary took orders for coffee and left them to it.

Rawlings scratched his head and cut to the chase. 'Press are hammering at my door and my bet is that they're looking for someone's hide to pin to it.'

Dixon laughed. 'It's a little early for that, John. They don't usually go scalping till they're done with all the sensationalism.'

'You're telling me this? Don't you remember how they gutted me after I had my dopehead son arrested?'

'I do.' He rolled his eyes sarcastically. 'Poor misguided fools thought you'd done it solely as a publicity stunt. Has Jason forgiven you yet?'

'We haven't spoken for two years.'

'Social media is already turning negative,' interjected Pryce, trying to get the conversation back to the Spree. 'We run two LAPD Twitter feeds – General Comms and Community Relations – and they're both trending with calls for us to catch the UNSUB and questions as to why we haven't. I have alerts on all the main portals and postings and I can see that the bloggers are starting to create a climate of fear and blame.'

Rawlings gave several *I-told-you-so* nods. 'Social media, Crawford

– that's the *new thing*. It changed with the Boston bombings, when you FBI boys started sending suspect alerts out on Twitter before even issuing media releases.'

'It's just quicker that way,' replied Dixon. 'Let's face it, these days the press are nothing more than middle men between us and the public.'

Rawlings laughed. 'You're right, but believe me, social media is like a never-ending laxative; the shit comes so much faster and lasts far longer than the traditional media ever managed.'

'We can manipulate some of the forums and chat rooms,' continued Pryce. 'By using a strong search engine optimization strategy and smart strategic blogging, we can get to planted hacktivists to influence key opinion formers.'

Jake couldn't hold his tongue any longer. 'How about we just catch the motherfucker who's killing people? That should put a positive "*spin*" on things, shouldn't it?'

Rawlings smiled. 'I favor that old-fashioned approach too, son. Which is why you and Connor here should make such a good team, instead of shit-mouthing each other. He can blow his hot air at all that digital shit heading our way, and it'll buy you a little more time to nail the aforementioned fucker of mothers.'

Jake eased himself out of his chair and shook out the creases of the grey suit he'd found in Angie's wardrobe. 'Given the delicacy of our position, might I be excused so I can make sure my teams are making progress?'

'Sit down, cowboy.' Rawlings pulled at his jacket cuff. 'You told my man over there that you want SKU to lead, so now you lead. And that includes dealing with the rattlesnakes under the boards as well as riding bareback down the middle of town shooting your big guns in the air.'

Jake looked to Dixon but his boss just smiled and left him hanging.

Rawlings patted Jake's arm as he sat back down. 'Life isn't all bad. You both did well with locking up that basket case Chandler over at the Observatory. I could have bruised my hands applauding you on that one.'

Jake resisted enlightening the chief about Chandler and his probable post-traumatic stress disorder.

'The only good thing about Sun Western,' continued Rawlings in a patronizing tone, 'is that for the moment it makes the public forget that they ought to be asking what the fuck happened over at Strawberry Fields.'

'Thank God for small mercies,' said Dixon.

'I shall, Crawford. Believe me I shall. But right now, we have to use all this search-engine-shit-blocking-blogger bullshit that Pryce is talking about to our advantage – and you, Special Agent Mottram, you need to use your military skills to bring this asshole in before the men with hammers and nails come for me.' The chief took a beat, then added, 'Just so you're all in no doubt about what's going on here, let me fill you in. Two months from now, there's a vote coming for the role of police commissioner and all I wanna hear when I throw my hat in that particular ring is loud cheers. No questions. No doubts. Certainly no fucking boos. Just big whoops of freaking delight. I hope I've made myself clear, gentlemen. Because believe me, if my rise to fame ends because of the sorry shit that brought us all here today, then, gentlemen, rest assured all of yours will as well.'

Chapter 51

C hips came in wearing a blue T-shirt that said, I HATE YOU GOD. HATE YOU LIKE YOU REALLY EXIST.

'Inappropriate,' said Angie, even though she didn't have the energy to fight with him.

'You think so?'

'I know so.'

'It's Graham Greene. I think.'

'I don't care if it's Mr Pink. Turn it inside out or we'll have the politically correct mob hauling your ass out the door.'

He stripped and turned the shirt inside out.

She wolf-whistled playfully. 'Good abs, bro. You been working out some?'

'I suppose you could call it *working out*.'

'FTMD.' She covered her eyes in mock embarrassment. 'Far Too Much Detail.'

They both laughed.

Angie waited until he finished dressing. 'Do me a favor, grab what you can from the SKU servers on the Sun Western shootings.'

'Grab as in *steal*? Or grab as in ask permission because you're not being sneaky?'

'Grab as in steal.'

He smiled. 'Okay – but only if you make coffee. I was late and didn't have time to hit Starbucks.'

'You got it.' She heard him sit and power up his terminal as she headed to the pantry.

Angie brewed coffee. Thick and dark for Chips and the thin color of rusty water for her. She remembered how she used to down shots of espresso like whiskey chasers and drink cappuccino thick enough to stand a spoon in. Now she couldn't stomach either.

Something else was bugging her.

McDonald's comment about her being a 'glory hunter'.

What a cheek.

Had the woman been serious? Could she really not see that some people looked at crimes in a light other than that they could serve their own careers?

Chips was answering her phone when she re-entered the office, balancing two beakers and wishing she hadn't filled them so full.

She hoped it was Jake.

He took a mug off her and whispered, 'Lieutenant O'Brien.'

She put her drink down and picked up the receiver. 'Angie Holmes.'

'Morning. I could really do with your help, Doc.'

She could hear he was on a car phone. 'What can I do?'

'The daughter of Sally Mesche – the third victim – just contacted us. Her mom has remembered something about the UNSUB – about his smell. Can you come and sit in on the interview?'

'She down at the station?'

'No. I'm on the way to her home. I can pick you up in fifteen, if that's okay?'

Angie hesitated. She was supposed to be seeing Suzie Janner for lunch and baby talk. 'I've got plans. Can we do it mid-afternoon, early evening?'

'Can't. The old lady only has a couple of hours. She has to go to a funeral. I wanna catch her before the dark clouds of grief descend and mess up her memory again. I can go on my own.'

'No, I'll come. I can cancel what I'm supposed to be doing.'

'Thanks. I value your help.'

'Enough to have rethought holding back discussions on the offender's race?'

He let out a long sigh. 'Let's see what Mrs Mesche says, then we'll talk about it.'

Chapter 52

'Crazy, timewasting, pencil-headed pricks!' Jake hurled his jacket into the corner of the office.

Ruis Costas had seen him coming along the corridor and was a step behind. He picked up the jacket and dusted it down. 'Problems?'

'You could say that.' He took the garment back. 'Thanks. Rawlings took more than two hours reading the riot act, lecturing me on leadership while that brown-nose nerd Pryce chirped in with claptrap about bloggers and digital platforms. Then they got in "media managers".'

'Media managers?'

'Glorified press officers. I had to sit through shit about "messaging to the public" and "image control of individuals and respective organizations".'

Ruis couldn't help but smile. 'With great power comes great bullshit.'

Jake still wasn't done. 'Do you know what the *unholy trinity* is?'

'Iraq, Iran and Afghanistan? Syria, Libya and Egypt?'

'No!' Jake laughed. 'According to Rawlings, the unholy trinity is "political fallout", "social media contamination" and "conventional press backlash".'

Costas broke up.

Jake looked at the plastic bag in his colleague's hand. 'From the mall?'

'Point forty-five ACP.'

Jake knew it well. 'Did Ballistics say what it came from?'

'From the marks, they guess a MAC-10.'

'When I joined the Marines I got my ass kicked for calling it a MAC. Old school say M10, then they go all historian and tell you it's a Military Armament Corporation Model 10 developed by Gordon B. Ingram back in 1964. Know your history, your weapon, know your enemy.'

'It help at all?'

'Some. You've fired one of these, right?'

'Sure. Not my choice, though. Like you, I prefer the H&K.'

Jake turned on his computer. 'Gangbangers love them. Some go raw, some pimp them up with Uzi conversion kits. Noise is suppressed, they're compact, there's not too much kickback and these days they're easier to find than a politician with a conscience.'

'M11's more the fashion now. I was thinking that maybe the 10 used at the mall has history. Perhaps someone sold it off cheap because they guessed rifling marks might bring some grief their way.'

'Be great if we get that lucky.'

'I have one of the team running the records.'

Ruis held up the baggy. 'The slug is Blazer Brass. Walmart used to knock out a box for less than ten dollars. I've seen people buying twenty or more boxes of this stuff when promotions have been run.'

'Any luck with fingerprints?'

'Not that I've heard.'

The computer was still loading programs. 'This thing really is junk.' He slapped the side, then picked up a charger cable off the desk and plugged his phone in – it had all but run flat at Angie's. 'Check for DNA too – you'd be amazed how many punks play with the rounds, kiss the tips as part of some ritual.'

'I'll tell the labs.'

'Forensics find anything else at the scene?'

'They're still picking their way through stuff. The floor was soaked in more than a dozen-and-a-half intermingled pools of blood. On top of all that jam came dropped dollars, purses, wallets, credit cards, receipts, you name it. You wouldn't believe what shit got kicked in from outside when people were running for the exit.'

'Have someone do overview checks on the crime scene stills and video while Forensics get granular. We're up against the clock.'

There was a knock at the door.

Both men swung their heads.

A young dark-haired man with a camera around his neck stepped in. 'I'm trying to find a Special Agent Mottram.'

'You found him,' said Ruis, pointing at his boss.

The youngster smiled. 'I'm here to take your photographs, sir. Bureau Media Office says it needs new stills of you. Shouldn't take more than half an hour.'

'How old are you?' Jake asked.

'Twenty-three, sir.'

'You're a little young to recognize a bad moment, so I'll help you. If you want to make twenty-four, get the fuck out of here while you still can.'

Chapter 53

The front room of the run-down townhouse smelled of dead flowers, boiled food and old cats.

Angie sat alongside Cal O'Brien on twin wing chairs covered in a faded floral fabric. Opposite them, squashed together on a matching two seater, were Hannah Vander and her seventy-two-year-old mother Sally Mesche.

Vander was what Angie called a suicide blonde – hair dyed by her own hand. She was early fifties, fighting the lines with a little too much make-up, and had given up on her waistline. She ran a local grocery franchise and her cheap cotton skirt and blouse said she tried hard and worked hard. Her bitten fingernails said she worried a lot, mostly about her mom.

Sally Mesche was a smaller, thinner, older version of her daughter, only her blue eyes were clouded with cataracts and her spine curved in a way she'd never imagined when she'd won the dancing trophies that stood on the back windowsill overlooking the yard where she'd been raped.

'The doctor's changed my medication,' the old lady confided. A ginger tom appeared from beneath the sofa and wound its way around her ankles. 'Things have started coming back to me. Things about that night.'

'She's on painkillers and still waiting for hip surgery,' added Vander. 'The attack's made the replacement all the more urgent.'

Her mom waved her down. 'They don't need to know about that. They're not interested in my hip, Hannah.'

Vander gave them a *see-what-I-have to-put-up-with* look.

The cat jumped and settled on the old lady's knee. 'Anyways, I think clearer now. Sleep longer too. And I remembered something about that man who attacked me.' She picked the tom up and dropped him back to the floor. 'Just a minute.' She tried in vain to reach one of the drinks her daughter had brought in on a tray with a plate of ginger cookies.

Angie passed a coffee to her and watched the cat cross a mat and disappear into the kitchen. 'Here you go, Mrs Mesche.'

'Thank you, honey.' She leaned back and her face said she hurt in multiple places. Her bony hand shook as she raised the white mug to her lips and sipped. 'My, that's hot,' she said with disappointment. 'You made it too hot, Hannah. You'll be scalding me with drinks like that.' She rested the mug on the arm of the couch.

Her daughter intervened. 'You'll leave a ring, Mom. Let me put it down on the tray so it can cool down.'

'Leave me alone. I can cope.' She moved the drink out of Vander's reach.

Angie fought back a smile and waited patiently. Old folks needed time. She was sure Sally Mesche would get to the point soon enough.

The grandmother cleared her throat with a raspy cough and began, 'The policewoman who came and interviewed me after I was attacked said I was to call if I remembered anything. Said it didn't matter how unimportant I thought it was, I had to call.'

O'Brien jumped in. 'She was right, Mrs Mesche. We're happy to hear whatever you have to say, and we appreciate you going through all this again.'

She looked at Angie. 'Could you pass me a cookie, honey?'

'They look good, don't they?' Angie lifted the plate for her.

'From my store,' said Vander proudly. 'One of our best promotions.'

'She means they're past their sell-by.' The old lady took three and stacked two like casino chips. 'I went out with a boy from Louisiana. He lived with his poppa. Name was Charlton Brazer. He had a chest as big as Texas – and other parts of him weren't so small either.'

'Momma!'

Angie and O'Brien laughed.

'Charlton's pa did all the cooking and I ate round there a lot. Time was when I practically lived with them. That was before I found Charlton with Lizzy Smithson, then I never went near the hound again.' She bit some of her biscuit and chewed slow. 'Charlton's old man cooked real well, but there was only one meal he could make. At first you thought, hell this is a good dinner. Then when you'd been a few times you got mighty sick of it. The smell started to turn your stomach. It was a stink that didn't come and go. It just stayed.' For a moment the old lady seemed to wander back to another time and place. One when her body didn't ache everywhere and Charlton Brazer had only had eyes for her.

She put the remains of her cookie down. 'It was a smell that wouldn't stay in a kitchen either. It climbed out onto the porch, crept its way upstairs into your bedroom, got in the bath with you and lived in your clothes and your hair.'

She tried her coffee again.

It had cooled enough for two sips.

Angie watched a brown spill slide down the outside of the mug and stain the fabric below it.

Sally Mesche knew they were waiting for her. Hanging on every word. She gave them three.

'Southern fried chicken.' She squinted through cloudy eyes at the two investigators. 'The man who attacked me never said a word. I never so much as saw him. But I'd know him if he was stood behind me now. He smelled of cooking oil, spices and fried chicken. It was in his skin like he bathed in it first thing every day and last thing at night.'

Chapter 54

They found a Subway a few blocks east of Sally Mesche's house and grabbed what passed as lunch.

O'Brien had a bucket of coffee to go with his twelve-inch steak, egg and cheese. Angie took a Diet Coke with ham and salad.

Between mouthfuls, the cop called his office and ordered fresh interviews of all the victims, with a view to them describing – 'unprompted', he stressed – what the UNSUB had smelled of.

'How's your sub?' he asked Angie.

She tried not to think of the lunch she should have been sharing with Suzie Janner. 'It's next to tasteless, but at least it's filling a hole.'

'You want some of this?' He waggled the half-eaten stick in her direction. 'I could happily give you a good four inches.'

She tried not to smile.

'Go on,' he urged. 'You could cut me a little slack and laugh.'

'It's not *that* funny, just juvenile.'

'I know, but you're one icy lady and I'm just trying to make a bit of a connection.'

'No need. Truth is, I respect the job you're doing. I just don't like your view on the race angle.'

'Still that?' He put his sandwich down and wiped his hand. 'You get why, though? You understand how in our racially tense tinderbox part of the world the idea of a black man raping white women out of hate might stir up a whole hornets' nest of trouble?'

'Yeah, I get the why. But that doesn't make withholding the details from your team and the public right. My observation isn't prejudiced or racist, it's just factual.'

'And inflammatory. It gets leaked to the press and there'll be no shelter from the shitstorm.'

'I'd rather a shitstorm than another rape.'

'And what if you're wrong?'

'I'm not. All the victims are white and elderly. All have been violated in the most aggressive and personal ways. These are hate crimes—'

He held up a hand to stop her. 'I know your argument and I'm starting to see it that way. But can we just get this round of new interviews out of the way before we disclose the twentieth point on your profile?'

She shot him a withering look.

'This afternoon we're going to start a sweep of all fast food workers in the locale. Kentucky Fried, Southern Fried, Dixie Fried, Chicken Fried – we're going to pull in each and every one of them and work your profile against all males on the books. I'll personally serve you with a suspect list and I'll personally look out for the factor that you've shared with me, but I'm begging you, Doc, just give me time on this one.'

'You mean *more* time.'

'Yeah, I do.' He picked up his coffee and watched her for a response.

Angie could see how the new info that Sally Mesche had given them needed to be processed. If it threw up suspects, then maybe there was no need to apply an extra filter at too early a stage. 'Okay, you got it.'

'Bless you. You are an angel.'

'Far from it,' conceded Angie, 'but I see sense in what you're saying. Can I ask you something?'

'Of course you can. Your gesture of goodwill wins you the right to one question completely of your own choosing.'

'I was going over the geographic profiling and I wondered whether there had been any attempted rapes in Lawndale?'

'Lawndale?' He frowned. 'None of our victims were from Lawndale.'

'I know. I didn't ask that. I asked if there had been any *attempted* rapes there.'

He took a second to think about it. 'No, not to my knowledge.'

'Or maybe violent but non-sexual attacks on elderly women?'

'To be honest, I wouldn't know.' He played with his sub and wondered if he should eat any more or leave it. 'There'd most probably be a bag snatch or break-in linked to a senior, but I only get detailed rape and homicide so I don't have details. I can check for you. Why?'

'I thought I'd worked out a pattern to the offender's attacks, but then it fell apart because there had been no incidents in Lawndale.'

'I don't follow.' He wrapped the food and pushed it away so he wouldn't try to finish it.

'Hang on.' She slid a small, lined notebook out of her purse and pulled the cap off a fiber tip pen with her teeth. Quickly, she divided the page vertically with the 110 and horizontally with the 105.

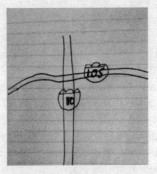

'From what we know, the UNSUB committed five offences in five different places. Inglewood, Huntington Park, Hawthorne, Lynwood and of course Compton, the Lindsey Knapp homicide.'

'Right.'

Angie marked them on her sketch. 'So what do you think?'

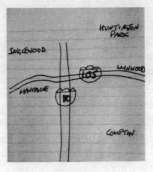

'I think what I always thought. The sick fuck runs up and down the 110 and back and forth along the 105.'

'Maybe. But there's more to it than that.' She scribbled again. 'Look what happens when I put in the order in which he attacked the victims.'

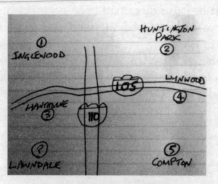

O'Brien began to see what she was driving at. 'You think he alternates? Started left of the 110 at Inglewood, then went right to Huntington, then left to Hawthorne . . .'

'Well, that kinda makes sense until he gets to Lynwood. Then from Lynwood he doesn't cross the freeway but goes straight down to Compton.' She marked it up for him.

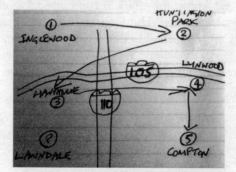

O'Brien tapped the bottom left of her sketch. 'This why you asked about Lawndale and put a big question mark over it?'

'That's right.' She reached into her purse for a different pen.

'Offenders are like sports stars. When they're on a winning streak they don't change the basics of what they've been doing.'

'If it ain't broken, don't fix it.'

'Exactly.' She ran a red pen over her notebook. 'After Lynwood, it really should have been Lawndale and then Compton.'

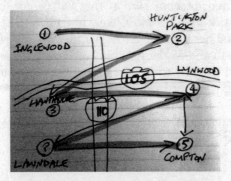

Angie took a belt of Coke to help banish the taste of bland ham. She bent over her sketch and drew all the mileages in, marking the distances between the sequence of offences. She pushed the book back to O'Brien. 'Look at this and you'll see his attacks are evenly spaced. There are twelve miles between Inglewood and Huntington. Nine point four between Hawthorne and Lynwood and ten point six between Lawndale and Compton.'

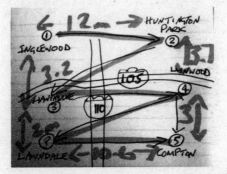

He took it all in. Looked a little defensive. 'We kept a map of early attacks on the wall in the incident room. But we didn't interpret the offending in the way you have. We saw it more as his strike area, his comfort zone. We certainly didn't see the zig-zag pattern that you have marked out.'

'Don't blame yourself. It's not always possible to see the emerging behavior.'

He tapped her notebook. 'From what you've got there, where do you think our sick friend is most likely to live?'

Angie planted her index finger high above the top of the notebook. 'He's living north and working south. Few offenders actually kill their way towards their own front porch, so I have him in the opposite direction, living north of Huntington and Inglewood.'

'Wonderful,' said O'Brien dryly. 'Out of the twenty million people housed in Greater LA's four hundred square miles, we've narrowed things down to a mere eight or so million.'

'It's a start,' said Angie. 'At least it's a start.'

Chapter 55

California

Shooter had slept well.

He did these days. Now that it had begun. Now that it was out of his head and had become reality.

Bed was nothing more than a mattress on the floor and a sheet to cover himself with. He didn't need anything else. Didn't crave comforts. There was no natural light inside his sanctuary and more than anything he liked the dark. He made his way to the bathroom in the blackness. Like a blind man, he'd learned every inch of the place. He could sprint in the dark and never touch a wall. He could find a switch or a gun in a split second without falling or faltering.

In his control room, he diligently checked the security cameras. They were all fine. None broken or interfered with.

It was already baking hot outside. Shadows on the ground told him the sun was high and it was just after midday. He stood for a moment and hit superfast rewind on a digital recorder. It was slaved to cameras showing split feeds north, south, east and west of the property. Watching the overnight footage always took fifteen minutes. Time he used to perform basic yoga stretching exercises for his spine, legs and arms. Fitness of body equaled fitness of mind. It was part of his discipline. His focus.

The recording revealed nothing alarming. Nor had he expected it to. The old unit was ringed with high metal fencing and padlocked.

He'd strung rusty razor wire along the top and thrown all manner of trash around the outside of the place. For months he'd tossed food there to encourage rats. Even street bums stayed away from vermin.

One of the inner rooms he had created was a large closet jammed with old clothes. Rich people had dumped them outside shelters, soup kitchens and charity stores. He'd taken what he wanted. Everything from denims to suits, workers' overalls, shirts, sweats, long and short coats and all manner of footwear.

Today he dressed blue. Low-riding jeans, old Converse trainers and a sleeveless T with a white Gold's Gym logo on it – a muscular bodybuilder lifting a weights bar so heavy it bent in the middle.

Shooter put on fake Oakley shades, grabbed cash, a bottle of water and a rucksack.

By one of the exit doors he picked up his pushbike, checked the video monitor to make sure his route was clear and then pushed his way into the dazzling sun.

It was half an hour before he stopped cycling. He didn't buy more than one newspaper at a time, but by the time he was done he had finished the water and jammed the rucksack.

He rode back slowly and spent the time people-watching. Most of them were robots. They glided from cars to buildings as though they were on rails in an automated assembly plant. Their brain-chips were programmed – HOME, WORK, HOME, SPEND SOMETHING SOMEWHERE, HOME, WORK, HOME, SPEND. Living was wasted on them. No wonder they made such bad decisions. Did such bad things.

From a small grocery store he bought eggs, juice, milk, sugar and bread, then he cycled round the block before he was happy no one would see him re-enter his sanctuary.

On a two-burner picnic stove, powered by a cartridge of Gaz, he cooked French toast. He ate it straight from the pan while drinking OJ from the carton and reading the papers cover to cover.

Once he was done he washed up. He spent extra time on the *Financial Times*. The rest of the papers he took to the room with the handmade sign on the door that said Death Row. He'd thought long and hard about what to call the dark heart of his hideaway.

Shooter pushed open the door and stared at the faces on the corkboard. 'Well hello there, Gina, Zach and little Amy. I've brought you some friends to play with.'

Chapter 56

SKU Offices, LA

Jake's day had gone from bad to worse.

After chasing off the photographer he got hauled into Crawford Dixon's office. Not only did he get told to go and pose for the head shots the young snapper had wanted, he got his ass kicked for trying to get Angie involved in the investigation.

'I didn't!' he protested. 'We haven't even discussed the case.'

'Then why was Sandra McDonald doing a war dance in her office while she had me on the phone?'

'I've no idea.' Jake looked exasperated. 'She and Angie have history. Maybe the AD's trying to cause trouble for her.'

Dixon shook his head in dismay. Office romances were always problematic. 'Danielle Goodman was at this morning's briefing. She's our unit psychiatrist; you want profiling help, use her.'

'I *am* using her. Ruis is with her now. Matter of fact, as soon as I walk out of here I'm joining them to see what she's come up with.'

'Glad to hear it.'

Jake saw his boss weighing him up. 'Honestly, I never discussed the case with Angie. We don't speak work as a rule – that is unless you count bitching about our bosses.'

Dixon laughed. 'I don't. Now get outta here and conjure up a way of keeping that bastard Rawlings off my back.'

'I'll do my best.'

Jake took the stairs back to his floor. He phoned Angie en route but it went straight to voicemail. He didn't leave a message. Best voice his concern in person.

Down the corridor he found Danielle's room. He hated this place. She'd had it painted cornflower blue and lit by special lights that she claimed mimicked natural sunlight. The woman herself was an oversized version of an off-diet Oprah and so proud of her extremely large presence that she always dressed in the brightest of primary colors. Today, the forty year old was wearing a poppy red jacket over a mid-length blue dress and red heels longer than some hunting knives Jake had used.

She and Ruis were gathered around a TV monitor. A freeze frame of the mall killer hovered between them.

'Danny's got some interesting thoughts,' said Costas as he saw his boss.

She smiled pearly whites at him. 'How are you, Special Agent Mottram?'

'I'm good, Danny, what've you got?'

She floated a hand to a chair. 'Please take a seat and I'll recap.' Danielle tapped a red-painted nail on the monitor. 'This is a very dangerous young man. His body language shows exceptional self-control and his actions display enormous violence. The combination is not a good one.'

Jake creaked back on his chair. 'I could have told you that, Danny.'

She ignored his tone and continued, 'He has remarkable confidence and dedication of purpose. Agent Costas says you both believe he is not military or police trained, which makes his use of a concealed weapon in an open space all the more astonishing.' She stared at them both. 'Tell me, gentlemen, how do you currently categorize a Spree?'

Ruis was first to speak. 'The definition changes every few months.'

'Which is why I stressed the word "currently".'

He shot Jake a look that said *what a ballbreaker*, then gave the classic FBI terminology. 'A Spree is someone who commits two or more homicides without a cooling off period between the killings.'

Jake could tell what she was driving at. 'I'm guessing you're intrigued by why the UNSUB ran away and how long his cooling off period might be.'

'Indeed I am.' She got up from her chair and waddled to a cornflower blue filing cabinet at the far end of her room.

Ruis caught Jake's eye and simulated holding Danielle's wide hips while taking her from behind.

She turned around with a file in her hands and almost caught him. 'You guys need to read this. It's a case from the 1950s and fits your UNSUB to a T.'

She pushed the file into Jake's hand. 'Enjoy.'

He looked down and stared at the name. 'Christ, Danny, you're not serious, are you?'

'More than. The guy in there is the world's most notorious spree killer. His string of homicides lasted two months and his debut kill started small – a storekeeper and a petty row over a stuffed animal.'

Jake held up the file so Ruis could see. 'Lincoln, Nebraska, 1958. You think we have another Charles Starkweather on our hands?'

'Read it,' insisted Danielle, 'then call me. It's a story about a punk transformed into a monster. How a kid with a grudge and a gun brought fear to most of America.'

Chapter 57

The mugshot of Charles Raymond Starkweather stared at Jake from his desk. Pretty much every cop in the world knew the story of how the teenager with a speech impediment and a chip on his shoulder grew balls the size of Mars once he got a gun in his hand. It had been immortalized in films such as *Natural Born Killers*.

Starkweather was born in Nebraska, the third of seven children. His mom and pop had been poor as dirt but they'd also been decent, hardworking folk. Young Charles struggled at school and other kids bullied him. He was academically useless and dropped out early. His love life was just as bad and he struggled to connect with girls of his own age.

By eighteen he was unemployed, homeless and centering his affection on a besotted fourteen-year-old girl. Then one day, Fate took a truckload of manure and threw it into the face of a hurricane. Starkweather snapped. Out shopping for a furry animal, he settled an argument with a storekeeper by shooting him. Nonentity Charles was suddenly somebody. The emasculated had been empowered.

Starkweather was on a roll. All fired up, he then went round to his young girlfriend's house and killed her disapproving parents and baby sister. When she came home from school they set off together on a road trip to hell that saw them shoot, stab and strangle everything from a dog to a baby.

Jake hoped to God that wasn't what he was up against. He grabbed the phone and dialed the unit psychologist.

Danielle Goodman answered with a laugh in her voice. 'Agent

Mottram, I've already got a date tonight, so don't you come pestering me with flowers an' all your sweet talk.'

Jake realized she'd seen his extension number on her display. 'I promise not to. Danny, listen. I just finished the Starkweather file and I'm praying his ghost hasn't blown into LA. Can you tell me exactly how you think our UNSUB is like him?'

'You mean *aside* from the cruelty, the meanness, the sociopathic explosion of violence, the disregard for young and old, the killing of kids and seniors, plus the fact that he fled the scene and we both know he's just brewing on where to strike again?'

'Yes.' He half-laughed. 'Apart from all that.'

'Well, I would expect our UNSUB feels he's been the subject of a huge injustice. It's probably something you or I would see as inconsequential, but it's fired him up and triggered his rage. He may have some physical affliction like Charles Starkweather, maybe problems with his eyesight, and it could well be that a store assistant in the opticians previously mocked him. Or perhaps he's been wrongly accused of shoplifting at that particular outlet. Something set him off and now he's going to run and kill.'

'Any thoughts where?'

'Your guess is as good as mine. I think he'll run far. Once he got through those LAPD roadblocks I reckon he just kept going until he felt it was safe to hole up and de-stress.'

Jake's memory stirred. 'Isn't Starkweather's ex still alive? Didn't I read something about her being in a bad car accident?'

'Yeah, over in Michigan. I'll have to check.'

'If she's okay, see if you can talk to her. Get some insight.'

'I'll try.'

Ruis burst through the door. 'We've got something.'

'Sorry, Danny, I need to go.' He dropped the call and looked to his number two.

'There's intel on a Hells Angel – well, to be precise a *wannabe* Angel. He got knocked back by the Santa Monica charter. They saw him as bad blood and he's been hiding out and acting wild ever since.'

'Too wild for the *Angels*?'

'Yeah, hard to imagine. Apparently they like their craziness controlled these days. They're trying to shake off the organized crime label and they have this motto, *"When we do right nobody remembers, when we do wrong nobody forgets."'*

'My, how public minded of them.' Jake flipped open a notepad. 'Who's saying what about this dirt bag?'

'Contact in Anti-Gangs has a CI working the charter. He says a snot-nosed kid called Wayne Harris started bragging about killing people with his machine pistol. One of the charter *acquaintances* called him a bullshitter. Wayne pulled a MAC-10, shot him in both feet then rode out of town.'

Jake got interested. 'Where and when did this go down?'

'Charter bar, out on the coast, about three hours ago.'

'What do we know of Wayne?' Jake underlined the name in his book.

'We're still learning. He's twenty-one and has a juvie rap sheet for assault, DUI and drug use. Broken home, no siblings, a girlfriend called Emma-Louise Bakker – she's sixteen and has been with him for a year or so.'

'Shit.' Jake put down his pen. 'Danielle must have some crystal ball; this is Starkweather all over again. Do we know where Wayne is?'

'Holed up in a shack in Rustic Canyon with the girl.'

'Okay, get some people over to her family. Set up phone traces on our man and this Emma-Louise. I'll give a heads-up to Pryce and the local cops, sheriff's office, et cetera; we don't want to be falling over each other on this. Meanwhile, you get one of your best surveillance teams to find and scope out the shack while we put a plan together.'

'I'm on it.' Ruis headed off.

Jake picked up the phone and called Angie. 'Hi. Sorry about this, we've got what might be a break on the mall shootings. I'm gonna be late, probably *very*.'

'That's good news – the break I mean, not you being late. You want to run the suspect by me for an opinion?'

He hesitated before answering. 'Best not to. Dixon chewed my ass because of something you said to McDonald.'

She winced. 'Sorry about that. I wouldn't normally stick my nose in. It's just that I've got bad feelings about this particular offender and I think I could help.'

175

He tensed up. 'Thanks, but Danny Goodman's already all over it.'

'Humm.'

'*Humm*? What does that mean?'

'Danielle relies too much on case studies and not enough on original thought.'

'Me-ow!'

'Hey, I'm not being catty, Jake. Please be real careful about this guy. He's a grade A sociopath.'

'That's what Danielle said.'

'She also say he's not a Spree?'

'Shoots like a Spree. Runs like a Spree.'

'I know, but I don't think he is. His level of planning and execution is more Serial than—'

He cut her off. 'He's a Spree, Angie. Believe me. Danny thinks he's as much a Spree as Charles Starkweather was.'

Alarm bells sounded in her head. 'Let me send you some thoughts.'

'No.' His tone was harsher than he'd wished. 'Please don't. Dixon read me the riot act. Let me run this with Danny and we'll talk later.'

'O-kay.' Her tone was flat.

He could tell she was pissed with him. 'This weekend – how about we take a boat out from Marina del Ray, go down and spend the night at Redondo? Forget work and find the time to talk about all our stuff?'

The gesture was enough to make her feel better. 'I'd like that. Just make sure you take good care between now and then.'

'I will. See you later.'

Chapter 58

FBI Field Office, LA

Angie got Chips to order sushi for her before he left for the night. She had rolls of spicy tuna, shrimp tempura and salmon. They never sent enough soy sauce and wasabi for her liking, but tonight she found raw fish was another thing she was going off.

Notes from O'Brien pinged into her mailbox. Most of the time she ignored them. While she ate a little of the rice she'd pulled away from the fish, she studied the footage of the mall that Chips had 'acquired'.

Danielle Goodman was wrong.

She was sure of it.

The perp she watched on camera was a fledgling serial killer. He'd planned his strike meticulously, carried it out with the coolness of an assassin and then vanished like an escapologist. This wasn't a dumbass venting rage. This was someone perfecting his craft.

One particular thing intrigued her.

It was the methodical way he walked around the store and finished off victims he'd already shot. She could see his lips moving as he passed among the corpses. At first she thought he was cursing them. Then she realized he was counting. Angie wondered if it was a compulsion. Some people had to repeat certain phrases over and over again when they encountered moments of stress. Or maybe he was literally just counting – making sure he'd killed the exact number that he'd planned to – that he'd fantasized about.

She wasn't yet confident enough to finalize her notes. But when she was, then she'd send them to Jake, whether he wanted them or not.

Finally, she looked at the latest missives O'Brien had mailed her on the rape-homicide.

She'd been right.

There *had* been an attack in Lawndale.

Ten days after the Lynwood assault, the fourth in the series, seventy-year-old Eva Hart had been knocked to the ground in the side passageway of her house. She'd been attacked from behind and her clothing pulled up over her head. Next door's car alarm had accidentally gone off and frightened the assailant away. Miss Hart had reported the incident as an attempted robbery and housebreaking, but as she'd lost nothing the crime report didn't find many interested eyes.

Angie checked her calendar. Four days later, the rapist had struck in Compton and killed Lindsey Knapp. The thwarted attempt would explain his surge in violence. He'd needed release and this time he had used too much aggression.

She pulled out her notebook and looked again at the sketch she'd made for O'Brien.

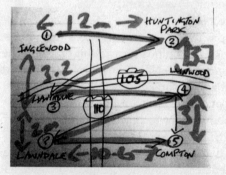

The double Z formed by her red pen showed a clear habit of moving west to east and north to south. It indicated such a fluid repetition of behavior that she doubted he would abandon or significantly alter it. In her mind, he'd do one of two things to claim his next victim. Either he'd cross the 110 again and strike in an area up to five miles south of Lawndale, or he'd go back to Lawndale and find another victim there.

Angie pulled up a Google map. Torrance lay four miles south of Lawndale, and like every other place the UNSUB had struck was within easy reach of the 110. But the more she thought about it, the more she favored Lawndale.

Lawndale represented failure to him.

Failure was something she was sure had triggered his offending. Something he could no longer live with.

Chapter 59

Rustic Canyon Park, 22:00 hours

The intel on Wayne Harris had been good enough for Jake to send his best teams out into the bush and dust.

From what he and Ruis could piece together, after the shooting at the bar, the punk had scored several ounces of Angel Dust and run for the hills. Harris had broken into a ramshackle workmen's hut and parked his Harley round the back.

The couple had hung there for a few hours, no doubt blowing the drugs and fooling around, then they'd gotten bored and decided it'd be fun to ride out to Sullivan Fire Road and shoot squirrels and birds out of the trees. Now they'd moved on. They'd ridden the motorcycle into the grounds of a derelict power station. A building with a rap sheet even worse than Harris's.

Murphy's Ranch was the unassuming name given to the fifty-acre site that during the 1930s was being developed as the base for a self-sustaining Nazi community. The multi-millionaires behind the scheme had hoped it would become the headquarters of American fascism. Like Hitler's Aryan dream, it now lay in ruins.

Jake and his teams had already started an approach from all four sides. They had parked their ops vehicles way back and hiked the mountain trails up to the site.

High in the starlit night sky, an FBI helicopter hovered out of earshot, ready to provide extra surveillance should the target start a high-speed chase across the arid Californian landscape.

Harris and Bakker had a fire going in the concrete-walled old station. It crackled loudly and spat reds and oranges through busted windows. SKU were watching and listening to everything. The two runaways were laughing so loudly and talking such crap it was clear they were either still high or had been hitting the booze as well as Angel Dust.

Jake gave the order for all four units to close in. They'd been set at angles to ensure they didn't catch each other's crossfire, and only one of the four would actually enter the building.

As boots moved across dried earth, the light from the fire suddenly went out.

There was silence.

Then the roar of a motorcycle engine.

The Harley burst out of the compound, spitting grit.

Its headlights were off. Automatic gunfire sprayed out of the blackness towards Jake.

He returned fire.

There was a screech of rubber, the sound of metal scraping blacktop and finally the dull thump of bike and body against a tree.

Jake's team moved on the wreckage. As they did, a powerful arc light lit up the site and exposed them all.

SKU men squinted rabbit-like into the blinding whiteness. It was more powerful than a security light and it took Jake a second to place it. The mangled remains of the motorcycle glinted in the snow-white beam. The body thrown over the bars was that of Emma-Louise, not Harris.

By the time Jake swung his gun to the top of the old power station it was too late. The wannabe Hells Angel was firing down on them.

The intel had been wrong.

He had two automatic weapons, not just the MAC-10.

Bullets rained on Jake and the three exposed SKU men. They drenched arms, legs, chests and heads.

Ruis Costas opened fire and popped Wayne Harris's head like a melon.

But he'd been too late.

Far too late to save his colleagues.

Chapter 60

A ngie decided she'd rather drive around than sit at home worrying about Jake.

The I-405 from Wilshire took her into Lawndale. She wanted to get a little first-hand experience of the neighborhood. Check out the streets and pathways that the UNSUB might have prowled.

She took Manhattan Beach Boulevard under the San Diego freeway and drove the backstreets around the block where Eva Hart lived. One side of the Boulevard was for petrol-heads. It was lined with body shops, tune and lubes, brake and tire centers and gas stations. The other side hosted the area's public works depot, a railway line, a storage center and small mall.

Off the main roads, most people were settled for the night. It would have been easy for the criminally minded to pick a target. Two cars on the driveway told their own story. As did children's posters and stickers slapped on front windows. Kids got the small rooms in the house, usually facing the road. Older folk took the bigger rooms at the back, overlooking a square of grass and a little more peace and quiet.

Angie parked up and walked 159th. She was out on the street at the same time the UNSUB had attacked the spinster. She knew that what she was seeing was what he had seen. The sidewalks were empty. At the bottom of McBain stood a school and patches of ground where dog walkers let their animals toilet before turning in for the night.

Eva Hart's house was on a long, tree-lined, badly lit street. All the houses were single story. Most smartly maintained, some run-down. Angie guessed a lot of old folk lived in the less well-kept dwellings, their limited cash going on basic necessities rather than regular repaints.

She walked the sidewalk on the opposite side of the street to Eva's place. Even though there was a full moon, thick canopies of trees created deep black pools that an offender could sink into. Angie leaned against a tree and looked around. The night was warm and she could smell grass cut earlier in the day. Folks had cracked their windows to let in fresh air and save on air-con costs.

It was too late to knock on Eva's door, but there was no harm in ambling over and taking a snoop.

The house to one side was empty and up for sale. The one on the other side was in blackness with no cars on the drive. Angie felt uncomfortable about the old lady being so isolated. She walked the short drive and saw a light at the back of the house. A TV played so loud she guessed Eva was hard of hearing. Another giveaway of a senior living alone.

The house was small and the passage down the side barely wide and long enough for a car. She walked it and stepped into a square of paved yard. There were strong smells of lavender, roses and jasmine. And something else. Something she couldn't quite place.

Fried chicken.

She turned. A shadow moved just feet away.

A man of her height and build.

Wearing a black ski mask.

Moonlight caught the edge of the metal bat swinging towards her.

Chapter 61

Angie had been caught by surprise.

The man in the mask had a baseball bat across her throat. His hands gripped both ends and he had her trapped against the back wall of Eva Hart's house. She was eye to eye with him and his smell was all over her. Cheap cooking oil and southern fried chicken.

If she didn't act quickly she knew she'd pass out.

Her FBI training kicked in and she kicked out. Drove her right knee into his testicles.

The scumbag woofed in pain and the bat slackened enough for her to wriggle free. She shifted her balance and swung a low kick at the back of his legs.

He stumbled into an even darker part of the yard.

Angie followed with a crisp left-hander that clipped his right cheek.

He was beaten and they both knew it.

One hard punch with her right and this cowardly punk was going down spitting teeth.

She stepped forward to swing and felt a blow from an unseen enemy – a trash can.

Her balance went. She stumbled. Dropped to her hands and knees.

The attacker kicked a supporting arm and sent her sprawling.

Angie felt pain shoot from wrist to shoulder as she collapsed.

He kicked at her head and body. Booted any part of her he could see.

She slid the one good arm across her stomach to protect the baby.

A foot rocked her head. She tasted salt and iron. Blood flowed over her teeth.

Light cracked from the back door.

Angie's heart sank. If the old lady was there he was certain to turn on her. Finish what he'd started.

There was a gunshot.

And another.

Then a crashing sound.

The noise of fence panels being climbed or broken.

Another shot rang out.

Then silence.

She lay in pain. Fluttering fingers touched her face. They smelled of night cream. A hesitant voice asked, 'Are you all right?'

Angie struggled to sit upright. 'I think my arm's broken.'

'Oh dear.' The old lady waved the gun dangerously. 'Are you police?'

'No, I'm not, I'm FBI, ma'am.' She stared down the barrel being shaken in her face. 'Can you give me that gun please and call 911.'

'Oh yes. Yes, of course.' She handed over the weapon and slipper-shuffled back inside.

Angie got herself up and was able to sit on the back step. She spat out blood and got her breath back. A few feet away lay the overturned trash can she'd knocked into. Just to the right, half in and half out of the light, there was something else.

A black rucksack.

Involuntary grunts escaped as she got to her feet and wandered towards it. She was pretty certain she knew what it contained.

His rape kit.

Chapter 62

Murphy's Ranch, Rustic Canyon, LA

Jake had been hit by several rounds from the MAC-10. He lay stunned and waited for pain to erupt in various parts of his body. It never came because layers of Kevlar had done their job.

He rolled out of the blinding glare of the roof-mounted xenon and looked towards the derelict power station. SKU were still 'sweeping' the rooms inside. Shouts of 'Clear' broke the warm night air.

Ruis Costas appeared, concern etched in his brow. 'You okay, boss?'

'I'm fine.' Jake's voice gave away his disappointment. He got to his feet and saw at least two of his men had been hit.

Chuck Warren had a hand on his right thigh and was pushing hard to stop a bleed. A copter blew up dust. Ruis had to shout above the noise. 'Medic will be with you any second, just hang in there.'

Jake knelt alongside Sammy Nicholson, a rookie who'd taken two in the helmet. Kid had been fortunate; neither had gone through, but he was sat up in the dirt, his face white as a sheet.

'You've been lucky,' said Jake, peering into his eyes. 'A bit of concussion, that's all. Tomorrow night you'll be downing shots and bigging it up with your buddies.'

'I don't feel so damned lucky,' Nicholson managed.

Jake left him and went over to the crashed motorcycle.

Emma-Louise Bakker was dead. There was no need to even check for a pulse. She'd hit the tree head first and broken her neck.

He kicked the gun lying in the dirt alongside the corpse of Wayne

Harris's teenage girlfriend. It was a micro-Uzi. Fashion toy for the bad guys.

Ruis joined him and wiped blood on his combat pants. 'Harris is dead too.'

Jake shielded his eyes from the still glaring light of the giant xenon on the top of the old building. 'Where the hell did that thing come from?'

'Come and see.' He walked his boss towards the old power station. 'There are two dead guys inside. Looks like they were filming here when Wayne rode up. The big light is part of their equipment.'

The SKU men entered the building and Jake saw the bodies in a far corner. It was easy to work out what had gone down. The walls around them were covered in graffiti and blood. Harris and the girl had herded them over there with the guns. Paper handkerchiefs, discarded wallets, small photos and coins lay around their feet. They'd been robbed. Emma-Louise had taken their phones, cards and cash while her crazy boyfriend had pointed his machine pistol at them. Jake finished the last of his thoughts out loud. 'Punk just killed them for the sake of it.'

'Looks that way,' answered Ruis. 'There's a camera and tripod over there.' He pointed to the opposite corner. 'I think the girl filmed it, snuff-movie style.'

'Fuck.' Jake remembered orders he'd given. 'Hadn't we checked this area for filming permits and suchlike?'

'We had. Not everyone who films has a permit. They must have just winged it. Planned to save a few bucks because they were doing something cheap.'

Jake saw a clipboard against the wall. He picked it up. Several sheets of paper flapped. It was part of a script. 'They were filming something called *The Big Scare*. Names on the top are Luke Henrik and Joey J. Aston.'

Ruis was bent over the bodies. He spotted a photo ID in a gritty pool of drying blood. 'One on the right is Luke.'

'Someone best find their next of kin and call the cops. Make sure that camera footage stays with us. I don't ever want to see a frame of this on YouTube.'

Chapter 63

Lawndale, LA

E mergency services arrived at Eva Hart's house within ten minutes of being called.

The local cops hit the streets and got a copter with night sun lighting and thermal imaging to comb the area for the perp.

Paramedics patched Angie up. She had dislocated her right elbow and there was a chance of a hairline fracture or chipped bone as well. She'd need an X-ray and possibly a cast or sling. Aside from that, there was extensive bruising to the shoulders and face. Her lip was split but no teeth bust and she didn't need stitches. Most importantly, they were confident the baby was unhurt.

Angie refused a ride to the hospital and promised to go later. She wanted to comfort Eva, who'd gone to pieces after she'd been told the man she'd shot at in the dark was most likely the one who'd previously attacked her.

Two female officers were helping calm her down when Cal O'Brien turned up. He stood in the back doorway talking to a CSI and gave Angie a look that said he wanted a private word.

She excused herself and joined him.

His eyes immediately roamed her torn clothes, bloodied face and bandaged arm. 'Please tell me the other guy looks worse than you.'

'He does. But that's not thanks to me. Our brave old lady shot him.'

'She hit him?'

'There's blood in the yard, so I'd say yes.'

'Good for her.' He looked back to the yard. CSIs were bagging and tagging under a blaze of lights. 'Maybe we'll catch a break.'

'Bad choice of words.' Angie lifted her bandaged arm and winced.

'Sorry. Did the old girl see him?'

'No. She just came out frightened and firing. She's one plucky lady. From what I could learn, she's got no one to come and stay with her. Can you fix protection and social support?'

'Can try. Best protection is to catch this scum.'

'I've got something that might help with that. Take a look at that rucksack, he left it.'

O'Brien dug in his jacket pocket and pulled out gloves. The top of the sack was buckled down, inside tied with a drawstring and toggle. He opened it and tipped out the contents.

The heap of objects included a pair of sex shop handcuffs, five or six lengths of cut rope, rolls of silver gaffer tape, a hunting knife, a pair of pliers, and a thick roll of black bin liners.

O'Brien moved the bags.

Underneath was a length of wood about eighteen inches long and two inches square.

They both silently considered the stave and the lives that had been ruined with it.

'Please God,' implored O'Brien, 'let me find this lowlife, let him resist arrest and give me good cause to blow his fucking head off.'

Chapter 64

Rustic Canyon Park, LA

It was gone three a.m. when SKU finished at Murphy's Ranch.
As Jake drove to Angie's he reflected on how they'd found the young film-makers' van parked at the back of the power station, out of camera shot and deep under a canopy of trees. Ruis Costas had been right. They'd cut corners and come filming without a permit. It had been a short cut that saved a few bucks but cost them their lives.

Jake hadn't called Angie because he'd presumed she'd be asleep, so he was surprised to find the light on when he crept into the apartment. He was horrified to find her sat in PJs on the sofa, with her arm in a sling and her face cut and bruised.

'Jesus Christ, what happened to you?' He dropped his jacket and knelt down beside her.

She put her head on his shoulder. 'I got myself beaten up.'

'What?'

She knew he'd be cross. 'I took a ride out to Lawndale to see where the rapist had failed during an attack, and he came back.'

'You what?'

'Please, don't start up with a lecture.'

'And you tackled this guy?'

She sat up and grimaced. 'I had no choice. I was checking out the old lady's house and there he was in the yard, complete with freaky ski mask.'

190

'I'm guessing from your injuries he's now downtown having what's left of him patched up?'

'No, no he's not.' She sounded tired and strained now. 'I fell over a damned trash can.' She looked at him. 'Don't you dare laugh at me. I was just about to plant a punch that would have knocked him all the way to the bullpen when I fell over it and ended up taking an air shot.'

'I wasn't going to laugh.' The twitch in the corner of his mouth said otherwise. 'How bad's the arm?'

'Not as bad as it looks. He kicked me and I thought he'd broken the elbow but he hasn't. It's a dislocation and bad swelling. O'Brien ran me to the hospital. Hurt like hell when they reset it.'

He tweaked her bandage a little. 'What's under the sling? Plaster or splints?'

'Splint – a neat little fiberglass number.'

'You almost make it sound sexy.'

She gave him a stay-away look. 'Don't even think of coming near me for the next few days.'

'Not even to kiss away your bruises and bring you drinks and snacks whenever you need them?'

'Yeah, I guess that would be allowed.'

'Any other injuries?'

'None to worry about, Doctor Mottram.'

He put a hand tenderly to her face. 'You know, pregnant ladies shouldn't be fighting in the street.'

She leaned into his big, safe hand. 'Yeah, I'm sure I read something in the books about not fighting homicidal rapists late at night during the first trimester.'

He kissed her head and stroked her hair the way he knew she liked it.

Angie grew somber. 'I scared myself tonight, Jake. Right in the middle of the fight I forgot all the training, all those years of martial arts I'd done. I just curled up in a ball to protect the baby and let him kick away. If this sweet old dear, Eva Hart, hadn't come out shooting like Annie Oakley, God knows what would have happened.'

'You were thinking like a mom, not a trained soldier, that's only natural.'

'I know. But it means the piece of shit escaped. Someone else is going to get hurt – maybe raped or killed – because I didn't tough things out.'

Jake shifted alongside Angie and carefully wrapped a protective arm around her. 'You're being stupid now. If anything, it sounds like your intervention saved an old lady's life.'

'Maybe.' She couldn't help but feel sad and exhausted. 'I just wish I'd got him.'

'You will.' He prised himself free, stood up and offered an arm to help her off the couch. 'Come on, let's get you to bed.'

Angie took it and made faces as she got to her feet. 'How was your night?'

'Eventful,' said Jake. 'I'll tell you when you've had some sleep.'

Chapter 65

S hooter had managed to finish work early.
He'd started his shift faking a dose of flu, and after five hours of coughing, nose blowing and acting listlessly, his boss had sent him home.

There had been good reason for wanting the time off, and it had nothing to do with feeling ill or simply swinging the lead like so many of his co-workers did.

He had history to make.

And making it required him to do something special.

FOCUS.

Right at the beginning of his *mission* he'd writ the word large. Cut his finger with an art knife and daubed the blood on a sheet of white cartridge paper until he'd completed the five letters.

FOCUS.

You could do nothing without it. Ask great athletes. Consult business gurus. Talk to spiritual and yogic leaders. They'll all tell you the same thing.

FOCUS is everything.

So much of Shooter's early life had lacked it. He'd wasted so many years of his life because of desperate rage that couldn't be vented.

Then he'd learned.

The hard way, of course. The way the best lessons of life are drilled in and remembered for ever.

There'd been a teacher, a powerful bear of a man who'd made his life hell. He'd failed him on tests. Humiliated him in class. Threatened privately to 'beat the living crap' out of him. For a whole year, this teacher had ground him down.

Shooter had thought long and hard about what to do – how to clear the pain from his mind and assuage the anger eating away inside him.

He'd waited two long months to put his plan into action.

On the last day of term, art teacher Harry Hennessy had kissed his wife and kids goodbye. He'd driven his old Chevy convertible off the drive of their modest home and set out early to beat the traffic into school.

A mile out he'd hit the brakes.

A mile and twenty yards out he'd careered across an intersection and slammed into a wall.

Hennessy hadn't died.

Nor had Shooter intended him to.

He *had* been crippled, though. The impact had thrown him through the windscreen, broken several bones and blinded him.

Shooter had seen the way Hennessy drove – fast, reckless, never buckled up. The thought of an art teacher not being able to see, not being able to criticize – well, that was too delicious to resist.

So he'd focused on it.

He'd waited until the night before the last day of school. Then he'd rolled under the car and cut the brake pipes. Not all the way through, of course, just enough for them to work once or twice before failing. He'd rightly figured that the teacher would be happiest and most careless on his last working day before the long summer break.

That day had changed Shooter's life.

It had empowered him. Shown him the alchemy of taking base thoughts and turning them into golden memories.

Now he was ready to focus again.

Shooter showered and changed.

There was no time for food or rest. He went straight to the room he called Death Row. He erected a shelf below the corkboard and placed electric candles there to create a greater sense of occasion when he opened the door. The effect was wonderful. Everything he'd hoped for. Little Amy looked so lovely in the flickering light. Gina too. And

Zach was handsome. Handsome and proud of the new ladies in his life. His *afterlife*.

Sadly, the twelve newcomers, the ones from the mall, didn't seem at home yet. They looked displaced. Awkward. Even uncomfortable at being there. Strangers in a strange land. But not for long. The world was getting to know them – to ask why they'd been united in death – and once he'd focused, truly focused and delivered what he'd promised himself, Shooter would reveal all the answers.

Chapter 66

Douglas Park, Santa Monica, LA

Jake left Angie propped up on a pillow and sleeping while he showered and shaved.

It had taken her an age to doze off. Normally, she slept on her side, but the busted elbow had stopped her doing that. Dawn had broken by the time she finally closed her eyes and drifted into anything like a restorative rest.

He pulled on a soft, taupe-colored shirt and smart black jeans, kissed the top of her head and left a note by the side of the phone.

I'll call your office on the way into SKU and tell them what happened and why you're NOT going in today. Let me know if you want me to get anything for you. I'll fix dinner tonight, so don't worry about that. Rest up!

Love you,

J x

The note said much more than he'd written.

He knew Angie would interpret his commitment to be there and look after her as a growing acceptance of the baby.

And perhaps it was.

Deep down, he still wasn't fully on board with that idea. But he knew he had to be. He loved her, so he had to accept it and grow to love it.

And he would.

He was sure he would.

During the drive to the office, he thought of work and what had to be done. He needed to see Dixon and explain the bloodbath last night at Murphy's Ranch. Wayne Harris's death wouldn't be a problem. No one was going to shed a tear for the drug-crazed scumbag. But Emma-Louise Bakker was different. The press might try to paint her as a victim of trigger-happy law enforcement officers.

Fortunately, the ME had last night confirmed she hadn't been hit by any of the SKU bullets. The teenager had simply lost control of the big motorcycle while simultaneously firing a machine pistol and being off her head on PCP. Jake had never understood why they called phencyclidine Angel Dust. Devil Dust would be a much better name for that brain-frying shit.

Once all that paperwork and ass covering was done and dusted, he'd be able to buckle down and do the important stuff.

Hunt two Sprees.

He needed to review the Strawberry Fields shootings and appoint a senior SKU agent to run possible leads on that inquiry, while he and Ruis concentrated on the Sun Western slayings.

Jake turned the radio on and learned a memorial service was going to be held at the mall tonight, out of respect for those killed there. It was a nice gesture but he'd be expected to go show his face and that meant leaving Angie on her own longer than he'd hoped.

He turned down the news and called Terry Gibbs, the unit medic. 'Sorry to hit you early, Tex; I'm just wondering how our guys are?'

Gibbs was an early riser and had just come out of the shower. He spoke as he toweled his hair. 'No problem, boss. They're both doing good. Young Sammy didn't even go to hospital. I walked him around awhile after you'd gone and the concussion cleared. He'll have a headache this morning but will be fine.'

'And Chuck?'

'Yeah, I spoke to the hospital. They dug out the slug and kept him in overnight for observation. Whole place is scared shitless of these MRSA bugs so they don't want to risk infection. Plus it tore up a bit of muscle and they want to check him again this morning.'

'Sound like a long layoff?'

'He'll need a lot of physio, that's for sure.'

'Okay, thanks, Tex. Let me know of any changes. I'll call Sammy later and cut some time this afternoon to go see Chuck.'

'I'm sure he'll appreciate that.'

As Jake hung up he was hit by an impulsive thought. One strong enough for him to call Ruis and act on it.

Unlike Tex, Costas was not an early starter. He answered still sounding asleep, his voice like a dying motor. 'He-ll-o . . .'

Jake put on his brightest tone. 'Morning, buddy! How you feeling this *fine* my-ass-is-still-here summer day?'

'Little rough.' He coughed a couple of times. 'Too many tequila shots. Too little sleep. The guys and I sank a few late ones after we wrapped in the hills.'

'No harm in that. D'you think you and your hangover could go and slump over my desk for an hour or so? I need to sort something out before coming in.'

'Yeah.' Ruis felt like death as he looked at his watch. 'We can be there by ten. Does that work?'

'It does. Thanks. I'm on my cell if or when a shitstorm breaks. Don't worry about Dixon, I'll text him and ask him to call me. We can sort out the paperwork on last night when I get there.'

'Already looking forward to it.'

Jake smiled and hung up.

He thought a little more about his sudden impulse. Maybe it wasn't such a good idea after all.

Nevertheless, he found himself driving straight past the office.

Chapter 67

Angie's cellphone rang.

Far off, in the distant world, on the other side of her shuttered lids, it trilled like an exotic wild bird.

Angie woke and felt like she was having a heart attack. Her body wasn't ready for movement. She stared across the bedroom. It was flooded with daylight. To her surprise, she was sat up. The pain in her right arm filled in the blanks. All the horrors of last night hit her like a bucket of cold water.

She eased her legs out of bed and felt dizzy. The ringing phone was on the dressing table across the room. It would be her office. They'd be wondering where she was, why she wasn't in. The bird trilled persistently as she took slow steps across the carpet.

'Hello.' She was surprised by her own voice, how it sounded as weak as she felt.

'Doc, it's Cal O'Brien.' He'd picked up on her tone as well. 'How you doing?'

Her bleary eyes read Jake's note as she answered him. 'I guess I'm okay. Hang on.' She pulled out the padded chair that matched the dressing table and sat on it. 'How can I help, Lieutenant?'

He gave her the news. 'A few hours ago, a young male with a gunshot wound was found collapsed in the street. A couple going home from a party had been driving by and guessed he'd been the victim of a gangland hit. They called 911 and he was taken to the emergency room.'

'You think it's our guy?'

'Pretty certain. The slug dug out of his bicep matches the caliber Eva Hart fired, but we still have to do rifling checks and prints on it. Get this, though – a beat cop who turned out with the parameds found a ski mask in a dumpster ten yards from where the punk was picked up. It had the word RAPIST on the forehead.'

Angie was fully awake now, her brain back in investigative mode. 'Forensically, can you tie it to him?'

'No, not yet. We've got hair and skin from the mask and a warrant to take body samples from him, so we're on the way. CSIs are all over the rape kit you found. No prints, but they *will* find DNA – they always do. I'd say sometime soon we'll have strong links to the mask or rape kit, as well as irrefutable ballistics on the slug.'

'I can't help but ask, was he of mixed race? I've been guessing white mom and black father.'

O'Brien blew out a breath. 'Yeah, yeah he is. How'd you know?'

'Well, the extension of the profile, the racial component you were sensitive about, predicts his father is black, pure black though, and is involved in local gangs.'

'Then you were right. You want in on the interview when he's fit to talk, or you too beat up for that?'

She eased herself out of the seat and headed for the shower. 'What do you think?'

'I'll let you know where and when it is.'

Chapter 68

S hooter worked hard all morning.

He scrutinized his planning and double-checked all his physical preparations. What he'd learned from his two separate sprees was that nothing went *exactly* as he imagined.

Take the baldy teacher and the fat kids.

They should all be dead. But they weren't. They'd escaped because he'd *presumed* the bullets had killed them. 'Presumption' wasn't a mistake he'd make again.

In the mall, he'd done better. He'd counted the victims and finished them off.

Shooter paced his sanctuary and wondered about the world outside. It was disappointing that no one had yet made the connection between the Strawberry Fields massacre and the Sun Western slayings. Granted he'd used different guns, and the mix of victims had probably thrown the media, but he'd assumed the cops or the FBI would have spoken about possible links.

And the note.

At first he'd been upset that there'd been no mention of the cute little message he'd left in the mall. Then the penny dropped. The LAPD must be keeping it secret from the public. They'd seek to use it to eliminate cranks who rolled up at a precinct and claimed to be responsible for the killings. If someone didn't know what was on the note, then they'd be immediately flung out on their ears.

He took a bottle of water with him as he left the sanctuary. It was important to be properly hydrated. The brain functioned better that way. A busy afternoon lay ahead. There were people to see. Arrangements to be made.

By tonight, everything would be perfect.

Dead perfect.

Chapter 69

Angie's arm hurt too much for her to drive so Chips had fixed a cab to North Los Angeles Street, where the wounded man, his arm also in a sling, sat waiting in an interview room with his State-provided lawyer and two cups of the world's worst coffee.

O'Brien met Angie in reception. 'His name is Alfonso Cayman,' the cop said as he guided her through to the interview suite. 'He's twenty years old and hasn't said anything except that he wanted an attorney and more painkillers.'

'Any progress with the DNA and ballistics?'

The lieutenant smiled. 'Bullet is a perfect match to Miss Hart's .22 and prelim DNA says the scumbag's head was in the ski mask.'

'Then I guess the interview is more a plea bargain than anything.' Angie waited for him to open a door for her. 'Thanks.'

'I hope so. Would be good to know that what he admits to is everything he's done, not only what we know of.'

'Which, I guess, is where I come in?'

'If you don't mind.'

'Glad to help.'

He lifted his hand and passed over a beige folder. 'These are rap sheets. Kid has no previous, but his old man is a different story.'

'Let me guess – wounding, drugs, guns . . .?'

'The full set. Seven kids by four women. Never paid a dime to help raise them.'

'Real nice guy.'

O'Brien halted outside the interview room. 'I'd like to play things in two stages. First off, I run through the evidence with him and his lawyer. Once he sees there's a world of grief heading his way, I call you in and you open him up for full disclosure. Are you okay with that?'

'Uh-huh. I'll just sit the other side of the glass, read the rap sheets and sort out my interview strategy.'

He smiled. 'You have a strategy?'

'Yeah, the FBI like to do it that way. You should try it some time.'

'Sounds too advanced for a lowly cop like me.' He opened the door to the mirror room for her. 'I think I'll stick to forensics, polygraphs and beating confessions outta people.'

Angie wandered into the darkened room. It was cool and dusty. Stank of others who'd stood there. Cheap male cologne. Old damp jackets. Cigarettes. Through the glass she saw Cayman.

This was the guy who'd tried to choke her.

A man who would have raped and maybe murdered Eva Hart if she hadn't been there.

He didn't look like a monster but he was everything she'd thought he'd be.

Not a giant or a dwarf.

Not fat, thin, ugly or overly handsome.

His whole body and demeanor shrieked with what he was not, rather than what he was. And then there was the biggest *not* of all.

His race.

He wasn't black. He wasn't white. He was caught mid-color.

Mixed.

And therein lay the answer to the young man's rage. What had set him against the world and made him angry enough to rape and kill.

Angie knew LA's streets well. Mixed-race kids were dogs that got kicked by both black and white gangs. Alfonso would have been constantly brutalized. And when it came to blaming someone, he'd have laid his victimization at the door of his white-ass mother – after all, she'd diluted his blackness, made him what he was. But boys are boys, and for a plethora of psychological reasons, beating Mom wouldn't have been an option. So the anger displaced a generation and passed back to his deepest surviving root, his mother's mother.

Angie saw her breath mist the interview room glass. She backed off a little and listened as O'Brien went through all the standard niceties with the scumbag's attorney, a sour-faced woman in her fifties. The brief was dressed in a plain blue, long-sleeved top and the kind of flared bold-print trousers she should have been arrested for even looking at, never mind wearing.

The lieutenant laid out the evidence – hairs, fibers, DNA, ballistics – the full lexicon of implied guilt. He let every word sink in. Nothing was rushed. Second by second the young man across the table grew increasingly worried. Finally, O'Brien got round to saying he wanted a colleague to join them, an FBI profiler who'd been working the case. Mrs Sourpuss said she had no objections.

As Angie walked in, she caught Alfonso's eye.

He looked straight at her and then away.

She settled in the seat alongside the lieutenant.

O'Brien had seen the moment between them. 'You recognize Doctor Holmes, don't you, Alfonso?'

He shrugged.

Angie kept her eyes locked on his. 'How is your arm?' she asked sympathetically.

He stretched the sling a little but didn't answer.

'I'm asking, not because I give a damn, but because I'm wondering what the hard black boys in County are going to say when they hear you got capped by a frail old white lady.'

His eyes widened a little.

'Tough gangster boys – like your pop – they're going to be mighty amused.' She saw him close his mouth and mask his fear. 'Come to think of it, some guys in the can maybe ran the streets with your old man. Tyler Cayman's been around some. What do you think, Alfonso?'

'Shut up 'bout him!'

Angie put the folder down and slid the rap sheet out. She spun it round so a mugshot of the father faced his mug of a son. 'Tyler Cayman: Crips soldier, drug dealer and all-round bad guy. Nothing he wouldn't do and no one he wouldn't do it to.'

She pushed the picture across.

Alfonso sat back in his chair. Stared down as though even the celluloid might hurt him.

'Tell me about your mom, Alfonso.'

'Fuck you, bitch.'

'Hey!' O'Brien stepped in. 'Talk nicely to the lady.'

Angie's eyes were burning holes in Cayman's skull. 'How did the pure *white* girl from Brentwood end up with the bad *black* man from Watts?'

He started a slow rock on his bolted-down seat.

Mrs Sourpuss woke up. 'Is this *really* evidentially relevant?'

Angie ignored her. 'Must have been rough for you as a kid, Alfonso. Your old man is hardly around. He has a rep on the street like some kind of hero. But when he comes by your crib, he doesn't want to know you – because, let's face it, you're not like him. Hell, you're not even like your mother.' Angie studied the pain in his eyes. 'I guess after a time he stopped calling. Left you home alone with Mommy. Only by then, Mom's a wreck, spaced out on crack and other crap. She's an addict and useless. Worse than that, you have to look after her. And you hate her for that. Hate her weakness. Hate how she made you a color that's not black like your big, tough daddy.' Angie watched him as he gripped the edge of the table, holding it like he might fall off the edge of the world if he let go. 'Grandma could have helped, couldn't she?'

Alfonso jumped to his feet.

'Sit down!' O'Brien was already standing opposite him.

Angie twisted the knife. 'Only Grandma didn't want anything to do with either of you – did she?'

His fist balled and knuckles whitened.

'Sit, Alfonso.' The cop stepped around the side of the table. 'Don't make me ask again.'

The sourpuss attorney looked terrified.

Angie waited until he'd lowered himself into his seat. 'What happened, Alfie? I guess your mom called you Alfie and not Alfonso – the name your old man gave you?'

He'd clammed up again.

'Way I figure it, she took you round to her parents' house and Grandma turned you both away. Slammed the door in your faces. That was enough to make your mom fall apart. And to this day it's a moment you'll never forget.'

He sank his head.

'You couldn't hurt her, could you? Couldn't take your anger out on your mom because you're not wired nasty like your pop. Oh no, he could do that in a blink.' She snapped her fingers. 'But you sure as hell could hurt that bitch who shut you and your momma out.'

'She's to blame.' He banged a fist on the table. 'She cudda helped us, man. She had the money an' she was blood. Blood shud help blood.'

'I agree. So why didn't you attack *her* then?'

Alfonso gripped the table again.

A thought occurred to Angie. 'You did, didn't you?'

'No, man. She had a gun like that bitch last night. And her old man was around. I thought he was away on business, but he come back and chased me in the yard like you did. We was there fightin' on the ground and he grabbed this wood that was holding up some plant or bush or somethin' and stabbed me with it, like I was some fucking piece-of-shit vampire.'

'That was the stave you took with you on your attacks?'

Mrs Sourpuss touched his arm. 'You don't have to answer that, Alfonso.'

He palmed her off. 'Yeah, that was it. He stuck me with it so I stuck them white bitches with it.'

'Why those particular women, Alfie? What made you pick them?'

'They didn't tip.'

The comment threw her for a moment. 'I don't understand.'

'I was running for Alabama Chicken. Delivering round Inglewood, Huntington and Hawthorne. Took da bitches their food and they'd never give me nuthin'. No spare change, not a cent; not even a dime at Christmas. They was just like that bitch in Brentwood.'

'Your grandmother?'

'Yeah.'

'What took you down to Lawndale and Compton?'

'Same thing. Manager laid me off but said there was a job going at a branch in Lynwood, so I worked there a time.'

'And Mrs Knapp, the lady you killed, what happened with her?'

Attorney Sourpuss stepped in quick. 'I advise you not to answer that, Alfonso.'

O'Brien sensed this was the make or break moment. 'That's not a good call.' He leaned across the table and made sure his gaze hooked the young man's. 'If I walk you past our CSI unit you'll be deafened by the sound of high fives and back-slapping going on in there. From ballistics to DNA and back again, they're putting enough together to see *you* fry – worse than any chicken you ever delivered. So I suggest, Alfonso, you play the co-operative scumbag card and answer the lady's question.'

O'Brien leaned back and let his words sink in.

Angie followed up. 'What happened with Mrs Knapp, Alfie?'

He chewed his lip and considered his options. Finally, he gave it up. 'I lost it with her.' He shrugged. 'I can't explain. It's like when I'm hitting the women, this pain inside me gets smaller.'

'I understand,' said Angie. 'You felt strong.'

'*Strong*, yeah. Like I was in control. Only fucking moment of my life I felt like my shit was together.'

Angie knew she had to get him to be more specific. 'Did you *mean* to kill Lindsey Knapp?'

'No!' he snapped.

'So tell me how it was.'

He swallowed and looked down at the table. 'It was like I said. I just beat her.' After a few seconds he tilted his head up at Angie. 'The more I hurt her, the better I felt. I couldn't stop. Once I'd started I just couldn't stop.' He dropped his gaze again. 'I'm sorry.'

Angie looked across to O'Brien. His eyes said he had heard enough. 'Listen, Alfonso, you need to go through it all. Everything you did. Not just to Mrs Knapp, but to all your victims. You do that, put it all in a full statement to the lieutenant –' she looked to the attorney –'and I'll see you get some psychiatric help.'

The lawyer nodded her consent and Angie rose. 'You understand me, Alfie?'

He nodded.

'You ready to give that statement?'

He put his free hand to his face and mumbled, 'Yeah, I'm ready.'

'Then I'll leave you to it.' Angie started to walk away.

'Wait!'

She turned.

'I'm sorry 'bout last night – about your arm an' stuff.'

Chapter 70

SKU Offices, LA

I t was gone lunchtime when Jake called Angie's cell.
'Hi there.'

He could tell from the background noise she wasn't at her apartment – the place he'd hoped she'd be. 'Please tell me you've not gone into the office.'

'I'm not *at* the office.'

'But you're somewhere, right?'

'Everyone's *somewhere*, Jake.'

'You know what I mean. You're somewhere *working*, rather than somewhere *resting*, like you know you should be.'

She smiled at his concern. 'I'm fine. I'm with O'Brien. We just got a confession out of a guy for the Lindsey Knapp homicide and the serial rapes.'

He knew better than to tell her off and mar the moment. 'Congratulations. Now can you please go home and rest?'

'Yeah, I can.' She softened her tone. 'Hey, thanks for your note this morning, it was a nice thing to wake up to.'

'I'd rather have woken you myself.'

'I bet you would.' She pictured what that might have been like. 'What time you going to be back tonight?'

'I'm not sure. There's this memorial service down at the mall. I guess I'm going to be expected to put in an appearance.'

'I'll come with you.'

210

'No, you're not. You're going to put your feet up. I gotta go now but I'll call you later.'

'Make sure you do.'

Just as she hung up, Danielle Goodman knocked on Jake's door and opened it.

'You got a moment for me?'

He put the phone down. 'Looks like I have.'

She floated in, wearing a buttercup yellow dress that was ludicrously bright.

'I've written up a profile on the Sun Western slayer and wanted to run it by you.'

'Glad to hear it. We need all the help we can get on this one.'

'Like I said to you and Agent Costas yesterday, I still think you're after someone in the Starkweather mold.'

'Like Harris you mean?'

She tensed. 'Profiles often fit more than one suspect – you know that. Just because he wasn't your UNSUB doesn't mean the profile was wrong.'

'I take your point. I'm not blaming you.'

'I'm relieved to hear it.'

He nodded to the paper in her hand. 'So – do you have any further ideas of what kind of stressor set our guy off?'

'I still favor it being something to do with that particular store, maybe a row with an assistant or a sacking from a position there. Here – look at my profile.' She handed it over. 'Point number three suggests a physical deficiency; it might be eye-related and connected to the store.'

'We're checking their employment records.' Jake looked through her jottings.

1. MALE 18–25.
2. AFRICAN AMERICAN.
3. HAS MINOR PHYSICAL OR MENTAL AFFLICTION THAT MAKES HIM SELF-CONSCIOUS.
4. STRONG SOCIOPATHIC TENDENCIES.
5. LIVES ALONE IN RENTED ACCOMMODATION.

6. UNDERACHIEVER.
7. HIGH SCHOOL EDUCATED.
8. OWNS MOTOR VEHICLE.
9. UNEMPLOYED OR IN MENIAL LABOR.
10. HAS ISSUES WITH AUTHORITY.
11. HAS BEEN/IS MEMBER OF GUN OR RIFLE CLUB.
12. MAY HAVE GANG ASSOCIATIONS AND ACCESS TO ARRAY OF WEAPONS.
13. IS MOVING FROM STAGE ONE (GUIDED) OF SPREE ACTIVITY INTO STAGE TWO (RANDOM).

He put the paper down and gestured for her to take the seat opposite. 'Can you talk me through points eleven and twelve?'

'Be glad to.' She pulled out the chair. 'At the moment, I see them as an option. *Either* the UNSUB was a member of a gun club and had access to weapons, maybe even permits, *or* – and I do favor this more – he was a gang member who got belittled by the leaders and wanted to demonstrate his dangerousness.'

Jake wasn't convinced. 'I'm not sure either holds water.'

'Why?'

'Well, I didn't see any amazing gun skills out there in the mall. The cowardly sonofabitch used a weapon powerful enough to wipe out half an army from only a hundred meters. It was total overkill. A gun enthusiast would have used something smaller, more tailored for the job. A pro shooter wouldn't have had a MAC in a bag, he'd have had a Glock in a holster.'

The psychologist nodded. 'So, option two – the gang link?'

'I'm struggling there as well. Gang shootings are usually gang on gang. When civilians get wasted there's generally a good reason why – they crossed, disrespected or threatened someone. I can't see that being the case in the mall. Another thing – gangs are always hierarchical; soldiers don't go on sprees like that to show their prowess to bosses, it just brings the kind of heat no one wants.'

She looked offended. Her prime theories had just been shot down in flames. 'I'd urge you not to discount these observations too easily.'

'I don't and I won't. I'll think and rethink every point you've made and believe me, I'm grateful for all your input. One worry I share though is your final point. You think he's on the shift?'

'I do. You know that in the Guided Phase, Sprees stay in their geographical comfort area?'

'Yeah, they usually kill their way towards a specific target. The most important hit is the last.'

'Exactly. Well, I think the mall was his big hit, or his last, but he may have drawn so much attention that focus on whatever targets he had set has been lost.'

'So now he goes random? On the run, out of state, but still with murder in mind?'

'That's the theory. The Spree loses direction, control and purpose. The next kill will be a rush of blood, spontaneous and disorganized. Then you know what happens.'

'Suicide by cop.'

'If you're lucky. Only I don't think this guy's going to go out alone. He'll want to take as many uniforms with him as possible.'

Chapter 71

'Oh my God!' Chips jumped out of his seat as Angie walked into the office. 'You look terrible.'

'You sure know how to make a girl feel good.'

'Why on earth are you here?'

'*Here* is where I work.' She shrugged her purse off her good arm.

He pulled her seat out for her. 'Sit down. Let me get coffee, water, pillows.'

'Don't fuss!'

'Sister, I *need* to fuss. I was born to fuss.'

Angie hit the power button on her computer as he headed to the pantry. 'Hang on!' she shouted. 'Show me your T.'

Chips turned and smiled. The shirt was Coca-Cola red. It featured a full frontal can of soda and the question DO FAT DRUG DEALERS SELL DIET COKE?

She smiled. 'It's okay. Go get the coffee.'

'Still black?'

'Yeah.'

'And are you still off chocolate and ice cream?' He rolled his eyes knowingly.

The comment threw her. 'Yes, as it happens I am.'

He tilted his head inquisitively. 'Do you have anything to share with your loyal and highly discreet co-worker?'

'How about a few bruises and a bust arm?'

214

'I'm getting the coffee.'

Angie watched him go, then put her hands on her waist. It didn't feel like she was showing too much weight. Not already. She squinted down at her breasts. They felt tender, but right now everything felt tender. Maybe it was wishful thinking but they looked bigger. Rounder. Better. Yeah, she *was* kidding herself. She'd always wanted bigger, rounder and better, but with her luck, pregnancy wouldn't even grant that wish.

The computer took an age to load, and when it had, she wished it hadn't. Her mail was jammed with all the stuff she hated: reminders for monthly reports that she had to submit; research papers to read; inter-departmental tele-conferencing requests.

Chips saved her from having to make a start. 'There you go, black and hot, just like an ex-friend of mine.'

'You're getting worse.'

'I know.' He headed to his desk. 'I've got something that I think you might find interesting.'

'Are you trying to be intriguing?'

'Do I have to try?'

'Much harder.'

He grabbed his laptop and returned to her desk. 'This is something I edited from the mall footage.' He put it down and pressed play.

Angie watched the screen. It was CCTV footage from Judy-Ju's. 'I've seen this.'

'I know.' He was used to her impatience. 'Watch again.'

She studied the grainy shots of the young black man moving from wounded shopper to shopper, executing them in cold blood. 'Sorry, I don't get it, Chips.'

'Wait.' He pointed at the screen. 'Here you go. See what happens after his last victim, watch the guy who tries to tackle him.'

Angie watched. A man in his thirties, who had been protecting his toddler and wife, got shot to pieces. The killer turned and walked out. But right after it Chips had edited a reprise, in slow-motion, not of the victim but the shooter.

Something fluttered from his left hand.

She hadn't seen it at normal speed. It had been lost in the body turn. All attention had been on the bag with the gun in it.

'What do you think?' Chips looked excited. He rewound it and played it again. 'It could be an accident but I don't think it is. Look closely and you see he's still got something in his hand. It's a tissue or a note.'

Angie bent so close to the monitor she almost rubbed her nose on it. 'No, it's no accident, Chips. Watch his face. He checks that he's dropped it. It's something we're meant to find.'

She dialed Jake's cellphone.

It tripped to voicemail. She replayed the footage at normal speed as she left a message. 'Jake, I just saw some footage from the mall. You probably know this already, but the Spree drops something. Right before he walks out of the store, he dips in his left pocket, takes out some paper and lets it fall. It's *not* an accident. If you view the tape you'll see he glances at it as he heads out. Call me, I'll talk you through it.'

Only as she hung up did Angie remember her boss's warning to stay out of the case.

Chapter 72

SKU Offices, LA

Jake and Ruis had just finished a team briefing when he picked up Angie's voicemail.

'Damn!' He clicked off the phone and slid it back into his pocket.

'Trouble?'

'Yeah, kind of. Do me a favor, get on to the labs and kick their asses.'

'For some specific reason? Or do you just feel the urge to know an ass is being kicked?'

'There's a suggestion the UNSUB dropped something at the mall, right after he executed the last victim.'

'A suggestion? From whom?'

'Doesn't matter. Find out if there's a note, a card, a slip of paper among all that trash that got picked out of the blood.'

'I'll do it now. Catch you back in the office.'

'Thanks.' He shouted at Ruis's disappearing back, 'I've got to see Crawford about some press stuff.'

'Lucky you!'

A few minutes later, Jake entered his boss's office and found him with sleeves rolled up, minus jacket and tie. It was a bad sign.

Dixon looked up at his visitor. 'Tell me something *good*, Jake. I need an illegally high fix of positive news, to keep me from slashing my wrists and taking a warm bath.' He motioned to a seat.

Jake took it. 'Coconut water can be used in emergencies instead of blood plasma.'

'No way. Are you shitting me?'

'Not at all. The water, not the milk, is liquid endosperm. It's sterile and has an ideal pH level. I learned it in the army.'

'Never taught me that in the air force.'

'Should have joined the Marines. Anyway, are you off the suicide list now?'

'Just about.' He sat back in his chair and took off his glasses. 'We're gonna face more cutbacks. I've spent the afternoon trying to make a yard go a mile.'

'We're down to the bone, Crawford. You cut anything more and you cause the kind of damage that might be permanent.'

'I know.'

A knock on the door stopped their conversation.

FBI Media Manager Ryan Fox walked in. Mid-thirties with thinning blond hair, dressed in a suit as blue as his eyes.

Dixon turned to Jake. 'Ryan's been fielding calls all day. Bit of a siege from what I understand.'

'The peasants are certainly revolting. *LA Times* wants to ride along with SKU. *USA Today* is setting a feature for the weekend on why LA is becoming the Spree capital of the country.'

'Great,' said Jake, sarcastically.

Ryan ticked the rest off on his fingers. 'CBS News is doing a live broadcast from out on Wilshire as we speak. NBC and Fox have both got requests in to film in the incident room. I've done holding pieces on a million radio news bulletins and they're all running phone-ins on "how safe are our streets". Unless Obama gets caught screwing a hotel maid or Donald Trump comes out as gay we're going to be top story and hammered for the next few days.'

Jake could feel bad news coming. 'So what have you in mind?'

Ryan looked to the section chief to deliver the message.

'You need to front up a presser, Jake.'

His face said that wasn't something he'd relish. 'I'd rather you did it. You're the one who has a way with words.'

'Not this time,' said Dixon. 'After your heroics at the Observatory, seeing you in front of a camera will reassure people.'

'We'd like to schedule something for tomorrow,' added Fox, enthusiastically. 'How about *late* morning?'

Jake knew he'd been set up. 'Fine. Though Christ knows what we're going to say.'

'Give them some of Danielle's profile,' suggested Dixon. 'The press loves profiles. It'll keep them slobbering until next week.'

'Can I get a copy?' asked Fox.

Jake shook his head. 'No offence, but I don't want the full profile seen by anyone non-operational. I'll mail you a summary.'

'Thanks. Is it an idea to have Danielle there as well?'

'It is. A very *bad* idea.' Jake explained himself to Dixon. 'We don't see eye-to-eye on some points. Best not to have us rowing in public.'

'It is *usual* to have the profiler there,' said Fox unhelpfully.

Jake shot him a scalding look.

He held his hands up in surrender. 'Okay, I'm just here to advise you.'

'Advice noted,' said Dixon. 'No profiler, Ryan. I guess we're all going to this memorial service tonight, so let's make sure no one says anything to any reporters. The three of us should meet at nine in the morning and finalize what we're going to say. Okay?'

They both nodded and Fox headed for the door.

Jake wanted a private word before he followed. He waited until the press guy had gone.

'Something on your mind?' asked Dixon.

'Yeah. There's been a development.'

'Good or bad?'

'I'm told the UNSUB may have deliberately dropped some paper at the scene. Labs are processing it at the moment.'

Dixon rubbed tired eyes. 'If it's a note, you know what it means, don't you?'

Jake frowned. 'I'm not sure I do.'

'Killers that communicate are the worst kind. Think Son of Sam. Think BTK. It means our whole nightmare just moved to Elm Street.'

Chapter 73

Chips had done more than just 'acquire' and edit the mall footage. He'd set up a spreadsheet showing thumbnails of what pictures had been shot from what cameras at exactly what time of day. There was an accompanying plan of the mall with all the camera positions numbered and marked, along with a red dotted line indicating the path the UNSUB had taken.

The first thing that jumped out at Angie was how pre-planned and well executed it had all been. The gunman had walked briskly in and out of the mall, pausing only once. He'd been efficient, ruthless and unemotional.

Now that the rape-homicide she'd been working was done and dusted, she desperately needed a new challenge to sink her teeth into. And this case was it.

Despite the warnings to stay away – or maybe because of them – she knew this was going to be one of those investigations that got talked about for decades. It would be up there with Kemper, Bundy and the rest.

Tomorrow she'd have another go at her boss. And at Jake. If what Chips had spotted on the video turned out to be a note left by the UNSUB, then that was a clear sign she was right about him being more Serial than Spree. Plus, she'd be more adept at interpreting the meaning of the note than Danielle Goodman.

Her right arm was all wrapped up in a sling and using her left was taking some getting used to. Even the two calls she took in the cab on the way back to her apartment felt awkward.

The first was from Suzie Janner suggesting lunch and a pregnancy planning talk next Monday.

The second was not one she'd wanted or expected.

'Angie, it's Sandra McDonald.' Her tone was brusque. 'Are you in the building?'

'No, I just left. I'm on my way home to change for the service at the mall.'

There was a slight hesitation before her boss continued. 'I heard from Jake that you took quite a beating and weren't coming in?'

Angie pieced things together. McDonald was pissed she hadn't called her. It meant there was a good chance she knew about the Cayman case as well. 'Yes, I'm sorry, I should have updated you. I dislocated my elbow and took a few whacks. I would have stayed off work and called you, but Cal O'Brien wanted me to help on the rape-homicide.'

'I know. I just got a message from the deputy chief at the LAPD, voicing appreciation for your help. Why didn't you at least tell me the case was closed?'

'My bad. The interview only went down a couple of hours back and he hadn't been formally charged and processed when I left the Detention Center.'

'Well he has now. And I expect that report tonight, along with a full explanation of how you ended up getting assaulted at a victim's home.'

'I'll do it straight after the mall memorial.'

'Do it before. I'm your immediate boss; I need to be in the know *before* anyone else asks me about it. Do you understand?'

'Yes, ma'am.'

'Good. And let's meet in the morning. We need to speak about a few matters.'

The line went dead without so much as a goodbye.

Angie had to do more left-hand conjuring to pay the driver.

She dropped her door keys twice while trying to get into the apartment.

She kicked off her shoes and felt more like slipping into bed than typing up a report and getting ready to go out. Ordinarily, she'd shower and put on fresh make-up, but the pain in her banged-up arm had gone off the scale.

She slipped off the sling and struggled out of her work clothes. In the wardrobe was a mid-length black dress that she only ever wore for funerals. It took her an age to get into it. The contortions left her needing to raid the bathroom cabinet for extra-strength Advil. She sat on the bed with a glass of water, took two tablets and spent the next half-hour on her laptop writing the mail McDonald wanted.

The clock on the nightstand said 19:05.

A physically hard and mentally draining day was still a long way from being over. She risked closing her eyes for five minutes.

An hour and a half later she woke up.

The memorial service was about to start.

Chapter 74

SKU Offices, LA

Jake always kept a plain black suit in his locker at work. It was a failsafe for funerals, big meetings with FBI top brass and visiting the homes of victims.

It took him several attempts to get a good knot on the plain black tie and at the same time not end up with one of the tails a yard longer than the other.

As he and Ruis headed to the Sun Western mall he had mixed feelings about the memorial service. It had been arranged at alarmingly short notice by a combination of State Governor and City Mayoral offices. As a result, it felt more like a bid to boost commercial confidence than a respectful event to remember those who had died.

By the time the two men got there it was twilight and cool out on the streets. The blue-black sky buzzed with circling news and police copters, the streets below filled with thousands of black ants, all marching to the same central spot.

Since the shootings, people had been spontaneously laying flowers on a spread of lawn near the Citibank side of the mall, off the Avenue of the Stars, and this was the focal point of the night's ceremony. Giant video screens had been positioned on all the surrounding streets to relay footage to those far away.

Ruis dipped a hand into his pocket and grabbed his ringing cellphone. He eased away from Jake as they walked and put a finger in his ear to block out the street noise. Meanwhile, Jake scanned the crowds and wondered if the UNSUB was among the mourners. Danielle was certain he was already out of town but Jake wasn't sure. He'd remembered Angie talking about how serial murderers liked to go back to the scene of their kills, to relive the thrill of what they'd done, and he figured a Spree might not be too different.

One of the huge street screens came alive with aerial footage of the gathering crowds. Jake was moved by the sight of thousands of flickering candle flames, symbols of sympathy for those who'd died.

Ruis came back to his side. 'Some good news.'

Jake's eyes drifted from the screen. 'That I could do with.'

'Look at this.' He passed his boss his cellphone. 'I just got it from the labs.'

Jake studied the display. It was an opened JPEG.

'What exactly am I looking at?'

'It was a note, found in pooled blood at the mall. The techies had to clean it up to read it.'

Jake angled the phone so he could see better. 'Why is the color so pale? It looks like sherry more than anything.'

'The victims' blood got diluted by gallons of water that flooded the place after the gunman shot out one of those big water dispensers.'

Jake handed it back. 'And you're sure this was dropped by the UNSUB?'

'Not a hundred percent. We still have other bits of litter to match to victims, or just trash from outside. But none of the other pieces of paper have hand-written messages on.'

Jake looked puzzled. 'Judy-Ju's is the shop name. Why would the perp write a note warning of danger after the event?'

'Because he's a crazy, mad sonofabitch?'

The two men fell silent as the mayor of LA, Mike Lewandowski, stepped up to a podium microphone. 'This city has been united in grief.' His voice echoed across the streets. 'The atrocity in the mall has joined the hands of every church leader, every politician, every social class and every man and woman, not just here in Los Angeles but across America. And tonight, as we bow our heads and pay our respects to the innocents lost here, we send the perpetrator of this obscenity a loud and clear message. We *will* find you and we *will* bring you to justice.'

Jake listened to the slow thunder of applause as it spread down the jammed sidewalks and roads. It was spine-tingling to hear the city motivated block by block. Not that fine words and public outrage would stop the UNSUB. Just the opposite. He'd watch tonight and leech off the energy. All that public anger and fear would make his dark secret seem all the more important.

As the applause died down, church and gospel choirs started up. Victims' families and loved ones headed a long, candlelit procession; they would walk the whole block and return to a spot now christened Memorial Square, where they'd lay new flowers and messages.

More local politicians hustled up to the microphone and spotlight to have their say.

'This eulogizing is going to go on for ever,' Ruis whispered. 'Every vote-grabbing goon in LA is gonna want to shed a tear out there.'

Jake didn't reply. He'd just spotted Angie checking through an LAPD control point. He shook his head. 'I knew it was too much to hope she'd take it easy and stay at home.'

Ruis gave him a knowing pat on the shoulder.

Angie read Jake's face as she approached. 'Before you ask, I'm feeling a lot better.'

'You don't look it,' he answered.

'Gee, thanks.'

He kissed her. 'I didn't mean it like that.'

'Congratulations,' said Ruis once they'd finished. 'Getting a rape-murderer off the street wins big applause in my book.'

'*Thanks*. I'm glad it's closed.'

Jake changed subjects. 'Ruis, show Angie the paper from the lab.'

He lined up the image and passed her his BlackBerry.

Angie tilted it for a better view. 'Is that blood all over the note?'

'Blood and water,' explained Ruis. 'Bullets burst one of those big drink dispensers and flooded the place.'

She passed the phone back. 'Judy-Ju's was the name of the store, right?'

'Right,' confirmed Jake. 'We were just talking about that. I don't get why he sends a written warning when the deed's already been done.'

Angie thought on it. 'Serials often feel compelled to make contact with law enforcement—'

'Spree,' countered Jake.

'He's more serial than you think.'

He could see she was in no mood to concede the point. 'You eaten?'

'No.'

Jake looked to Ruis. 'The procession will take an age. You mind covering while I take the good doctor for a slice of pizza?'

'Sure, but bring me back something spicy.'

They started walking. Jake turned and shouted, 'We'll get you a large pepperoni, ham, sausage and egg.'

Ruis gave him the thumbs up. 'I love you, man.'

Jake laughed and shouted back, 'Love you too, buddy.' He waited until he and Angie were out of the crush of the crowd before he asked the obvious question. 'So, how are you *really*?'

'Exhausted, but I needed to be here for this. Like everyone else who's turned out, I want to pay my respects.'

He took her hand and squeezed it. 'You're a very special lady, Angie Holmes.'

'I know that. I have to be to put up with you.'

He stopped and kissed her. Warmer and longer than before. A kiss that said he'd be there for her.

She leaned into him and for a brief moment all the pain vanished.

Someone across the street wolf-whistled. They broke with smiles on their faces.

Jake draped a giant arm over her shoulder and guided her along a side street. 'You feeling anything with the baby yet?'

She curled her one good arm around his waist. 'It's way too soon for that, you idiot.'

'It is?'

'I'm *seven* weeks, that's all. You don't feel kicks and punches until about sixteen, maybe eighteen weeks. Though I may punch you, if you carry on like this.'

He laughed. 'I feel safe because you've only got one functioning arm and you punch like a child with your left.'

Now she stopped the walk. 'And I feel safe because I get the impression you're growing used to the idea of being a father.'

His face turned sad. 'I'm really sorry about how I reacted when you told me. And to be honest, I'm not all the way there yet with the idea, but I'm far enough to know I'm going to be.'

'*How* do you know that?'

'Because I'm not a *complete* idiot – only a partial one. And I realize many people go through life never finding true love and never having the chance to raise a family. So I'm lucky. Very, very lucky.'

'Me too.' She got on her toes and kissed him even longer this time. Kissed him like their lives depended upon it.

Chapter 75

Sun Western Mall, LA

Pizzafazt was as close a rip-off of Pizza Hut as you could get without actually stealing their tables and staff.

The eat-in queue was Disney-ride long, so they decided to order takeaways for themselves as well as the one they'd promised Ruis.

Angie went for a thin-crust vegetarian special. Jake ordered his usual quattro formaggi plus what was billed as 'A Beast of a Meat Feast' for his SKU colleague.

While they waited, TV news played on a large flat-screen mounted high on a wall. It was predictable stuff from the ceremony: helicopter footage of the crowds, comments from politicians, flashbacks to the bedlam when the shootings had happened, close-ups of the families and friends making their way around the block.

'I love the way so many people have just come out with candles,' said Angie. 'In a small way it restores your faith in human nature.'

'Most folk are good folk,' said Jake. 'They know it could have been them in that mall and they're counting their blessings.'

'It's an anagram.'

He frowned at her. 'What is?'

She dropped her voice so no one else could hear her. 'The note that was dropped. DANGERJUDYJU – it's not some stupid post-event *warning*, it's an anagram. That's why he left it.'

'Anagram of what?'

'I don't know. I've not worked that out yet.' She fell silent and began trying to unscramble the letters.

Jake could see she was getting absorbed in thought. 'Angie, don't waste your time trying. You can't work this case. Dixon's already got a wasp in his hole about you even suggesting it to McDonald.'

Someone turned the sound up on the TV. Mourners had started arriving at Memorial Square. Most held placards bearing photographs of dead relatives and friends. Happy faces, snapped in favorite pictures, hung eerily in the darkness of the night.

The guy behind the pizza counter shouted out, 'Takeaways for Pawlik, Voigt and Pavlovic.'

Up on the screen, a father and a young teenage boy put down a poster-size picture of a blond woman who until the mall shooting had been the center of both their lives. The child held it together at first, but when the tears broke there was no stopping them. His pop had to smother him in his arms and carry him away from the cameras.

'Takeaways for Kuentzle, Kessler and Jensen.'

More mourners appeared in front of the news cameras. Elderly women. Housewives. Students.

Then a young black kid who looked no older than nine.

He walked through the crowds with a big picture of a kindly looking old lady pasted on the back of a cereal packet. He also carried a little clay model he'd made of her. Camera lights flashed all around him as he tenderly laid down his homemade tribute.

Jake pointed to the guys collecting boxes at the counter. 'I'm sure they ordered after us.'

A deafeningly loud noise erupted on the TV.

The window of the pizza place smashed. Alarms sounded. The whole building shook and the power shut down.

Heads ringing, Jake and Angie rushed outside.

A bomb had blown a crater in the street. Plumes of grey smoke spiraled in the night sky. Bodies lay everywhere.

Chapter 76

Glass crunched beneath Angie and Jake's shoes as they raced to help.

The streets were full of panic. Survivors rushed madly away from the heart of the explosion. The attack had all the hallmarks of the new breed of al-Qaeda terrorists. Bomb opportunistically. Cause maximum repulsion as well as maximum death.

Jake could smell a stomach-turning acridity in the night air. The bomb had engendered primal fear in the crowd. It was like the massacre at the mall all over again. People were fighting to get away, falling over each other, almost killing each other, in order to escape.

In the distance, cops shouted instructions through megaphones but they could barely be heard above the cacophony of car and burglar alarms, sirens and the frantic mob.

From where Jake and Angie stood they couldn't see the center of devastation, judge how big the bomb had been or tell whether Ruis was okay. An LAPD helicopter buzzed through billowing grey smoke, shining a beam over Memorial Square. Dust and debris swirled high into a hundred-foot pillar of white light.

There was another loud bang.

Plumes of black and orange flame flared two hundred yards to their right.

'Oh my God!' a voice shouted. 'Look! Look what's been hit.'

The remains of a news copter belched black smoke.

'Motherfucking A-rabs!' someone screamed.

A series of smaller bangs and fireballs followed. The air turned chokingly dense. Jake guessed flames from the fallen copter had reached a gas station down the block.

They pushed through the crowds to an LAPD area command vehicle. Jake badged busy officers and turned to Angie. 'You wait in here until I come back for you. Don't come out. Don't wander.' He could see she didn't like being spoken to like that. 'Please, Angie, you have a busted elbow and you're pregnant. Just for once don't fight me.'

Reluctantly she stepped into the open back of the van and struggled with her feelings of powerlessness.

Jake's time in Afghanistan had taught him that surprise strikes like this usually came with a high risk of secondary IEDs. The sooner the Bomb Squad, K-9s and robots arrived the better. The former Marine was tall enough to see over everyone in front of him and able to pick his way to an unmarked 'telecoms' van that he knew was an FBI ops vehicle. To his relief, he saw Ruis inside.

'Guess you forgot my pizza,' he said, nodding at Jake's empty hands.

'Tomorrow I'm gonna buy you one so big it'll take a year for you to finish it.' Jake plucked a radio out of a charger and pulled a pair of high-powered military field glasses off a line of emergency equipment pegged to the wall. 'I'm gonna find some high ground and see how I can help. Call me once someone has a plan.'

As he exited the truck he could see cops had already shut down surrounding streets and begun shaping the slow, sticky flow of the crowd away from the blast zone. Jake put his eyes to the cups of the glasses. His vision filled with the blue and red flares of lights flashing on top of patrol cars. Fire trucks swam into view. A crew at the far end of Santa Monica Boulevard was hosing down a line of parked cars that had caught aflame. Memorial Square was now nothing more than a steaming black crater. Around the crusted ring lay charred corpses and debris.

Jake pulled focus. Shards of glass twinkled under the glare of lights and he started to see people moving. Out on the periphery, a handful of brave bystanders were tending the injured. He wanted to be there too. This was a battlefield and all his instincts urged him to rush into the thick of it and lend a hand. But that wasn't safe and it wasn't his job.

Keen to see who was watching, he scanned east along the Boulevard, out towards where it eventually hit Wilshire and hosted the Beverly Hilton. Dark shapes loomed large and small, blurred and sharp. They flowed through his constantly shifting lenses. Jake's brain processed the jumble and desperately tried to discern something or someone suspicious.

He caught a glimpse of Connor Pryce arriving and talking to a uniform. A paramedic's van pulled up onto the sidewalk. Its back doors spilled light and men began unfolding steps. Jake shifted the glasses again and lost clarity for a few seconds. Eventually, he picked out a huddle of gang kids watching the show. One of them pulled hard on a reefer and it lit up in his mouth like he was chewing a firefly. Next came blackness. Emptiness. Nothingness.

Then a glint of light.

Jake swung the lenses back.

Three, maybe four hundred yards away, a man was standing back, far away from everyone else, almost hidden in a clump of trees.

He was watching through binoculars.

Jake's instincts tingled.

People brought candles and flowers to a memorial service, not field glasses. There was a chance he was part of the terror cell. Maybe their escape route had got jammed up and he was scanning for a new way out.

One eye to the lens, Jake cut a route towards him.

The distance between them slowly closed.

He was no more than a hundred yards away when the man spotted him. For a second he stood and stared.

Then he ran.

Jake let the glasses drop to his chest and gave chase.

The guy disappeared into blackness behind some fencing.

Jack sprinted across the Boulevard, the FBI radio to his lips. 'This is Special Agent Jake Mottram. I'm in pursuit of a suspect, heading north across the LA Country Club grounds in West Hollywood. I need an eye in the sky and units east and west of Santa Monica Boulevard. I repeat, there is a lone suspect and he may be armed.'

A reply crackled back but Jake was sprinting too hard to make out anything other than the fact that it was Ruis's voice. The carriageway was shut off so it was easy to cross.

Jake climbed the barrier and fought his way through a clump of bushes. He dropped down a banking. Felt the earth spring soft beneath his feet. Sprinklers had soaked newly cut grass. He raised the glasses and switched them to night vision.

Nothing.

As far as he could see.

Nothing.

An owl broke from a tree and made him spin left. Desperately he scanned the blackness. Through the green fog, he saw rabbits run for cover.

Up above him came the clack, clack, clack of rotor blades. He knew the sound well. It was a Eurocopter AS 550 Fennec. A burst of white light erupted from the night sun attached to the FBI craft.

A figure broke from a thicket and ran right-to-left sixty yards ahead of him.

Jake sprinted as fast as he could. Being tall and heavy made him slow over the first ten yards, but then he was like a train.

Ruis's voice came through the ear-piece. 'Suspect heading west towards Comstock, Jake. West, west, west.'

The gap between them shrank to thirty yards.

The FBI man started to think of how this might end. He reached across his chest and slipped a service issue revolver from its holster.

Another ten yards and he'd give the call.

The man stopped.

Jake threw himself to the ground. If he was going to be shot at, he wanted to be as small a target as possible.

The helicopter swooped low and showered the runner in dense white light. A voice boomed through the onboard Tannoy. 'This is the FBI. We are armed. Put your hands up and get on your knees. This is the FBI, put your hands up now or we will shoot.'

Jake saw the man's silhouette stretch and kneel.

The SKU leader kept his pistol trained on the suspect as he got to his feet and headed over. The downdraft from the copter shook his balance.

Five yards separated them.

Jake could see the guy wasn't armed.

Nor was he Arabic or black.

He was middle-aged, stocky and white.

Mr Average.

And he was terrified.

Jake still wasn't taking chances. He pulled a pair of plastic restraining cuffs from his pocket and shouted above the noise of the copter, 'Hands behind your back.'

They went back.

Jake pushed him into the turf and cuffed him. He rolled him over and patted him down.

No gun. No knife. No trace of detonators or explosives.

Just field glasses and a face full of fear.

In one pocket he found car keys, a BlackBerry and a wallet. The other yielded a pack of Kleenex and a small bottle of baby oil.

Jake got the picture.

He'd stumbled on a Peeping Tom. A pervert who'd been distracted by the bomb while out watching courting couples in cars down the back roads off Santa Monica Boulevard.

Chapter 77

For a second, Shooter looked away from the TV on the canteen wall and studied the faces of his co-workers as they watched the news. These were life's bottom-feeders, the dregs of society, none of whom would ever be more famous than they were now. Perfect companions on a night like this.

'Jesus fucking Christ,' shouted an older man. 'Some people have no respect. To bomb a memorial service, what the fuck has the world come to?'

A young redhead who worked the switchboard started crying.

Shooter felt stranded.

He knew he had to seem sympathetic. It was important not to look out of place. But he couldn't match this extremity of emotion.

A driver pointed to the screen. 'Turn it up. Someone turn the damned thing up so we can hear what's being said.'

The remote was close enough for Shooter to grab it and adjust the volume. He was grateful for the chance to somehow seem involved.

'We are coming *live* from the Sun Western mall,' announced a gravel-voiced male anchor, 'where the shootings of forty-eight hours ago have been followed by another massacre – this time at what is believed to be the hands of callous terrorists.'

The screen filled with juddering aerial footage.

'Death came,' continued the anchor, 'in the form of an explosive that had somehow been placed at the very spot where the flowers and tributes were laid by friends, family and mourners.'

Aerial shots cut to ambulances speeding from the scene, sirens whooping to clear the roads.

'Eyewitnesses say there are at least fifty people either seriously injured or dead. Casualties include city officials and policemen, hit either directly by the explosive or by glass and metal from the mall and cars parked nearby.'

A studio director mixed to an X-rated scene that turned the stomach of just about everyone in the room.

Except Shooter.

A young redneck swore at the set. 'Motherfucking al-Qaeda. We should have blown up the whole goddamned country, not just that bearded prick Obama.'

'Osama,' shouted a woman. 'Obama's our President. You mean Osama bin Laden, you jerk.'

People laughed.

Shooter didn't.

He was transfixed by the carnage. A collage of life and death. Such vivid colors and immense emotions.

A camera picked out the clothes of the last little boy to be seen before the bomb went off. He had laid down a clay model he'd made for what people had supposed was his grandmother.

Shooter watched the idiots around him go mawkish and sentimental.

The supervisor entered the room. A big, fat Polish guy called Januk Dudek who stank from never washing and had a wife-beater's temper.

He glanced at the screen and his round, sweaty face was unmoved. 'Turn this shit off. There's work to do. 'Less you fuckers want me to find other people to do it?'

Chapter 78

Sun Western Mall, LA

The runner with the field glasses turned out to be a forty-year-old minor sex offender called Shane Garvie. He lived alone and had a string of convictions for lewd and indecent behavior in public places.

The night's one brief moment of amusement came when everyone realized Garvie had thought he was the sole focus of an FBI manhunt.

Without being prompted, he'd confessed to being in possession of hard-core pornography, using teenage prostitutes and having three ounces of dope in the glove box of his SUV.

Soon after two-thirty a.m., the Bomb Squad finished with their robots and Labradors and declared the immediate area around the mall and blast site to be free of secondary devices. They needed a short break before sweeping the inside of the mall. Thousands of shop workers were going to have an unexpected day off tomorrow.

Jake was impressed to see Chief Rawlings walking the scene. Okay, so he was a renowned political fox, but it was still good to see him putting in the street time. Crawford Dixon was there too, even though anti-terrorism wasn't under his brief.

Predictably, Angie wasn't in the truck where he'd left her.

To his relief he found her out on a patch of fried grass, squatting in the middle of a group of grieving relatives. She was trying to help them through what would undoubtedly be the most difficult moment of their lives.

Angie looked up and saw him. Managed a smile. One that said *give me a minute.*

He hung back and checked messages on his phone until she was done. Finally, he saw her hug several women before they went their own tearful ways. By the time she came over to him, she looked more exhausted than he'd ever seen her. Jake lifted his arm so she could rest up against him as they walked. 'How you doin', hon'?'

She pressed close. 'Take me home, baby. Take me to our bed and hold me until I sleep.'

They walked through debris and saw Dixon and Rawlings, deep in earnest conversation. The two men looked up and saw them.

Crawford waited until they were up close and spoke directly to Jake. 'NIA have just had a communiqué from al-Qaeda saying the bomb was nothing to do with them.'

The former Marine looked shocked. 'Then who? Syrians? Iranians? North Koreans?'

The section chief shook his head. 'Bomb Squad says the blast was from a device activated in the open *above* ground level, not sunk in earth or hidden in a vehicle.'

Jake pulled a face. 'What does that mean? We're talking a suicide bomber in the crowd?'

'Too early to say,' answered Rawlings. 'Problem with this event is that every fucking thing was thrown together last minute.' He grew crosser than he intended. 'Mayoral office and Governor's office have been falling over each other's freaking egos, fighting about who does what, who says what, who stands freakin' where. Bottom line – I'm betting checks that should have been done didn't get done.'

'What about motive?' interjected Angie. 'Stood over there with survivors and victims' relatives, I've been asking myself who stood to benefit most from an atrocity like this?'

Rawlings looked perplexed. 'And did you give yourself an answer?'

'I did. And it's one hard to accept. The only person I could link motivationally to this memorial is the shooter in the mall.'

Crawford Dixon grew agitated. 'Angie, you know as well as we do that bombers are a different breed to Sprees. The first is meticulous, the second impulsive. Their signature is as dissimilar as they come.'

'That's not completely true and this man is not a Spree.' Her voice was insistent. 'Believe me, it's a big mistake to think of him like that.'

The TV light of a news crew flickered less than twenty feet behind them.

'This conversation's over,' said Dixon angrily. He leaned close so he couldn't be overheard. 'Doctor Holmes, I told your boss directly, now I'm telling you. I do not want you trying to work this case – directly or indirectly. That's an order.'

Chapter 79

Januk told everyone to stay late. It was their punishment for idling around in front of the TV set and not doing their jobs properly.

'Too much talking, too little working!' he shouted across the canteen.

The big Pole marched over to the monitor on the wall, pulled out the plug and tore it off the flex.

'Hey, man, there's no need to do that. We're on a break.' The protest came from Stevie, a young driver with black, greasy hair and biker tats on his arms.

Januk stomped his way across and hurled the plug at him.

Stevie jumped to his feet. 'You fucking mad Polack.'

Januk grabbed him by the front of his overalls and hauled him over the table, knocking food and drink everywhere.

Shooter watched in fascination. The big supervisor had so much raw and wonderful rage but no control over it.

Such a waste.

Januk punched Stevie in the head.

A woman screamed.

The supervisor yelled into the driver's face. 'You call me a Polack? You piece of American *shit*.' He smashed his forehead into the man's nose and dropped him to the ground like a sack of trash.

Stevie lay moaning. His hand touched his busted nose and he stared in disbelief at the blood flowing over his fingers.

Januk's fists were balled tight. Veins in his neck rippled like ropes. He turned slowly and glared at the watching crowd.

Shooter could see the brutal moron was clearly enjoying his moment in the spotlight. This guy wanted to fight everyone. He wanted to pull down the sky and smash up the earth.

No one was stupid enough to challenge his rage.

Except Stevie.

Stevie was mopping blood and simmering with humiliation and hatred.

Shooter looked at him and knew what was going to happen.

The driver reached for a steak knife still lying on the table.

He grabbed it and rushed the back of the supervisor.

The blade rose.

Came down in a vicious arc.

Shooter crashed into him.

He got there a split second before steel found flesh.

They tumbled to the floor. The knife clattered across the tiles. Stevie stretched for it.

Januk had turned. Now he understood what was happening.

He stamped on the driver's wrist.

A roar of pain filled the room.

People ran for the exit.

Two of the older men closed in on the supervisor. 'Enough now, boss. Come on.'

Another driver went to help Stevie.

Shooter got to his feet and picked up the knife.

Januk watched him cautiously.

Everyone tensed.

Shooter placed the knife on the table. The click of steel on wood was the only sound in the room. He looked from one man to the other. 'How about you say this never happened?'

Stevie's nose dripped blood into his hands. 'What?'

His friend passed him a wad of table napkins. 'That way you don't get done for attempted wounding.'

'And Mr Dudek here don't get prosecuted for assault,' added one of the older men.

'Then we have a deal?' Shooter asked.

Januk nodded.

Stevie blotted blood and managed, 'Yeah, I guess so.'

241

Shooter left the room, conscious that the supervisor was following a few feet behind him.

Januk shouted in the corridor, 'Hey, wait.'

He turned.

'I want to say thank you.'

'There's no need.' Shooter walked on. As much as he'd have liked to have seen one of the men kill the other – *it didn't matter which* – he knew that would have meant the police coming to interview everyone, and that was something he really didn't want to happen.

Chapter 80

Douglas Park, Santa Monica, LA

It was five a.m. when Jake woke and found the bed empty.

He wandered through to the lounge and found Angie awake. She was sat in her PJs on the sofa with a laptop across her thighs. Her right arm was out of the sling but still bandaged and hanging limp. An empty coffee cup on the floor said she'd been working when she should have been sleeping.

'Morning,' she managed brightly. 'What woke you?'

'You not being there, baby.'

'How sweet.' She tilted her head so he could kiss her.

He obliged, then added, 'You should still be resting, not doing that. What is it anyway?'

Angie ignored the rebuke. 'Coffee's still hot, if you want some.' She smiled and lifted her mug so he could refill it as well.

Jake took it. 'What did your last slave die of?'

'Sexual exhaustion.'

'Not a bad way to go.' He headed into the small kitchen. 'You didn't answer my question.'

'I know. I was being evasive not forgetful.' She lifted her arm protectively and swiveled around so she could see him while she spoke. 'I think I cracked the anagram.'

He froze at the cupboard, one hand on a clean mug. 'Maybe I'm going mad but I thought just a few hours ago my boss told you to stay the hell away from this case.'

'Yeah, he did.'

'And that made it irresistible?'

'Kind of. You want to hear my theory?'

'Theory?' He topped her mug up and filled his own. 'We've gone from an anagram to a whole *theory* now.'

She carried on tapping left-handedly on her keyboard until he came in with the drinks and settled alongside her.

'So go on.'

'Judge and Jury.'

'That's the anagram?'

'Yep. Danger Judy-Ju makes a few other things, but nothing as clean and clear as Judge and Jury.'

The words settled in Jake's brain. 'And you think – what? That this was his statement to the world?'

'I do. I think he's saying he is going to be society's Judge and Jury. He will decide who is guilty and innocent. Who lives and dies. He's showing us his absolute power.'

Jake thought on it. 'It's certainly the crazy kind of shit killers come up with.'

'Serial killers.'

'Oh my God, just because he plays anagram games, that doesn't make him a Serial.'

'It pretty much does. He *is* a Serial, Jake. Serials move from location to location too.'

'So do Sprees, and they also communicate. They send notes. They make calls and they run and hide just like Serials.'

'But Sprees are generally dumbasses. They get caught quick, whereas Serials don't.'

'Mostly,' he conceded. 'But then there are the likes of Charles Starkweather.'

'What?' She hoped she'd misheard him.

'Starkweather. He went on a two-month spree.'

'Is this the shit that Danielle Goodman is feeding you?'

He didn't answer.

'Christ, Jake. The woman's way out of her depth. This Starkweather shit was what led you to almost getting killed by Wayne Harris.'

'No, you can't hang that on her. Bad intel was what got people hurt that day, not anything Danny said.'

Angie still wasn't done. 'Aside from the anagram – and that should be enough to convince you – there are so many other things screaming Serial and not Spree.'

His voice said he was tired of arguing. 'Like what?'

'How many people died in that store?'

'Eleven.' He corrected himself. 'No, twelve.'

'Twelve. Exactly. And how many letters in the anagram?'

'I don't know.'

'Twelve. And on a floor plan of the mall, which number shop is Judy-Ju's?' Her stare provided the answer before she did. 'Twelve.'

Jake laughed. 'I think they gave you too much procaine at the hospital. How many letters are there in your full name, Angela Holmes? I'll tell you, twelve.'

'Okay, I get it. You're skeptical. There are coincidences. But what about the message I made from the anagram?'

He shrugged. 'Yeah, that's interesting, I give you that. And I buy the power and control stuff – the idea of him being Judge and Jury.'

'So you'll take it to Dixon?'

He closed his eyes and imagined telling his boss about Angie's overnight thoughts on the case he'd warned her off. 'Yeah, I'll take it to him.'

'You don't have to say it was me. I just want you to catch this guy.'

'Oh, I'll catch him, honey. Don't you go worrying your little procained brain about that.'

Chapter 81

Skid Row, LA

Locals in LA say the city is divided into 'Bucks'.

'Big Bucks' is home to the thousand-dollar-an-hour law firms, the marble-floored investment banks and blue glass skyscrapers of the multi-national businesses.

'Shopping Bucks' is the air-conditioned oasis where glitzy brands hang and get hunted by hordes of platinum-carded designer junkies.

'Anything-for-a-Buck' is the block or so where hookers will do whatever anyone wants, providing they have enough dollars to buy lunch or their next fix.

Then there's 'No Bucks'.

'No Bucks' is another name for Skid Row. It lies between 3rd and 7th and is just a short walk and a whole world away from everything else.

Even crack whores don't fall that far.

Today, the trash-strewn sidewalk was hot enough to cook eggs on. A raggedy old man with clumped, unwashed hair bent his world-weary shoulders over a supermarket trolley and squeaked it towards a patch of shade. In it was everything he owned: a sleeping bag, a pullover full of holes and lice, and garbage that he'd picked from dumpsters. He'd come across a store trashing a tray of sandwiches and they'd let him have them.

Christmas in August.

He couldn't believe his luck.

SPREE

Old Joe steered his trolley towards two blankets spread in an alley back of Seaton. The red-checkered one was home to Wheelie, a diabetic in his sixties who'd lost a leg because he couldn't afford his meds. At night, he chained himself to his chair so people didn't steal it and sell it for scrap.

The mustard-brown blanket opposite belonged to Fat Mamma Cas, and not many people were fool enough to try to steal from her. She'd punch their lights out. But Old Joe knew he was welcome.

'I got something to eat,' he announced as he parked the squeaky trolley against the alley wall. 'Woman down at the sandwich shop was throwin' stuff out. Can you believe that?' He fished in the rusty wire basket and pulled up a part of his catch, careful not to show the rest of his precious haul. 'I got toona and mayo-nayze. I got ham. An' I got somethin' odd called bry. It looks like sick-assed cheese'n'pickle but without any pickle.'

Fat Mamma cracked a yellow smile. 'Man, you got a beggars' banquet there. What you do, sell that body of yours?'

'Wouldn't have got three sandwiches for a rack o' ribs like his,' snorted Wheelie, rolling himself forward. 'He wouldn't have got crumbs, never mind sandwiches.'

'Ain't you the funny one,' answered Joe. 'So who's wantin' to share my food and who's wantin' to bad-mouth me an' go hungry?'

'I think you're a fine, *mighty fine* lookin' man, Joe,' beamed Mamma Cas. 'An' the only thing I want more in my mouth than you is that sweet tuna mayo.'

Joe tossed her the sandwich. 'Which means you get the bry, Wheelie, coz hungry as I am, I ain't eatin' that shit.' He tossed the wrapped triangle onto the disabled man's lap.

Wheelie squinted at it. 'Ain't no *bry*, you fool. It's *Brie*.' He laughed. 'You done give me the most expensive sandwich there is, that's how piss-stupid-dumb you are.' He cackled again and started unwrapping it.

'I got some water for us,' said Mamma Cas. 'Bitch from the Mission came by and left some.'

'Not until she'd gone and prayed the holy living shit outta us both,' added Wheelie, sucking Brie off his stumps of teeth. 'She says to

247

Mamma, our church is prayin' for you and Jesus has a special place in his heart. You know what Mamma said?'

Joe knew he had to ask. 'What'd you say, Mamma?'

'I said, if it's just the same to you, lady, I'd like to swap my prayers for an all-you-can-eat dinner and trade the place in Jesus's heart for a condo down in Glendale.'

They all laughed then set about chewing.

'Mmm. It's *real* good, man.' Wheelie lifted the half-chewed sandwich in a gesture of thanks. 'Can't remember when I las' tasted somethin' like this.'

Mamma unscrewed the cap on the two-liter bottle of water and passed it around. By the time she got it back there was so much bread floating in it, it looked like a fisherman had laid down ground bait.

The sound of tinny music spilled around the corner from Alameda.

Single instrument. Brass. A B-flat trumpet. Out of tune.

Everyone knew what it meant.

'Finish quick,' said Mamma. 'Trumpet Man is a comin' an' he's one food-stealin' mother.'

Backlit by the blistering sun, a thin black guy appeared at the end of the alley.

He was dressed in a dusty brown suit that finished three inches above bare ankles and busted boots. On his head was a tatty trilby that never left him, not even when he laid his daft old skull on the sidewalk at night.

Trumpet Man raised a dented old brass to his big, scabbed lips and blew hard. Out came the only tune he knew – 'Family Guy'.

Old Joe got to his feet somewhere between a mangled E flat and a murdered D. 'I'm gonna roll. I ain't got time to have my ears blasted by that fool.'

Neither Wheelie nor Mamma Cas questioned his exit. Joe rolled in and Joe rolled out. You had to respect other people's ways.

'Take care, man,' shouted Wheelie, sucking the last of the cheese from his gums. 'Thanks 'gain for that *de-lish-us* Brie.'

'Bring doughnuts an' coffee tomorrow,' hollered Mamma with a laugh in her voice. 'An' may the good Lord keep a place in his heart for you, brother.'

They both roared as he pushed his trolley away.

Joe lifted a hand in acknowledgment. Dust rose as the trolley wheels cut along the blacktop.

He was done for now.

He'd lapped several blocks and shown his face to all the regulars.

Kept up his identity, one of his back stories.

Now he could return to his other life.

The one the whole of America was talking about.

Chapter 82

SKU Offices, LA

Jake was on his way in to work when he got the call from Crawford Dixon. The one he knew was going to screw up his day.

His boss needed to see him. Urgently. It was too important to even mention over the phone.

None of this was good news.

Jake found the section chief grim-faced at his office desk. Opposite him was a large African American man, who'd planted his feet and set his shoulders like a former soldier.

'Jake, this is Tom Jeffreys from the Bomb Squad. He has news on last night.'

'Heard a lot about you, Jake.' He rose and shook the SKU leader's hand. 'I had a friend served with you, said nothing but good things.'

'Your friend's probably a very generous and forgiving man, sir.' Jake took a chair opposite them both.

Jeffreys rubbed a palm over his bald head. 'We found enough chemical traces to discern that the bomb was ninety percent cyclotrimethylene trinitramine. Diethylhexyl was used to plasticize it and then polyisobutylene added as a binder.'

Jake recognized the ingredients. 'We're talking C4?'

'Yes. Composition Four. Plastic explosive. From the blast pattern and rerunning the TV footage, we pinpointed a clay statue put down by a kid who said he was the grandchild of a Mrs Tanya Murison.'

Jake looked surprised. 'A kid?'

'Uh-huh. He'd turned up late and flustered. A cop looked at it, saw the tag that said "Grandma, I'll always luv you" and ushered him through.'

Jake was still stunned. 'Did the kid detonate it?'

'No. He was a patsy. Some asshole sent him in there with it. There was a timing-based high-energy detonator cap inside the clay.'

Jake could see how that would have worked. 'C4's heavily controlled,' he added. 'Whoever got it and detonated it had to have special contacts to obtain it.'

'In theory, yes,' said Jeffreys. 'Distribution *is* strictly monitored and needs end-user certification. But quantities go missing. And you can buy the chemicals separately through companies and countries that aren't as scrupulous as they should be.'

'Last night, al-Qaeda denied any involvement,' Jake recalled. 'Has anyone claimed responsibility yet?'

The two bosses shook their heads.

'And the kid's family? Have they shed any light on who he's been hanging around with, who might have set him up as a walking bomb?'

'We've been working overnight with the LAPD,' explained Jeffreys, 'and we've managed to ID the kid as eleven-year-old Leroy Danziel. He was certainly no rebel or political activist. Lived out in Watts. No father. Mother is either on the game or on ketamine, or on both. Neighbors said the boy came and went as he chose. No one to account to. No one to account for him. He lived mostly on the street, doing whatever people wanted him to in return for food or cash.'

'So we're thinking, what?' asked Jake. 'Some heartless crazy just paid him a shitload of cash to carry the clay tribute?'

'That's the main theory we're looking into,' said Jeffreys. 'That and a feeling that maybe the crazy is the UNSUB who shot up the mall.'

'That's what Angie figured last night,' Jake said to Dixon.

'She did,' he conceded. 'Did the labs come back to you on that piece of paper you thought might be a note he left?'

'They did.' He wasn't sure he should disclose it in front of the Bomb Squad commander.

Jeffreys sensed the uncertainty. He put his hands on the chair rests

251

and made to stand up. 'You guys need privacy and I need to go. I'll call you later, Crawford, please keep me apprised.'

They all stood and shook hands.

As soon as the door closed Dixon wanted the story. 'Okay, Jake, out with it.'

'The labs cleaned up the note and through the bloodstain you could make out twelve letters that said DANGERJUDYJU.'

'Judy-Ju being the name of the store?'

'That's right. Angie figured it was an anagram and worked it out to be Judge and Jury.'

'Angie? She's been doing a lot of figuring on this case I told her to forget.'

Jake skipped the trap. 'Her theory is that the killer is setting himself up as a supreme power over the State. One with the right to decide who lives and dies.'

'Let's back up a second, Jake. Do you and Dr Holmes remember my remarks last night about her not working this case?'

'I do. Of course I do.'

'Then for now, forget them. I reserve the right to change my mind during times like this. Pull together a full briefing for late this morning. Ask Jeffreys back. And Pryce too. I want all bases covered. I'll talk to Sandra McDonald and have her okay Angie's attendance – but to be clear, it's just to *voice her theories,* that's all. This is still Danielle Goodman's case – you may want to help prepare the ground on that basis.'

'I will.' He got to his feet to leave.

'I pity you, Jake. Crossfire between Angie and Danielle could be worse than anything you faced in Afghanistan.'

Chapter 83

A call from the press office gave the SKU leader the only good news of the morning. He was off the hook vis à vis facing the cameras. The mayor and the governor were both holding media conferences before midday and the Bureau figured everyone would benefit from staying out of their spotlights.

Instead, he was able to spend most of the morning chasing operational loose ends and calming Danielle down. The news that Angie Holmes had theories on 'her' case and had secretly watched footage of the shootings in the mall had sent her into orbit.

Peaceful hours passed, until the two women came face to face at eleven a.m. in Briefing Room A. Jake witnessed an exchange of laser-beam glowers across the long dark wood table and he was thankful their respective bosses, Dixon and McDonald, were there to keep the peace. Jeffreys settled down next to his number two, Katherine Mitchell, a tall, long-faced woman with dark hair pulled back in a ponytail. She was dressed in an old jumper and jeans and the discomfort on her face gave away that she had worked most of the night and not expected to be bumped into a high-powered meeting like this one. Opposite her was the immaculately blue-suited Connor Pryce, who as well as being LAPD SWAT was now also Chief Rawlings' personally appointed liaison officer on the joint-inquiry with the FBI.

Jake settled into a seat next to Ruis Costas and kicked things off on a note of solemnity. 'I've just been told that unfortunately the Sun Western death toll has risen again. Two of the bomb victims in ICU didn't make it. Total count for both incidents at the mall is now twenty-nine dead. It will most probably clear thirty by the end of the day.'

Dixon briefly interrupted. 'In a couple of hours' time, there will be public announcements that all known terror groups have denied responsibility for the latest attack. That will let the White House off the hook as it clearly means the incident is a *local* problem, not a foreign policy one. There is no country for us to attack, no religious fundamentalist to vilify, so the President will stay out of things – for now. But you can bet your asses we're gonna get calls from his office, and the mayor's and the governor's. In other words, the shit is on our shoes and everyone is going to blame us for the resultant mess that gets spread, so we need to clean up fast.' He nodded to Jake to carry on.

'Okay, I'm presuming you've all read and understood the briefing from the Bomb Squad?' The faces around him said they had. 'A clay model put down by a child at the scene contained C4 and a shockwave detonator. Top of our agenda is the question of whether the same man was responsible for the shooting spree and the bombing?'

Danielle Goodman jumped in. 'I think it would be very dangerous to go along those lines. I've already submitted a detailed profile on the "Sun Western Slayer" as the press are calling him. I think psychologically it is at odds with the psychopathy of a bomber.' She pitched to Dixon. 'The UNSUB is impulsive and emotional. He is of low intelligence and probably derived sexual satisfaction from killing at close quarters. Watch him on the footage and you can see he is a sexual voyeur enjoying an orgy of violence. While the bomber, well, he is totally different. He clearly has intelligence, know-how and expertise. I think he'd been planning an explosives attack for some time and simply seized the moment. He may even have been annoyed that the Spree got so much news coverage at a time when he was planning to strike, so he sought to use the Memorial Service as a way to upstage him.'

'Dear God,' Dixon responded, 'please don't tell me there's a possibility of *two* lunatics trying to outdo each other in some sick competition to see who can create the biggest atrocity.'

'Why not?' she answered. 'Given their completely different profiles and MOs, it's the only explanation.'

Angie could no longer restrain herself. 'That's bullshit.'

Jake dropped his head. All her promises of staying calm and not winding up Danielle had obviously been forgotten.

'Say what?' Danielle had a face like thunder.

Angie calmly locked eyes. 'Let's start with the child and his model of the grandmother. Are you saying the bomber made this model of the dead woman, inserted explosives into it and then recruited a street kid to carry it to the Memorial Ceremony all within such a short period of time? I really don't think so.'

'It was a *clay model* and not a very good one,' retorted Danielle. 'It looked as much like my grandmother or anyone's grandmother as it did the dead woman.'

'Ladies . . .' McDonald intervened. 'Let's keep this respectful. Disagreement is good – even vital – for teasing out the basis of theories, but remember we're all on the same side here.'

Danielle hadn't finished her defence. 'I think he could have had that model ready as a gift for any occasion and he just adapted it. Let's be honest, you can get a street kid to run any errand in the world these days if you pay them a little upfront and promise them a whole lot more once the job's completed.'

'That last bit I concede,' said Angie.

'Good, then you also have to see that there are two different offenders at work here with two completely different MOs.'

'*With respect*, I think you're wrong.'

'Why?'

'What about Anders Breivik? He shot up a whole island of kids in Scandinavia and bombed a town center. Maybe this UNSUB is America's Breivik?'

'*That* was politically motivated,' said Danielle dismissively. 'He wanted to be caught so he could expound his race hate claptrap. There's no indication of that here.'

'Maybe there is.' Jake was glad to get a word in between them. 'Maybe that's what's behind the note.'

Danielle jumped in again. 'I want to go on record saying I'm unhappy I wasn't told about this note until this morning. I think it's unprofessional that I wasn't looped in earlier.'

'Duly noted,' said Dixon dismissively. 'Now let's get on with what it might mean.'

Angie gave her explanation. 'I take it to be an anagram of the words Judge and Jury, something the killer is setting himself up as. He wants us to see him not only as having the power to decide *who* should be found guilty and punished, but also as the person to dispense justice – the executioner.'

Sandra McDonald wasn't so sure. 'Perhaps it wasn't an anagram but was the UNSUB's idea of a sick joke, a piece of bad taste sarcasm.'

'Could be code,' speculated Jeffreys. 'Bombers like codes. It would be interesting to see what the Bureau's cryptologists make of it.'

Dixon nodded. 'They're looking at it, Tom. Tell me, from what you've just heard, are you feeling that there might be a connection between the shooting and the bombing?'

'We were already thinking along those lines.' He nodded towards Angie and Danielle. 'I agree with some views of both psychologists, namely that the clay model and the hidden bomb suggest long-term planning and opportunistic execution. Maybe even specific targeting of that woman for some reason.'

'Her name was Tanya Murison,' added Katherine Mitchell. 'She was a Christian but her surviving husband is a Muslim.'

'Extremist?' asked Jake.

'No, not at all. A kindly man from what we've found. We're still digging into their backgrounds in case there's a racial or religious aspect.'

Jeffreys knew what the group was thinking. 'We've checked

denominations of the dead and injured at the mall. There were only two Muslims in total, the rest were Christians and Jews. That doesn't rule out the bomber having some twisted theory about punishing Muslims and those who associate with them.'

'Then I'd expect the note he left to be more religiously skewed,' said Danielle.

'And I would too,' concurred Angie.

An unconnected thought occurred to Dixon. 'Before I forget, where did you guys get with the baseball cap the UNSUB was wearing?'

Ruis let out a long sigh that signaled extreme disappointment. 'In short, nowhere. We pulled in some help from the LAPD but they've drawn blanks. Actually, that's a lie. So many of those caps got sold, it's going to take an age to make matches. They've got a team working first on the Lakers' own outlets, profiling purchasers within our suspect's age-range who visited stores within the last two months. From that pool – and we're talking hundreds – they're chasing down surveillance tapes at checkout registers and seeing if they get lucky.'

Dixon rubbed his tired eyes. 'Very lucky. Let's face it, that's just the start. From there they've got to progress to dozens of other franchisees.'

'Then there are the counterfeiters,' added Jake. 'A zillion caps get knocked out for sale on street corners on game days.'

A blonde secretary opened the door and signaled to Ruis.

'Sorry,' he said to the room as he waved her in. 'I asked Jane to bring a report she just mailed me about.'

The secretary laid down a green file and flushed because people were looking at her.

'Thanks.' He looked inside and checked a few of the papers.

'If it's worth interrupting the meeting, then let's hear what's in it,' said Jake.

'Of course.' Ruis took out a black and white photograph and held it so people could see. 'This is a shot of a female cleaner working the mall. It was taken the day before the shootings, in the elevator that our killer escaped in.'

Everyone studied the print of a fat, old black woman in navy blue jacket and pants. She was carrying a red bucket filled with cans of polish, sprays of cleaners and disinfectants, sponges and cloths. On her chest was a name badge declaring her to be LETITIA-ANNE.

'The service elevators get cleaned every day,' continued Ruis. 'But not by Letitia-Anne. She's never been seen before – or since. And she's dressed in a uniform very similar to one used by members of the cleaning company that has the contract – same color jacket and pants – but not identical, not the official issue.' Ruis put down the still and took two more out of the file. 'Here she is polishing the steel walls.' He switched to another shot. 'Then she produces a glass cleaning spray and squirts the camera. Soaks it good and proper. Only she forgets to polish off the cleaner, so when she walks away the camera is left wet. In time, it dries, but the lens goes foggy in patches. Of course, no one in security really notices or gives a damn. The mess they see on their monitors in the control room could be anything – condensation, spit, spray from a can of Coke opened by some idiot heading out on a break. So they leave it be. Hell, they guess the cleaner will sort it tomorrow.' He pulled a sheet of paper from the file. 'Lab report just in. It shows the camera and housing were sprayed not with glass cleaner but with hydrofluoric acid. This stuff is highly corrosive. The king of corrosives. It can even dissolve glass, it's that strong. The glass cleaner wasn't the only fake, so too was Mrs Mop – she was our Spree.'

Chapter 84

Skid Row, LA

Shooter had picked most of the daily papers from the trash cans down on 7th where the Greyhound buses lined up.

Back in his sanctuary, he spread them out and then publication-by-publication went through every report concerning him.

He highlighted key words with different colored text markers, and when he was done, sat back and weighed up what the world thought of him.

The most commonly used descriptions were despicable, cold-blooded, disgusting and inhumane.

Given time they'd change their minds.

He'd see to it that they did.

No one had mentioned the note he'd left at the mall, so he guessed the cops were still keeping quiet about it. Although they seemed so stupid, he didn't rule out the possibility that they hadn't even found it.

All the newspapers mourned the 'double tragedy' that had hit the mall, but none were bold enough to suggest that only one person might have been responsible for both. What really annoyed Shooter was that there were almost as many pictures of the kid, Leroy Danziel, as there were of him. The way Shooter figured it, that piece of gutter trash hadn't deserved a single line of print. The kid had been running crack bags to cruising cars for a corner gang. Shooter bought a deal and with it the boy's willingness to run other errands.

USA Today urged people not to forget the victims of the store because of the even more emotive murders at the Memorial. It reminded its readers that they were looking for 'A black, twenty-to-thirty-year-old male, of average build and height, probably living alone.'

The description made him laugh. He'd worn clothes beneath his oversized T-shirt to appear fatter and broader. He'd been careful in layering up, so the cops couldn't see creases or other garments beneath the big white T. They'd got far more wrong than right.

He used specialist craft scissors to cut out the report. Then he excised every photograph he could find of himself.

Not out of vanity.

Out of caution.

It was important to know how the world saw him. Who they thought they were scanning the sidewalks, bus seats and grocery stores for.

Ninety percent of the stills had come from CCTV footage in the mall. The reproductions were mainly grainy and shaky, often out of focus and usually too distant to be really telling. The remaining ten percent were better. It was the Judy-Ju's footage and in good color and sharpness. But there wasn't much of it. He had moved around a lot in the store and the camera had only caught his face a couple of times. Studying the shots, it was plain to see that the cops had blown them up because they were pinning all their hopes on someone recognizing the fat-faced black boy in the white Lakers cap with his Afro-American hair tucked back beneath the brim.

Good for them.

That's exactly what he'd wanted them to do.

The pictures looked nothing like him. Nothing like Letitia-Anne the cleaning lady. Nothing like Old Joe. Or any of the other people he could be. They could search all their lives for that fool kid in his cap and Nike T and they'd never find him.

He held a magnifying glass over the shots, just as he knew the cops would. There was no evidence that he'd fattened his face with cheek implants, or that he'd dyed his eyebrows to perfectly match the false hair he'd glued to the edge of his cap. Hair he'd collected from the back of a barbershop off East 6th and Gladys where the black brothers liked to go.

Shooter felt something approaching pride as he stuck the

photographs to black cards and then pinned them to the pegboards in Death Row.

He turned off the light and walked a few paces to the room next door.

It was filled with garbage bags and the stench hit him as soon as he walked in.

Each bag had been labeled, dated and the contents listed.

He picked a few up and then found the one he wanted. It brought a smile to his face. Her name always did.

Shooter had work to do.

Another shock to prepare.

Chapter 85

FBI Field Office, LA

I t was mid-afternoon when the knock came on the door. Angie had been expecting it.

Sandra McDonald walked in, wearing her killer smile, the one she always produced when she was about to behave like a bitch.

She shut the door with a flick of her wrist and no backward glance.

Angie watched it hit the frame and bounce a painting on her wall, an acrylic of the ocean that Jake had bought for her. She turned to Chips. 'Give us the room for five.'

He covered the slogan on his green T-shirt that said I USED TO BE SCHIZOPHRENIC BUT NOW WE'RE OKAY and headed out.

The AD watched him go, pulled out a chair and sat before finally speaking. 'I don't like being disobeyed, Angela. I don't like being worked around or manipulated. And I don't like the way you're causing inter-unit friction with your interest in the mall cases.'

Angie didn't answer. She was studying her boss. Her hands were together on the desk and she was controlling her breathing so she didn't lose her temper. A wiry vein throbbed in her neck and showed her heart was beating like a bongo at an island party. She'd started smoking again. Red nail polish was chipped on her thumb from flicking the stub and she smelled of Menthol Lites.

'Do I make myself clear?'

'Perfectly.'

McDonald sat back. She was a long way from finished. 'I'd like you to spend the rest of today and tomorrow writing up your theories and your notes. Make three copies. One for me. One for Section Chief Dixon and one for Danielle Goodman. When you've done that, I want you off this case. If SKU need you, then they'll have to go over my head to get you.'

Angie stayed silent.

Again McDonald repeated the question. 'Do I make myself clear?'

'You do.'

'Good.' She slapped her hands down on the table with an air of finality and got to her feet.

'For the record,' said Angie, 'I'll be making fourth and fifth copies of those summaries. One I will personally deliver to the area director, the other I will be having Fed Ex-ed to the office of the director general of the FBI. If I'm moved off this case and other people die, then it's going to be on your head not mine.'

'My head?' McDonald laughed over the desk that divided them. 'Every death on every case in every unit I'm in charge of is on my head. I go to sleep with those rats of guilt gnawing my conscience every damned night of my life. Get this straight, I call the shots, lady. Sometimes I'm right. Sometimes I'm wrong. But *I* decide how things get run. I don't have people like *you* deciding on my behalf.'

Angie replied matter-of-factly, 'Danielle Goodman's wrong. Not a little wrong. Badly wrong. And there's going to be a whole extra nest of rats in your head if you follow her advice.'

McDonald spotted an open file on Angie's desk. Crime scene photographs of the Strawberry Fields shootings. She picked one up and shook it at her profiler. 'What are you doing with this?'

'We have had three unsolved multiple murder cases in almost as many days; I was looking to see if there was a link.'

'Dear God.' She threw it back onto the table. 'In the past seventy hours there have been four other gun-related homicides in LA. You want to bundle any or all of those into the inquiry as well?'

'No.'

'Then listen. You did a good job on the rape-homicide. Damned good job. Aside from getting yourself busted up, that is. Put your notes in on the mall murders. Take some sick leave and get healthy. There's a profiling conference next week in Toronto, hosted by the RCMP. I'd like you to stand in for me as one of the keynote speakers. It'd be good experience and it'll help your career.'

It was a clever pitch. And both of them knew it.

Angie was exhausted and her body still ached from the battering Alfonso Cayman had given her. The conference was a biggie. It came with a cast of global experts she'd long admired. The chance of speaking there was tough to turn down.

'I really want to work this case. It's not that I'm trying to be a pain in your ass, or Danielle's for that matter. It's just that I know this is the work of one man, not two. And I know he's a Serial not a Spree.'

'So you think it should be taken off SKU?'

Angie had stepped into a trap. 'Technically, yes.'

'Then put that in writing to me. Of course, it's up to you whether you want to give Special Agent Mottram a heads-up that you're asking for the case he's worked so hard on to be yanked out his door.' McDonald studied the profiler's face.

Angie studied her boss's.

'Write up your notes. Book your tickets to Canada. A week from now the world will be a whole different place and you'll be so glad you didn't fight me on this.'

Chapter 86

T he clock over the door said four p.m.
 Jake had been dreading this moment.

It was the time he'd agreed to see Danielle Goodman.

At ten seconds past, she knocked and breezed in. She was wearing a floating parachute of orange with matching shoes and a color co-ordinated document folder.

Jake jokingly shielded his eyes and reached for some Ray-Bans next to his car keys. 'Danni, wait until I put these on else you're gonna blind me.'

She laughed as loud as the dress and then put on a pretend Southern accent. 'I just wanna bring some sunshine into your life, *Meester* Jake. You look so tired and stressed.' She sat on the opposite side of his desk and fluttered batwing eyelashes.

Jake took off the shades. He liked Danielle. She could be as stubborn as a mule but at least she had a sense of humor. 'As a *trick cyclist*, I hope you see the jam I'm in. You and Angie each have a lot to say on the shootings and bombings and I think it's only right that you both get the chance to have your views heard.'

'I agree. But I'd have preferred that she'd come direct to me, Jake. Privately, behind these closed doors, we could have discussed her theory in more professional depth.'

'Or you could have dismissed it more easily.'

She smiled. 'Yeah, maybe that as well. But I really do think she's wrong.

I can quote you countless serial murders where profilers were adamant only one UNSUB was responsible and it turned out to be two. None of those experts were any less professional than Angie Holmes.'

'Point taken.'

'And I'm really pissed about you not giving me that note from the mall.'

'Angie's assistant spotted it. He told her and when she told me it was late at night. I wanted to see if the labs turned anything up before I mentioned it to you.'

'Because you knew I'd be pissed at your lady snooping in my case.'

It was his turn to smile. 'Something like that.'

'Can I get a promise from you that from now on I'm first on your information list?'

'You have my promise.'

'Thank you.' She smiled her sweetest smile. 'Within the hour, our boss, Mr Dixon, is going to call to tell you that you have to front a media conference tomorrow.'

'I thought I'd got out of that.'

'You got a postponement, that's all.'

'Okay. So, I believe the plan is to give the media some snippets of your profile.'

'That's right.' She warmed to the conversation. 'Only the plan's changed a little. It will be a joint press conference with the LAPD – just you, me, Chief Rawlings and Commander Pryce.' She anticipated his objection. 'I know you told the old man we didn't quite see eye-to-eye, so I shan't speak. But I have to be there. Are you able to live with that?'

'I guess so.'

'Good. The first part of the conference will be a public declaration from Rawlings that the FBI is taking the lead in both mall cases. Then Section Chief Dixon and I have a personal message we want you to deliver to the UNSUB responsible for the shootings.'

'We're still going to talk about two UNSUBS for the murders and bombings?'

'We are, if we're pushed. But in relation to your prepared speech you will only address one – and you'll do it very personally.'

'I'm fine with that. What's the message?'

She opened a slim document file and slid a single sheet of double-spaced typing over the desk.

Jake speed-read it. 'It's certainly very personal.'

She knew where his comments were leading. 'It has to be *exactly* like this, Jake. No alterations, no watering down by our mutual friend Doctor Holmes. Can you please do this without having to seek her approval?'

He waved the paper. 'Has this been run past Dixon and Fox and the LAPD?'

'Everyone's approved it. We just need you to deliver it.'

Chapter 87

FBI Field Office, LA

If Angie had to back out of the case – the one she knew she shouldn't really have shunted her way into in the first place – then she was determined to leave behind the best notes she'd ever written.

Geography usually played large in her offender profiles. Normally, the crime scene gave a lot of clues to the UNSUB's behavior and lifestyle and she used those basic facts to build a pyramid of assumptions. She'd generally know whether the offender used a car or not. Where the position of the death scene was in relation to major roads and footpaths. What social groups congregated in the place where the attacks had happened. Those answers mostly pointed her in a particular direction.

Not this time.

No one understood how the offender had left the mall. The Sun Western complex could be just as easily exited by car, motorcycle, bus, bicycle or on foot.

It was pretty much a block on its own, bordered by the Avenue of the Stars, Century Park West and then Santa Monica and Constellation Boulevards. By car, those routes could take you north, south, east and west out of LA. An offender could have been in Pasadena within thirty minutes, Malibu within forty-five or Anaheim within the hour. Indeed, if Danielle Goodman was to be believed, this was exactly what had happened.

Only Danielle was wrong.

Angie was sure of it.

In fact, she figured the UNSUB hadn't used a vehicle. At least not one parked nearby and not during the crazy rush to get away. Given how well everything had been planned, he would have known that the parking lot would have jammed up once the bodies started falling. He would probably also have known that in an area like Sun Western, a car was not the best mode of transport. Traffic was always as thick as syrup and once cops got an eye in the sky, there was no escape. On top of that, car license plates could be as damning as fingerprints and no matter how careful you were, just sitting in a vehicle left enough DNA in there to prompt a crime lab to throw a party.

Nope. Angie was sure the UNSUB had simply walked away on foot. The question was, in which direction?

She pulled up a Google map, one marked with every building, shop and bus station.

The InterContinental stood bottom right of frame, the Hyatt Regency, center frame, and Stars Inn, top left of frame. They were all only a few minutes' walk away. If the perp had somehow managed to get out of the clothes he'd worn in the mall, then he could have gone to any of those hotels and disappeared into one of a thousand rooms.

Angie tried to think it through some more.

He would also have had to leave the hotel in different clothes as well.

It made her wonder if they should be looking for a guest. An out-of-towner enjoying what the FBI referred to as 'recreational homicide'. He could have holed up after the hits, then checked out when the heat died down. Danielle might be right – by now he could be out of state, or out of the country via LAX.

The other possibility was that he was a hotel worker. A maintenance man or cleaner. The uniform would have been perfect for getting in and out of the hotel, maybe even passing unnoticed through the mall.

She ran through how that might have worked.

He could have stashed the clothes somewhere in the mall – or even in the sports bag.

That was it.

The holdall hadn't only been to conceal the weapon; it had been to carry his getaway clothes as well.

It made sense.

Again she had the thought that he might be a manual worker. Employed and living nearby.

She turned her attention to the map and eyed the usual housing catchment areas for lower-paid city workers. They weren't so far away. You could catch a 28 bus from Avenue of the Stars, make a quick change at La Brea and Olympic and then be out at Inglewood within an hour.

She looked across the timetables. There were plenty of buses regularly leaving Santa Monica Boulevard. With a couple of easy changes, the number 4 would get you as far north as Sherman Oaks within sixty minutes. Conversely, going east, you could be Downtown within the hour, and going west you could ride out as far as Santa Monica itself within thirty-five minutes.

Angie sat back and reviewed it all. Before the first cops had even reached the mall the UNSUB could have been holed up in a hotel minutes away – or out of town and almost into another state.

More than ever, she was sure that Danielle Goodman had got it all wrong. This was not a killer on a road trip, no modern-day Charles Starkweather. He was a thousand times brighter and more dangerous than that. He was a new breed of homicidal monster – a hybrid of a Spree and a Serial. Maybe the deadliest category of criminal ever identified.

Chapter 88

Time drizzled away and Jake never got ahead of the curve. Every minute of every hour, someone was at his door or on his phone.

It seemed to him that Crawford was under so much pressure the old guy was in danger of having a heart attack.

No way would he ever want *that* job.

Less than an hour ago the head of the FBI had talked to the office of the President.

Shit had started to fly.

And people were arranging the wind tunnels so it came thick and fast in the direction of the LA Field Office. The talk was of 'heads rolling' if there wasn't a quick result.

It was eight o'clock when Jake shut down his computer and called it a day. He had a date with Angie and wasn't going to miss it. They'd made progress the last day or two and he wanted to build on that. Ruis was under strict instructions not to call. Not unless the UNSUB struck again or they had an address for a door to go and bust open.

The restaurant was called EPOC and it was the place Jake had first taken Angie when they started dating. It was a lot less pretentious than its name suggested. Teak flooring, vanilla walls with spot-lit paintings by local artists, and round tables draped in starched white and brown cloths. The food was a long way from Michelin starred, but there was a hearty range of steaks and a hot chocolate soufflé to die for.

271

He arrived early. And nervous. It reminded him of their first date. Way back then, his emotions had been more sexually loaded. The attraction had been blisteringly physical. He just had to look at her and he'd been in trouble. Nowadays she still thrilled him but it was different. The excitement was a steady buzz, the attraction somehow richer and deeper than just being physical. And when she wasn't around he felt incomplete. Like he'd run into battle without a gun. Life was just wrong when he was without her.

Jake's chosen table was in the corner with his back against the wall. Some habits die hard. Through the window he saw her on the sidewalk, hair flowing, tan bag over her shoulder, a far-away look on her face. She was still as slim and beautiful as a swimwear model. No hint of the baby inside her.

His child.

The thought had taken some getting used to. But he had. He wondered if that was how Nature worked. Once you'd gotten over the Taser shock of being told you were a parent-in-waiting, some odd hormones kicked in and started to make it seem desirable.

The restaurant door opened. Angie looked around, spotted him, smiled and made her way over. 'Hi,' she said from a distance, her face full of color from the walk.

'Hi yourself.' He got up and kissed her clumsily. This was even more like his first date than he'd thought.

Angie looked at him quizzically as they settled.

A waitress handed out the cards and introduced herself. 'Hello, folks. I'm Sandy and I'll be looking after you tonight. Can I get you something to drink while you're making up your minds on the food?'

'Just some mineral water,' said Angie.

'I'll have a beer.'

'What kind, sir? We have Miller, Peroni, Bud—'

'Any. You choose.' He just wanted her to go. Needed to talk to Angie. Get things said.

'Large or small, sir?'

'Any. Whatever you decide. Please just leave us for a minute.'

Sandy gave him a startled look, found her waitress smile then vanished.

'What was that all about?' asked Angie.

'This.' He slapped his big hands in the middle of the table then moved them away.

She stared at a small, open velvet box and the gold and diamond ring sparkling there.

'Angie Holmes, will you please make me the happiest man in the world and be my wife?'

Chapter 89

Douglas Park, Santa Monica, LA

They made love all night. Slower. Gentler. More meaningfully than they'd ever done.

Their bodies tied a bond. Made a vow. They were to be a family. A family.

Jake had never known one. And Angie wished she hadn't known hers. Now they were going to start their own. Be parents. And not screw up. It was as scary as fuck and he knew she was just as excited and simultaneously freaked out as he was.

But she'd said yes.

Said it and cried when he'd put the ring on her finger.

Now he slept. A deep sleep that wasn't populated with politicians and photographs of dead people. In his drifting dreams he pictured the wedding. The birth. The child in Angie's arms, pressed to her breast then, full and sleepy, handed over to him and laid across his chest to love and cherish.

The dream didn't stretch any further. He didn't know the sex of the child. Didn't see the first steps or hear the first words. All that was being saved for future dreams and future days.

Jake woke with Angie stuck to him.

She'd fallen asleep with her injured arm laid across his stomach like it was a pillow.

He moved slowly and peeled her off so he didn't wake her. It was six-thirty a.m. Through the window he could see the day was already blast-furnace hot.

Jake got up, made coffee and scrambled eggs. He shaved and showered then dressed in a lightweight grey suit with crisp white shirt and grey tie.

At seven-fifteen, he squeezed a jug full of fresh orange juice and put together a bowl of chopped fruits with snowy dollops of low-fat yoghurt. He brewed more coffee and went in to resuscitate Angie. 'Wakey wakey, Sleeping Beauty. Believe it or not, it's time to go again.'

She squinted at him. Groaned. Tentatively stretched her bad arm. Grimaced.

'Breakfast is served.' He raised the tray to her bleary eye-line and approached the bed.

'Hrrm. Thanks.' She pulled herself up. 'Was last night really real?'

His smile lit up the room. 'Really, really real.' Jake laid the tray next to her. 'I love you, Mrs Mottram.'

The name sounded odd to her. 'Holmes-Mottram. We'll hyphenate it.' She kissed him then playfully pushed him away. 'Now get me a T-shirt, I don't want to dribble food all down me.'

'Oh I don't know, could be fun.' He dipped a finger in yoghurt and smeared her lips.

She licked it away and said firmly, 'T-shirt! You damned near busted my arm again last night, you animal.' She pulled up the covers and noticed the diamond on her finger. 'The ring you got is beautiful. Did I tell you that?'

'You did. I'm glad you like it.'

'Come here.' She put a hand around the back of his neck and kissed him again. 'Forget the T and get your ass back in bed.'

Chapter 90

C hips had finished early the day before and, as was his way, he'd come in early to make up the lost time. For the past hour he'd been plowing through more of the mall footage and had stuff to flag up to his boss.

Angie came in wearing a powder blue jacket and skirt with matching shoes. But that wasn't what caught his eye.

'Whoa! Whoa! Whoa!' He rushed to her side as she approached her desk. Then he squealed with delight. 'Oh my God, you're engaged.' He grabbed her hand and lifted it for inspection. 'It's so *bee-you-tee-full*!' Then he smothered her in a hug, careful not to crush the damaged arm.

Angie came out panting for breath. 'Wow, I think Jake should have asked you. That's an even hotter response than I gave him.'

'Sister, I would certainly have said yes if that hunk of man had asked me.'

'He's taken – just you remember that.' She saw his T for the first time. It was mauve with white letters that asked CAN DYSLEXICS READ BETWEEN THE LINES?

'That's not funny,' she said, half-seriously. 'Not if you're dyslexic.'

He smiled mischievously. 'Ah, but if you *are* dyslexic then you won't be able to read it, so there's no chance of it offending.'

Angie shook her head in despair. She could see an empty coffee cup on his desk. 'I'm gonna make myself some Joe, you want another?'

'No, thanks. 'Fore you do that, I have to show you something.'

She followed him to his desk.

'I've been going over the footage again.'

She didn't have the heart to tell him that they were being forced off the case. 'What have you got?'

'It's this bit that interests me.' He hit play on his media controller and the screen filled with the silent, all-too-familiar images. 'It's when Mr Sicko has shot everyone and walks around finishing them off. First, he makes sure that Mrs Murison is dead.' Chips tapped the screen. 'Even though he's not closest to her. Now, why do you think that was?'

'When I first saw it, I thought maybe just because she was an old lady and perhaps there was a tiny spark of humanity inside him and he wanted to put her out of her misery.'

'And now?'

'Jake told me the bomb was planted by a kid pretending to be a relative of hers, but you keep that to yourself, it's not to leave this room. Right?'

He drew a pretend zip across his lips.

Angie gave him her fuller answer. 'Now it looks like the UNSUB may have deliberately targeted her. And perhaps after killing her he always had it in mind to desecrate her memory, defile her even after death.' She looked at the frozen picture of the killer on the screen. 'Does he behave oddly with any of the other victims?'

Chips nodded. 'Not with his victims. Not specifically. But there is something.' He fast-forwarded the footage. 'Look at this and tell me what you think.'

The section played. It was a moment after the killer had finished shooting. The sports bag on his shoulder slumped down and he lifted out his hand. The weight of the weapon made the bag point to the floor. The UNSUB was heading out when he stepped in blood. He looked down, wiped it off his sneakers and then walked on.

'I don't see the significance of this,' said Angie. 'Is it the blood on his shoe that I'm supposed to be interested in?'

'Uh-huh.'

She looked again at the screen. 'I guess he's wiping it off because he's reasonably smart and forensically aware. He knows CSIs will look for footprints and maybe trace him from the tread pattern.'

'It's not that. Let me show you.' Chips got up and paced to the middle of the room. 'I'm the killer, right. Bag over shoulder.' He dropped his shoulder and held his hands as though there were a gun on his right side.

'Other side,' said Angie, straight away. 'The UNSUB had the bag slung so it hung on his left side, meaning he's either left-handed or ambidextrous.'

'Sorry. I'll make the switch.' He moved the imaginary weight to his other hip. 'I'm walking out. I step in blood. I look down and realize it. Now watch what I do.' Chips put the flat of his foot down about six inches away from where he'd trodden, then he dragged his leg back and forth three times like a dog scratching earth. 'Look correct to you?'

'I guess.'

He rushed back to his computer and hit play. 'That's *not* what the UNSUB does. He steps into the blood. Sees it's on his foot and then, he doesn't step out or make the motion I did.'

Angie leaned closer to the monitor. 'Run it again.'

He played the section. 'See? There's no scraping of the sole. He points his toe, like he's a ballet dancer, brings it down at an angle, then upwards almost as though he's drawing a hockey stick in the blood.'

'Again.'

He replayed it for her.

'You're right.' Angie sat back. 'But it's more like he's a painter than a ballet dancer. He makes his toe the tip of a brush then he does that tick.'

'Tick – that's it!' Chips looked animated. 'He's drawn the Nike swoosh. Look at his T-shirt. I should have realized it. He's living up to the slogan JUST DO IT. He's cracking a sick joke in the midst of the bloodshed.'

Angie studied the freeze frame. Chips had hit on something but she wasn't sure he was *quite* right.

'I don't think it is a *commercial* reference,' she said. 'I reckon he's checking the kill off his list. His Tick List. And you know what that means, don't you?'

Chips did. 'He's only part way through. There is a lot more to come.'

Chapter 91

The press conference was set to be the biggest the LAPD had ever staged.

The two communication chiefs, Ryan Fox of the FBI and Jamie Luttings of the LAPD, had been overwhelmed with attendance requests from national and international news teams.

Rawlings had insisted the announcement was handled by his team and made from force HQ on West 1st Street.

Jake let Danielle Goodman drive him across town so he could take calls and run things through in his mind. He hated press conferences and they made him oddly nervous. Action was what he was comfortable with, not words.

He was also stressed by the fact he hadn't even mentioned the media event to Angie. The night had gone so perfectly he hadn't wanted to ruin it by raising Danielle's scheme and inevitably debating what should and shouldn't be said.

They parked up and Marjorie Dalton, an ageing blonde in a pale pink jacket and matching trousers, was waiting in police reception to meet them. 'You're late. We're on in ten. Follow me.'

'Marj isn't big on the polite stuff,' explained Danielle as they headed up stairs, down corridors and past the conference room where rows of cameras were already set up.

They stepped into a small room next door.

Jake was surprised to see Rawlings sat in a chair, with a young lady powdering his face in front of a mirror.

'Glad you could make it,' said the chief. He looked at the reflection of the redhead prettifying him. 'Short of a hair transplant and cosmetic surgery, I think you've done all that can be done there.'

She smiled at him and unfastened the make-up cape she'd draped over his chunky torso.

Rawlings stood and turned.

Jake had to choke a laugh.

The guy was in full uniform with a chest full of ribbons that you got for doing next to nothing. His hair was dyed an unbelievable black, and his brown eyes sparkled in greedy anticipation of all the publicity he was about to receive.

The make-up girl checked Jake out then smiled at Marjorie. 'You don't need me for this one. He seems pretty close to perfect.' Her eyes twinkled as she reached up and dabbed powder across his forehead, down the bridge of his nose and on the ball of his chin. 'There you go, sir. That's you done.'

Jake was too nervous to flirt. 'Thanks.'

Rawlings opened the door. 'C'mon then, Mr Handsome, let's go through. We have a packed house. No point keeping them waiting.'

Even in the corridor, Jake could hear that the room was jammed with journalists, camera crews and photographers.

As he walked in, cameras flashed, chairs scraped the floor and the noise died down to a rolling mumble.

He and the chief took their places at a table with their name cards pasted over the edge. Rawlings cupped his mouth with his hand and whispered to him. 'Remember, CNN, Fox, Sky and the like will be cutting to us live.'

Live.

Jake had thought it would all be recorded.

He'd done press conferences before. Plenty of them. But never this large and never *live*.

Jamie Luttings stood out front, made the introductions then backed away.

The chief started his pitch-perfect address. 'The Los Angeles Police

Department has only one aim – to secure the safety of all its citizens. We pride ourselves on our professionalism and our pledge to protect and serve. This is why we unhesitatingly asked the FBI to add their expertise to our relentless drive to find the perpetrator – or perpetrators – of the terrible crimes of the last few days.' He paused and gestured towards Jake. 'Alongside me is Special Agent Jake Mottram, the head of the Bureau's Spree Killer Unit. A couple of years back the President of the United States pinned the Medal of Honor on his chest because of his heroism, his dedication to his job and his determination that good would triumph over evil, even if it cost him his life. As of now, Agent Mottram will be taking operational control of the Sun Western slayings, and I will be ensuring that he has the full support of the LAPD and all its officers and resources.'

Mutterings broke across the room as hacks prompted their photographers to snap the moment.

Rawlings was experienced enough to wait until the noise died down, then continued, 'To avoid any misunderstandings, I want to make it clear that this act of co-operation was instigated by myself and has been backed unconditionally by the LAPD Board of Police Commissioners. Rest assured, together with the FBI, we *will* make our city safe again. I pass you over to the safe hands of Special Agent Mottram.'

'Thank you, Chief.' Jake took a reflective beat and made sure his tone respectfully matched what he was about to say. 'My sympathies, and those of my colleagues, go out to the families and loved ones of all those who have died.' Camera flashes almost blinded him. 'I have come across many enemies in my time, but only the most evil of creatures strikes at civilians in a way as cowardly as this. To shoot men, women and children as they shopped, to blow up mourners as they laid flowers and paid tributes at the Sun Western mall – these are acts that rank as the most despicable I have ever witnessed. The mind behind these acts is a cowardly, spineless, gutless one. It is housed in a body that has no place in our society. We are speaking of the lowest of the low, the kind of person parents would disown, the kind that society is most ashamed of. You'll notice that I haven't used the words "human being". That's because *the creature* responsible for these homicides is not worthy of the words. The worst criminals in prison would consider him too vile to be allowed a cell alongside them. It might even contravene their human rights to be put in close proximity to such an abomination.' He took a pause and immediately wished he hadn't. A lightning storm of camera flashes blinded him. It took several seconds for him to blink away the burn from his retinas. 'I'll be honest with you. I'm not good with words, I'm no politician or orator, but I think I speak for the American public when I say this to the UNSUB who has ruined the lives of so many good people. You will be hunted to the ends of the earth. There is nowhere you can hide. No lengths that we won't go to in order to catch you. Dead or alive, you *will* face justice.'

The cameras clacked and flashed again. Jake closed his eyes and saw only white snakes wriggling across the backs of his lids.

Luttings once more stepped forward and took control of the massed media. 'The chief and Agent Mottram have a few moments for your questions.'

The hand of a stubble-bearded, middle-aged man went up. 'Leo Vogel, *LA Times*. Has a psychological profile of the offender been constructed, and if so, can we be told what it is?'

Rawlings batted the question away. 'I think that's best answered by the FBI.'

'We do have a profile,' answered Jake, 'but we are not in a position to share it with you. Photographs of the suspect have been distributed and we would like to talk to anyone who knows someone who fits that description.'

'Why can't you share it?' countered Vogel.

'Because the suspect may well read your newspaper and watch TV. And – as a result of learning the details of our profile – he would undoubtedly seek to alter his behavior and evade capture.'

A woman's hand went up and Luttings picked her out.

'Tina Bolz, CNN. What exactly is the difference between a spree killer and a serial killer? And what specialism do you bring to the case that the LAPD doesn't already have?'

'Sprees don't have cooling-off periods like Serials do.' Jake had answered this question many times. 'Serials go months, sometimes years between their early kills, and the gap generally shortens only when they get careless, lose control and begin to make the kind of mistakes that lead to their capture. Sprees start with little or no gap. They shoot two or more people. Then they quickly kill again – often within the hour, sometimes within the same day. Now let me address your second point. The LAPD is among the most professional police forces in existence. They were the first in the world to create a SWAT unit and the first in the USA to introduce female police officers. They have a very fine behavioral science unit and an exemplary bomb unit. The officers in those divisions are second-to-none. They do, however, have to attend multiple types of crimes, whereas my team at SKU investigates only spree killers. Day in, day out, that's all we do. That singularity of focus – and the streamlining of resources to serve only that end – is what makes us different, and what we hope will make the difference in these cases.'

'One more,' said Luttings.

A slim, dark-haired woman stood up. 'Anna Arit, Associated Press. Chief, can this "creature", as Agent Mottram called him, be caught before he kills again?'

'That's our intention,' answered Chief Rawlings. 'Like Special Agent Mottram said, we're going to catch him and bring him to justice, dead or alive. For the record, my personal preference is dead.'

Chapter 92

Jake's cellphone rang the second he stepped out of the media room and turned it off mute. He was ushered into a small office at the end of the corridor and given some privacy.

The display said it was Angie.

He took the call and braced himself. 'Hello—'

'What the hell, Jake? What in God's sweet name were you thinking of?'

'Angie—'

'Why on earth didn't you tell me you were going to do that?'

'Angie—'

'Don't do one-to-one interviews. Please, please, please don't talk any more to the press.'

He finally got to say more than her name. 'There's no plan to do anything else. Rawlings will do some interviews, but not me.'

'"Plan"?' she snapped. '"Plan" implies some thought had gone into this madness. Correction. What I just saw on the TV was reckless and irresponsible, not madness. Mad people can't help themselves. Was this all Danielle Goodman's doing?'

'Not only her. It was vetted and supported by Dixon.' He felt defensive. 'The idea is to infuriate the UNSUB. Force him into a spontaneous reaction. One that hopefully people around him will notice and cause them to report him to their local cops or FBI office.'

Angie was shouting an abusive response when Ryan Fox cracked the door open and stuck his head through the gap. 'Amazing piece, man. The press are going wild. They love you.' He put his hands wide apart. 'You're going to make big headlines. BIG, BIG headlines.'

Jake scowled and showed him the phone. 'I'm talking.'

'Sorry.' He smiled and disappeared.

'Angie . . .'

The line was dead.

'Fuck.' Jake banged a hand on the wall and left a dent in the plaster-board. He'd guessed she'd be upset when she found out, but he hadn't expected her to go so far off the scale.

The door opened again.

A middle-aged secretary hovered patiently until he looked her way. 'Special Agent Mottram.'

Jake recognized her from Rawlings' office. 'Yes, I'm sorry – I was miles away.'

She smiled professionally and announced, 'I have a call for you, in the chief's office.'

He was too churned up to speak to anyone else for a few minutes. 'Could you please take a number and say I'll call back when I return to my office.'

'I don't really think I can do that, sir.'

He frowned. 'Why not?'

'Because it's from the office of the President of the United States.'

'I guess you can't.' Jake followed her into the corridor and down to the corner office with Rawlings' name on the door. The secretary let him in and signaled towards the big brown desk and leather executive seat lit by a warm angle-poise lamp. 'I'll put it through to the desk set.'

The door shut behind him and the phone rang.

Jake picked it up. 'This is Jake Mottram.'

A male voice on the other end replied, 'Please hold for the President of the United States.'

The two men had met only once before. It was when America's Commander in Chief had pinned the Medal of Honor to his chest, in respect of heroism in the Yemen – the result of an operation that had gone wrong. A covert strike on an al-Qaeda base had been screwed up by a communications error in another regiment. Jake had been forced to hold a position on his own and lay down covering fire to get his men out of the death trap. In the process, he took two bullets in his shoulder and was left for dead in the scorching heat. Split from his unit he stuck himself full of morphine and soldiered on. En route to the evac. zone he ran into a two-man enemy recon unit and almost bled out in the firefight that killed both of the enemy.

A click on the line brought his reminiscences to an end.

'Special Agent Mottram, how are you?'

He felt an odd surge of nerves. 'I'm fine, sir.'

'I just watched you on television and like most of America was moved by your words.'

'Thank you, sir. Though I have to confess, I was pretty much sticking to a script that had been written for me.'

The President laughed. 'As do we all, Jake. We need a hero right now and, script or no script, I'm comforted that a man of your distinction is leading the hunt for this killer. Bring him in quickly, soldier, then let's talk again when you have done your job. My party could do with a man like you in its ranks.'

Chapter 93

Skid Row, LA

Shooter was angry.

He'd wanted to finish his shock surprise. The special one he'd been diligently creating with scraps collected from trash bags. With those kinds of materials he only had one chance to produce the masterpiece he had in mind. But now his mood was ruined.

Zapping between news channels, he'd found the studio anchor on Fox announcing 'A major development in the hunt for the Sun Western slayer.'

Annoyingly, he was having to wait until after the break to discover what it was.

He sat as patiently as he could.

When the 'special report' came on, it really didn't seem so special. Rehashed videotape from the mall, close-ups of his disguised face, shots of ambulances ferrying away the wounded, a long view of open-backed black coroner's vans swallowing bodies draped in white sheets.

Shooter had seen it all before.

Then came a hard cut to the fat LAPD chief in his ridiculous police uniform, plastered with so many badges he looked like a cartoon character. Mr Medal headed into a press conference alongside a giant of a man. A stiff-backed Neanderthal as broad as one of those brain-dead football players.

The chief posed for the cameras, then kicked things off. 'Alongside me is Special Agent Jake Mottram, the head of the Bureau's Spree Killer Unit . . .'

Shooter stared at Mottram's face.

There was a hardness to it. A look that only came when you'd taken the life of someone else. When you had stared Death in the face and had run for cover.

It came as no surprise to see pictures flashed up of him in full camouflage uniform, a machine gun looking small in his huge hands. The voiceover said he'd fought in Afghanistan and Yemen, been wounded in battle, had killed an enemy recon unit and still escaped.

Shooter was amused.

The guy was described as a war hero but he was no more than an action figure. A soldier doll. Mr Grunt to go with Mr Medal. He was all body and no brain. Shooter had grown up in neighborhoods full of idiots like that. They'd never been any trouble to him.

'As of now,' continued Mr Medal, 'Agent Mottram will be taking operational control of the Sun Western slayings, and I will be ensuring that he has the full support of the LAPD and all its officers and resources.'

Now that *was* interesting.

The report was turning out to be quite special after all.

Shooter had expected the FBI to get involved but not so soon.

Grunt was talking now but Shooter wasn't fully listening. They'd called him a spree killer. It wasn't really a term he liked. It belittled what he did.

Revolutionary.

Protestor.

Avenger.

Artist.

They were all more accurate than the denigrations used by the press and police.

The camera angle tightened and Shooter started to pay attention. A slow zoom during a news piece was always a sign that the guy talking had finally become interesting.

'I have come across many enemies in my time,' said Grunt, 'but only the most evil of creatures strikes at civilians in a way as cowardly as this.'

Evil?

Cowardly?

The soldier doll was out of line with that. It was disrespectful. Ignorant. Downright rude.

'The mind behind these acts is a cowardly, spineless, gutless one. It is housed in a body that has no place in our society. We are speaking of the lowest of the low, the kind of person parents would disown, the kind that society is most ashamed of.'

Shooter balled his fists and shouted at the screen. 'My parents? You dare mention my parents, you motherfucking piece of establishment shit.'

Jake seemed to answer him back. 'You'll notice that I haven't used the words "human being". That's because *the creature* responsible for these homicides is not worthy of the words. The worst criminals in prison would consider him too vile to be allowed a cell alongside them.'

Shooter grabbed the flat screen and shook it. Banged it against the wall until it fell from his hands. Still Grunt refused to shut up. Still he spouted nonsense. Then there were pictures of him leaving the police HQ and being followed in his car by the press, like he was some freaking movie star.

Shooter ripped the monitor off its bracket and crashed it to the floor.

'Dead or alive,' repeated the upturned newsreader.

Those were the last words the TV spoke before it died.

It seemed prophetic.

Shooter said them aloud over the busted screen. 'Dead – or – alive.'

He stood in the pooled LED glass and crushed it. Ground it under his heel. Digital dust to digital dust. 'I choose "dead", Mr Grunt. I choose "*dead*".'

He swept his foot through the powdered ashes and made a perfect tick.

Chapter 94

SKU Offices, LA

J ake's cellphone rang all the way back to the office. He ignored it. The attention was almost as annoying as Danielle Goodman's permanent grin. If she congratulated him one more time he was going to lose it with her.

Somehow he kept his temper and made it to his corridor.

Most of SKU were lined up outside his office and clapped as he rounded the corner.

Jake wanted to fall through a hole in the floor.

His embarrassment grew with every step and every shouted comment.

'Well done, boss.'

'Way to go, Mr M.'

'Let's get that piece of shit.'

Ruis Costas shook his hand and followed him in. 'Man, that was quite a speech. You sure tore a new hole in that scumbag.'

'Talk's cheap – you know that. We need to double our actions now. Cancel all leave. Everyone works this weekend. I don't give a damn about the overtime; we do what we have to do. All these politicians are going to have to put their money behind all this.'

Angie was in the doorway. 'That might be the first smart thing you've said today.'

Ruis could feel the tension. 'I'll give you guys some time.' He put an imaginary phone to his ear. 'Call me when you're ready, boss.'

Angie walked in, heard the door close behind her then let fly. 'I don't know what I'm angrier about. That you kept me in the dark about this insane press conference, or that last night, when you proposed to me, you knew you'd be spouting all that crap today.'

'You're being ridiculous.'

'Am I?'

'Yes. One is work and one is personal.'

'They're the same now, Jake. When you pledge the rest of your life to someone, you do it on a basis of *complete* trust and honesty. You held back on me, you deliberately kept things secret because you knew I'd have objections. That's not trust, that's manipulation, and I sure as hell am not going to enter into a marriage of manipulation.'

He tried to mitigate. 'I meant everything I said last night. And I meant everything I said today. There was nothing dishonest in any of my words. I love you, Angie, and I want to spend the rest of my life with you and with our baby. And I hate this creature, this *monster*, that can kill in the way he does. Believe me, I'd personally put a bullet in his head and sleep soundly, given half a chance.'

She shook her head in dismay.

Jake could see fury still building inside her.

'This is not a war, Jake. Hunting him is not a personal challenge to you. It's a *job*. A J.O.B. It's what you get paid for – not what you should risk your life for.'

'We all risk our lives, that's why we carry guns not flowers.'

'Don't be so damned flippant.'

He headed her way. 'Come on, you must be able to see my difficulties here. That was a speech my boss and my unit psych wanted me to make. What was I to say?'

Her face reddened. 'No! That's what you should have said. NO, NO, NO! The speech was ill thought out. It was tabloid bullshit, designed to grab cheap headlines, to rally the troops and buy politicians time. And I bet that bitch Danielle knows all that too.'

Now he was cross. 'Cut her some slack – she's doing her best.'

'No, she's not! She's doing what is politically smart, for her, for Dixon and for the Bureau.'

'Well, excuse me, but how's that a bad thing?'

'Because, you stupid man, you're being played. They're making you their scapegoat. It's your head that will be sacrificed if – or when – all goes pear-shaped, which it undoubtedly will.'

'Thanks for the vote of confidence.'

Angie took a deep breath. 'Jake, he's not a Spree. You shouldn't even be . . .' She bit her tongue.

'What?' He gave her an accusing look. 'What shouldn't I *be*?'

'McDonald asked me if your unit should even be working the case and I said technically, no.'

'Gee, you really are a fan of mine.'

'Grow up. She wanted me to write a detailed report as to why I was convinced the killer was a Serial and file a recommendation that it was taken off you.'

He backed away from her. 'Jesus! And you accuse *me* of keeping secrets.'

'This is different.'

'Why?'

'Because I *didn't* write the report – though I wish I had. And it isn't as simple as that. He's not a Spree and not a Serial. He's a Hybrid. A new breed that still needs properly defining.'

'Oh, and Doctor Holmes is just the person to do that, not dumbass Danielle Goodman, I suppose.' Jake's voice bounced with sarcasm. 'And I guess in future, everyone will remember how you recognized this new category and you'll be up there with the Robert Resslers, John Douglases and all the other founding fathers of profiling. Right?'

'Fuck you, Jake.' She made for the door, then stopped. 'For your information, before your little show on TV, I told Sandra McDonald I wanted off the case. That was a decision I made to make life easier for you – not me. Now I'm going to write up all my notes tonight, and I'd like to do that on my own at home, without interruption, so it'd be good if you gave me that space and stayed the hell away from me until I'm done.'

'I'm sorry.'

'So am I, Jake. So am I.' She resisted the urge to slam the door and shut it gently behind her.

Chapter 95

The rest of the day dragged.

Not an hour went by without fragments of the row blowing into Jake's mind. He'd thought it had been smart to separate work from his personal life.

It hadn't.

He'd felt obliged to comply with Danielle Goodman's request for him not to discuss the speech with Angie.

He shouldn't have.

Even though Dixon had approved it, he should have told her 'no' and insisted he write his own words. More than anything, he should have put Angie first, just as she had apparently done with him.

Lessons learned. The hard way. As per.

At least she hadn't thrown the ring back at him. There was some comfort in that.

He had to work late tonight, so maybe an evening apart wasn't such a bad thing. Besides, he needed some sleep because, pregnant or not, Angie had worn him out and he needed some shut-eye.

As the night wore on he called her cell to apologize again, but she didn't pick up. He left a simple message. 'Sorry.' Then added, 'When you're done being mad at me, remember, I love you.'

Just after ten-thirty p.m., Ruis Costas rubbed fire from his eyes and declared he was done. 'Hey, boss, I have to go. If I don't hit the sack soon then I'm going to be worth shit tomorrow.'

'Go. You're worth shit to me anyway.' Jake jokingly waved his number two away. 'Get yourself home, buddy, and thanks for everything. I really appreciate you staying on so late.'

'No problem. I'll be in around eight.'

'Drive safely.'

Jake's cellphone rang within minutes of Ruis leaving. He looked for Angie's number but caller display threw up a blank. 'Mottram.'

'Jake, it's Connor Pryce. I'm about to walk into your reception. Can you have them clear me to come on up?'

'Sure.' He wondered what warranted a personal visit rather than just a call.

They both hung up and Jake buzzed the guards on reception to let the lieutenant come on through. He walked to the pantry to check there was coffee brewing and then waited by the elevator down the hall.

It dinged and Pryce stepped out. Despite the lateness of the hour, his tie was still tight to his immaculately white collar and he looked freshly shaved and smartly suited.

'I just made a fix of caffeine, you want some?'

Pryce smiled. 'No, I'm good. Any more and I'll be able to fly home.'

'Maybe I should skip too. Either that or file my flight path with LAX.' Jake walked him back to his office and they took seats at the desk.

The cop dug in his jacket pocket and pulled out two evidence bags. 'This is a MAC-10 cartridge case.' He dangled bag one. 'And this a MAC-10 bullet tip.' He held up the second bag. 'Both were found in connection with a shooting in Compton eighteen months back.' He tossed the bags across to the SKU man. 'First, take a look down the side of the cartridge and at the rim.'

Jake slid the seal open. He held the remains of the round between his thumb and forefinger and lifted it to the light.

Pryce guided him a little. 'See the front to back diagonal striation?'

Jake tilted it until the barreling mark glistened. 'Yeah, just.'

'Flip it over and look at the end.'

Jake knew what to expect. Californian law meant firing pins had to micro-stamp the cartridge with the make, model and serial number of the weapon that fired it. To stay anonymous, crooks removed the stamp, but doing that always damaged the pin and left its own unique mark. 'Looks like a little moon.'

'It does, you're right. We found that, along with several more spent cartridges, in a sports bag at a suspect's house.'

'A sports bag?'

'Yep, but it wasn't the same as the one we saw at the mall.'

'Still, it's a gun in a sports bag with the same type of weapon.'

'It's better than that. Look at the bullet tip.'

Jake opened the second evidence pouch. He lifted out the shiny business end of the bullet and rotated it until he found a barreling mark. He picked up the cartridge case again from the other bag and aligned the grooves. 'Same caliber, same striation lines. I'm no ballistics expert but they look like twins to me.'

'They are.' He watched Jake's face as he revealed the big news. 'And they're the same as the ones in the bodies at the mall.'

'What?'

'The bullet tips are the same. They bear the same striation marks. They were fired from the same gun, a MAC-10. They match the cartridge there in your hand.'

Jake felt the air bend.

It was a connection.

The first physical, forensic connection in the case. 'So you know who the UNSUB is?' He held up both evidence bags.

The cop's face said the answer wasn't going to be that easy. 'Like I said, this case goes back a year and a half. It led to us arresting a young black guy called Aaron Bolt. He hung with the Pirus gang, affiliates of the South Side Crips. We were pretty sure Bolt had gunned down a sixteen-year-old who'd disrespected a senior gang member. It was his first kill. His initiation. We had full IDs and eyewitness on him. Bolt was heading to the big house.'

'Was?'

'Main witness got wasted before trial. As did his two-year-old son who was in his arms when the shooter came through his door in the early hours of the morning. Once word of that got out on the streets, the other eyes recanted. Said they'd been mistaken. Case collapsed.'

'No witness protection?'

'None at all. Local cops said they'd asked and got told there was no budget for it. No staff. No overtime.'

'No fucking kidding. Do you know where Bolt is now?'

'That's the bad news. We don't. I've had men in the hood all night. Right from the moment ballistics flagged a match with the mall murders. There's no sign of him. We'll keep checking, but we're told he's been missing from the street for about a week now.'

Jake knew he was grasping at straws. 'And the MAC-10?'

'Never found it. When we arrested Bolt and interviewed him he said he thought a MAC was a computer.'

Jake gave a wry smile and realized he'd missed out the most obvious question of all. 'What does this Aaron Bolt look like? Does he fit the photos of our guy?'

Pryce knew that one was coming. He put his hand inside his jacket and pulled out two photographs. One was an LAPD mugshot. The other a gang photo. Tellingly, Bolt was stood there in baggy black shorts, a white Nike T and a white Lakers baseball cap on his head. He was posing moody and sullen for the camera, a Glock in each hand, the barrels aimed right down the lens.

Chapter 96

Douglas Park, Santa Monica, LA

Aside from needing a cooling-off period, Angie hadn't been lying about the necessity of some time on her own to write up her notes.

She *was* dead beat.

So tired that she had to wind down the window of her old Avensis to make sure she didn't fall asleep at the wheel.

As she headed home, she was still annoyed that Jake had been so crudely manipulated and that she had been unable to help and protect him.

And after today's monumental cockup, things were only going to get worse. Rawlings and Dixon were bound to dodge all future heat and let Jake fry if it meant protecting themselves. Weak bosses always liked to have someone like Jake around to blame. Someone bold, brave and stupid enough to think he was doing the right thing.

On top of all that, her mind was buzzing with personal stuff. The baby. Her maternity leave.

A wedding to fix.

Mad as she was at him, Jake Mottram was still the man she wanted to spend the rest of her life with. He just needed some training, that was all.

Wedding – before or after the baby?

It was a question she hadn't thought of until today. *After* seemed best. That way, there was a chance she could get into a decent dress and make a real event of things.

Maybe a ceremony on a beach.

Barbados? The Bahamas? Miami?

Or somewhere more traditionally romantic.

Venice? Paris? Rome?

Better still, marry on a beach and honeymoon in Europe.

Angie was still smiling as she banged the car door shut, zapped on the central locking and climbed the stairs to her apartment.

Jake's stuff was everywhere and she instantly felt soft towards him. The army hadn't managed to get him to be tidy so she doubted she would. She shifted shoes in the hall and put them on a rack. Picked up a glass he'd left on the floor and put it in the dishwasher. Shifted a sweater from the back of a chair and put it on a shelf in a wardrobe he'd claimed for himself.

Angie got salad from the fridge and made herbal tea. Her phone was off and it was staying that way. If she turned it back on there'd be a message from him, she'd call back and then he'd come round and the notes wouldn't be written. Or they'd argue again.

The phone stayed off and she settled with a mix of greens and chamomile and for the next hour wrote up a preliminary profile. It was good but not quite right. She decided to review it first thing in the morning, when her head was clear of emotional junk and she could see it in a fresh light.

Just before midnight, she poured herself a glass of water, found a soppy historical romance book on the rack beneath the coffee table and headed to the bedroom. Hopefully, she'd be asleep within a chapter or two.

She took off her make-up and tried not to think of the killer. Scrubbed her teeth and tried not to think of her row with Jake or how much she wanted to call him. She slipped into black pajamas and tried not to think what she'd look like when she gained all that extra baby weight.

The bed felt cool and soft. The pillow was plump and comforting and the book so wonderfully and ridiculously romantic that she was dozing within three kisses and an unbuttoning of a corset.

She felt good now.

In the morning, she'd call her idiot fiancé and everything would be all right.

Chapter 97

SKU Offices, LA

It was gone midnight when Jake finally walked Connor Pryce through reception. To his horror, a hardened media cadre was still camped out on Wilshire Boulevard.

The peaceful dark of night was suddenly broken by the blinding white of TV lights.

Jake shielded his eyes and went back inside. Pryce no doubt loved the attention but he hated it. They'd trailed him in Danielle's car all the way from the LAPD HQ, but that was hours ago and he'd presumed they'd gone.

He spent another fifty minutes at his desk, writing follow-up notes for the morning and sending briefing notes to Crawford Dixon. He didn't want his boss to be behind the curve. Pryce had already tipped Rawlings that there was a possible name to put in the frame, so there were bound to be frantic conversations down the FBI and LAPD corridors of power first thing in the morning.

Aaron Bolt featured large in everything Jake wrote.

It was good to finish the day with a suspect. Especially one so strongly linked to a previous killing. One where ballistic evidence tied 'his' gun to the mall murders. An added bonus was the photo of Bolt in clothes virtually identical to the ones the UNSUB had been pictured in on the CCTV footage. Jake stared at Bolt's picture one last time. He and the UNSUB could easily be the same person. Photographs always looked slightly different to the real thing.

Jake shut down his computer and headed to the garage where his old Lancer was kept. He fired it up. Enjoyed hearing the throaty engine echo through the empty parking bays. He got the old girl moving and swung past the front of the building where, to his relief, he saw that the press had gone. It was good to know that even they went home sometimes.

Jake turned the radio on but made sure it played music not news. He'd had enough news to last a lifetime. Alanis Morissette sang about God and love and what you might ask the Holy Father if you had just one question. She was one of Angie's favorites and it made him think of her, made him want to ring his wife-to-be and share the big news of the breakthrough with her. More than anything, it made him pledge to himself that from now on, there'd be no secrets between them. Not even if the President himself told him not to say anything.

He drove with the window down to catch some air. The Marines had made him hate desk life. He longed for real light, not nicotine-yellow artificial crap. He craved real air full of pine and grass, not the warmed sock stink that was piped from office to office. And openness. He yearned for plenty of space above him as well as out front, to the side and behind him.

There were only a few cars on the road and the drive went quickly. He parked outside his condo at Mar Vista, a stone's throw from Santa Monica airport and barely four miles from work. Maybe he'd persuade Angie to make a marital home down at Westchester, or if they found a little more money further west at Marina del Rey, with a view of the water and an old boat to take out on the weekends.

He slid up the window, killed the ignition and stepped out onto the empty sidewalk. It felt good to be the only one up and about. The road was so quiet he could hear his footsteps. The sky clear and black and endless. Stars sparkled like they'd been chipped from a diamond and sprinkled on black velvet.

He caught rose scent as he walked the borders to the front of his apartment block. A couple of lights burned in neighbors' homes. Some distant traffic hummed. A car door clacked behind him.

He turned.

The fucking press.

He couldn't believe it. A camera light blinded him.

'Hey, buddy, enough's enough.' Jake stepped forward. 'Please turn that thing off before I do it for you.'

The light bobbed. Grew brighter if anything.

Okay. He'd asked nicely. Now Jake was going to stuff that light where its beam wouldn't shine.

A sharp, hot pain erupted in his right thigh.

Then his stomach.

And his chest.

Jake dropped to his knees.

He knew what had happened. Knew it before he heard the sound. Before he smelled the acrid smoke from the automatic weapon. Before the light dipped and a voice said, 'Dead or alive, Mr Grunt? I choose *dead*.'

Another burst of gunfire tore holes in the silence of the night.

This time, there was no Kevlar to protect him. All Jake Mottram saw was blackness.

Chapter 98

Douglas Park, Santa Monica, LA

Angie woke with a fright.

She'd been in the deepest of sleeps. Floating in a black tank of restful, restorative peace.

Then came the noise.

A thump.

A bang.

Heavy hands hitting her door.

'Angie.'

The voice was muffled.

She looked at the red lights on the bedside clock.

03:05.

'Christ alive, I'm coming.' She was going to kill Jake for this. She'd asked him to give her tonight on her own to finish her work. No doubt he'd finished late himself, got drunk and decided to push his luck.

She clicked on a light and squinted in the painful glare as she padded barefoot across the boards.

Before slipping the chain, she widened a bleary eye and tried to focus through the spyhole.

Ruis?

Not Jake?

The SKU man was stood to one side of the hall, staring at his shoes.

Angie knew the look.

Her heart hammered as she fumbled the chain. Lumps filled her throat by the time she cracked it open.

Ruis's face spoke volumes.

Her legs turned to jelly.

'Jake's been shot.' He took her by the shoulders before she fell. Slowly backed her into the room. An SKU shortwave radio crackled on his hip. Her world was full of static.

'It's bad, Angie. Multiple wounds and they don't think he's gonna make it.'

'Oh my God.' Her eyes stung with tears.

Ruis held her. 'You need to get dressed and hurry – if you want to see him.'

She bit her lip. Chewed so hard she drew blood. It was something she hadn't done since childhood. Something she hadn't needed to do since she laid out the man who'd beaten her mother and abused her.

The blood in her mouth gave her strength. Physical pain always masked mental pain.

She rushed to the bedroom and stripped. 'He'll be all right,' she shouted to Ruis. 'Then I'm going to kick his ass for scaring me like this.' She pulled on grey track pants, a matching hoody and a pair of sneakers she'd meant to put in the washing machine.

In less than sixty seconds Angie had her keys and had banged the door shut behind her.

Chapter 99

'Hey!'

The shout stopped Shooter in his tracks.

'Where have you been?'

The question came from Januk, the big Polack supervisor. It seemed to those who worked for him that the only sentences he ever formed were questions.

Shooter was out on the parking lot. Walking away from the door of a work van that he'd just slapped shut. There was no point denying he'd used the vehicle. The keys were dangling from one hand, a sports bag from the other.

He was going to have to lie about the reason for breaking a basic company rule.

'I had an errand to run.'

'On company time? You think I pay you to run errands?'

'I'll work my break.'

'Why you do errands in a company vehicle, using company gas?'

Shooter dipped into his overalls and pulled out a scrunched up twenty. 'Look, I'll pay for it. It was an emergency.'

Januk slapped the money out of his hand. 'This emergency – did it have big tits and a wet pussy?'

'No.'

'What you take me for?' He walked up to Shooter's face. 'You think because you play the hero one day, you can play the cunt the next?'

Shooter wiped spittle from his cheek. 'No I don't. It was an emergency. My mother's alarm had gone off and she was frightened.' He got out his cellphone. 'You want me to call her, so she can tell you what happened?'

Januk stared at him. He could see the lie in his eyes. 'This once I forget what happened. Just this time.' He kicked the sports bag. Noticed his foot hit something heavy. 'What's in that?'

Shooter froze.

'Show me.'

That was something that couldn't happen. It contained the gun he'd shot the Fed with and the camera and recorder he'd filmed it on.

'It's personal.'

'Then don't bring to work.' He reached out to snatch the bag.

Shooter swung it away.

'Show me.'

Shooter stepped back and threw him the van keys. 'I quit.' He turned and walked.

'You quit, you don't get paid.'

He kept walking but slid the zipper back on the bag. Januk was crazy. If the big douchebag came rushing him he'd have to shoot the fuck. Part of him wanted it to happen. To see the look on his big moon face as he opened up on him.

'Wait!'

The voice was where he'd left it.

Shooter turned.

Januk scratched stubble on his cheek. 'I owe you one. Take your bag of secrets and get back to work. I can't afford to be a man down.'

Shooter nodded his compliance and Januk threw the keys back. The pitch was short and they fell in the dark. Steel glinted in a pool of security light on the blacktop. The young man bent and picked them up but not for one second did his eyes stray from his supervisor.

Januk watched him with disdain and then disappeared inside.

Shooter counted twenty before he followed. Without hesitation he went straight to his metal locker and stuffed the bag in there. It was a sports holdall but nothing like the one he'd used in the mall. He was a long way from being that stupid. He banged the dented and scratched door several times to make sure it was shut and then he walked away. There was half a shift left to work. That was a long time to stay away from Januk and all the dangers he represented.

Chapter 100

UCLA Medical Center, Santa Monica, LA

Angie sat on the floor near the surgery doors. Her back was to the wall and her hands pressed to the thin plasterboard that separated her from the man she loved. The only man she'd *ever* loved.

This was the closest they'd let her get to him.

Through her fingers she could feel the vibrations of the room. The hum of electricity, the friction of medics walking the polished floor. As distant as it was, she was still in touch.

Ruis stood bolt upright next to her. Sentry straight. As alert as any soldier. Ready for the enemy when it came. As he knew it would.

Six bullets.

Two bursts of three.

The first set low and debilitating, catching the legs and gut.

The second more tightly grouped. Focused. All on the left side of the torso.

Gut. Ribcage. Heart.

There was no way anyone survived injuries like that.

Angie had insisted on knowing.

The math was stacked against Jake. Any one of those wounds could prove fatal. A combination was undeniably lethal. It was a miracle he was still alive. All that height and mass had probably saved him. Given him a fighting chance.

Angie shut her eyes. She didn't believe in any particular God, but now she was willing to. She'd believe in one or a thousand if Jake could survive this.

Time moved with funereal slowness and Angie wondered how long he'd lain there outside his apartment before someone had found the courage to go to him. Ruis said a neighbor had heard the shots and called it in but had insisted they had not seen anything. No one ever saw anything these days.

Already she blamed herself.

If they hadn't rowed over that stupid press conference Jake would probably have stayed at her place. In which case, none of this would have happened.

The wall beneath Angie's fingers vibrated. Someone banged a cart against the other side of the plasterboard. She put her ear to the wall and heard muffled shouts. Clear, loud voices. Earnest, cold, resigned. Machines bleeped. Metal fell against metal. Steel instruments in steel bowls. And the worst sound of all – silence.

The hospital had wanted to put her and Ruis in a private room; they'd said it would be the best place for them to wait until there was news.

But there had been no restraining Angie.

She'd wanted to be right inside the theater. Gowned up. Holding Jake's hand. Helping him pull through.

Sitting by the doors had been the only compromise she'd accept. The gurney-battered doors and the noisy, draughty corridor was where she and Ruis had been brought almost an hour ago.

The first rays of a new Californian day rubbed hesitantly against a small window. The morning was still pencil-shade grey and the sun too weak to outshine the insipid blue of the overhead tubes in the hospital.

Angie stared up at the ugly, thin light boxes. They ran like stitches down the endless ceiling. The corridor where she sat, where she clung to hope, was one of the hospital's main arteries leading to the operating theater, the heart – the building's ultimate source of life and death. Suddenly the lights went out.

As she watched, the lights flickered, buzzed, then went out with a heavy clunk.

Angie jumped.

'Daylight timer,' explained Ruis. 'Everyone's trying to save a little energy these days.'

She spread her fingers to the plasterboard and searched again for the pulse of the theater.

A steady hum tingled in her palms.

That was good.

Then there was a thump. A loud bang.

The doors swung open.

A woman stepped out. She was in green surgery scrubs. Blond hair poked through a small, tight hat. A white mask hung loose around her red neck. Blue eyes looked icily across the corridor.

Angie's knees cracked as she stood.

Ruis took a sentry step closer.

'I'm very sorry . . .'

'No!' Angie felt the ground crack beneath her.

'. . . I'm afraid your friend has died.'

The word dropped like a stone. Its impact fractured whatever was being said.

'He suffered too much blood loss . . . too much damage to the internal organs . . . too much trauma . . . we did everything we could . . .'

Ruis took hold of Angie. Kept her upright as her legs trembled. The nurse was still speaking but her sentences seemed fragmented and unbelievable.

'. . . the injuries were not survivable . . . really nothing more we could have done . . . very sorry for your loss . . .'

Angie broke away from Ruis.

The theater door was still ajar.

She pulled it wide and rushed through.

This was all nonsense. If she could get to him it would be okay. She'd *make* it okay.

Startled faces turned her way. Medics were at the outer edges of the room, not in places where they were supposed to be. They were pulling off gloves. They thought their work was over.

Someone tried to stop her. Angie two-handed him in the chest and he staggered back and fell.

Voices were shouting around her.

Ruis was shouting back at them.

Angie got to Jake.

She reached his head. His beautiful dark hair. His wonderful mouth. She knew what to do. Kiss of life. CPR. That would fix it. That would open his eyes. Make him look at her. He'd cough a little. Gasp. Then his big chest would heave. His heart would beat. His smile would come.

He wasn't there.

As soon as she touched him she knew he'd gone.

His lips were lifeless.

Even his smell had gone.

They'd already rubbed his essence away.

She put her hands to his blood-smeared chest but didn't press. There was no point. He wasn't there. He'd run out on her. He was gone.

A scream escaped Angie's mouth.

It felt like it didn't belong to her.

It was so loud and shrill it couldn't be hers.

She knelt in Jake's blood and took his giant hand and put it to her lips. She rested her head against the cold steel of the gurney and closed her eyes.

Now neither of them was there. They were both far away. United. Together again.

Angie could hear the sea crashing, feel the sun on her face, the breeze in her hair.

There were people all around them. Friends, familiar faces. Jake had his hand in hers and was saying how beautiful she was in her dress, and she was thinking how handsome, how gorgeously handsome he looked, as he stood by her side in his wedding suit.

Chapter 101

O ne of the old-timers had gone home sick. It meant Shooter ended up busier than he'd expected to be. In many ways he was grateful. It kept him out of Januk's way and made the shift pass more quickly.

He worked an hour longer than he should and never said a word. He hoped it would keep that madfuck supervisor off his back.

The rising sun was already steaming the back lot where the vans had been hosed down. There was no TV in the canteen any more so he wasn't sure whether the Fed's death was already news or not. He suspected not. The place was so full of gossips someone would have mentioned it if it had been.

Shooter took a leak then washed his hands in one of the cracked sinks. As his hands dangled beneath a dryer he wondered whether the Fed had actually survived the shooting. It was unlikely but not impossible. He remembered how the big grunt had taken the first shots as though they were slaps from a girl. It had been quite something to empty three rounds into another human being and see him barely flinch. But all that bravado had disappeared when he'd served up another three portions of lead.

He couldn't wait to see the footage.

The art of life and death. That's what he'd call it after he'd edited it and set it to music. Maybe he'd post it on YouTube and see how many hits his hit got. *Hits*. The wordplay made him laugh.

He stood back from the sinks and checked himself out in the restroom mirror.

He looked different.

Changed.

There was a glow to him. A halo. An aura that set him apart.

He opened the door and headed to the lockers.

Januk was leaning against them. Waiting for him. A half-moon smile illuminated his grubby full-moon face. He lifted his hand from his overalls and shook a thick bunch of keys.

Keys to every door in the works. Including a master key for the lockers.

As Shooter approached, the supervisor swung open a metal door and pulled out the sports bag. 'I'm going to take this into my office and you're going to follow me. Then you tell me again about that personal errand you had to go on.'

Chapter 102

UCLA Medical Center, Santa Monica, LA

Ruis kept them away for as long as he could. But now it had gotten serious. Two security men and a surgeon were crowding him. There was nothing more he could do. He walked to the center of the operating theater where Angie was still kneeling, holding Jake's hand.

'We have to go.' He touched her shoulder reassuringly. 'They need to clean up, there's another case coming in.'

She heard him but it didn't make sense. There was no way she could let Jake's fingers slip from hers. If she kept hold he'd come alive. The miracle she'd hoped for would happen. She just had to keep believing. 'A little longer. Please.'

A senior nurse came to her side. 'We'll bring him to a room for you, honey. You can be there on your own with him for as long as you like.'

She looked at the unresponsive hand in hers. The hand that had put a ring on her finger. The hand she'd hoped to hold for another thirty or forty years.

She let go and stood up.

Blood had soaked into her track pants and the grey cotton stuck to the tiles and tried to pull her back down again. Someone in the corner indelicately fired up a spray hose and prepared to clean the floor.

'Switch it off!' shouted Ruis. His tone of voice would have made an armed robber drop a gun.

'It's okay.' Angie turned to the group of waiting medics. 'I'm sorry

315

to have held you up. Thanks –' she almost choked – 'for doing everything you could.'

Ruis walked her out into the corridor. She felt stiff and disorientated
as he sat her on a molded plastic chair. The big guy stepped away,
talked to a nurse, and then came back and took her hand before he
spoke. 'In a minute, they're going to move Jake to a private room and
they can leave him there with you for as long as you need before they
take him to the morgue.'

Morgue.

The word hit her like a fist.

Ruis squeezed her fingers. 'They'll come and find us when they're
ready for you to be with him.'

'But I won't, will I? I won't ever *be with him* again.'

'I think you'll *always* be with him, Angie. You only have to close
your eyes—'

'Don't!' She pulled her hand away. 'Don't you dare tell me how to
remember him.'

'I'm sorry.'

She hung her head. 'No, I'm the one who should apologize. I didn't
mean to snap.' She looked at the blood on her knees and rubbed a
palm over it. The contact made her wince. Her heart thumped so
hard her chest was sore. She took long, slow breaths. Never in her
life had she felt so hurt and helpless.

Time slid like a truck on an icy road. The silence before the crash.
The painful, slow-motion wait.

A nurse came and talked briefly to Ruis.

She drifted away and Ruis came back and crouched in front of
Angie. 'They're ready for you.'

The words didn't seem to make sense, but she let him guide her
down a soulless corridor. Disinfectant filled her nostrils. Muffled voices
bounced around her. The whole place was hot and stuffy. She felt
weak and dizzy. Needed air. Needed to lie down before she fell down.

Angie stopped and put a hand to the floor. The world tilted. Her
head smacked the hard tiles.

But it was Jake who picked her up, not Ruis.

They were together again. Their first Christmas filled her mind.

316

Sliding ice at the Rockefeller Center in New York. She was laughing her ass off. So was he, but even then there had been kindness and care in his eyes. They'd spent the night together in a little hotel off Broadway and had got giddy on champagne for breakfast. They'd shopped on Fifth Avenue like tourists. The Christmas tree at The Rock had been the biggest and most beautiful she'd ever seen.

Angie had been looking up at the lights, the twinkling angel pirouetting at the top, when a child fell in front of her and she went down in the pile-up.

Jake broke up laughing. He put down his big hand and she put hers in it and he pulled her back up as though she weighed no more than a feather. This man made her feel safe. He could protect her from anything. Or anyone.

She'd never thought of who'd protect him.

Now Jake was gone and it was Ruis's hand that was in hers as he sat her up against the wall. 'Are you okay?'

She stared glassy-eyed at him.

'Angie, are you okay? You fainted.'

She nodded. He was there because Jake was dead. It came back to her. She was on her way to see his bullet-riddled corpse. In a private room before they took it to the morgue.

'Yeah, I'm okay.'

Ruis brought her a plastic cup of water. It went down in a single swallow. Her body was on fire.

The baby.

Their child.

She thought of the trauma, the shock, her racing heart. She worried that all of this nightmare might affect the baby.

Her inner voice told her she had to be strong for the child. She couldn't fold. Couldn't collapse and cry her heart out like she wanted to.

Angie took Ruis's hand and let him haul her to her feet.

'Take it slow,' he urged.

She had no option. Her body had only one speed now. Everything was numb. She couldn't feel the floor beneath her feet. Signs flashed over her head. People streamed by. They were aliens from another

317

world, babbling incoherently and inconsequentially. Nothing mattered any more.

Ruis tightened his grip on her.

She felt like a prisoner being led to a cell. A terrible punishment awaited.

A life sentence. One without remission.

Chapter 103

'**O**ffice' was the wrong word to describe the unventilated hole that Januk sank out of view into. It was occupied by a tiny desk with room for only one chair, a lockable metal cabinet and a square filing cabinet that was topped with old newspapers and a soccer ball signed by some obscure Polish team.

The supervisor dropped the bag on the table and unzipped it.

Shooter stared into the gap. He could see the contents had already been taken out and put back in a different way.

Januk tipped them onto the table.

Shooter stepped back and pressed his heel against the door to click it all the way shut.

Januk laughed. 'You think people come in here without me asking them to?' He picked up the MAC-10 and shouted, 'RAT-A-TAT-TAT!' Then he laughed so hard he looked like he might wet himself.

He put the weapon down and picked up the digital recorder and the compact HD video camera with mounted light. 'So what did you do? Use the gun to rob this equipment from a store?'

Shooter let out a long sigh. Long enough to give the impression that he was ready to come clean and tell the dumb fuck the truth. 'You were right in the first place.'

Januk frowned. Then he remembered what he'd said. 'Pussy?'

Shooter picked up the recording equipment and put it back in the bag. 'Porn. I was shooting porn.' He lifted the MAC. '*Pussy with Pistols.*' He checked the mag and slammed it back. 'Gangsta gals. Baaaaad-ass girls. Shooty-booty.'

'Show me.' Januk grabbed the bag again. He turned to the cabinet behind him and pulled open a drawer. 'I have vodka and I have finished my shift too. We can watch together.'

Shooter cradled the MAC. He was fairly sure no one else was in this part of the building. One spray with the baby in his hands and jabbering Januk would shut the fuck up.

The Super produced the vodka and another of his moonbeam smiles.

Shooter raised the gun and aimed it at his head.

'RAT-A-TAT-TAT!' shouted Januk again, then fell about laughing as though it were the funniest joke ever.

It took Shooter all his self-control not to squeeze the trigger. He slipped the weapon into the bag and smiled. 'I can do better than show you porn. I have three girls coming round to where I live, to film the last scenes of my movie. Give me a lift home and I'll let you watch – *maybe* even join in. I'll make sure it's the biggest *blast* you've ever had.'

Chapter 104

UCLA Medical Center, Santa Monica, LA

The world became muted.

The moment Angie's eyes fell on Jake's lifeless face, the soundtrack to their lives stopped.

With the silence and Jake's permeating stillness came a terrible pain.

Every second of looking at the corpse of the man she loved was unbearable torture. To never touch him after today. To never kiss and stroke and love him. To never hear his laughter or be moved by his kindness – it was pain more brutal than any knife or hammer could inflict.

Angie tried not to weep. Told herself she had to become calm and strong for the sake of the life growing inside her – and because that's how the extinguished life in front of her would have wanted it. Jake had made her stronger. Every second she'd spent with him had fortified her, seen her grow and blossom.

Now he was gone.

Officially gone.

The sheet tucked neatly around him to hide the bullet wounds. The wiped clean face. The drawn curtains in the room. The box of tissues left close, in case she broke. All signs that told her it was over.

She swallowed the baseball-sized lump in her throat and looked to Ruis. 'Who could have done this?' She almost broke. 'The mall killer?'

He was struggling too. With his own grief and with the pain he could see in Angie's eyes. 'Maybe. Whoever it was, we'll find him, I promise you that.'

'Make sure you do.'

A tear dripped off her face as she bent over the cold body. 'I love you, baby. Love you so much more than you ever knew. I'm so sorry that we fought – so sorry that I didn't tell you to come home last night.'

Ruis used a knuckle to wipe away his own tears. Watching Angie was ripping him apart.

She pulled herself upright. Bit down on the agony and wiped her eyes with trembling fingers.

'I'm done, Ruis.' She struggled to speak. 'There's nothing here for me now but hurt. Take me home?'

'Of course.' He put out an arm.

Angie saw the wetness on his cheeks. 'You okay?'

He gave a reflex smile, in the hope it'd dam his own tears. 'No, not really. Jake and I were tight, you know.'

'Yeah, I know you were.' She took his hand and held it all the way to the Jeep he'd taken from the motor pool.

In the passenger seat, she pressed her boiling head against the cold glass of the passenger window and let the early morning light smear against her face.

She pictured Jake with his eyes open. His full of life, bright as the sky, sexy-as-fuck eyes. Those pools of blue had developed a thousand ways of looking at her. Ways that said he had something funny to say, that he was excited because he had a present for her, that he wanted to share something small, something childish and wonderfully silly. Ways that said he needed her help to decide something big and brave, or that he wanted to shut out the whole mad screaming world and undress her.

And most recently, ways that said he loved her. Wanted to spend eternity with her. Was ready to help her raise their child.

Angie knew all of those ways. And already she missed them.

In the cruel world outside her muted grief, Ruis talked in a sad, hushed tone, traffic honked rudely and the radio played inanely, a distraction from silence that weighed more than a battleship.

The car stopped, the brake went on, the engine died and doors opened. Angie's feet and body moved, air shifted and her aching heart thundered again. Ruis guided her through the communal entrance, up the stairs and into her apartment.

She stood looking at him in the doorway. He hadn't moved from where he'd been just a few hours ago when he'd brought the news that wrecked her life. She couldn't believe it had happened. One knock on the door. One word. It had changed everything.

'Angie?'

She looked at him. His face said he was waiting for an answer to a question she'd missed. 'Sorry?'

'It's all right. I just asked, would you like me to come in and stay with you a while?'

She thought about it. 'No, thanks. I think I just need to be on my own and fall apart a bit. You know – let it all out.'

'I understand.' He hugged her and then held out a brown bag.

She hadn't noticed it until now. 'What's this?'

'Jake's wallet, some cash, keys and stuff.'

She took the bag and unwrapped the top.

His smell hit her and she let out a small cry.

It was on the wallet. On his keys. His writstwatch. It was as powerful as if he was next to her.

She rolled the top of the bag closed, tried to put the memory genie back in its bottle.

Ruis saw fresh tears in her eyes. 'I can come in, Angie.'

'No.' She sniffed. 'I've got to face this. I might as well start now.' She deflected the attention. 'What's being done to find who killed him?'

'Don't worry about that. They're doing everything and more.'

The answer didn't satisfy her. 'Tell me *everything*. Who's heading the inquiry? Who's in charge? When will they want to speak to me?'

'Angie—'

'What can I do to help, Ruis?'

He guided her deep into the apartment and towards a sofa. 'It's all in hand. You don't need to think about that kinda shit. Just rest and . . .' he stopped himself saying 'take it easy'.

'*Shit?* It's not *shit*. For now it's the most important thing there is. Maybe helping catch this motherfucker is the only thing I *can* do at the moment.' She put the bag down, grabbed a tissue from box and blew hard. She had to think straight. Get her act together. 'Thanks, Ruis – for coming over, for being there and helping me at the hospital. It was good of you to go through that with me.' She pushed him towards the door. 'I need to shower now and get outta this crappy tracksuit.'

He could see a change in her, a sudden resolve, like a kneejerk reaction, and it worried him. 'I'm not very happy about leaving you.'

'Don't stress. I'm all right.' She backed him into the corridor. 'I need space. I just have to get myself together in my own particular way.'

'Okay, but you call me when you want.' He took a step away. 'I'll look after the other stuff.'

Other stuff.

The words almost knocked her over. She was a long way from even being able to think about *'the other stuff'*.

Chapter 105

Januk's vehicle was an old station wagon that was rusted from roof to wheel rims. Keyed down one side, it was badly dented on the other and the windshield was peppered with stone cracks.

Shooter sat uncomfortably on the torn front passenger seat and plucked biscuit-colored foam from busted seams. The all-incriminating sports bag was between his feet. He'd made the mistake of glancing into the back. Fast food trays glistened with fat and stank of cheap spices. The floor mats were covered in hand-crushed beer and soda cans. Balled tissues lay everywhere and looked grey and hard from wiping God knows what.

'You fuck hookers sometime?' Januk asked casually in disjointed English as he drove one-handed.'I know where there's cheap European pussy. Maybe they do your movie for free?' His moon shone.'I take you to see them. Introduce my new friend, *the movie director.*' He laughed. 'Maybe they blow me for free just to be in your film. What you think?'

'I think for now, we have all the girls we need.'

The Pole wasn't giving up that easily. 'I like you to meet them anyway. They work an apartment block together not far from here. We drive by just for you to say hello.'

Shooter knew he had to take control. 'Afterward, not now!' He twisted in the seat so Januk could see how determined he was.'Filming porn takes a lot of setting up, man. I haven't got the time to screw around meeting your wannabes. Now we do this my way, or you drop me right here and forget being involved.'

The supervisor didn't look fazed. 'Okay, Mr Director, we fuck your pussy first. This is no problem.' He turned his radio up and picked his nose with a thumb and forefinger. Anything he got he either rubbed on his overalls or put in his mouth.

Shooter looked away and watched the pale new day slide by the side window. He directed the slob of a driver down a twist of backstreets and made him park a good block from his sanctuary.

'Where your place?' Januk locked the wheeled dumpster and stared curiously at the industrial buildings around him. 'I don't see no movie set. No Hollywood.' He coughed up phlegm and spat it hard by his feet.

'We need to walk a bit.'

'I don't like walk. God made cars so I don't need to walk.'

Shooter ignored him and strode on ahead. His mind was focused on how to get rid of the pain in the ass. He was big and strong, which meant the simplest and least risky thing would be to sit him down and shoot him in the back of the head.

It would be messy though.

Blood and bone flew further than he'd imagined. He'd learned that from the mall. The MAC was certainly too powerful. It'd kill Januk no problem but tear a hole in a wall as well. He'd probably have to use a handgun and try to shoot downward. Even then, there was a chance of ripping up part of the floor.

'How much further we go?'

'Couple of minutes, that's all.'

'Minutes?' he moaned. 'Why couldn't we drive nearer? Why we have to walk this far?'

'Nowhere to park, you'd get your vehicle towed. I'm doing this for you, so be grateful.'

Januk fell quiet and wheezed for the rest of the way.

Shooter halted at the chain link and produced a key for the padlocks. The sooner he got the guy inside and whacked him the better. If he'd had to walk another block he was sure he would have killed him in full public view.

Januk stared at the old factory. 'I know this place. They used to make shoes here. I bought boots very cheap once.'

Shooter swung the gate open and let his boss through. 'I just rented it. I told the authorities I was renovating, but I'm not. I only use it to shoot pornos.' He shut the gates and the padlocks.

Januk shrugged. 'You close everything? You stupid? How will your girls get in?'

He took out his cellphone and waggled it. 'They'll call me and I'll come and open up.' He swiped a finger over the screen, accessed a security app and keyed in an alphanumerical sequence to deactivate the booby-traps.

Januk looked up at the CCTV cameras on the flat roof and waved. 'I like cameras and films. One day I buy a 3D television and watch porno on that.' He stretched out his hands and twisted them mid-air. 'You can feel the tits through the tube, yes?'

He was still laughing and groping imaginary breasts when Shooter punched in a further set of numbers on an old security door and pulled it open. He flicked on an internal light and they both stepped inside.

'I need shit,' announced the unwelcome guest. 'I shit same time every morning. Habits are good for you. Where's your place to shit?'

Shooter led him to the old toilet block and pushed open a door. 'Make yourself at home.'

Januk playfully slapped his face on the way past. 'Then I get fucked, yes?'

Shooter smiled. 'Oh yeah, you're definitely going to get fucked.'

Chapter 106

Douglas Park, Santa Monica, LA

Angie's head was the most messed up it had ever been. Only thing she knew for sure was that she wasn't going to wear black.

No freaking way.

Jake was still alive. At least in her head and that was how she was determined to keep him. Upright Jake. Bright-eyed, warm-handed Jake. Not the cold-limbed, sheet-wrapped and shot-to-death Jake they'd tried to palm her off with at the hospital.

That was their bogus Jake.

Fake Jake.

And Angie had no time for him.

Her real Jake needed her now. Needed her brain, her drive and her determination to find the triggerman – that cowardly waste of skin and bone who'd cut him down.

And she would. She knew she would because she was angry. And she and Anger were old friends. They went way back to the early days of her childhood when her world was full of all kinds of serious shit and shitters. When the going got tough, Anger had always been there to give Angie a brutal edge and help her fight her corner.

She opened the closet and decided on hard business cottons. Dark navy jeans, a plain grey top and a long, loose grey cardigan that would cover the gun she planned to belt to her hip. The bottom of the closet offered a store's worth of shoes. She went for sneakers rather than her favorite Prada pumps – comfort and speed rather than style and grace.

Once she'd tied her hair back and found shades to cover her blood-shot eyes, she and Anger were ready to kick ass.

Chapter 107

The toilet flushed. There was silence and then it flushed again. A tap ran and Januk hollered from the washroom, 'I think I block your john!'

Shooter was waiting outside, sickened by the laughter in his boss's voice.

He'd removed the bulb in the short corridor. Changed into old overalls. Now he lay in the dark.

'It is the meatloaf from work that I have left you as a present,' shouted Januk as he came out. The door banged shut on its spring and he added, 'Hey, there are no lights here. Where the fuck do I go?'

Shooter stayed quiet. He heard the dumb Polack's hands slap against the wall so he could feel his way along the corridor.

'I can't fucking see.' Januk bumped a wall and swore in Polish. 'Kurwa!'

Shooter could smell him now. The stink of his body. Salt. Sweat. Stale semen.

Soon there'd be blood.

'Where the f—'

'I'm here,' he said calmly. 'Stay still, I'll guide you along.' He put a reassuring hand on his boss's shoulder, got his body bearings, then jammed a five-inch hunting knife into Januk's gut.

Clothing blunted it. Held up its deadly passage. Prevented it going in as far as he'd expected.

Shooter leaned forward and pushed harder.

Januk gasped out air. 'Hooh.'

Harder.

'Hooooh-hooooh.' He sounded like a steam train starting up.

Shooter felt the steel nick a rib. His hand punched Januk's belly. The blade was all the way in now.

'Hoooooooh-hoooooooh.' He doubled up. Grabbed at clumps of darkness.

A desperate hand caught Shooter's wrist.

Despite being wounded, the big man had a grip like a vice.

Shooter could feel him forcing the knife out.

The effort started the train noises again. 'Hoo-hoo, hoo-hoo.'

Januk dug deep. His survival instinct kicked in. He snaked a second hand onto the knife arm. Forced the blade down. And out.

Shooter stumbled backward. Hit a wall. Felt pain slap the back of his skull.

Januk went woozy from the exit slash and sudden rush of blood. He lurched and staggered. His desperate hands clawed the dark. Found his attacker's face. Fat fingers searched for a grip. An eye to gouge. A mouth to force his hand into, so he could break the jaw like a clamshell.

Januk found a pillar of flesh.

A neck to break.

A throat to choke.

Shooter stabbed upwards in the dark. Hit unseen meat. Once. Twice. Blood spurted over his hand. The knife twisted in his wet fingers. Fell away. Clattered into the darkness.

Januk's fingers tightened around his attacker's neck.

Shooter's legs went. His windpipe was shut by iron thumbs.

The supervisor came down on top of him. Grimy hands kept their choke hold. He was unable to breathe and was blacking out.

The fingers suddenly slackened. The heavy body on top of him went limp. The big moon of a head dropped from the black sky and hit him in the bridge of his nose.

Januk twitched and spasmed.

A last huff of foul air escaped.

Shooter felt blood seep from Januk's corpse.

He pushed the dead weight off him. Rolled it onto the floor. Lay panting as fear filled his crushed lungs.

He stayed on his side for what seemed an eternity.
Finally, he laughed. Laughed hysterically.
It had been a messy start to the day.
But Shooter knew it was about to get even messier.

Chapter 108

FBI Field Office, LA

Angie drove to work. She knew it was crazy. Knew the expected thing was to stay at home and be consumed by grief. But she wasn't going to do that. Not yet. Not until she'd done all she could to help catch Jake's killer.

She traveled with the radio off. News of Jake's death was bound to be on the bulletins and she didn't want to hear it.

The route she took down Wilshire was one she'd done a zillion times but today it felt like unknown territory. She was on edge. Apprehensive. Thrown by where and when she had to turn. Her internal compass was totally screwed.

Life had fundamentally and irrevocably changed.

But only hers.

Everyone else seemed to be ploughing their usual furrows. Deliciously stuck in comfortable ruts. She looked across the traffic and saw a woman in a business suit putting on make-up behind the wheel of a Lexus. A tired mom in a Ford was half-turned, trying to soothe a crying child in a baby seat. Two young girls in a Fiat were flirting outrageously with stubble-bearded guys in an open-topped Merc level with them.

If only they all knew how lucky they were. How special their status quo lives were. How priceless it was for life to stand still.

The parking garage at work seemed bigger and emptier. The elevator ride slower and more claustrophobic. Her office felt like it already belonged to someone else.

Angie made coffee and turned on the computer. Chips had left her a note. 'WILL BE IN EARLY. LOTS TO TELL YOU! X'

She had lots to tell him too.

Reassuringly, the coffee turned out to be as bad as it had always been. She put it down and thought about Jake's killer. Instinctively, she was sure it was the UNSUB behind the mall atrocities. But experience had taught her that she could be wrong. It could just as feasibly be a publicity-seeking crackpot, a seriously deranged psychotic, or maybe someone seeking revenge for an arrest Jake made years ago.

Angie pulled paper out of a printer tray and grabbed a pen. She knew she was physically and mentally wasted, so making a list of the simple stuff was a way to make sure she didn't miss anything.

Jake's death was a homicide, so the LAPD would be involved as well as agents from the FBI – the Bureau wouldn't rest until justice was done.

She stayed focused, began to write slowly and carefully.

1. WHO'S WHO – LIST OF CONTACT NUMBERS FOR CASE INVESTIGATORS.

Angie knew that the CSIs would already be at his apartment and have the dope on the weapon used.

2. CSI REPORTS.

She'd want copies of their findings and any other cross-refs they'd made.

3. BALLISTICS.

4. TRACE.

Angie wrote the words in capitals because she couldn't form joined-up writing with her left hand. It slowed her down and the clock was ticking. Soon people would be coming in. They'd be all over her, telling her to go home, back off, stay out.

5. THE SCENE.

She would have to go to the apartment block, see where Jake fell, look at where the triggerman had stood.

6. PRE-MEDITATION?

Had the UNSUB already been there, lying in wait for Jake to return? How did he even know where Jake lived?

7. FOLLOWED?

She ran her pen underneath the letters. Jake's phone number was unlisted and his address tough to unearth at short notice. He must have been tracked from work. CCTV cameras on the FBI building might have caught the UNSUB or his vehicle.

8. SECRETS.

Angie hesitated. She tapped the pen on the desk like a child with a drumstick. She knew Jake better than anyone, but her experience as a profiler – and a woman – said there were still going to be secrets, things and people she had been unaware of. Investigators would need access to his computer, phone records, diaries, notebooks, desk drawers. And if she was going to help catch his killer, she needed all that data as well. She wrote down:

9. MEETINGS, MOVEMENTS, CONTACTS.

Again she hesitated. Another two beats with the drum pen.

Lovers?

She couldn't write it down.

Was she really the only one?

This doubt had sharp and twisted roots and they burrowed painfully through her aching brain. They'd had their rows, their weekends and nights apart, their mini-break-ups. He was so good looking, charming, decent and downright fuckable – did she really think she was the only woman in his life?

She did.

She absolutely did. With all of her soul and all of her heart she knew that was how it had been.

But before her, there most certainly had been others. Numerous others. Too many to list on her single sheet of paper. Maybe there was someone who still carried a torch for him. A lunatic woman with an even more lunatic boyfriend or husband who'd snapped when they'd seen Jake on TV.

Angie wrote it down:

10. EX-LOVERS & THEIR PARTNERS.

Undoubtedly, the press conference had been the stressor. She'd need to carry out a detailed examination of all those stupid words that stupid Danielle Goodman had put in his beautiful mouth.

11. MEDIA CONFERENCE TRANSCRIPT.

She drained her coffee, held up the beaker and dripped out the last bitter dregs.

12. THE HYBRID?

Had the UNSUB killed Jake?

Only someone with the cold audacity to bomb mourners would have the boldness and badness to take the life of someone as good as Jake.

But there was no shortage of other bad people to suspect and no stone could be left unturned. Jake's life inside and outside the Marines had seen him make powerful enemies – military-trained criminals capable of anything from rape, abduction, arson, bombing and homicide. The more she thought about it, the more she had to consider the possibility of an ex-soldier settling an old grudge. It certainly fitted with an MO that included surveillance, tracking, ambush and execution. Maybe the bungled shots were deliberate. Misfires to make investigators believe a pro hadn't been involved.

The door opened slowly.

Angie looked up from her list.

Chips stood there.

There was no T with a smartass slogan today, just a plain white shirt over black trousers. He looked like an intern. An intern who'd been crying.

'Angie?'

His voice was slow with pain. It was obvious he'd been told the news.

'What are you doing here?'

'I'm working.' She filled up. 'And boy, could I do with some help.'

He stepped close and embraced her. 'You've got it. All the help you need.'

Chapter 109

Shooter replaced the bulb in the corridor.

The bright light made him squint and showed the mess to be more terrible than he'd expected.

The walls were covered in spatter. Smears and scuffmarks on the plaster showed where they had struggled. Body meat dripped from the ceiling.

Before he did anything else, he got his video camera and filmed the dead man. He took wide shots and low shots. But most of all he took close-ups. Later he'd add filters and effects. Saturate the color. Make it look like it had been shot on grainy 8mm film.

The corridor stank. It was rank with the smell of their fight. The sweat. The fear. And now the post-mortem blood and gases.

Januk's body looked like a beached whale. The guy was massive. And he had to be moved.

Shooter cursed himself for not having thought more about this aspect. He'd never had to dispose of a corpse before. He'd always walked away after the kill and left the mess to others.

Now it was his problem.

It was clear that he couldn't conceal a six-foot-four-inch, three-hundred-pound male on the premises. Nor could he carry – or even drag – it any meaningful distance.

He'd have to either use Januk's vehicle. Or one from work.

Shooter put his hands around the dead man's ankles and pulled. He moved an inch. Maybe two. That was all he could shift him.

Shooter let go. The heavy leg hit the floor with a thump. He studied the cooling cadaver.

There was only one thing he could do.

And he was completely unprepared for it.

Dismemberment.

Chapter 110

They came for her as a group. As Angie knew they would. Mob-handed. A band of do-gooders, intent on shooing her out of the building and keeping her away from what she did best.

Did better than any of them.

'No one knows Jake –' she corrected herself –'*knew* Jake better than me.'The past tense stung but she didn't stumble.'No one understands Serials like I do and no one can work this case as well as me.'

She was sat on the edge of her desk, Chips stood protectively at her side. Opposite them were Sandra McDonald, Ruis Costas and their surprise recruit, Suzie Janner.

The assistant director called the shots.'Angie, you know you're too emotionally connected to this. You shouldn't even be here today let alone be thinking about working.'

She felt her fingers curl around the end of the desk, almost as though she were ready to physically resist them.'I should. And I think if any one of you had lost someone like I've just done, then you'd be at your desks too.'

Suzie Janner took her turn to try to make her see sense. 'Honey, there are a lot of good people already working this case; colleagues of Jake's who are fired up and getting things going. You can trust them to do a good job.'

'You can't go breathing down people's necks,' added Ruis.'You might slow things down, force them to make mistakes.'

'I'll stay in this room.' Her knuckles whitened. 'Just give me the data I need. I'll run everything through you.'

'This isn't negotiable, Angie.' McDonald's voice was firm but sympathetic. 'I want you to take compassionate leave, starting right now. Please save whatever files you have been working on, turn off your computer and go home.'

'Let me stay until the end of the day.'

'That's not going to happen. We have to think about the integrity of the inquiry and we have a duty of care towards you, too. Doctor Janner and I have discussed this and we're both of the mind that it's best if you're not here.'

Angie looked lost.

Chips put a hand reassuringly on her arm. 'Let me sort out your computer while you get together whatever you have to.'

She nodded.

'I'll drive you home,' offered Suzie Janner.

'No need. I drove myself in. I can drive myself out.'

'Then I'll come back with you and we can chat.'

Angie was too annoyed to argue. She pulled a carrier bag out of a bottom drawer of her desk.

'Not files, I hope?' said McDonald.

'Personal books and photographs,' Angie lied. She held out the bag. 'You want to check?'

'No need.' Her boss fixed her with a steely gaze. 'I'm hoping I can trust you, so don't let me down.'

Chips clacked away at her keyboard. The monitor fizzed to black and he stepped away. 'All done.'

Angie grabbed her cardigan from around the back of the desk chair.

Chips hugged her warmly, tried to squeeze some strength into her. 'I'll call you later.'

Ruis opened the door. 'You need me for anything, I'm right here for you.'

'Thanks.'

The mob walked her out of the room. Janner and McDonald lagged behind, talking in hushed voices that Angie could still hear. They were discussing her mental state. The strain on the baby. Whether she really would stay out of the case. All good questions. Ones she'd been asking herself.

Angie thought about the copy of her checklist that she'd given to Chips. He'd already been around to SKU and emptied Jake's office drawers; the contents were in her carrier bag. Copies had been made of his computer files, and later Chips would mail them from his private PC to her private Mac.

The mob turned the corner with her and waited by the elevators. There was a ding and a car opened.

Danielle Goodman stepped out.

She froze.

Angie saw horror fill the woman's eyes. *She knew.* That waste of space knew exactly what her stupidity had resulted in.

'You're one lucky bitch.' Anger took over. Pulled Angie's arm back. Delivered a hard sharp punch to Danielle's nose.

Blood bubbled from Danielle's nostrils and she cried in horror.

Angie shook the tingle out of her knuckles. 'Don't be around when my good arm's fixed, I might really hurt you.'

She walked into the lift and turned around. The last thing she saw before the doors closed was Goodman kneeling on the floor, blood pouring like spilled tomato soup down the front of her ridiculous white dress.

Chapter 111

He stood and looked at the body for what seemed an eternity. The printed paper in one hand was of the human skeleton – a guide to where to cut. In the other hung the tools for the job – hammer, chisel, saw, knife.

But Shooter couldn't do it.

He could kill with a pistol, with a rifle, even with his hands. But he couldn't dismember another human being. A few feet away stood buckets, water, sponges and cloths. Everything to clean up the mess that would inevitably be made.

But he couldn't do it.

Mutilating a dead body was crossing a line he'd never even considered going anywhere near.

But Januk was problematically big.

Severing his head wouldn't be enough.

Even taking off his legs would leave a mass too heavy to lift and easily conceal.

Shooter looked again at the anatomical drawings he'd printed.

There would have to be five cuts. Neck. Both legs. Both arms.

He slumped to his knees and began.

Chapter 112

Douglas Park, Santa Monica, LA

Angie drove in a daze. The emotions of the day had tired her out and the incident with Danielle Goodman was a warning sign that she couldn't take much more. She didn't normally give in to anger like that. Not since her troubled teens had she lashed out when the pressure had got too much.

She parked and waited at the curb outside her apartment block for Suzie Janner.

The medic arrived about fifteen minutes later.

'How is Danielle?' Angie asked as they walked together to her front door.

'She'll live. I've sent her for an X-ray. I'm fairly sure you broke her nose.'

Angie said nothing. She wasn't going to fake remorse or apologize when she didn't really mean it. She opened up her front door and ushered her friend into the two-bedroom rental.

'I should just warn you,' added Suzie, 'she was talking law suits when I left her.'

'Funny you should say that. I'm thinking of actioning her – for professional negligence resulting in murder. I reckon there's no end of attorneys who'd like to handle that case and go for punitive damages.'

Suzie looked shocked. This was so unlike the smart, cultured psychologist that she was used to.

'Listen,' protested Angie, 'I get that she didn't kill Jake, but what she made him say resulted in him being killed. The least she deserves is a broken nose.' She headed to the kitchen. 'You drink tea not coffee, right?'

'Black with no sugar, please.' Suzie settled at a dining table adjacent to the kitchen area and two soft cotton sofas. They'd been arranged for a couple to sit close. There were matching cushions and stacked car and house magazines, two books on two small side tables and a thin, neat flatscreen hung on the wall like a picture frame.

Angie set water boiling and looked for clean crockery in the dishwasher.

Jake's Dodgers mug gleamed at her.

It was only one among many cups, plates and glasses, but it was all she could see.

His lucky mug.

On game days he'd insist on all his drinks being made in it.

She snagged two plain beakers from a top rack and filled one with instant coffee and the other with tea.

'There are so many reminders of him lying around.' She placed the drinks on coasters on the table. 'Part of me wishes they weren't here. Some of me wishes there were more.'

'That's understandable. Balance will come.'

'I know. I'm mentally mapping myself through the grief process – first there's shock, then anger, then sadness and finally a fresh view of the world. I know the route.'

Suzie picked up her tea. 'Judging from the punch you threw, I'd say you were stalled at stage two anger.'

'Yeah, and I'm probably going to stay there until I find Jake's killer and fix him a nice cell on Death Row.'

The tea was too hot and Suzie put it back down. 'This is where I remind you that your boss sent you home so you wouldn't work the case.' The tone indicated she knew that wasn't likely.

'Reminder duly noted.'

'Seriously, though, your head is going to be everywhere for the next few days. Grief fills you with doubt. It makes you question everything you believe in. You'll sleep badly, dream horribly, maybe even hallucinate. Have you got anyone who can come and stay with you for a few days?'

'I'm not big on girlfriends. I'll do just fine on my own.' She picked up her coffee but like her friend's tea it was too hot. 'Suzie, I really appreciate you coming over, but honestly, I don't need my hand holding through this. Please don't go mentioning grief counselors you can recommend or homeopathic anti-depressants you think I should take.'

Suzie laughed. 'I won't. But if you need some help making arrangements or you just want to chat, then let me know.'

'That's kind of you.'

'Not at all. How are you feeling about the baby?'

'Mainly good. I think Jake and I had found a way through things.' She struggled for a moment. An involuntary image hit her – an imaginary one of Jake at her bedside, holding the baby just after birth. She tried to block it out. She knew she had to throw Suzie off track, otherwise she'd go probing her emotional state and that would be more than she could take. 'The fight I got into, not the one with Danielle –' she raised her still bandaged elbow – 'the one with the rapist, it scared me.'

'That's understandable.'

'I know, but I was scared for the baby not me. Even after I was checked out and told everything was okay, I still felt worried.'

'Maternal instinct.'

'You think?'

'I know. Being at home for the moment is better for both you and baby. Your condition is the child's condition. When you're strung out or in danger, so is the fetus.'

'I get the message.'

'Good, but don't go underestimating the ordeal you're going through. Bereavement and a first birth aren't supposed to happen together. Carrying a new life does strange things to you physiologically. Losing someone you love does odd things to you mentally.'

'I know.'

'I know you know. As a psychologist you must realize both carry risks of depression; they pressure your identity and personality and they can leave you imagining things, hallucinating and feeling desperate.'

Angie grabbed her coffee for comfort. It was cool enough to sip.

Talking about the baby and her need to care for it had momentarily distracted her from the agony of losing Jake. But now the grief was back. Welling up like a sickness in her stomach. 'I don't mean to be rude, but I'd really like to be alone.'

Suzie ignored the hint to leave. 'You're in shock and your anger is making you internalize. Don't lock people out and bottle things up. It's not healthy, you know that. You're going to create problems for yourself.'

Angie stood up. 'Thanks. I'll take the advice but right now I need to crash and get some rest.'

Suzie let out a sigh and gathered her stuff. 'Okay. But I'm going to call you and pester you. And you ring me night or day.'

'I promise.' She walked to the front door and opened up. 'Thanks for coming by.'

'You know you're welcome. I'm a friend, and I'm only trying to look after you.'

Angie nodded.

Suzie took one last shot at making her see sense. 'Think on this – you're in your first trimester. Your baby is growing fast. Little fingers and toes are forming. Eyelids are almost fully developed. Nerve cells in the brain are branching out and connecting. Lungs are shaping and developing. The miracle of life is in full flow. Please don't let Jake's death distract and damage you. Focus on the new, on the future, not the poison of the past.'

'I will.'

They briefly hugged and Suzie left.

Angie closed the apartment door and felt the last of her energy go. She was empty. Depleted. Beaten.

Tears started to flow and she tried to fight them. She told herself she was *not* going to fall apart. She needed to be strong.

But the tears still came.

She took a long, slow breath and shut her eyes.

Anger was building. Unstoppable rage. Coming to the boil beneath the salted tears.

Angie opened her eyes and smashed her left fist into the door. She hit it once, twice, three times. Not until she saw blood and split skin did she stop what she was doing. Not until her heart and body hurt as much physically as they did emotionally did she let her hand hang by her side.

Then she wept. No holding back. No slow seeping tears. She cried her heart out and slid down the door. Curled up on the floor like she'd done as a child. Made sure no more hurt could get in.

Chapter 113

The dismemberment took Shooter most of the day. If he hadn't vomited and lost his nerve several times he'd have finished much earlier. But the emotional trauma stopped him repeatedly.

Five cuts. Six pieces. It had sounded so easy. Now, with the torso hacked into bloody chunks there was one final problem.

Where to get rid of the pieces.

A plan was forming in his troubled mind, but for it to succeed, he needed to work carefully. Make sure there were no mistakes. No more unexpected setbacks – like the dismemberment.

Shooter washed each ragged limb under a shower hose, bagged it, bound it with tape, put it in a second bag and taped it again. He rammed stacks of newspapers into the open wounds and holes of the torso and bound the great hunks of meat in multiple garbage bags.

When he was finished, he was confident he could handle all the pieces without telltale splits or leakage. His intention was to load Januk's station wagon with the body parts and drive to a dump. Puente Hills, America's biggest landfill, lay less than twenty miles and under half an hour away. If he could get over there under cover of darkness then he had around a thousand acres of waste to hide the limbs in. He'd read that the site was so full they'd stopped taking new garbage for a while, maybe forever, but there were still dozers there and staff burying and shaping millions of tons of waste into something that one day may not be so much of an eyesore.

The way Shooter figured things, he'd go into work as normal. There'd be chaos when everyone realized the supervisor wasn't around. It would take senior management at headquarters hours to find out Januk had gone AWOL. He would call them and offer to keep an eye on things until they got a new face over to run the show. Around midnight, he'd take one of the work vans and come back to the Polack's station wagon. He'd drive home, load it with the big fat Januk jigsaw and take the Pomona freeway out to Puente. The site was fenced but there were sure to be security holes that locals got through to drop their own trash. He'd cruise the terraced trash hills until he found one. Most probably down near the Rio Hondo bookstore or off Workman Mill Road.

Once he got there, he'd dispose of the body parts, drive back to Skid, pick up the van and return to work. If he caught a break, he'd do it all within a ninety minute stretch. If he was unlucky and got caught, everything he'd devoted his life to up until now would be ruined.

Chapter 114

Douglas Park, Santa Monica, LA

A ngie filled a sandwich bag with ice and held her smashed-up hand inside it to take down the swelling. She used to feel guilty after a violent outbreak. Even dirty. Not today. The explosion had been all that had kept her sane.

Her phone rang all afternoon with calls from well-wishers who'd seen Jake's death on the news. Somehow their sympathies just added to the strain.

Crawford Dixon called and wanted to come by, but she managed to put him off for at least a day.

Angie wandered around the apartment like a dazed and dangerous animal in a cage. Around five p.m. she plumped up cushions on the sofa and fell asleep through exhaustion. She woke an hour later and found she was holding a shirt of Jake's that she'd been taking from the bedroom to the washing machine and had decided she couldn't let go of. Maybe this was the craziness that Suzie Janner had warned her about. She held the white cotton to her face and felt hopelessly close to her dead fiancé.

Her door buzzer went. At first she ignored it. After the second buzz she wearily went to the intercom screen on the wall and was relieved to see it was Chips outside and not anyone else.

She clicked him through and left the door open while she hid Jake's shirt in the bedroom.

The young assistant came in breathless. He was hauling a suitcase, a laptop and a bag of groceries.

'What's that?' she asked, reappearing from the bedroom, her eyes on his clutter.

'More files, my laptop, food and an overnight case.' He put them down. 'I'm not going to take no for an answer. You can kick me out in the morning if you want, but I'd like to be here for you tonight.'

'There's really no need.'

'There's every need. And if you send me home, then I'm only going to stay up all night worrying about you.'

She gave in. 'Thanks. That's very considerate of you.'

'That's the kind of guy I am.'

'I've got to warn you, I'm a bit temperamental.' She lifted her swollen hand.

He went over to comfort her. 'God, was that from hitting Danielle?'

Angie looked ashamed. 'No. The door.'

He looked surprised, then followed Angie's eye-line to where he'd just come in. The back of the MDF door had multiple holes in it.

'Sweet baby Jesus, remind me never to upset you.' He picked up the brown bag of groceries he'd brought and headed to the kitchen. 'While I make something to eat – because I'm sure you haven't had anything since yesterday – you need to call Lieutenant O'Brien.'

'Why?'

'He's been made lead officer on Jake's case.'

'That's good news. O'Brien is human enough to share a little off-the-record information.' She picked up her cellphone and called straight away.

'Cal, it's Angie Holmes.'

'Hello, Doc.'

She could tell from his tone that he was surprised to hear from her and thrown by how normal she sounded. 'I just heard you're running Jake's case.'

'Angie, I'm really very sorry for your loss. We're busting our asses to find whoever did this.'

'I'm sure you are. I'm glad you're the OIC.'

O'Brien knew *why* she'd called and where this conversation was headed. 'Before you say anything else, I should tell you that I've already had your boss on the line, asking me to make sure you don't try to co-investigate this case. Now, that's not why you're calling me, is it?'

'I need to go to Jake's apartment but wanted to make sure you had finished with the scene before I drove over.'

'CSIs wrapped there about an hour ago.' He thought for a moment and then added, 'When are you planning to go over?'

'Within the next half hour.'

'Then I'll be there for you.'

Chapter 115

Halfway down an all-too-familiar street, Angie saw Jake's face staring out from an LAPD poster pinned to a tree. It was an appeal for information in relation to last night's shooting. The picture was one she hadn't seen before and it hurt to see something new about him made public. It was as though she'd already lost her unique closeness to him.

She pulled up behind the old '58 Swept Wing he'd lovingly restored.

There were cops all over the street but no one stopped her unlocking it and sliding into the driver's seat. Angie flipped open the glove box and found an old manual, five of his CDs, a dried-up leather screen cloth and a pocketbook. She pulled the book and put it into her purse without even looking inside.

Angie checked the door pockets and beneath the seats, painfully knocking her right elbow in the process. Down the side of the seat, as though dropped from a jacket, or maybe put down while driving and forgotten, was a cellphone. It wasn't Jake's. Least she'd never seen it. She pressed the on button but the battery was dead. Angie put it in her purse and wondered whose it was.

She'd only just climbed out and taken a long reflective breath when O'Brien's car pulled in behind her Avensis.

He looked even more ragged than usual. Tufts of uncombed hair signaled that he'd been called out in the early hours and the facial stubble said he hadn't managed to shave for quite a while.

'How you doing?' He walked towards her.

'Holding up.' She kept the reply deliberately short. Any further discussion could so easily result in her falling apart. She swung the car keys. 'You need to check Jake's vehicle?'

O'Brien nodded and took the keys from her. 'You want us to drive it over when we're done?'

'Yeah, that'd be a help.' She started towards Jake's apartment. 'You got an idea how it all went down?'

He hesitated.

'Come on. At least give me that.'

He fell into step with her. As they got nearer, he pointed to the entrance doors at the foot of the stucco building. 'Witnesses on first and second floors both heard two bursts of gunfire. A gap of a few seconds between them.'

Angie knew what the timing and shot sequencing meant. 'Let me guess. The first burst cut him down. Second finished him off. The second were the more tightly clustered chest shots.'

'Are you okay talking about this? Really?'

She opened up a little. 'It's what's keeping me sane. The only positive I can focus on at the moment is catching this piece of shit.'

He nodded. 'I can understand that.'

'Good, you may be the only one that does.' She pressed out a thin smile. 'Any news on the weapon?'

'Uh-huh.'

'Can you tell me?'

'Rounds were nine mill, from a G18.'

Angie knew the Glock well. 'Classic gun for three-round bursts when set on auto.'

'So I'm told. Once the labs get into things, they should be able to calculate the exact distance it was fired from. Along with the angle of entry, we hope to work out the gunman's height.'

'I'm no medical examiner but I suspect the autopsy will say the second burst was fired at closer range. Given Jake was wounded and probably immobile from the first shots, it meant the UNSUB stepped closer, so we're talking an execution here; executions mean pre-meditation, premed means grudges.'

'I follow your logic. My initial thoughts are the same as yours but we shouldn't go jumping to conclusions.'

They walked further and now Angie could see where the blood stained the pathway. She stopped mid-step. Her veneer of eerie calm shattered. This was the exact spot where the man she loved had been shot down and her whole world had been kicked off its axis.

O'Brien saw she was struggling. He stepped slightly away and gave her some space. No amount of professional fatals prepared you for personal grief.

Angie bent low and examined the smeared pathway. She wanted to dig it up and take it home. It wasn't right that any part of Jake was washed away or walked on.

Residents had already laid bunches of flowers with cards and messages around the spot. She was too raw to look at them. There was a job to do and she needed to concentrate. Jake had to become just another poor soul she was seeking justice for if she was going to get through this without falling apart.

Angie stood up and turned to the lieutenant. 'The body wounds I saw at the hospital and the spatter here indicate he was hit by a gunman standing to the front and a little to the left.' A shadowy image formed in her mind. A disturbing vision of the killer catching Jake unprepared and opening up on him. She angled her head to the side. 'Looking at where Jake's vehicle is parked, what I just said would be consistent with the UNSUB tailing him, parking some distance behind, then running up and making the shots.'

O'Brien weighed it up. 'Why couldn't he just have been lying in wait for him?'

'Lots of reasons.' Angie paced as she talked. Her eyes flicked across the street, apartment blocks and parked cars. 'Let's assume the killer knew Jake's home address – which is a hell of an assumption – then the one thing he wouldn't have had any idea about is the time he'd be home, or even if he was coming home. So he would have needed to wait out here in a car for maybe hours or days. That posed a big risk of being seen and his plate remembered. The kind of guy with the balls to kill one of us doesn't take risks like that. He looks to strike quickly and be gone before anyone realizes what's gone down.'

O'Brien connected the dots. 'Jake was on TV earlier in the day, so it's possible he was followed from the press conference. The UNSUB sat out on Wilshire and waited for him to come out, knowing he'd have to head home.'

'Sounds plausible. My money is on the mall killer.'

'All the smart bets are.'

She got his drift. 'Which means we have to be careful not to rule out someone else.' She walked to the front door. 'Okay if we go inside?'

'Sure.' He stopped after a pace. 'Would you like me to give you a minute on your own?'

'I'd appreciate that.' She slipped in a key and opened up.

Just walking through the door sent her heartbeat haywire. Jake's giant shoes lay in the hall. His jackets and coats dangled from pegs. Angie pressed herself between two of them and remembered leaning against him as they walked and talked, holding hands or with arms around each other. A whole relationship-worth of memories swelled in her mind and she had to remind herself to ignore them and stay professional. There would be time for grieving later. *Much* later.

She went into the bathroom. It was full of his soaps and aftershaves. Jake had always smelled of pine and mint, as fresh as wind through a forest. She looked down at the floor where they'd made love, wrapped in white towels as thick as sheepskin.

The bedroom threatened to derail her all over again. A wall of mirrored robes had often shown tantalizing flashes of their unions. The bed slats had broken during one wild session. The dressing table still contained a bangle she'd left behind months ago and he'd asked to keep because it always made him think of her.

Angie sat on the edge of the bed and almost choked. There was so much Jake in here she could barely breathe. His clothes and character were all over the place. His atoms still moved in the air.

Finally she gave in and lay down. Let her face rest on his pillow. Allowed her soul the reconnection it craved.

The moment was piercingly painful. But addictive. Like the self-harming cuts on her wrists as a child.

Tears flowed through her closed eyes and she let them. At first because they couldn't be stopped. And then because she wanted them gone.

Didn't want to get caught like this again. She needed to purge them. It felt like she was wringing vulnerability from every fabric of her being.

Almost breathless, she sat up and pulled tissues from the nightstand to wipe her eyes. Then she got herself together and resumed the search.

She went through all his drawers. There wasn't much. Most of it had found its way to her apartment. There were odd socks. Underwear that had grown tatty and should have been thrown out. Shirts she'd never seen him wear.

The closets bulged with unfashionable jackets and jumpers that she'd stopped him wearing. The pockets produced a few dollars, tickets from football and baseball games, receipts from restaurants visited years ago.

At the back of the last closet, she discovered two metal gun boxes. One made for a rifle. The other big enough for handguns and ammunition. She examined the key ring Ruis had given her inside the bag of personal belongings and found two that fitted.

The big box didn't contain a rifle, but was stacked with three pistols and enough rounds to start a war. The smaller one held photographs and letters.

She'd never seen any of them.

Like it or not, Jake Mottram had kept things from her. Maybe something that had gotten him killed.

Chapter 116

Cal O'Brien was talking to a couple of neighbors when Angie reappeared. She'd filled a recyclable shopping bag with the smaller metal box she'd found plus some framed photographs and a handful of bills that were due.

The lieutenant finished up and wandered over. His gaze panned from what was in her hands to her tear-reddened eyes. 'Are you okay?'

'Yeah, I'm done.' She lifted the bag to show him. 'I've taken some photographs, letters and bills.'

'For personal or professional reasons?'

She thought about lying. 'Both.'

He studied her face again. 'Let me know if there's something in the letters.'

'You don't mind me taking them first?'

'Let's be honest, you're probably the only person who can spot anything significant in them.'

'I'll let you know. And thanks again for coming over and playing it straight.'

'Stay in touch.'

'You too.'

The only thing she could think of as she drove back was the metal box. It was filled with his past. The years before they'd known each other. Pictures from his days in the Marines. Men she'd never seen or heard of.

And women.

Photographs of beautiful women.

And letters.

Letters he'd kept.

Angie parked outside her apartment and for a while just sat there with the engine off and the dull hum of traffic rubbing against the glass of the Toyota. Twenty-four hours ago, life had been so different. So certain. Now every hour threw a new punch.

She closed her eyes and put her head back. But there was to be no respite. Brutal images crowded her inner blackness. Jake in a pool of blood, unable to move or speak, neighbors stood over him calling 911. The shadowy figure of the killer turning away, smoking gun dangling from his hand.

Angie vanquished the demons and forced herself to think beyond the emotion.

Six shots in two bursts. The second three fatal. Several seconds between those and the first burst. It meant the killer wasn't a pro. Not military. Nor was he a trigger-happy spray-and-pray gangsta. He'd fired only body shots – big target hits – but he'd shown a certain calmness.

He wasn't fleet of foot, experienced in covert strikes. Jake had heard him. Turned from the door he was about to open.

She pictured the love of her life catching the first burst and going down.

The gunman hadn't seen exactly where he'd hit him but he'd known it was bad. It had given him the confidence to move in for the kill. But he needed to be up close because he'd been afraid of bungling it. Either that or he'd wanted to see Jake's reaction as he finished him. Beat him. Maybe settled a grudge.

Angie opened her eyes.

Danielle Goodman had been right. The words she'd put in Jake's mouth had been arrows that wounded the Sun Western Slayer. They found his Achilles' heel and enraged him. Only way beyond what she'd expected. It had sent him over the edge. The big question was – why? Exactly which part of Jake's speech had touched a nerve so sensitive that the UNSUB had risked everything to kill him?

Chapter 117

Things went better than Shooter planned.

Management asked him to supervise the local depot that night, then come see them when he finished his shift. It was no big surprise. They ran the whole outfit on basic minimum-waged staff and simply had no cover to send over.

None of his co-workers were sad that Januk wasn't around. No one seemed to mind Shooter stepping into his shoes. Especially given the fact that he was hardly a kickass kind of guy who was going to crack the whip and make them work harder.

By one a.m. he'd found an open gate at the Puente dump and by one-thirty he'd scattered Januk's bagged body parts far and wide. He hadn't tried to get to the centre of the dumpsite. It was too far away and too high up the pyramid-like terraces. At its peak, Puente reached something like five hundred feet and he wasn't about to scale it in the dark. Instead, he'd just spaded open a few old dump areas that had been grassed and covered with trees and flowers. Only the torso had taken any rigorous burying. The rest popped in, sweet as seeds in fresh soil.

Shooter dropped the rusty old station wagon far away from the sanctuary in a place that suited him very well. Then he drove the van back to work. He waited until the day supervisor arrived and used it again to cross town and meet with senior management. Apparently, they'd called Januk at his home and on his cell but without answer. They believed the Pole would turn up tomorrow, but would be grateful if Shooter would be prepared to step in if he didn't.

Shooter told them he was always prepared.

By the time he dropped the van and headed out of the gates, he hadn't slept in twenty-four hours. Soon he'd be resting up, but not at the sanctuary.

He needed to make an early start tomorrow. Needed to be close to his prey.

Chapter 118

Douglas Park, Santa Monica, LA

I t was five a.m. when Angie woke.

For a split second, she'd thought everything had been as it was.

Almost perfect.

Then she had seen Chips lying on the sofa, his head tilted back on a cushion, mouth open, loud snores rattling like some small creature had crawled inside his throat and was cawing to get out.

The floor was littered with files. Both their laptops were open and cables snaked towards power sockets. The table was still stacked with stuff from the dinner that Chips had made – Caesar salad with salmon and glasses of beetroot juice, which he insisted were good for her blood pressure.

Angie yawned and stretched. She scraped fingers through a scrub of hair and the greasy feel made her realize it was more than a day since she'd stepped into a shower. As she stood, she noticed a wad of drawings and notes piled around the foot of Chips's sofa. He'd clearly carried on working long after she'd crashed out, not that she could remember when that was. Her brain had just shut down, like someone had pulled a plug and all power had gone off.

Angie tiptoed to her bedroom and saw the bag of stuff she'd brought from Jake's place. Last night, she'd been unable to go through it. Now she knew she had no choice, especially if she wanted the complete picture of Jake, his final movements, and maybe even some personal things about him that he hadn't shared.

She climbed onto the king-size bed and took out the metal box she'd found in his closet. It reminded her of Pandora's Box.

The one that was never meant to be opened. But of course it was and out flew envy, hate, and every form of badness imaginable. But the worst of all was hope. Because once let out, it was lost forever.

Angie felt she had no choice but to take the same risk. She flipped the lid and poured the contents onto the quilt. First, she separated pictures of men and women. The men were soldiers. All in uniform or standard white T-shirts. She didn't know any of them.

Next she assembled the women. Two blondes and two brunettes. Two photographs were single headshots, very old by the look of the hairstyles and quality of the prints. The other two were wider shots with men in them – not Jake, but maybe friends of his.

Angie turned over the head and shoulders of the blonde.

On the back was the faded word MOM.

It took her by surprise.

She turned it and looked again. The woman was pretty, and now Angie could see Jake's pale-blue eyes staring out at her. He'd never spoken of his parents, except to say he'd understood from the children's home that his mom had died early. Angie guessed the picture had traveled with him when his father had given him up.

She picked up the shot of the brunette and now realized it was the same woman. Dark was her natural color. She flipped it and saw Jake's faded writing again.

MOM.

The lady with Jake's eyes was in the other pictures too. And even though they'd been taken a good five years apart, the man with her was the same.

Angie turned them over and read the inscriptions.

MOM – & DAD?

It saddened her that Jake hadn't been sure about the man's identity and had died not knowing.

She stacked the pictures, put them to one side and lifted out a bunch of letters and postcards. They were mainly from friends and spanned the first three years of his life as a teenage recruit. Tough years. Lonely years by the nature of what she could read.

Most of the messages were the same. They asked about how he was settling in, who he was hanging with, places he and other squaddies went drinking. Some girls' names came up, but only in connection with other guys. This was Shy Jake. A Jake she'd seen glimpses of but barely knew.

Angie found a note without an envelope. It had been curved by wear in a pocket and was worn and frayed, filthy in parts and splitting at the creases. She unfolded it. On the top was a date she knew well. August 1st. The day Jake joined up. It was in his best handwriting, not the fast scribble of many of the other letters. She shuffled up the bed, so her back was on the headboard, and read:

To whomever finds this . . .

The phrase made her smile. It was so *un*-Jake. He must have copied it from a formal English document.

As she read through the immature, stilted language she realized what it was.

A young soldier's last wishes.

. . . if your eyes are on this page it is because mine have been closed. At least, I trust they have and I have not been left staring at some mosquito-infested foreign sky and will scare the life out of some kid from a dirt-poor village who comes along and finds my rotting remains.

If you're a fellow soldier, then I hope I have died in honor and taken some less honorable fucks with me. Man, there are so many of them. Killers of kids and women. Cowards that come from the shadows and attack those without weapons, those with only good in their blood.

If you're a buddy, you'll know I'm drunk while writing this – you have to be, right? – but you'll also know I mean every word. I'm not sure I believe in God, but I believe in doing good. I'm not sure I believe in Judgment Day, but I'm happy to be judged for the way I live. I've got a lot to learn but I already know freedom is worth fighting and dying for – my freedom and that of those I care for, and of those who cannot fight or care for themselves. It is the duty of the strong to protect the weak. The responsibility of the free to break the chains of those who are slaves.

I have no regrets. Life's been simply beautiful. Sunshine in the morning. Stars at night. Snow on the mountains. A wind out at sea carrying a boat in full sail. Never a day without food or drink. These are miracles enough. It would have been good to have found love. It sure as hell isn't at the end of the barrel of a gun and I haven't so far spotted it through any field glasses. Who knows, maybe if there's a life after this one I'll find someone special, someone willing to put up with me and my odd ways – before you say it, yeah, I know, she'd have to be exceptionally special.

If you're reading this and I don't know you, then I guess it might well mean that I've been killed in a city, maybe even by accident or natural causes rather than an act of war. If that's the case, then I apologize up front because I'm gonna ask a big favor of you. Do it for me and maybe some stranger may one day do a great kindness for you.

There's a little money put aside in a bank account and my lawyer has instructions to unfreeze it for you. His name and number are at the bottom of this page. It should be enough to make sure you're not out of pocket.

I'd like to be cremated. Then I want my ashes to be put in a candle lantern and launched high into the night at sea, from the tip of the Terranea Trail where it hits the curve of Pelican Cove, so I can float out across the North Pacific and roam far and wild. As I suspect you might be the only person stood there, I ask that you stay until the light has drifted so far that you can't see it any more. It sounds odd, but I like the idea of someone looking out for me during those last moments.

Whoever you are, thank you.

If there's a God, may he or she bless you and protect you.

Jake Mottram Soldier and Future Traveler of the Skies

Angie let out the long breath she'd been holding. They'd spent a weekend together at a spa near the Terranea Trail and they'd stood together on the very spot he'd written about. He'd pointed to the sky and said as a kid one of the care workers had told him angels stuffed clouds with dreams and all you had to do was identify one that looked like you and everything you ever wanted would come true.

Since that moment they'd always watched the clouds together.

Chapter 119

South Sepulveda Boulevard, LA

Four hours' sleep. That was all Shooter had managed.

The hotel he'd spent the night in was a small Best Western with paper-thin walls. It was jammed with noisy tourists and expense account delegates attending dinners and events at the Olympic Conference Center. The early crew had been rushed off their feet coping with them and Shooter had difficulty finding a discreet parking place for Januk's old Datsun.

He pulled back dusty drapes and morning light got sifted through even dustier grey nets. Instinctively, Shooter checked the street before he showered and dressed.

Today was a big day so he'd brought along one of his finest suits, a brown pinstripe that wouldn't look amiss on Wall Street, a sharp white shirt with a scooped collar and an understated chocolate and cream silk tie. Brown brogues and a faded leather briefcase completed the fashionable executive look.

He spent the next hour reading the newspapers he'd ordered and a complimentary copy of the *Economist* he'd found on a coffee table in the room. When he was done, he took a stroll in the now blazing sun. Not very far. In fact, a walk of exactly half a mile.

In less than fifteen minutes he was inside the air-conditioned luxury of the Olympic, thirty thousand square feet of event and banqueting space spread across three floors. He knew most of it intimately. He'd been here a month before, similarly dressed, and had collected floor plans from the Customer Service desk, under the ruse of possibly staging a conference.

Shooter made his way to the second floor. He passed the Capitol Room and entered the foyer near the Imperial Ballroom and its function kitchen. Along the main wall were washroom facilities, including a baby change room. He checked he wasn't being watched and slipped inside. There was an area to lay a child on, a sink to wash in and a shelf of complimentary products. Under the sink was a panel for plumbing maintenance. Shooter used a cufflink to unfasten the four folding screws. Inside the dark and dusty space was a black leather case. He replaced it with his brown one and fixed the panel back in position.

Minutes later, he returned to the public areas. An electronic board told him the location of the event he was interested in and where the attending delegates were having lunch.

He made his way to the Regency Terrace and asked a waitress on the door to find a specific delegate for him and ask him to come outside to sign some papers. He held up the black case and stressed the urgency.

The young woman checked her seating plans and drifted away.

Shooter stepped back out of view. From behind a pillar he watched her head to a table almost at the back of the room. She spoke to a man in an expensive dark green suit. He got to his feet and obediently followed her. He was tall, early fifties, dark hair turning white at the sides, a little flab jostling his pale green shirt over an expensive black leather belt.

Shooter had got the ID he'd wanted. He slipped away from the restaurant, passed the cloakroom and hid himself among a bank of people using payphones at the north end of the conference hall.

He stayed there for the next fifteen minutes. At ten to two, everyone started back into the four-hundred-seater hall. Shooter scanned the hordes. Dozens of people were hanging around in the corridors, swapping business cards and hurriedly making final calls before the afternoon session started.

The man in the green suit appeared. He veered away from the hall and headed to the men's room.

So did Shooter.

Chapter 120

Douglas Park, Santa Monica, LA

Once Chips left for the office, Angie rearranged her living area. It was no longer home. It was a murder incident room with soft furnishings.

She took down an oil painting she and Jake had bought. Printouts of locations and stills of crime scenes replaced the impressionistic view of the Himalayan peak they'd climbed last year.

Her elegant glass dining table became a crowded desk. Instead of flowers, she'd set up a printer, laptop, phone, notebook, files and a jug of purified water – an attempt to cut down her caffeine intake.

Angie settled down and marshaled her thoughts. She was convinced Jake's killer was the man responsible for the attacks on the mall, and maybe even the school trip to the strawberry fields, though she was still struggling to find anything forensic to link them. Chips had transcribed Jake's press conference address and sent her a private email. Working through it was top of her priority list.

She read the transcript several times. Selected sections. Copied and pasted them onto a separate document so she could see the remarks in isolation. Thirteen lines had references that disturbed her.

1. . . . I have come across many enemies in my time, but only the most evil of creatures strikes at civilians in a way as cowardly as this . . .

2. . . . these are acts that rank as the most despicable I have ever witnessed . . .
3. . . . the mind behind these acts is a cowardly, spineless, gutless one . . .
4. . . . has no place in our society . . .
5. . . . the lowest of the low . . .
6. . . . the kind of person parents would disown . . .
7. . . . the kind that society is most ashamed of . . .
8. . . . *the creature* responsible for these homicides . . .
9. . . . the worst criminals in prison would consider him too vile to be allowed a cell alongside them . . .
10. . . . such an abomination . . .
11. . . . you will be hunted to the ends of the earth . . .
12. . . . nowhere you can hide . . .
13. . . . dead or alive, you *will* face justice.

Danielle Goodman had clearly sought to destroy the feelings of power and fame that the UNSUB would have been experiencing as the whole country began talking about and fearing him. But the strategy was crudely inflammatory. She'd tried to explode his self-worth, and if he had any sense of mission to divert him from it. Most probably, she'd expected him to post a letter to a newspaper explaining his grievances and justifying himself. This would have led to personality clues and maybe even forensic hints as to his whereabouts. Instead, the stupid woman had tipped him over the edge. Pressed a psychotic trigger. Made him react violently instead of verbally.

The thirteen lines Angie had isolated fell into two main categories – insults and warnings. Lines one to ten were insults, lines eleven to thirteen warnings. She was sure the stressor, the very thing that enraged him enough to kill, lay in those first ten lines.

Angie sub-divided them into generalizations and specifics. References to 'creature', 'lowest of the low' etc. were generalizations. Many of those were prosaic insults that got hurled around by all kinds of groups about all kinds of people. She was sure the key lay in the specifics – lines three, six and nine. Angie reviewed them again:

3.   . . . the mind behind these acts is a cowardly, spineless, gutless one . . .
6.   . . . the kind of person parents would disown . . .
9.   . . . the worst criminals in prison would consider him too vile to be allowed a cell alongside them . . .

Only line three stood out. It questioned his masculinity, his principles and power. Shooting strangers with a high-powered weapon and bombing mourning families were undoubtedly cowardly acts, but that hadn't been how the UNSUB had seen them. To him they'd somehow been justified and glorious.

She picked up a copy of the UNSUB's picture from the mall footage, taped it to her wall and stood back.

The young black man she stared at was around six foot, maybe a little too heavy for his size, but looked as though he was big and tough enough to handle himself. He seemed at odds with the image of someone who could be enraged by being called a coward. He looked as though he'd take something like that in his stride. Had no doubt been called much worse out in the hood.

Annoyingly, her cellphone rang. She was in no mood for distractions, especially if they came in the form of more well-meaning people offering condolences.

Caller display showed it was Chips.

She picked it up. 'Hi.'

He knew better than to ask how she was doing. 'I've just heard that Agent Costas talked to Connor Pryce and the LAPD has pulled a suspect in the mall case.'

Angie felt her heart jump.

'It's supposed to be hush-hush,' added Chips, 'but it's the only thing anyone's talking about round here.'

Chapter 121

The Olympic Conference Center, LA

The businessman in the smart green suit waited patiently in the washroom. A cubicle to the right came free and he glanced at his watch as he drifted in.

He was about to close the door and relieve himself of too much lunchtime wine when it banged hard in his face. He stumbled backwards holding his head. By the time he'd stopped himself falling over the john, Shooter had raised a silenced pistol from beneath the cover of the briefcase. 'Sit the fuck down and give me your watch and wallet.'

The delegate forgot about the bump to his face. He sat and clicked the steel Rolex off his wrist.

Shooter bolted the door behind him. 'Put it on the floor at your feet.'

He did.

'Now your wallet.'

The dapper green jacket flapped open and a calfskin billfold came out along with a matching cardholder. He started to put them down.

'Get your driver's license out and hold it up for me to see.'

The man pulled the card and made to pass it over.

Shooter waved the pistol. 'Just hold it up.'

He pinched it between his thumb and forefinger.

Shooter read the name. 'Sean Thornton. Your wife's Mary, right?'

The question drew a frown.

'Mary, Mary, quite contrary.' He enjoyed seeing the shock on the man's face. 'Only Mrs Thornton *wasn't* contrary, was she?'

'I don't understand.' Fear showed in his eyes. 'What's this about? What's it to do with my wife?'

'Everything.' Shooter dipped into the briefcase and took out a roll of seal-lock plastic bags. He passed two over. 'Put your money, watch, wallet and whatever's in your pockets in there.'

Thornton let out a sigh. Being robbed in a washroom was embarrassing as well as peculiarly scary. He'd heard about a spate of West Side stick-ups in expensive hotel parking lots but hadn't expected boldness like this. Desperate times apparently bred desperate crooks. He filled the bags. 'You want them sealed?'

Shooter nodded.

Thornton lined up the click-together edges and sealed them tight.

Shooter produced a roll of duct tape. 'There are pre-cut strips on there. Pick them off with your fingers. Put one over your mouth and another over your eyes.'

He hesitated.

Shooter gestured with the pistol. 'Do it quickly! Then I'll be gone. This will be over in less than five.'

Thornton turned the roll in his hands until he found an edge he could get a thumbnail under. He pulled off a strip and his eyes narrowed as he smeared it over his mouth.

'And the second one.'

He dug some more. Peeled off another length of tape. It snagged his eyebrows and he tried not to stick it too tight.

Shooter stepped forward and pressed it snug.

Thornton tried to push him away.

Shooter smashed the pistol handle onto the top of his skull.

There was a muffled grunt of pain and he rocked on the seat of the john.

Shooter waited and listened. Someone came into the restroom. They urinated and whistled. A sink tap ran. A hand dryer blasted hot air. Doors flapped closed.

Then came silence.

Shooter pulled a folded plastic sheet from his briefcase and quickly tented himself. He put the gun to Sean Thornton's head.

Then he shot him.

Twice.

The red mess that spread across the white-tiled toilet walls persuaded him a third bullet wasn't necessary.

He rolled the plastic sheet up, slid it into a third seal-lock bag and put it into his briefcase.

He was almost done.

Just one more box to tick.

Shooter ripped a long length of toilet tissue from the hanging roll. He made a thick pad and in a single sweep wiped the spattered wall, firstly downward at forty-five degrees, then upward so it formed a perfect tick.

Chapter 122

R uis Costas had expected the phone call.
  Just not so soon.

'Angie, I don't know a lot.' He sought to head her off early. 'Seems Jake and Pryce met the night he was murdered and discussed a suspect, the one that's now in custody.'

'You there now?'

'Yeah, I am. The guy's insisted on lawyering up and Pryce's in with someone from the DA's office.'

'Can you ask him to call me? I could help with this. Interrogation strategy is one of my specialties.'

'Angie, you're not even supposed to be ringing me, let alone trying to work this case or any others.'

'Hey, if that's Jake's killer, I want in on the interview. Please don't let me be squeezed out of that.'

'It won't be my call, Angie. Hell, it's unlikely I'll even get in there.' He really felt for her. 'I know you think the same guy's responsible but we can't make that leap yet. We have to let Pryce—'

Angie jumped in. 'It's him, Ruis. Danielle's words provoked him. She had Jake belittle him and then threaten him with justice – "dead or alive" – it was like he was calling him out.'

He tried to calm her down. 'Good luck with using that argument in court. I can just see the DA saying, "Ladies and gentlemen, there are no forensic links to the suspect but our psychologist has a red hot theory."'

She ignored his sarcasm. 'Will you ask Pryce if I can sit in?'

'No, Angie, I won't.'

'Please, Ruis. As Jake's friend and hopefully mine too.'

There was a pause. 'Even if I wanted to, I can't. I was there, remember, when McDonald sent you home. She's spoken to Crawford and they've both warned me not to help you – I shouldn't even be having this conversation.'

She was shocked. 'What's wrong? Have you already put in for Jake's job? Is that it? You don't want to rock the boat and ruin your chances?'

'That's unfair.'

She thought about it. 'You're right. I'm sorry, that was an awful thing to say. But hell, can't you see I'm desperate here. Come on, as a friend, bend the damned protocol and ask Pryce to call me.'

He was angry. She was manipulating him but he understood why. Understood he'd probably do the same thing if their roles were reversed. 'I'll think about it.'

The line went dead.

Angie slammed her phone down on the table. She wondered if O'Brien knew about the suspect, whether he was also seeing links between Jake's death and the other murders.

She called his cell but it tripped to messaging. 'Lieutenant, it's Angie Holmes, call me when you get this. I have some information for you.'

She hung up and paced. Bit on a nail. Poured a glass of water and paced some more. She hated this isolation, lack of involvement and drought of information. She wondered why Jake hadn't mentioned that he and Pryce had zoned in on a suspect? The cop must have contacted him late in the evening, after they'd spoken.

Remorse began to raise its ugly head. She couldn't help but think what would have happened if she hadn't told Jake she'd wanted to be alone that night. The truth was hard to live with. If they'd been together then, they'd still be together now.

Her phone rang.

She snatched it off the table. 'Hello?'

'This is Connor Pryce.'

'Commander, I'm told you might have a suspect in custody in relation to the mall incidents?'

'In relation to the *shooting*, yes. Not necessarily the *bombing*.' He hoped he didn't sound indelicate. 'Doctor Holmes, I'm very sorry for your loss. I didn't know Jake that well, but from our little time together I could tell he was a good man and a very fine agent. I hope this difficult time passes quickly for you.'

'Thank you.'

'I'm sorry but I have to go now, we're about to interview the suspect.'

'Commander, I think the man who shot those people in the mall also killed Jake.'

Pryce ran the possibility through his head. 'Do you have any proof of that?'

Angie wasn't done. 'And I believe he may have carried out the mall bombing and the Strawberry Fields massacre.'

'Proof?'

'Not *forensic* proof. Nothing physical. But I'm starting to see strong psychological connections between the cases.'

He let out a sympathetic sigh. 'Doctor, I think you know that even if I agreed with you, which I don't by the way, then I'd need more than psychological assumptions to charge someone. Now forgive me, I really do have to go. Again, my condolences for your loss.'

Chapter 123

The Olympic Conference Center, LA

Shooter rolled Thornton's trousers down around his ankles and used them to soak up the blood pooling at his feet.

He unraveled two toilet rolls and tamped the flow before he climbed the partition that separated the locked cubicle from the vacant one next door. He slithered down onto the toilet unit and stayed still, in order to listen and make sure the washroom was clear. It seemed everyone was back in the conference hall. No doubt the afternoon session had begun.

He walked to the sinks, washed his hands and checked himself in the mirrors.

No blood. No mess. No clue as to what he'd just done. He glanced down at the locked cubicle floor and for the moment no blood was visible.

Shooter walked out into the foyer. It was empty now. Doors to the nearby hall were closed. Behind them, businessmen no doubt listened intently to some bullshit about quantitative easing and stock market confidence.

Before leaving the Center, he took the stairs back to the baby change room, opened the panel beneath the sink and swapped briefcases. Inside the discarded one lay the gun and plastic sheet that had protected him from the spatter. It had all gone well. Smoothly. To plan.

Fifteen minutes after fatally shooting Sean Thornton, Shooter walked back into the Best Western and returned to the room he'd hired for two nights.

He turned on the TV news, stripped off his clothes, wrapped them in a hotel laundry bag and pushed them into his suitcase. He pulled a pillow out of its case and used it as a giant mitt to cover his hands while he emptied the two plastic bags that contained the dead man's belongings.

Only Thornton's driving license and around three hundred dollars in cash were of any interest. The picture would make a unique souvenir for his wall while cash was always welcome. The guy had numerous credit cards, including an Amex Black, but Shooter wouldn't be using any of them. ATMs had cameras and cops could get your fingerprints from the keys, even when messed up by hundreds of other prints. He'd grown up knowing all about police and what they could do. He'd even heard some CSIs could get DNA from surfaces that you'd only breathed on or coughed near.

Shooter showered and put on cheap blue jeans, an old brown sweat and scruffy black bomber jacket. He looked like an average working guy as he strolled outside the hotel.

Clouds masked the heat and the streets smelled of scorched rubber as he walked past Januk's Datsun and caught a bus back to Skid.

Before approaching the old shoe factory he walked the block. Checked out the parked cars and people on the sidewalks. Only when he was sure it was safe did he unlock the gates and make his way inside the litter-strewn compound.

Shooter disabled the alarms and traps. The smell of bleach stung his nostrils as he entered the cool, dark building. Bleach and death. A pungent reminder of his dismembered supervisor.

The tapes in his control room showed there'd been no suspicious activity while he'd been away. He poured a glass of water and pushed open the door to the room he'd christened Death Row.

'Hello, my friends. I've missed you.'

Rows of dead eyes stared back.

'I have someone new for you.' He held up the driver's license. 'This is Sean Thornton. You all know Sean – course you do – he's the husband of that bitch of a sheep, Mary.' He smeared glue on the back of the license and slapped it on the wall next to the photograph of Tanya Murison. Pride of place. 'Welcome, Sean.' He pressed again. Wiped squashed glue away with his fingers. 'Make yourself at home.'

Chapter 124

Douglas Park, Santa Monica, LA

The moment Angie began writing on her apartment wall she knew she was never going to be normal again.

Not unless she caught Jake's killer.

In thick black felt pen she marked out four separate sections of what she saw as one single inquiry: STRAWBERRY FIELDS, SUN WESTERN SHOOTINGS, SUN WESTERN BOMBING, and one just called JAKE.

Try as she might, she couldn't bring herself to write the word MURDER next to his name.

Beneath the headings, Angie listed all the crime scene locations, the number of dead and injured, the dates and times of the attacks and the weapons used.

At first, they seemed vastly different and unconnected. One was mid-morning, one early evening and one in the dead of night.

The Strawberry Fields massacre was almost fifty miles from the Sun Western attacks. It was rural, not urban. An AR rifle was used, not a MAC-10. Those kinds of weapons usually had very different personalities peering down their barrels. Then there was the bombing at the night-time memorial. And of course Jake's homicide, carried out with a Glock 18. The use of so many different weapons sent out confusing messages. In isolation, she'd speculate that the UNSUB was a gun enthusiast or someone with a military background, but the limited skill shown in using them suggested that perhaps he'd stolen, found or borrowed the weapons. The use of the bomb and his lack of emotional attachment to any single gun also indicated that he didn't have an arms obsession or weapon fixation.

Before Angie got distracted by examining details of the explosives or Jake's murder, she wanted to revisit the conclusions she'd come to while writing up her notes on the Sun Western shootings.

Physically, she'd seen the offender as a black male, twenty to thirty, around six feet tall, maybe a hundred and sixty pounds and in good health. He'd had no obvious limp, no curvature of the spine or any peculiar features that distinguished him. His clothes were baggy but his legs seemed slim and muscled. He appeared well-nourished and therefore he wasn't an addict of any kind. He'd had a plastic watch on his right hand but the sports bag had been slung over his right shoulder. This was confusing. Right-handed people usually wore watches on their left hand and right-handed shooters tended to sling bags over their right shoulder. She marked down the possibility that the UNSUB was ambidextrous. This would put him in an elite group of about only three percent of the population. It was also possible he had a dominant left eye or perhaps had suffered an injury to his right hand or arm and been forced to teach himself to use his left hand. Angie knew she was grasping at straws but right now that was all she had.

Psychologically, she homed in on three key areas.

1. His use of weapon.
2. The leaving of a note.
3. The level of planning and pre-meditation involved in the crime.

These factors more than any others indicated that he was articulate, intelligent, imaginative and driven. He was out to prove something. Teach someone a lesson. Show the world he was right.

Angie deduced that he had completed high school and perhaps even a college education. His report card would show him to be smart but rebellious, a student who could be Grade A when he wanted – and probably out of the class and on his way to exclusion when he didn't. He'd have clashed with authority. Probably got sacked from early jobs or work experience schemes.

Angie doubted he had any significant criminal record. Perhaps there'd be some recreational drug use, but nothing serious; certainly no violent or sexual offences.

She was sure he would have been too intelligent to have got sucked into gangs and manipulated by people of lesser intelligence but bigger muscle. Instead, he'd have grown isolated and developed chameleon-like skills that allowed him to become socially invisible and therefore not picked on.

The offender's lack of concern for other people and his willingness to kill and maim showed an absence of any decent male or female role models in his life. As a consequence, she thought it unlikely he would be in any long-term sexual relationship. The combination of troubled characteristics meant it was almost certain he would live alone in a low-income neighborhood.

Angie was pleased with what she was pulling together. Her overview summarized him as a highly organized, sociopathic offender with Machiavellian and egotistical tendencies who would repeatedly kill until he was stopped. Her filter chart for investigators suggested they looked for:

1. Black male, 20–30.
2. 6 feet tall, 160 pounds in weight.
3. Physically fit, well nourished.
4. Not substance-dependent.
5. Well educated and intelligent. Argumentative when challenged. Maybe works in job beneath his abilities.
6. Perhaps orphaned and institutionalized at early age.
7. Not in sexual relationship and lives alone.
8. Financially independent but not wealthy.
9. No sexual or violent criminal record.
10. Possibly ambidextrous or left-handed.

Angie reviewed each point and couldn't find fault with any.

She looked again at the text lines she'd isolated and prioritized from the transcript of Jake's speech.

Line 3.   . . . the mind behind these acts is a cowardly, spineless,
          gutless one . . .
Line 6.   . . . the kind of person parents would disown . . .
Line 9.   . . . the worst criminals in prison would consider him
          too vile to be allowed a cell alongside them . . .

She was drawn again to line three. Was this the key to the UNSUB's rage? Had one or both of his parents called him 'cowardly', 'spineless' or 'gutless'? The thought resonated. Maybe he wasn't orphaned. Mabye his father was a law enforcement officer, a man who hated criminals, who had disowned him because of his ways and had branded him as worse than many of the people he'd locked up? The thought fizzed like a flare in Angie's fogged and painful head. It would explain a lot. Especially if his father happened to be a serving officer – a senior lawman in LA.

She took it a step further.

Perhaps he was a *very* senior officer, like John Rawlings. A man who had publicly humiliated his only son by prosecuting him for smoking dope.

She called Chips. 'I've just been thinking, a couple of years back, the LAPD's venerable chief of police had his son Jason busted.'

'Yeah, I read about it. Kid had a blow habit. Shock, horror. What about it?'

'They fell out very publicly as a result. Rawlings Junior went off radar after that. No doubt took his grudge with him. Can you find out where he is now?'

'Probably. No one with a legit ID is invisible these days. What are you chasing?'

'A hunch, Chips. Just a hunch.'

Chapter 125

Douglas Park, Santa Monica, LA

It was late afternoon when Crawford Dixon arrived unexpectedly at Angie's place. He came dressed in respectful grey and that included the color of his face.

Angie saw him on the videophone door entry system, waiting in the block entrance downstairs. She couldn't let him in – the walls of her living room were plastered ceiling to floor with victim photographs, crime scene maps, UNSUB video grabs and countless notes scrawled in thick black ink.

She thought about pretending not to be home but that seemed weak and wrong. Instead, she grabbed her jacket and keys then went downstairs to head him off.

The FBI section chief was pacing by the entrance buzzer, waiting to be let in.

She opened up. 'Hello, Crawford.'

'*Angie.*' He fastened his jacket and became attentive. 'I just came by to see how you are.'

'That's kind. Do you mind if we walk a while? I'm going stir crazy up there.'

'Of course not.'

She led the way. They strolled the tree-lined street outside her block, sunlight bouncing through thick canopies of maple, cedar and oak. Despite her urge to, she knew she couldn't come straight out and ask about the arrest Chips had informed her of. 'Any developments?'

'Not in relation to catching Jake's killer.' He turned to look at her. 'But he *will* be caught. That I can promise you.'

'Can you, Crawford?' She made no effort to keep the skepticism out of her voice. 'Everyone seems to promise me that.'

He walked a few paces to take a break, then asked, 'Angie, have you given any thought to funeral arrangements?'

The question hit her like a kidney punch. 'A little.'

He sensed she was still raw.

'I know you and Jake weren't married, but Sandra McDonald and I have insisted you are treated as his next of kin, at least as far as the FBI is concerned.'

She tried to read between the lines. 'To what ends?'

'Well, with your permission, I'd like the Bureau to take care of him – of all the arrangements.'

She nodded. 'Thanks, that would be a help.'

'I've been talking to the director and we think it fitting to give Jake a hero's goodbye and lay him to rest at Arlington. We'll be petitioning for a memorial to mark his valor both inside and outside his time in the military.'

Angie frowned. 'I don't want to sound strangely ungrateful, but I'm not sure that's what he would have wanted.'

Dixon seemed shocked. 'What makes you say that?'

She didn't want to go into details. 'As a young soldier, he wrote about wanting to be cremated, having his ashes scattered high in the night sky over the Pacific.'

'Aah, a nice farewell for a young soldier, but not for the hero that he became.'

'I suspect Jake was always a hero. The world just took its time noticing him.'

Dixon could see this wasn't the time to **argue**. 'Will you think about it? Lots of people would like to show their respects and be there to honor him.'

'Yes, of course I will. I'll give it good thought.'

He smiled appreciatively. 'So how are *you* holding up? Getting any sleep?'

'Sleeping's not a problem. The pain isn't there when I sleep, but it's all over me like wasps on a trash can when I'm awake.'

'I understand. It'll take a while.'

'So I'm told.' She took a couple of silent steps then hit on him for information. 'A minute ago you said there was nothing new "in relation to Jake" – that kinda implies there is *something* new.'

He didn't answer.

'I'm guessing it's in relation to the Sun Western slayings.'

Dixon stopped walking. 'Angie, you should be resting and recovering, not guessing developments.'

'I know Jake and Pryce were chasing a suspect –' she played coy – 'so I suppose there has been an arrest and someone charged.'

'Not quite.' He let out a resigned sigh. 'But there is a man in custody.' He saw expectation in her eyes. 'Don't read too much into this, Angie. Ruis Costas is over with Connor Pryce at the moment and I expect, from what Ruis has said to me, there will be a joint statement this evening about a man being charged – but for now, *only* in connection with the mall shootings.'

Angie became agitated. 'Don't let them do that, Crawford. It would be a terrible mistake.'

'What?'

'It would be wrong, Crawford. The profile I started—'

'Angie, you've got to drop your obsession with this case. I don't want to be indelicate, but you're not thinking straight.'

Her face flushed with anger. 'Is there evidence to support murder charges? I really suspect not.'

He gave up more than he'd intended. 'There are excellent ballistic and forensic ties to a suspect. A suspect who has already been linked with previous murders and has been pictured in almost exactly the same clothes as the Sun Western UNSUB.'

The explanation took the wind out of her sails. That was a lot more convincing than she'd expected.

Either she was wrong.

Or the killer was even brighter than she'd thought.

Angie turned back to her building. 'I'll call you about Arlington. Give me a day and I'll give you an answer. Thanks for coming by.'

Chapter 126

The sun had long gone down by the time Chips rolled up with pizza.

Angie had hardly any appetite but knew she had to keep up pretenses and stay away from the dark clouds of depression that were closing in. 'Hey, my man. I'm disappointed to see you in a plain white T. I miss your slogans. You want beer or soda?'

'The Ts will be back – in good time.' He put the boxes on her table. 'Coke or Mountain Dew would be good.'

Angie pulled two of each from the cooler and grabbed plates for the food. 'I made up the spare room for you, but you don't have to stay. Hell, you don't even need to be here.'

He put his arms around her. 'Course I need to be here. And I *want* to be. Both for you and for Jake.'

She hugged tight, then had to push him away before she became emotional.

'Take a look at the work I've put on the wall and tell me what you think.'

He surveyed it like he was studying a new painting. 'Well, the profiling is not too shabby but I think you're gonna need a home makeover. That pen will never clean.'

'I know.'

He picked up a piece of pepperoni pie. Chewed as he mentally worked through the columns, lists, routes and intricate profile points. 'Social media. You've missed it out completely.'

'I can't stick Twitter feeds to a wall, there are so many of them.'

She decided to force down a sliver of veggytariana with extra olives. 'Besides, I'm not that interested in what the public has to say about him.'

'Maybe you should be. *He* certainly will be. He'll be watching and reading everything about himself. In fact, you once told me, people don't kill in public unless they want a public reaction to their killing.'

'I said that?'

'You did. And if you weren't so tired and stressed you'd be telling me this creep will be all over the social media spectrum, sucking up every mention of himself, trying to feed his ego.'

Chips had a point and she knew it. 'Okay. You're right. We've got a gaping hole there. I haven't been able to stomach watching the TV news, let alone read blogs and crazy chat-room rants.'

'You don't have to. I've made a compilation of top sites, postings and Facebook pages. We can run through them together and then I can work out a social media strategy to deal with him.' He grabbed the TV remote. 'Are you up to watching the regular news?' She popped the tab on a can of soda. 'I guess I have to be.'

He powered up the set and found a news channel. A report detailed a whole new batch of hurricanes rolling towards poor old Mississippi. Then came a story about the shooting of a businessman in the washrooms at the Olympic Conference Center. The studio anchor threw live to a smart young man in a dark suit, who held a microphone under his chin.

'Investment banker Sean Thornton was gunned down inside a stall in the washrooms early this afternoon, outside a hall where city bankers were holding their annual conference. The fifty-two-year-old was found as the day's session came to a close and colleagues searched for him. Unconfirmed reports say robbery may be a motive. Mr Thornton was found minus his credit cards, watch and wallet.'

Angie couldn't help but jump in. 'No one heard the shots?'

'A robbery in a john's pretty weird,' added Chips. 'Unless maybe a *"new friend"* came on to him.'

Angie pointed at the screen. 'He's married, look. Wife and two kids.'

'Marriage doesn't stop men having "*special*" friends, believe me.'

'Too much information, Chips.' After half a slice of pizza Angie felt like she was exploding. She put the plate down and took a hit of soda to wash the gut ache away. 'You have any luck finding the errant son of our revered police chief?'

He wiped greasy fingers on a napkin. 'Jason John Rawlings split from the family home right after his father had him prosecuted. Last year he moved out of LA and got hospitalized in San Francisco following an overdose of sleeping pills. He's been unemployed and living on welfare ever since. No fixed abode. He just drifts and scrounges. Cops I talked to say his old man never pulls favors to keep him outta jail. That said, the kid got pulled for illegal possession of a firearm and ammunition in Arizona and walked.'

'How come?'

'Official story is they messed up procedure and had no choice.'

'And the *un*official?'

'Custody sergeant used to work with his old man and did him the favor – maybe without even being asked.'

'Can you dig some more?'

'I can *try* but don't hold your breath.'

The TV filled with a caption announcing NEWS JUST IN.

Angie pointed at the remote near his hand. 'Turn it up.'

The anchor was now in front of a large background depicting the aftermath of the bombing at the mall memorial.

'Moments ago, the FBI and LAPD revealed they have arrested and charged a man in connection with both the shootings at the Sun Western mall and the bomb attack that followed.'

Up came the familiar and now famous photograph lifted from the grainy CCTV mall footage, showing a young black male in Lakers cap, T-shirt, baggy shorts and sneakers. The anchor explained, 'This is the suspect who has been subject to a nationwide hunt this week.'

Alongside the first picture came a second. It was also blurred but showed another black man in virtually identical clothes holding a MAC-10.

The similarity took Angie's breath away.

Was this really the monster that slaughtered all the people in the mall?

And Jake?

The anchorman added, 'The LAPD have now named him as twenty-three-year-old Aaron Bolt.'

Chapter 127

The young man in square-framed glasses and a cheap brown suit picked his way through the dank and dirty works depot and knocked on the open door of the tiny office that had belonged to Januk Dudek. He cracked a friendly smile at the seated occupant and said warmly, 'Hi, I've come to see how you're getting on.'

Shooter recognized him from his visit to Head Office. This was Gary Hawkins, the VP of operations, a corporate brown-noser and general lackey. 'I'm getting on fine.' He wiped his hand on his overalls before offering it politely. 'What brings you here at this time?'

Hawkins tentatively shook hands. 'As you know, most of our work is at these godawful hours. What the world messes up during the day, we put right at night. Can I sit down?'

Shooter pulled back the desk so there was enough room for the VP to slide a chair out.

Hawkins squeezed in and settled down. 'The thing is, despite a lot of effort, we haven't been able to trace Mr Dudek. Disappointingly, he hasn't responded to any of our calls, texts, mails, or even a hand-delivered note to his home.'

'That's strange.' Shooter did his best to look bemused. 'I've asked around here and no one heard him talk about holidays or going away.'

'We think he might have left town. We've been through all the data we have on file, even checked hospitals and medical centers. It doesn't seem he's ill or being treated anywhere.'

'At least that's good.'

'Yes. I suppose it is.' Hawkins sounded as though he didn't care.

'This morning, a colleague went to Mr Dudek's apartment block and found no one has seen him for some days.' His tone became even more officious. 'Given all those factors, it appears he's made himself unavailable for work. As I'm sure you know, prolonged and unauthorized absence constitutes gross misconduct and a breach of contract and is therefore a dismissible offence.'

'No. I didn't know that.'

'Well it does. And I'm afraid Mr Dudek has left us with no option but to terminate his employment.' Hawkins forced out a smile of zero sincerity. 'Mr Taylor, he's the EVP who spoke to you the other day, has sent me to tell you that he was very impressed with how you stepped forward and have kept things going. So, for a trial period of six months, we'd like to offer you the job of depot supervisor. What do you say?'

Shooter didn't want to say anything. The way he figured it, somewhere down the line the cops might come calling and the last thing he wanted was to get suspected of killing Januk for his crappy job. 'No, thanks.'

'Excuse me?'

'I don't mind helping fill the gap, but no thanks. I really don't want the supervisor's job.'

'Why?'

He shrugged. 'I don't know. I guess I just like being out on the road.' He put his hands down on a set of timesheets and sick notes spread over the dingy cheap desk. 'I hate all this stuff.'

'Oh, I see.' Hawkins paused and then eyed him suspiciously. 'Is this a money thing? Coz if it is, then of course there's a pay rise, but not a big one. I should warn you that we're not going to be held to ransom. There are lots of people out there looking for key managerial jobs like the one we're opening up to you.'

'I'm sure there are. I just don't wanna do it any longer than necessary.'

Hawkins looked worried. 'But you'll keep acting as supervisor until we find someone?'

'Yeah, I'll do that. But I want it on record that I don't want the job. And I have to tell you, if a month from now you haven't replaced Mr

Dudek, then you're going to have to replace me too, because I'll just walk outta here like he seems to have done.'

Hawkins gave the comment due executive consideration before replying. 'We have an agency who'll find someone. Someone with *ambition.*' He pushed back his chair, got to his feet and headed to the door. 'Oh, by the way, we have also informed the police about Mr Dudek's disappearance. I'm telling you because you might get a call from them. Be sure to let us know if you do.' Hawkins walked out without a goodbye.

Shooter went to the office window that overlooked the yard. He watched the lights of the VP's company Chevy blaze on and then float away into the blackness beyond the depot gates.

He snagged a set of van keys from a nearby row of wall hooks and headed out.

There were two hours before dawn. Three before the end of his shift.

He had just enough time to get things done.

Chapter 128

Douglas Park, Santa Monica, LA

After their late dinner, Angie and Chips began wading through all the social media comment on the four incidents – the Strawberry Fields massacre, the Sun Western shootings, the memorial bombing and Jake's murder.

Four hours later, they were still at it.

Chips had run a special software capture program that culled all topic-related comments and pictures from Reddit, Twitter, Tumblr, Flickr, Facebook, MySpace, Deviant Art and a dozen other portals.

He'd divided the haul into three categories: NEWS, and POSITIVE and NEGATIVE COMMENT.

NEWS contained a lot of user-generated content, mainly cellphone pictures and videos, plus tweets on body counts, roads closed, emergency numbers and speculation of who was to blame.

POSITIVE COMMENT was a heartwarming flood of messages from the public, thanking the LAPD and FBI for their efforts, offering help and assistance to families of victims and venting their anger at the atrocities and those who caused them.

NEGATIVE was a toxic collection of posts from cop haters, criminals, conspiracy theorists and general scum of the earth.

Angie had been locked in a pensive silence for the past half hour, writing notes and double-checking comments across various social platforms. 'Okay –' she stretched her injured arm as best she could and eased away a little cramp – 'I think I have some conclusions.'

'I'm all ears,' answered Chips.

'Let's do consensus first.' She rolled her shoulders to get rid of a crick in her neck. 'Most people commenting think the mall shootings and bombings *are* related and are the work of seasoned terrorists such as al-Qaeda. The Boston Marathon comes up a lot, people are still scarred from that, and you see it in repeated mentions of Chechen cells and Syria.'

'Strange, isn't it, until April 2013, most Americans had never heard of a Chechen.'

'And most still can't find Syria on a map.' She looked down at her notes. 'In terms of main interest, the public put Sun Western first, Strawberry Fields second and Jake low and last.'

He could see it hurt her to say that. But she was right; his death had been completely overshadowed by the other tragedies. 'Jake gets the most sympathetic comments,' he said encouragingly. 'I think there's near universal recognition that he was a good, brave man and his death is a hell of a loss.'

Angie could see that he was trying to lift her spirits. 'Thanks.' She pulled over some notes she'd made. 'One of the more interesting threads in the conspiracy chats is a suggestion that the attacks were a backlash against poverty.'

'Yeah, I saw that. CNN picked up on it and found some low-rent sociology professor to claim the mall represented America's rich and the UNSUB saw himself as the embodiment of the poor raging against the injustice of poverty.'

Angie had to stifle a yawn while she stared at the screen of her laptop on the dining table. 'I've been thinking over what you said earlier about the UNSUB reading everything online about himself.'

'I'm certain he is.'

'Me too.' She sat back and looked straight at him. 'Which is why I think there's a way to make contact with him.'

'Go on.'

'I need you to use your black arts, Chips. Create a virtual me. Give me a new face, name, identity, and build me some edgy false social media memberships and followers.'

'That's all easy stuff.'

'And when you've done it, can you also bounce my IP address to a rented house across the city?'

He smiled. 'Lady, I can bounce it to the moon if you like.'

Chapter 129

Shooter headed home just after dawn.

Everything had gone well. Quicker and slicker than he'd dared hope. LA would soon be waking up to a wonderful surprise.

The road was still quiet but there were god-awful noises coming from inside his compound. As he opened the gates he could see a pack of stray dogs had gotten in somehow. They were fucking and fighting like the end of the world was only minutes away. He loaded his arms with half bricks from a mountain of rubble and set about pitching hard.

A scraggy Alsatian got his rhythm ruined by a blow to the shoulder, and two dirt-brown Labs forgot their differences when chunks of brick skittled their legs.

'Get outta here! Go on, get the fuck away from my place!' Shooter closed on them with another barrage of bricks.

They got the message and scampered out of the open gates.

He dropped the rest of his ammunition, closed the compound and brushed brick dust off his hands. All he had to do now was find out how the little bastards had got in.

The answer came around the rear of the old shoe factory, in a far corner backing onto a deserted yard and beyond it a footpath and side street. Someone had opened a slit in the wire fence about a yard high all the way to the ground.

He bent low and examined the rusty metal mesh where it had been snipped. The links hadn't been severed by sharp, single cuts; they'd been chewed away by blunt, cheap wire cutters. Brute strength had been used to twist and snap the more stubborn strands. That sloppy MO ruled out the cops or Feds and probably meant it was either the handiwork of petty thieves intent on stripping the place for metal, or bums looking for somewhere to sleep.

Shooter opened up the app he'd developed for his iPhone and logged in to the building's surveillance system. He methodically examined each camera feed and only when he'd checked them all again was he content that nothing had been damaged and no one had managed to break in.

Cautiously, he circled the outside of the factory. Around the far side he found an old pallet angled against a wall. There were shoe marks up the outside of the building. Cardboard had been thrown over the coiled razor wire that he'd nailed just below the roof gutters.

Shooter stood on top of the pallet and spotted ripped denim and dried blood on the barbs. Someone had tried to climb it. There was no real sag in any of the strands so it looked like they'd given up.

He jumped down.

A hand hit the middle of his back. It threw him face first into the brick. A hard kick took his legs from under him. Suddenly he was face down in the dirt, his hand locked up his back.

'I'm a police officer,' said a male voice. 'If you resist arrest, I will use a Taser on you, and if you're still trouble after that, then I'll shoot the living fuck out of you, so stay very still.'

Chapter 130

Culver City, LA

Ruis woke dripping sweat.

In his dreams he'd been shot. Gunned down outside his apartment just like Jake had been.

He was no psychologist, but he knew it meant one of two things. Either he was developing a subconscious fear about his own vulnerability, or else he blamed himself for Jake's death.

Maybe it was a bit of both.

Had he stayed with Jake, they'd have gone for a very late drink together as they had so many times in the past. They might even have grabbed some food from a 24/7 diner. Either way, it could have saved his boss's life.

But he'd been tired.

Cried off early because he wanted to rest.

Now it seemed so weak. So wrong.

A look at the clock told Ruis it was almost seven. He'd tossed and turned most of the night, even gotten up twice.

He swung his legs out of bed, creaked off the old mattress and went to the bathroom. As he stood in the shower something else was preying on his mind.

The look on Aaron Bolt's face.

He'd spent years staring into the eyes of killers and there was no doubt the man they'd arrested had taken lives. It was in his unblinking stare, his hard, challenging gaze, and his cocky, arrogant look. All of that was consistent with a cold-blooded murderer, but when Pryce had gone into details about the mall, there'd been no hiding the guy's surprise. It hadn't been outrage at being linked to such an atrocity. It had been genuine shock. Bemusement, then blank but honest denial.

Pryce had felt differently. The cop had been absolutely sure he'd got his man. And that was worrying Ruis too.

He turned off the water and pulled on a toweling robe. Water ran down his legs and he left wet footprints on the imitation oak boards as he walked to the kitchen. He opened the fridge and grabbed a carton of juice. He swigged straight from the box and took it with him to the sofa.

For some minutes he sat there, his eyes fixed on a photo across the room in a silver frame.

It was of him and Jake. Arms around each other. Smiles as wide as a freeway.

It had been taken by one of the crew at the end of a charity marathon and they both had copies of it.

They'd finished the run together, side by side, neither of them wanting to better the other. Brothers in arms.

Ruis lifted the carton to his old boss. 'I'm gonna miss you, buddy. Miss you more than you'll ever know.'

He took a swig of the OJ and put it down just as his cellphone rang.

One thing he knew even before he answered – it was too early for the call to be good news.

Chapter 131

Shooter felt the cold steel of a handcuff ensnare his wrist. Pain blew up in his shoulder as the cop dragged his other arm into position and completed the cuffing.

The lawman rolled him.

Shooter stared up. He saw a guy his age but broader and a whole lifestyle more muscular.

'I'm arresting you for attempted burglary, you have the right to remain—'

'It's my place!' protested Shooter. 'I rent it.' He wriggled his legs. 'The keys are in my pocket.'

The young cop stopped reading rights and patted him down. 'So what the fuck were you doing halfway up a wall if you're a key-holder?'

'Someone cut the fence while I was out. I found wood against the wall and wanted to see if they were up on the roof.'

The rookie emptied a jumble of stuff out of Shooter's pockets until he found the keys and a driving license. 'Stay the fuck still while I find out if you're who you say you are.'

Shooter caught his breath, then slowly sat up in the dirt and watched him walk away a few paces and talk into his radio. This was going to work out okay. He was sure it would. Things were nowhere near as bad as he'd first feared.

The cop took an age.

Finally, he turned around and came back. The look on his face told Shooter he could stop worrying.

'Your story checks out.' He pulled him to his feet and dusted him down. 'I'm sorry I roughed you up. I'm Mike Hanrahan, I work this beat on my own and you can't take risks these days.' He got out his handcuff keys and freed flesh from steel.

'I understand.' Shooter rubbed his wrists. 'Better to say sorry than get yourself shot.'

'You got it.' Hanrahan stuck out a hand and hoped for a shake. 'No hard feelings?'

Shooter took it. 'None.'

'Thanks.' He silenced crackly chatter on his radio. 'We had a report from a security guard a block down. He said he'd come back from picking up some late night chow and had seen teenagers down the alley acting suspiciously. I mean, kids up at this time, that on its own is suspicious.' The big cop let his eyes roam over the building. 'So what do you do in here that warrants all the Colditz wire?'

Shooter stayed cool. 'I'm starting to build computers. Buying in components from Asia, assembling them here and selling the completed units online.'

'Sounds cool.' A thought hit him. 'How about this: in return for a deal on new PCs, I fix for a patrol car to prowl here every hour or so. What do you think?'

Unwanted as it was, Shooter didn't see how he could refuse. 'Sounds good.'

Hanrahan nodded to the door. 'Shall we seal the deal with a cup of Joe and I'll check around inside for you? Make sure no one got in through a gap somewhere.'

'No can do.' Shooter had to think of something quick. 'I don't have any coffee. Nothing to drink. Not until I've been shopping, later.'

The cop gave him an awkward stare, then smiled. 'Hey, no worries. I'll still check the place out for you. Would be nice to see your stuff, so I can tell the guys at the precinct what to expect.' He started towards the entrance door.

Shooter walked after him. 'Truth is, I'm whacked and a little shaky after you scared the shit out of me. Really, I just want to hit the sack.'

Hanrahan finally took the hint and turned to the gates. 'Okay. But if I were you, I'd get that fence mended quick as I can.'

'I will.' Shooter watched him turn his radio back up and kick dust all the way across the yard and out onto the sidewalk.

He sighed with relief.

A great day had almost finished terribly. He'd been sloppy. Careless.

It wouldn't happen again.

The lesson had been learned.

Chapter 132

Douglas Park, Santa Monica, LA

A ngie had fallen asleep at the table where she and Chips had been working.

He'd managed to sleepwalk her into the bedroom and get her to flop underneath her comforter, then he'd gone back to his MacBook and all her notes.

There were so many different victims, weapons, scenes and possible motives; he was going mad trying to figure things out.

Finally, he'd crashed out, just like his boss. When he came round he had a pain in his neck and an old piece of advice in his head. One Angie had given him.

The first kill was always the most important.

It was true with all Serials and even most Sprees.

He got up and stretched. Through the cracked door he could see Angie was still asleep. He hoped she was finding some peace and strength.

Chips took his keys off the table and slipped out of the apartment. There was no way he was going back to sleep, so he figured he might as well do a little research.

The sky was still pink and raw as he drove across town to Tanya Murison's house. She'd been the first victim shot at the mall and he'd seen dozens of crime scene photographs, but never any photographs of where she lived.

The neighborhood was run-down and the street filled with cheap, old cars. She and her husband had risen to the top of a very poor pile and had a corner plot townhouse opposite a big block of ugly apartments.

Chips parked his six-year-old BMW and got out. He used his smartphone camera to snap wide shots of the Murisons' house and surrounding buildings. Statistically, he knew, this was a hood that would be home to all manner of crooks.

Everyone was still asleep. No lights burned in any of the homes. The street was silent except for birds. He heard a diesel van struggling to start up a street away. Finally it chugged into life and drove off. Chips clicked more shots with his camera as he walked along the low privet hedge that skirted the front and side of the plot. It had been well clipped and he wondered if the old lady had been the gardener or her husband.

He pushed the gate and strolled down the side of the house. It would be good to get some shots at the back. See who overlooked the place. Angie's encounter with the rapist flashed in his mind and he stopped.

Finally, he found the courage to turn the corner.

'Holy fuck!' Chips put his hand to his thudding heart.

A woman's body dangled from the wrought iron bracket of a hanging basket over an open back door. A noose was around her neck. She was swinging gently.

'Jesus! Jesus! Jesus.' Chips started to panic. He dropped his phone. Bent quickly, grabbed it and stepped back.

When he looked again at the hanging corpse he realized it wasn't a body.

It was a dummy. Life-size.

Dressed in the clothes of an old woman. Black shoes had been fitted to tights, stuffed with what he guessed might be balled-up newspapers.

Chips stepped closer.

It was Tanya Murison.

Or at least a blown-up photograph of her face, stuck on a papier-mâché head. The mouth had been smeared with dark red lipstick. Mascara circled the eyes. Old broken spectacles had been glued in position. Black, African-American hair had been stuck over the skull and a worn navy bonnet pinned in place.

Chips looked at the gloved hands. Fingernail clippings had been fitted on the ends of each gloved digit.

His stomach flipped and he almost hurled. He looked away. Told himself to be professional. It was important he reacted properly. Captured the moment as quickly as possible.

He raised his smartphone and clicked off a shot. His hands were shaking but he was okay. He could get through this.

Chips stepped further into the back yard and clicked again.

Something caught his eye.

Beyond the swinging dummy he'd pictured, through the open back door of the townhouse, flat out on the ground was another figure.

An unmistakable human one.

Motionless.

Chapter 133

Inside the house, beyond the slowly moving shadow caused by the swinging life-size effigy of Tanya Murison, a man's body twitched and groaned.

Chips stood shaking from shock. He stared down at a black male in his late sixties, curled on his side, hand clutching his heart.

'I'm calling for help, sir. Don't worry, you're going to be all right.' It was a promise Chips wasn't sure he could deliver as he hit the phone. First 911, then Angie, and then, on her instruction, Ruis.

In between the calls he went back to the old man, comforted him and checked his pulse. The senior's face was creased with pain. He was sweating and so short of breath he couldn't speak.

Within ten minutes, sirens filled the early-morning air. 'I can hear the ambulance, hang in there.' Chips wiped the man's glistening brow and held his free hand.

A male and female paramedic soon rounded the corner of the Murisons' back yard, their eyes already scanning for the patient. They both did a double take when they saw the swinging female dummy.

'Don't ask.' Chips flashed his FBI ID at the nametags of Adam Miles and Su Fenton. 'The sick man is over there, inside the house.' He pointed into the kitchen beyond the open doorway. 'I think he's having some kind of heart attack.'

Miles ducked the dummy and made his way through.

Fenton, a brunette in her late twenties, hung back. 'Do you know how long he's been like that?'

'I don't. I've been here less than fifteen minutes. Guy was already down when I arrived.'

'Can he talk?'

'No, he's in too much pain, but he's been conscious all the time.'

'Did you give him anything?'

'A little water, but he could hardly swallow. There are no pills in his pocket, or in the bathroom – I looked.'

'Thanks.' She rounded the dummy, knocked it spinning with her shoulder and joined Miles with the patient.

Chips paced nervously. He was beginning to wish he'd stayed at Angie's place and stuck to pure theory. If this was fieldwork without the danger of an UNSUB shooting at you then it was already too scary for him.

The medics grabbed a roll-along bed from the ambulance and started to move the senior to the vehicle.

'We think he has a myocardial infarction,' explained Fenton as she walked. 'Pain's all over his chest and his heartbeat's irregular. We've given him oxygen and aspirin and it's starting to help.'

Chips walked to the curb with them. 'Is he going to be okay?'

She knew what he wanted to hear. 'There's a good chance he'll be fine.'

Ruis Costas's Jeep pulled up just as the medics left. The SKU man was dressed casual in black jeans and white shirt. He dropped from the driver's side to the blacktop and watched the ambulance disappear before joining Chips. 'Is he alive?'

'Just about.' He looked at the neighbors gathering in their doorways. 'Remind me to make a T saying how much I hate rubberneckers.' He led Ruis towards the house. 'The sick guy is Harlan Murison, Tanya's widower. I found his ID on a table in the kitchen.'

'Holy shit.' Ruis recoiled as he confronted the effigy. 'I know you said there was an effigy swinging in the yard, but man, that's freaky.' He circled it. Stared at the photo-face of Tanya. Squeezed the legs and lumpy body. 'There's rolled-up paper inside these tights and clothes, to make a human shape.' He examined the black gloves tied to the

409

ends of the arm stumps. 'Fuck, have you seen this? These are *real* fingernails stuck to the end.'

Chips cringed with revulsion. 'The hair strands?'

Ruis peered at them. 'Real as well. And the lipstick and mascara smeared on the face.' He stepped away from the thing. 'You think some local kids did this? Maybe the old man made himself unpopular with a gang?'

Chips pulled a sour face. 'No, I think the killer did this. I'm willing to bet that he made this out of Tanya's old clothes and stuff she'd thrown away and he hung it here to shock the husband and get more attention for himself.'

Ruis stared up at the noose around the effigy's neck. 'When CSIs are done, I'm gonna ask them for that rope, so when we catch this fucker I can string him up with it.'

Chapter 134

The music Shooter chose for the video edit was Marilyn Manson's 'Death Song'. The lyrics were fittingly full of cops, priests, candles and injustice. But what nailed it for him was the rapid cymbal slaps in the opening section. They were delicious reminders of the noise the G18 made when he'd shot the Fed.

The killing was on the news now, playing low on the TV while he labored over the computer and to his great enjoyment made Jake's lifeless body jump from frame to frame. It fascinated him how, with the power of rewind, he could bring the big man back to life, empty him of lead then shoot and kill him over and over again. When he grew bored, his eyes slid to the TV. Apparently, the husband of Sun Western mall victim Tanya Murison had suffered a heart attack but was recovering well in hospital. That was good. He hadn't wanted old Harlan to die. Not yet. The old bastard had to suffer a lot more first. And Shooter was most amused to find the studio anchor mentioning that police investigating the shooting of Sean Thornton at a bankers' convention in LA were now following leads that connected him to a Sicilian investment group prosecuted for money laundering. That came as a pleasant surprise. Hopefully it would mean even more grief for his widow, Mary.

There had been no mention of Januk Dudek. Not that he'd expected any. He suspected that he spent more time thinking about the missing Polack than anyone else did. Nor was there so much as a passing

411

reference to the Strawberry Fields massacre. It was amazing how quickly the press had grown bored with what had been front-page news only days ago.

Just after eleven, a police cruiser slow-circled his sanctuary.

Shooter watched it crawl from one security monitor to the other. Mike Hanrahan had been as good as his word. Which meant at some point, the cop was likely to park and come knocking, either for a favor or just to escape the sun and boredom of his job. Either way, he was going to be trouble.

Shooter watched the black and white disappear then went about his business. Today was a two-bag day. One for cleans and one for dirties.

And in a little over an hour, things were going to get very dirty.

Chapter 135

Douglas Park, Santa Monica, LA

A ngie had intended to drive to Tanya Murison's house to be with Chips.

While telling him to call Ruis, she'd struggled out of bed and made her way to the bathroom. Despite being exhausted and her injured arm hurting like hell, she'd had the shower running before she'd even hung up.

Then she'd seen it.

The reminder that had popped up on the smartphone. A note to herself that a week today was the anniversary of when she and Jake had first met.

It felt a lifetime ago.

Jake's lifetime.

But she still had the photo from that first night. The crazy loon had insisted on a waiter taking it at dinner; clinking wine glasses and smiling fresh faces over a white linen cloth centered with a red and yellow rose. He'd told her that in ten years' time they'd come back to the same restaurant and take a picture sat at the same table. Back then, Angie had thought it was just a line. Now it was what she wanted most in the world.

She wished the reminder had never come. Wished she didn't feel compelled to open the media gallery on her phone and look at the thumbprints of memories that spanned the past three years. Dozens upon dozens of pictures of her and Jake. She'd snapped him a thousand times. Shots in MacArthur Park, blossom behind his head, looking as soft as a puppy. Coming out of the ocean, tanned and ripped like a hard-case movie star. Head back and snoring like an old man in the rear of a cab after a late party out at Venice Beach. And there were videos too. Not that she was strong enough to look at any of them. The bravest and saddest thing she could face was replaying his last voice message to her.

'Sorry. When you're done being mad at me, remember, I love you.'

The words tore her apart.

And then there was that picture. The one the waiter had taken. She opened the file and felt an awful pain. They looked so good together. Eyes bright with lust and hope. All the future to look forward to. True love still a thousand steamy sex sessions away. Arguments and break-ups unimaginable. Pregnancy and marriage unthinkable.

She kissed the small frame of the phone. Kissed Jake. Kissed the whole damned restaurant, the moment and the memory.

The shower steamed behind her, but she couldn't stand, let alone step into it. She slid to the floor, back against the glass, phone to her aching chest, and felt wiped out. Empty. Hollow.

So this was grief.

It had come with stealth and hurt even more than she'd ever imagined. It went beyond wet eyes and unstoppable sobs, beyond regret, unfairness and injustice.

Angie snaked a left hand up to the rail by her side and pulled down a large, thick towel. She wrapped it around her shoulders and lay flat on the tiled floor. Her eyes were open but she wasn't seeing anything. Her mind was processing a million thoughts. She had to ride out the emotional storm. Wait for a break in the thunder and lightning.

It was a long time coming.

The doorbell rang twice and she didn't even blink, let alone get up and try to answer it. The hurt was everywhere. In her bones. In her blood. In her soul.

Gradually, she raised herself from the tiles, put down the cellphone and towel and slipped into the shower. The water felt like a thousand pins being stuck in her skull. She soaped and soaped. Tried to distract herself with the sharp smell of lemons and limes. Tried to wash away the sadness that was stuck to her.

Angie tilted her face into the spray and ran the shower hot.

She changed the pressure. Let it fall like soft summer rain before turning it into driving hail. She felt cells being stripped from her skin. Felt blood pump through her arteries.

Angie stayed there until she was dizzy from the heat, until she was so wet the skin on her fingers wrinkled and puckered. She shut off the tap and wiped her hands over her body to sluice off the water. Her palms found her tummy. Fingers gently circled the secret space where hope grew, where the baby slept.

Jake's baby.

Her baby.

Their child.

She stepped from the shower and toweled dry. Gently rubbed moisturizer on the slight curve of her stomach that cradled her reason to live. The clothes she picked for the day were loose and practical. Black leggings and a pink silk zip shirt with rolled cuffs.

She towel-dried her hair and decided against make-up, in case she had another emotional moment and it got messed. From the fridge she grabbed OJ and a tub of plain yoghurt. Chips could cope on his own. Ruis would be there to help him. There was no need to rush.

She peeled the top off the yoghurt tub and looked at the mass of photographs and profiles plastered across the living room wall. None of it seemed to make any sense. Her gaze slid to the power socket beneath the scribblings. Plugged in was the pay-as-you-go phone she'd found in Jake's car. It had been flat. Only late last night had she dug through a drawer of old cables and found a charger that fitted it.

Now it was fully powered. The display showed it had last been called on the morning of Jake's death. The very time she'd been with him in the hospital. The moment when he was dying.

There were three missed calls and one new message.

Angie played it.

A man's voice boomed out. 'Call me. You were right. I have what you want.'

She played it again to see if she'd missed a name. She hadn't. Nor did she recognize the voice. She flicked through the phone's directory. It was empty. No names or numbers listed. Nor had the caller used his own or Jake's name. The message was a mystery. It could refer to anything. Some goods he'd ordered. A part for his car. Maybe a present for her.

But then why use a burner?

And what had Jake been right about?

It had to be something sensitive. Something that couldn't be said on a traceable line, or jotted down in an email.

She racked her brains but couldn't remember him mentioning a case that was highly confidential or unusually dangerous. For several minutes she fumbled with the phone's buttons and then found the text message function. There were none in the received or sent folders. She checked the deleted folder and found two.

One from Jake: ANY NEWS? JM

And a reply: BPATIENT. JL

JL.

The initials meant nothing to her. There was a John Lindsay who worked in HR at the Bureau. But there'd be no reason for Jake to make secret calls to him. And a Jenny Lovett in payroll, who was a year off retirement.

JL?

She hadn't got a clue. But she knew how to search for one. Cal O'Brien had Jake's FBI cellphone; it was possible there'd be a JL listed on that. And Chips would be able to use satellite triangulation to at least find the place where the missed calls had been made from.

She was about to dial O'Brien when her own phone rang. The display showed a familiar FBI number. 'Hello.'

'Angie, it's Sandra McDonald.'

Her spirits sank.

The AD cut to the point. 'Where is your research assistant and why have you been digging around Jason Rawlings?'

Angie took a slow breath and bent the truth. 'I asked Chips to help me with something personal, and with regard to Rawlings, I thought that given his very public differences with his father and the chief's profile, he might be a suspect—'

'Jesus, Angie.' She tried not to snap. 'I've had his old man on the phone for ten minutes all but ripping my head off. Now I understand why.'

'I'm sorry, but it—'

'Please don't "*but*" me.' McDonald barely managed to hold back her anger. 'Everyone knows what a terrible time you're going through but you have to stop interfering in cases. I told you not to get involved and I expect you to respect that instruction.'

'You could do with the help. Arresting and charging Bolt was a mistake and in career terms for *some people* it could turn out to be a costly one.'

McDonald rode the verbal punch. 'There were sufficient grounds for Bolt's arrest, not that we need debate the issue with you. Just so there's no mistake between you and me, listen carefully: stay out of this case, Angela. Otherwise I'll have Chips suspended and sent home.'

'Hey, that's unfair; none of this is down to him.'

'Of course it is.' Her voice gave away her rising annoyance. 'He's been like a mole on acid, digging around all over the place for you. Sure, he's a smart guy and can hide his online investigations well enough, but when he goes calling precincts then he stirs up trouble.'

'Why are you so sure Jason Rawlings has no connection to the killings?'

'Because he's got a cast-iron alibi.' She sounded infuriated. 'He has been more than a hundred miles away in a residential addiction center for the past month. And before you dare ask, yes I have checked personally and he hasn't for one minute left the premises.'

Chapter 136

The LAPD and CSIs were all over the Murison place. Ruis figured he'd take Chips for coffee and breakfast before the kid turned any paler and fainted.

They drove to a place just around the corner from the FBI offices, an Italian joint that made cappuccino thicker than clotted cream. Ruis went to the counter and ordered for them both – pancake stacks with sides of bacon and sausage.

'They didn't have croissants?' asked Chips when the food came.

'Breakfast like a king,' quipped Ruis. 'Enjoy.' He picked up bottles of maple syrup and treacle and made to uncap them.

'King Cholesterol.' Chips rolled his eyes. 'Tell me that you are not going to put syrup *and* treacle on that, Agent Costas.'

'I am. Start the day sweet and it stays that way.' Ruis squeezed both bottles at once and zigzagged drizzles across his food.

Chips looked mortified. 'Think of the fat. Your waistline. Your heart.'

'They all love it. Those body parts are just squealing with excitement over what's coming their way.' He took a long and satisfying chew, swallowed, then asked, 'So tell me, how's Angie doing? Real answer, no bullshit.'

Chips sipped his coffee. 'Not so good. She's tensed up all the time. Won't relax and let everything out. She thinks it's weak to cry. Beats herself up if her eyes get more than moist.'

Ruis nodded as he chewed. Wiped his mouth on a white paper

serviette. 'Angie Holmes certainly has a tough rep. Tough and smart. If she didn't argue with her boss and punch co-workers she'd be a cert to climb the slippery pole.'

'That's just Angie. She has no censor button.'

'Jake was almost as bad. Two peas in a pod.' Ruis replayed a couple of instances in his head. People Jake had defended when others wouldn't. Risks he'd taken that no one would have expected him to.

Chips saw he was struggling. 'I guess you miss him both professionally and personally.'

'I can't tell you how much. Jake Mottram was like a role model for me. A real tough mother with a big, soft heart. Would kick your ass one minute then defend your life with his the next. Man, he was pretty special.' Ruis tapped his head with a stubby finger. 'In here, he's still alive. I can't actually believe he's dead.'

'I know, it doesn't feel real.'

'Not at all. It's like he's gone away on vacation.' Ruis laughed. 'Or one of those damned management courses he hated. He always said they seemed to go on for weeks.'

'How long had you known each other?'

'Let me think. About four years. I met the boss around six months before he got together with Angie. Hell, he was a real hardass back then. There was no softness at all to him until she came along. She did the whole unit a favor by taking his edge off.'

'That wasn't in SKU, was it?'

'No. We were in a kind of rapid response pool back then. Deployed on –' Ruis shrugged – 'well, you know.'

Chips understood. Agent Costas meant the kind of jobs that didn't get spoken about. Black ops. Wet squads. Off-the-book assassinations. 'Coffee's good,' he said, picking up his skinny cap, eager to move the conversation on.

'Yeah it is.' Ruis took a hit of his. 'You looked kind of grey back there. For a desk-jockey, I thought you did good.'

'Thanks.' Chips felt his face redden. 'I don't normally venture out in the field. You know, when I came round the corner into the yard and saw that "thing" dangling there, my heart was in my mouth.'

'You thought it was a person?'

'Yes, I did.' He took another hit of coffee.

Ruis forked some sausage and dabbed it in syrup. 'So, exactly why were you there? I mean, given that Angie isn't supposed to be working any cases at the moment.' He chewed the meat while he waited for the answer.

Chips's face completed the transition to a deep claret color. 'Er – well – let's say I was tidying up some loose ends and I, er –'

Ruis waved him to be quiet. 'Listen, Angie Holmes is a big girl. I think it's right that she got sent home on compassionate and given the chance to recover without the pressure of work. But hell, if work is what helps her recover, then that's fine by me.' He wagged an empty fork. 'Just don't tell McDonald or Crawford I said that.'

'I won't.'

'I know you're a good guy, Chips. You're looking out for Angie and that's great. If she needs help and is afraid to ask, you call me, right? I'm looking out for her as well, even though she might not fully believe that.'

Chips took a long look at Ruis.

The SKU man stared back, quizzically. 'What?'

'I'm just wondering – do you think Jake's killer will be caught? Honest answer, not a bullshit one.'

Ruis took a sip of his coffee then placed the mug on the table. 'No. No I don't. But hell, that won't stop us all trying our best to prove me wrong.'

Chapter 137

Downtown, LA

Jerry Zander had opened a restaurant on South Spring Street six months ago. He'd got a good deal on the rental, but launching in tough times had scared the crap out of him.

Jerry needn't have sweated.

JZ's Saloon had gone from strength to strength and today it had been busting at the seams from the moment its doors opened for lunch.

Themed as a Wild West eatery, it was full of dark woods and warm lights, with cowboys drawing drinks behind the bar, Indian squaw waitresses working tables, bows and arrows strung on the walls, and a menu offering cheap food and all kinds of 'moonshine'.

From the get-go, Jerry understood that locals wanted to have fun, but they didn't have a whole lot of money to spend. By giving them good-value burgers, steaks, fish and fries plus some free entertainment in the form of gunfights and Indian magic tricks, he'd started to clean up.

Right now, there were two kids' birthday parties in full swing and tonight there would be a 21st and several bachelor parties.

Jerry was in his late thirties and a little on the heavy side but reckoned he was tall and handsome enough to carry it. He swaggered in front of the long mirror behind the bar and adjusted the big silver star on his Stetson emblazoned with the word 'SHERIFF'. He stood statue-still. Snatched his guns. Leveled them waist high. Twirled them in sync.

Dropped them back in their holsters and winked at the man in the mirror.

Pitchers of lemonade were on their way to the kids' tables. Two of the waiters staged a mock gunfight with cap guns. The bad guy in black lurched left and right then staggered backwards. It took him thirty seconds and most of the restaurant floor to finally die. The other cowpoke blew the barrel of his pretend gun and the diners cheered.

A squaw waitress made sure the youngsters got all the Stetsons and headdresses they wanted. Girls always went for the feathered golden bands and boys snapped up the sheriff hats.

'Howdy pardners,' Jerry hollered across the long table. 'You all having a good time down here?'

'YES, SHERIFF,' shouted moms and kids together.

'Glad to hear it. Y'all let me know if the chow's not to your likin'. Have a good day now.' Jerry politely tilted his hat and his eyes fell on a pretty mom in her mid-thirties. He was pleased to see her hold his gaze and smile back. He'd make a point of moseying on down to her end of the table once the burgers and fries had been cleared.

Two squaws rain-danced out of the kitchen in leather mini-skirts and put bottles of ketchup, mayo and mustard down on the tables. Then the restroom door opened and a masked cowboy trotted out on an imaginary horse and shouted, 'Hi-ho, Silver!'

The kids cheered.

The Lone Ranger turned to the table where the pretty blonde sat and pulled his guns. Kid sheriffs reached for their weapons.

The Lone Ranger opened fire.

Blood spattered the windows. Not pretend goo but shocking suck-all-noise-out-of-the-room real blood.

The masked man fired indiscriminately. Pretty women became face-less corpses. Shouting children fell silent.

The outlaw lawman, champion of justice, turned and sprayed automatic gunfire at the screaming diners across the restaurant.

Jerry felt fire break out in his stomach and chest. By the time he fully realized what had happened he was dead.

Chapter 138

Shooter kept the black mask on for half a block. He ducked into a gap behind a hoarding that fronted the junction of South Main and West 3rd and unlocked his bicycle from the iron post he'd chained it to.

Half an hour earlier, he'd walked into the restaurant in jeans and a T-shirt and had gone straight to the restroom. In there, he'd stripped naked and put on painter's overalls and then added the cowboy costume, plus boots with lifts.

Now he removed the Lone Ranger outfit and was left looking like a decorator. He rolled the jeans, T-shirt and guns into his canvas shoulder bag and covered everything else with gasoline from plastic bottles he'd brought. Once he'd set them ablaze, he mounted his bicycle and rode off.

With any luck, he'd be back at his sanctuary in time to see the first of the news bulletins.

It would be interesting to discover how many he'd killed – in addition to the one that really mattered, the pretty blonde mom sat at the head of the table.

Chapter 139

Chips was relieved to be back in the office and safely behind a desk. What wasn't so satisfying was that when he called Angie and updated her, she sounded really down. Flatter than he'd ever known her. He guessed it was natural. Part of the process of getting over having your life torn apart.

He spent the rest of the morning doing things Angie couldn't and shouldn't, namely tracing and tagging all the crap that had been written about Jake's death on the social media platforms.

Ninety-nine percent of what had been posted had been kind and sympathetic. The remainder seemed to be from cranks and anarchists.

Both Chips and Angie figured the killer wouldn't be stupid enough to blog or even send a message, but there was no doubt that he'd be avidly reading about himself and maybe even downloading pictures and articles.

Chips called the Bureau's Cyber Intelligence Unit and found no shortage of analysts ready to help. They told him they had a disinfected and isolated server in a 'dead house' in Watts that would look like an unprotected IP address and lure in predatory users by exposing itself.

As well as running search and trace programs on all the questionable sites, Chips intended to create more than a dozen social media memberships under the identity Judgelysia. On top of that, he wanted to add years of back postings and have some of her mails and accounts blocked in case it was scrutinized. Finally, he needed to ping it all from the 'dead house' out in Watts.

If the UNSUB became interested in Judgelysia, he'd find on her Facebook profile that she described herself as the Fourth Judge of the Underworld, the only female to sit in power in the afterlife and decide the fate of souls that Cerberus allowed through. The Elysia part of her name was an allusion to the Elysian Fields, the blessed place that sprung from Greek mythology. Judgelysia would be discovered to have sent tweets about all manner of spiritual and paranormal stuff, and on her own blog ranted about injustices in modern society and how the government used poverty to control the masses.

Both he and Angie knew it was a wild shot in the dark. But for now, the darkness was all they had to shoot at.

Chapter 140

Douglas Park, Santa Monica, LA

A ngie saw the South Spring Street killings on TV and left her apartment so fast she didn't even turn the set off.

She flicked on the siren in her Toyota and ran the lights all the way across town. Ambulances passed her in both directions. Reports on the radio said a dozen were dead and even more injured. Eyewitnesses mentioned guns being fired by a single male, dressed as the Lone Ranger.

Angie instinctively felt it was their UNSUB. The cowboy costume was as much a disguise as the rapper boy clothes and Lakers cap in the mall. Up above her, police copters swept the sky, cameras and desperate eyes scanned the blocks below. In a city of four million people they had almost no chance of spotting the guy. He was a chameleon, a shape-shifting sonofabitch who was getting bolder and better with each kill.

Her car squealed to a halt yards before the LAPD cordon thrown around the restaurant. As she got out, she saw that the crime scene was virtually in the shadows of the HQ of the California Department of Justice. The anagram they'd found at the Sun Western mall saying 'Judge and Jury' suddenly had extra resonance.

A young cop wandered towards her. She was without her badge and any authority to be there so she had to wing it. 'I'm Doctor Holmes from the FBI.' She pressed keys into his hand. 'Please get my car off the street and lock up for me.' Angie didn't wait for an answer. She strode away just as two paramedics passed carrying stretchers laden with the wounded. One was an old man hit in the hand, the other a teenage boy shot in both legs.

Just outside the restaurant entrance she saw Crawford and Ruis. Before she walked over she got out her smartphone and snapped several photographs and mailed them to Chips. He'd know what to do with them.

'It's him,' Angie said as she headed over to the two FBI men. 'This is the same UNSUB as hit the mall, you know that, don't you?'

Ruis looked shocked to see her. 'What the hell, Angie? *You* shouldn't be here.' He put his hands on her shoulders and tried to turn her around.

She pushed him off and looked to his boss. 'Crawford, don't make another public mistake. Believe me, this is your guy. Let me inside. Let me see where he shot first, where he came from. You know you need me on this.'

The section chief looked her over, his face full of doubts. 'Ruis is right, Angie, you shouldn't be here. But you are. And you're right, your insight might help. I'm gonna give you ten minutes. Less if I think you're not coping professionally, or if you're getting in the way of the team.'

'Thanks.' She walked towards the restaurant's frontage and felt the enormity of the case rush at her like a howling grey ghost. Hundreds of droplets of blood had hit the inside of JZ's large front window and run down in vertical streams.

Ruis tagged her and added what he knew. 'We've got eyewitness accounts from a waitress and three customers.'

'Are they still here?'

'Yeah, over in our ops van.' He held back for a second. 'Danielle is talking to them.'

Angie cringed at the mention of the woman's name. 'Let's hope she doesn't screw that up. What story are they telling?'

'Customers saw a masked man dressed in a white Lone Ranger suit shout "Hi-ho, Silver", then he opened fire on a party table in the corner. At first everyone thought it was part of the show. There are pretend guns being fired all the time. After the initial shots, he turned and opened up on the whole restaurant.'

'Lone Ranger as in full Disney drag, or just kind of that style?'

'As in the recent Johnny Depp turkey.'

She looked around. 'And the UNSUB portrays the masked battler for justice, right here outside the Department of Justice. This mother sure wants to rub our noses in it.' She opened the door and walked inside.

There were bodies and blood everywhere.

The ME hadn't yet arrived and medics were still separating the dead from the unconscious. Angie presumed that, as usual, there'd been an agonizing delay before law enforcement officers had given the all clear for the helpers to go in.

The place had been wrecked. The long mirror at the back of the bar was busted into centuries of bad luck, the rich dark wood veneer splintered into a winter's worth of kindling.

Angie glanced right. A number of dead women and children were slumped like blood-spattered rag dolls over a long table. It was covered in popped birthday balloons and a stomach-turning mush of spilled drink, slopped foods and bodily fluids. Corpse flies had already found their way to the table and crawled over hands and faces. The sad combination of moms and kids pinched a maternal nerve.

Ruis drifted a hand across the carnage. 'That's where the first shots were fired.'

She cleared her head and took in the scene. There were two doors barely twenty feet away. One was a flap-hinged entry to the kitchen, so waitresses could bump it open with their shoulders or butts. The other led to the washrooms.

He followed her eyes. 'A waitress said the gunman came out of the restroom with a big shoulder bag. He dropped it, shouted his lines and opened fire. CSIs are already working the stalls and basins.'

'The bag will have contained his normal clothes. Any CCTV in here?'

Ruis looked to his left. 'Just at the registers and over the bar – in case of staff fraud.'

'And out on the street?'

'Plenty, but they're high and wide. LAPD have got a detail grabbing tapes and searching. There's a surveillance camera on the building opposite, but the sun was burning straight into it.'

She shook her head in dismay. 'Is this guy one lucky sonofabitch or what?'

'Luck runs out,' said Ruis optimistically.

Angie's eyes flicked across the room and took in the spatter on the walls, the pooling on the floor, the splintered furniture, smashed glass, burst balloons and bloody corpses. Her training rearranged it into a logical order. 'It looks to me like the UNSUB was focused on this one table.' She pointed at the corner where six dead boys lay close to six dead moms. 'There's more concentrated, close-up violence here than anywhere else.' Neither she nor Ruis spoke as they mentally blotted the scene. Seeing murdered children was always emotionally painful but this scene tugged at Angie more painfully than any others had done.

'You okay?' Ruis touched her shoulder.

She didn't say anything. Her mind was spinning violently. It was a centrifuge, separating personal and professional thoughts.

'Twelve.'

He frowned. 'Twelve what?'

'Just like at the opticians in the mall. There are twelve dead.'

Ruis counted. 'Twelve here but there are other fatalities across the room.'

'It's twelve,' insisted Angie. 'The others didn't matter. He just had to clear a way out for himself. He wouldn't have cared if they'd lived.'

Ruis was still looking at the moms and boys. 'It could be coincidence that there are twelve.'

She turned to him. 'Serials don't do coincidences – they do patterns.' She remembered that Jake had all but laughed at her when she'd pointed out how the number twelve kept coming up in the Sun Western slayings. He'd so convincingly knocked down her theory that she'd begun to doubt herself. Not any more. She let her eyes roam once more over the murdered moms and their precious kids. 'Ruis, I need to know exactly what these poor people were celebrating. Whose birthday was it? Who booked it? *When* did they book it? I want all their names, ages, addresses and everything you can find out about them. Don't leave out any scrap of information that you find.'

A thought hit Angie.

Scrap of information.

'The bastard's been going through their bins.'

'What?'

'It fits with the scene you and Chips went to this morning. That horrendous effigy of Tanya Murison had been made out of her cast-offs.'

'We don't know that for sure.'

'Believe me, you can bank on it. The UNSUB had gone through the old lady's trash, picked out her nails, her lipstick and make-up. That's how he knew she'd be at the opticians that day. Tanya would have gotten a letter through the post, or been given a card. She'd have marked it on her calendar then thrown it away.' Angie's eyes lit up. 'It hadn't been random. He'd known the exact moment she'd be there.'

Ruis could see the sense in her assumption. 'And what about here? You think he found something in someone's trash saying the party was happening at this joint?'

'Something like that. Maybe an invite, or home-printed cards that hadn't come out as neat as someone wanted and had been tossed.' She knew she was clutching at straws. 'We have to find out if there's a link between one of those moms and Tanya Murison.'

Ruis touched her arm again. 'Are you sure you want to get swallowed up in all this, Angie?'

She touched him back. 'I have to, Ruis. I'll fall apart if I don't.'

Chapter 141

Skid Row, LA

Shooter ran through his mental checklist. As far as he could make out, there'd been no mistakes.

Street cameras would have captured images of a young black man in jeans and hooded sweatshirt going into the restaurant carrying a canvas bag. Closer shots might highlight his smart designer stubble and a head of tight curls cut shoulder length.

Surveillance footage in JZ's would show a black masked 'cowboy' in white shirt and pants draw two Glocks from a holster and turn party time into murder time.

There had been no street cams covering the giant billboard where he'd left his bicycle, but to be safe, after torching his cowboy disguise he'd emerged from behind the board on the southern side of East 3rd in decorator's garb. He'd then cycled less than a mile east to the Little Tokyo/Arts District station and left his bike padlocked there. From the station he walked south into Skid and had been back inside his sanctuary in less than twenty-five minutes.

He was sure the cops would find the burned clothes but doubted they'd pick up on the bicycle. If they did, then he was comfortable that they'd be thrown by the circumlocutions he'd made on foot after chaining it up, and no way were they going to link his three different physical appearances.

Shooter's only worry was on the forensic side. He'd worn transparent gloves going into the restaurant and hadn't taken them off until he'd stripped to get into the shower. But he feared strands of fake hair he'd glued to his normally shaved head could have come off when he'd changed. His DNA was not on record, but instinctively he knew leaving any form of trace was bad practice.

He dressed in baggy black pants and matching short-sleeved shirt. He put the painter's overalls and sneakers in the canvas bag and then squashed everything into a backpack. On the way into work, he'd dispose of the lot.

Shooter poured a glass of Sunny D and ate granola straight from a box as he watched the TV news. The killings the lead story. He flipped from channel to channel. They were all working the same basic information – a single birthday party of twelve dead, plus the owner of the restaurant and two others.

He went online and found the shootings were already trending. A blog said he was the hottest social media crime story since the Bling Ring, the Hollywood teenagers who'd burgled the homes of stars like Lindsay Lohan and Paris Hilton.

Next, he read the FBI and LAPD Twitter feeds. They'd been appealing for witnesses and were already inundated with bogus sightings. One woman said she'd seen a cowboy boarding an alien spaceship in Beverly Hills. Another libeled several individuals in Compton, Culver City and Santa Monica as 'certain killers'. No one came remotely close to fingering a guy on his own in an old factory in Skid Row.

Shooter Googled 'JZ', 'JZ Slayings' and 'JZ Massacre'. He found a food review of the restaurant that gave it three stars. A lead article on Huff Post was titled 'Lone Ranger Kills Kids at Birthday Party' – it didn't have much detail, just hazy eye-in-the-sky video from a news copter that showed nothing. Then there was a link to a Facebook page that had quite a good amateur shot of blood on the restaurant window. Below it, a caption in gory red font declared: LAPD 0 – LONE RANGER 15. It made him smile. The same pic was doing the rounds on Twitter. A contribution there read: THINK BOUT THE VIKTIMS FAMLIES B4 U RETWEET YOU SIK FUCKS!!!! Shooter scrolled down and watched the vitriol roll in. Whoever had taken the picture and posted it had certainly invited a torrent of abuse.

Judgelysia was the name that he found, beneath a female silhouette.

There were links to her other social media outlets – Blogger, Mashable and Boing Boing. Shooter laughed. Man, she was a crazy-tongued bitch. Her rants were pure napalm and were all over The Daily Beast, Smashing and Fail Blog.

The Judge said she considered herself a hacktivist. She actively supported disruption by groups like Anonymous and called for people to crush and kill injustice before it crushed and killed them.

Shooter grew bored and was about to click away when he came across a day-old picture of Jake Mottram, posted by the FBI as part of an appeal for witnesses to his murder. Judgelysia had painted bullet holes in his head. In her trademark red font she'd written: HERO to ZERO!

Chapter 142

Downtown, LA

Angie came out of the restaurant exhausted but still in the zone. She took long, slow breaths to clear her lungs of the smell of death then scanned the street and tried to work out which way the UNSUB would have come and gone.

Crawford caught her eye and walked over. 'So what do you think?'

'I think it's our mall guy, I really do. CSI just found several short head hairs in a cubicle in the men's room.'

'I do believe men with heads and hair go into those stalls.'

Another day she may have laughed at his attempt to lighten the mood but not today. 'What's interesting,' she continued, 'is that they were not on the cistern or over the back of the toilet seat, they were found up near the door.'

Crawford got the significance. 'UNSUB put his bag of cowboy gear on the toilet lid and stood with his back to the door while he got changed.'

'That's what I'm thinking. This guy is a freaking master of disguise. Whatever we get on camera is only what he wants us to have.'

Ruis joined them. 'One of the uniforms followed up reports of a fire behind a big billboard less than a block away. Someone torched the hell out of something.'

'Clothes,' guessed Angie. 'It'll be his Lone Ranger gear. He did a fast change so he was free to mingle with the crowds.' She looked around. 'Makes me wonder if he's still close – even watching us.'

Ruis shook his head. 'He's gone in the wind. I can feel it.' He pointed to the river of traffic running twenty yards away. 'I'm betting he had a vehicle parked on a lot around the corner from that billboard. He simply got in and vanished. It's the obvious thing to do.'

'*This* guy doesn't do the obvious,' replied Angie.

Crawford chipped in, 'Wearing a Lone Ranger outfit in front of the Department of Justice isn't obvious?'

'Well, we didn't see it coming, did we?' She looked in her shoulder bag for a bottle of water and took a long drink. Her phone was in there and it reminded her to ask Ruis about Jake's official FBI device. She recapped the bottle and turned to him. 'Do you think I can have Jake's cellphone back? I guess you've downloaded what you want and checked his messages.'

He eyed her suspiciously and then looked to Crawford.

'She can have it,' said the section chief. 'Angie, while you were in the restaurant I spoke to Sandra and she says I can have you work the case, but it's my risk. So if you play on my team there are some rules. And they start with you not burning yourself out and not holding back on us. Understood?'

She nodded.

'You shout, you come clean if things are getting too much.'

'I get it.'

'Okay. Give her the phone, Ruis.' He looked towards her again. 'You find something on there, you let us know straight away, not *after* you've checked it out.'

Chapter 143

FBI Field Office, LA

The beep caught Chips's attention. 'I have to go, lover, I'll call you back.' He hung up and typed in the code to clear the screen lock on his computer.

Judgelysia had been getting a steady flow of tweets since he'd posted the photo Angie had sent him and the Hero to Zero comments they'd agreed to put out.

But the new one was different.

It wasn't abusive. It was smart. And intriguingly it came from someone called JudgeMinos.

Chips knew that Minos, along with Rhadamanthus and Aeacus, were the three mythological judges of the Underworld, ruled over by the god Hades.

The message left on Twitter said: ONLYU&IRFIT2JUDGE.

He felt a rush of excitement.

Instantly, he tried to trace the sender.

The Twitter account was linked to a dummy email address. Chips 'pinged' it – a way of sending a signal to the URL like a sonar signal.

Nothing bounced back.

No telltale IP address.

'Man, that's weird.'

He repeated the process to see if he had made a mistake.

He hadn't.

Chips opened a command console and ran an advanced 'ip-lookup' search. 'Come to Daddy, come on my little beauties.'

A series of numbers should have come up but didn't.

He sensed he was facing someone with computer skills at least as good as his own. 'So, my tricky friend, what are you hiding behind?'

He guessed the sender was using an advanced form of anonymity package.

'Let's see if you can beat this.' He ran a search program devised by the FBI's cyber crime specialists. It quickly shuttered through the tweet's coding.

Nothing.

'Now, that's smart.' He smiled in curious admiration at his imaginary enemy. He thought for a few minutes and guessed the sender was using a type of TOR package and somehow mirroring the Twitter feed. TOR stood for 'The Onion Router' and was a multi-layered encryption tool designed to protect the anonymity of a computer user. Chips had first come across it as a student. It continuously and randomly bounced an IP address across a volunteer network of thousands of servers all over the world. Tracking the origin of the bounce was impossible unless you had months and unlimited manpower.

Chips cracked his fingers impatiently and watched the screen. 'Come on, honey, where are my magical digits?' Usually a series of different numbers such as 12.34256.789 would show up, but he was only getting zeroes: 00.00000.000.

Blanks were the ultimate insult for a techie like him. It was the digital equivalent of being flipped the bird.

He looked again at the message: ONLYU&IRFIT2JUDGE.

Social protocol demanded he replied – and soon.

Chips wrote: BE JUST.YOUR ADMIRER.JE

All he could do now was sit back, wait and hope the smart asshole made a mistake.

Chapter 144

Skid Row, LA

BE JUST.

Shooter liked the comment. It had a ring to it. 'BE JUST'. Judgelysia stood out from the crowd. He liked that too. If only more people had the balls to speak their own minds and not behave like sheep.

YOUR ADMIRER.

He'd felt alone in the world until he'd seen that endorsement and read her blogs and comments. It felt good to know that someone out there thought like he did.

Shooter went to the Launchpad on his computer. Among his hundreds of self-developed apps were many that would protect his own IP address and enable him to trace others. As well as rummaging through his victims' physical trash cans, he also sifted their computer bins. He had devised his own mini botnet and pixeljacking programs so he could inspect and even control their browsers and mails. As a kid he'd been a loner and the computer had been his one constant friend and companion. There was nothing they couldn't do together.

He chose a geo-locator and ran it. Most GLs tended to be only around ninety percent accurate and were often hit or miss within fifteen miles. His was as on the money as a smart bomb. He hit longitude and latitude coordinators then dropped them into Google maps. Up came a big red arrow pointing at Elysia's location.

Watts.

That was close.

Shooter zoomed in. Pulled the little yellow Google man down onto the road and walked him along the curb. He could all but knock on her door.

She was less than ten miles away. He could see her face to face within the hour.

Chapter 145

Downtown, LA

Crawford Dixon arranged for a conference room at the Justice Department to be used as a temporary incident base. He walked Angie over to the corner table where Danielle Goodman was writing up notes following her interviews with survivors.

'Play nicely,' he told Angie. 'Ruis has already broken the news that you're back on the case and that's all I want broken.'

'I get the message.'

Angie saw the profiler's eyes had blackened and her nose was twice the size it had been before she'd punched her. 'Danielle.'

She looked up. 'Oh, dear God. You come back to beat on me some more?' Her response was muffled and nasal.

'Don't tempt me.' Angie pulled out a chair and sat. 'What can you tell me?'

Danielle self-consciously touched the bridge of her nose. 'Ruis said you were interested in the primary victims.'

'Particularly, who'd booked the table.'

Danielle looked down at her notepad. 'Evelyn Richards. Mother of Sam — that's as in Samuel not Samantha. It was his sixth birthday party.'

'When had she made the booking?'

'At least two months back.'

'How do you know that?'

'I interviewed two survivors, waitresses who'd been working the registers. They said they've been booked solid for the last ten weeks. Place had been doing really well.'

'Did they give you any behavioral information about the UNSUB?'

'A little. They hit the floor behind the counter as soon as they realized what was happening. Apparently, when he came out of the restroom they initially thought he was either a parent having some fun, or a new member of staff they hadn't noticed before. They were both under the impression that some kind of birthday stunt was going off because the UNSUB had gone straight to what they call Table One, which is the preferred party table.' She turned her notebook to show Angie the rough floor plan she'd sketched. 'As you can see, there were three tables directly facing him when he came out, yet he turned left and started shooting in the corner at Table One, the furthest away from him.'

'Did they see who was shot first?'

'One of the waitresses did. She said it was the mom who booked the party, Mrs Richards.'

Angie had heard enough. All her suspicions about the attack being a targeted hit rather than just random slaughter had been considerably strengthened. There was a link between Evelyn Richards and Tanya Murison; she just had to find it. She got up and started to walk away.

Danielle called after her. 'Angie.'

She turned.

'I just wanted to say how sorry I am about Jake.' She added extra emphasis to the last part of her apology. 'About *everything*.'

Angie took a pace back to the table and Danielle sat back out of fear. 'What you did, lady, was unforgiveable and unforgettable. Sorry doesn't get you off the hook. I'm going to have to live with the consequences of your stupidity every day of my life.'

'I didn't pull that trigger, Angie. It's unfair of you to blame me like this.'

'No it's not. Not at all.' She rounded the table and stood over her. 'You as good as shot Jake yourself. You created a verbal stressor for a psychologically damaged murderer. You manipulated him into a state of rage and you didn't anticipate the consequences.' Angie made a gun out of her hand and jabbed it in the middle of Danielle's forehead.

'That foolishness was the same as giving a pre-school child a loaded weapon and being surprised when he pulled the trigger.'

She hung her head. 'I'm sorry. All I can do is say I'm sorry and ask you to forgive me.'

'Forgive you?' Angie flipped the table and sent it crashing. Anger rose inside her. She wouldn't hit the woman again but she wanted to. 'I'm carrying Jake's child, you lousy bitch. It will be born fatherless because of you.'

'Oh God. I didn't know.'

'And if you had? Would it have made a difference? Would you have thought twice?' She studied her reaction. 'No, I thought not.' Angie turned her back and walked away before she had the chance to break the promise she'd just made and *really* lose her temper.

Chapter 146

South Los Angeles

The gang on the east corner rode beat-up BMXs and slid shiny step rails near a yellow fire hydrant. Across the blacktop, dope bags were being sold by pre-teens through windows of slow-moving cars. Even younger kids were running to the stash house for extra gear. Off in the shade, the older corner boys smoked, watched the deals go down and never let their hands stray far from the guns jammed in their belts and covered with sweat tops.

Further back, sat against walls where the soil stayed damp, were the wasted and the wasters. The cripples and the winos. The ones that were no threat to the young guns. Most slumped saggy-assed in groups and talked old bullet wounds and times in the pen. Those who sat alone tended to be drunks, sleeping off cheap booze and staying away from the curb where the LAPD's black and whites crawled and locked glares with the homeboys.

Far back in the dank leafy shadows, a wreck of an old man, white-haired and scarecrow-clothed, lay sprawled alongside a large empty bottle of cider. He was half in, half out of scrubbed earth, right where dog walkers toileted their animals. Not that it seemed to matter. His own pants looked more messed than the earth around him.

Everyone who passed gave him a wide berth. Even in Nickerson Gardens, LA's great unwashed were greatly ignored.

Which was the way Shooter wanted it.

For more than three hours he wallowed in the filth and watched the long rows of cheap houses. The comings and goings. He formed pictures of who lived where. The kids, the parents, the gun-toting teens.

Number 1644 was of particular interest.

Drapes were drawn upstairs and down. There was a newer front door, with reinforced hinges. Maybe the cops had busted the place recently and it had just been replaced. Up on the roof there was a small non-standard satellite dish that puzzled him. The IP provider linked to Elysia's address delivered their service by cable not satellite. Maybe she was smarter than he'd given her credit for. Much smarter.

He raised himself on one elbow and got up slowly and unsteadily. This was a neighborhood of hidden eyes. Someone somewhere would undoubtedly be watching him. He played the wino all the way to his feet, to his outstretched hand against the toilet tree, to the wobbly first steps and the slow stagger that took him far out of sight.

Chapter 147

Santa Monica Freeway, LA

The sun slanted low in the evening sky and the slow snake of traffic slithered to a stop, level with Baldwin Hills.

Angie sat in silence, her Toyota wedged between a battered pick-up and a pink-pimped Hummer. It wasn't only the traffic that was crowding her. It was everything. The new crime scene. The fresh blood. The dead children. Crawford's reminder that he needed an answer on Jake's burial at Arlington. Most of all, Danielle Goodman, thinking she could wash away a lifetime's guilt by just saying sorry.

She looked at her hand on the steering wheel and saw her knuckles were white. This was the bad side of her anger. She was so close to losing her cool. To exploding like she'd done as a child. But now she knew better. Understood that the rage only masked her true feelings – helplessness, unfairness and injustice.

Angie let go of the wheel. Put her hand to her mouth and tried to stop the cry rising in her throat. It was no good. It came out in shredded sobs. She began to cry the kinds of tears that can't be held back or stopped. They just have to run out.

Angie fumbled for tissues and hid her face from the car alongside. She blew hard into a Kleenex. As a psychologist she knew the value of just letting grief go, but it was a horrible experience.

Horns honked. Long, loud blasts. She lifted her head and saw the traffic move. A gap of ten yards opened up. More horn blasts. She didn't care. She wasn't moving until she was done.

Two more tissues were needed before she could see clearly, before the Toyota could continue the slow crawl home, down the freeway into West Los Angeles and the less fashionable end of Wilshire Boulevard.

It was a relief to park, to get out, to hide inside her own apartment and not have the world staring at her.

Angie poured a glass of water and sat down with Jake's phone. She wasn't going to be dragged down. Wasn't going to wallow in self-pity. She was going to stay busy and get to the bottom of who JL was.

She wired the phone into her FBI laptop. Opened a record and trace facility on her desktop. Accessed Jake's directory. There were a lot of names listed under J. Even more under L. Only three combined the two letters – James Lake, Jillian Lane and Joe Lamotta.

She rang the woman first and hit an answerphone: 'This is Jillian Lane, Bespoke Floristry. We're closed at the moment, please leave a message and we'll get back to you. Otherwise, you can visit us online at—' Angie killed the call. She remembered getting several birthday and 'sorry honey' bouquets from Jake via Jillian Lane. It was highly unlikely someone on their reception had been given the details of Jake's secret burner.

She called James Lake.

Again, another out-of-office message. 'This is James Lake Sports Injury Clinic. We're sorry no one is available to—' Angie remembered Jake's recurring hamstring problem and cut it off.

She thumbed her way through to the last JL listed. Joe Lamotta.

It dialed out.

There was no pick up. No automatic message clicked in.

She dialed again.

Once more it just rang in the wilderness.

She hung up and made a third call.

There was a click. 'Hello.'

She sensed that behind the deep male voice was some wariness, probably due to seeing Jake's number flash up on their phone display. 'Mr Lamotta, this is Angie Holmes. I'm a friend of Jake Mottram's.'

She counted two seconds of silence. 'Mr Lamotta, are you there?'

Finally he answered, and in doing so confirmed his identity. 'Yes. Yes I am. I'm very sorry for your loss, Jake was a fine man.'

'Please tell me how you knew him.'

Lamotta hadn't been at all prepared for this call. He cleared his throat and filled in some of the gaps. 'Well, we served together. You and I never met, but he spoke of you.'

'Did he?'

'Yes, and very affectionately. Jake and I didn't meet up much these days; certainly not as much as we'd have both liked, but I know exactly who you are and what you meant to him.'

Angie tried not to grow emotional. 'Sir, I wonder if you could help me understand something.'

'I'll try my best.'

A glance at her computer showed her call had been routed to somewhere in Fairfax County, Virginia. Alarm bells sounded. Fairfax was Spooksville.

'You had a question, Doctor Holmes?'

'I did, but given something that's just *come up*, I wonder if you could call me on another line so I can better deal with it?'

Joe Lamotta understood the connections she was making. 'Give me five minutes and I'll do that.'

They both hung up.

Angie sat in silence and stared at the computer screen. The call had gone through to a cellphone inside the George Bush Center for Intelligence at Langley, a place better known to the world as the headquarters of the CIA.

Joe Lamotta worked there. Jake had been calling him on an untraceable burner. JL had said he'd got the information that Jake had wanted. And then Jake had been killed. A new dimension had been added to the inquiry. Was she blundering into a situation she didn't understand? Getting hopelessly out of her depth?

She knew the answer was a resounding yes. But Angie felt she had no alternative but to keep probing.

The burner buzzed and made her jump.

She picked it up. 'Mr Lamotta.'

'Angie, you best call me Joe, or preferably nothing at all. I'll be in LA tomorrow for "business". Do you know Shutters?'

'Of course.'

'Then I'll see you there at one. I'll have a beach view table in the café and I'll be free for only thirty minutes so please don't be late.'

The line went dead.

Chapter 148

Douglas Park, Santa Monica, LA

Chips arrived at ten p.m. wearing a smile and a T-shirt that said NOTHING MEANS EVERYTHING.

Angie studied the white on blue letters as she let him in. 'I like that you're back in your fashion swing.'

He kissed her on the cheek. 'You'll like it even more when I tell you what it means.' He put down his laptop case and passed over a large yellow bag he'd been carrying. 'There's a little present for you.'

Angie was surprised. 'Thanks. You want a drink?' She walked him through.

'Cranberry would be good. I put some in that big old Frigidaire of yours, which, incidentally, is unhealthily bare.'

'I know. I'll shop soon.' She opened the bag on a kitchen worktop. It contained a yellow cup the size of a soccer ball filled with yellow and white daisies and roses. A Mr Happy face grinned on the side. Angie couldn't help but mirror the smile. 'It's lovely.' She put it on the windowsill next to a framed photo of her and Jake, then got juice from the cooler and a glass from a cupboard. 'I had soup for dinner – you want me to warm you some?'

'Soup? Dear me, no thank you.' He followed her into the small galley and took the cranberry. 'I'm good with just that, thanks. I hope you don't mind, but I ate with Leo before I came over.'

'Of course not.' She leaned back against some cupboards. 'You two still getting on okay? I hope coming here hasn't caused any—'

'None.' He stopped her mid-flow. 'He asked me to marry him.'

Angie went bug-eyed. 'Really?'

'Really!' Chips flushed with excitement.

'That's amazing. Come here.' She opened her arms for a hug. 'I'm delighted for you both.'

He put his juice down. 'I know, it's fantastic. I've never been so happy.' He hugged her, then realized he may have made a faux pas. 'I'm sorry, that was insensitive.'

'No, don't be sorry.' She scowled at him. 'Grab this happiness and enjoy it. Don't you dare think of hiding any of it from me.' Thoughts of Jake rushed her mind. The ring he'd bought her. The unplanned wedding. The baby. She hugged Chips again. 'I need to be around happiness – as much of it as possible.'

He could see she was struggling and he held her for longer than he'd ever done.

'Thanks,' said Angie. 'You know, I'd be lost without you at the moment.'

He felt himself welling up and wafted his face. 'Phew! Well don't you worry, girlfriend. We're going to kick the ass out of this "moment". You'll get through it, Angie Holmes.' He looked pointedly at her belly. 'You have to, for the little one.'

She'd never told him she was pregnant. 'How long have you known?'

'Ooooh, I'd guess since right after your medical. When you were as skittish as a kitty on a hot roof and about as much fun as McDonald during a budget review.'

'I was that bad?'

'Worse, and you left a pregnancy page up on your computer, as well.'

'I should be a blonde.'

'Anyway, ask me to explain the slogan on this fine new T-shirt.' He pulled up the front to show her.

Angie read it aloud. '"Nothing means everything." Nice but I don't understand.'

'Of course you don't. You've been far too busy for me to update you. While you were across town you got mail. Or to be more precise, Elysia got tweeted.'

'From the UNSUB?'

'Well, he didn't call himself that.' Chips picked up his juice again. 'His username was JudgeMinos, which I'm pretty certain is him.'

'What makes you so sure?'

'That brings me to the T-shirt. The *judge* went to such great lengths not to have his tweet traced that he gave away a lot about himself.'

'You need to explain that to me.'

'Well, he used a shielding program. Highly advanced. Way beyond TOR, TrueCript and Incognito. He'd mussed up the exit and entry nodes like I've never seen anyone do. You can't do that kind of thing unless you're smart and tech savvy, maybe a former IT or graphics student who's been on the edge of hacking or has hung with an arty, anarchistic crowd that were into hacking.'

Angie was struggling. 'I kind of get what you mean – you think he's some kind of supergeek.'

'More than that. Anyone who deploys encryption devices like he does wouldn't have tweeted us unless he'd checked out our IP address first.'

'Well, that kind of behavior fits with our UNSUB. He's been pretty meticulous so far.'

'Yep, but if he traced our false IP address then he must have used a geo-locator, which means he may know where the safe house is.'

Angie was shocked. 'Really? He could do that?'

'I think so. Of course, he won't know it's a safe house, he'll just think it's a normal home, and our past blogs and posts are consistent with living there.'

'Shit. This guy is an operator.'

'And he knows it. He's full of himself. His message said, "Only you and I are fit to judge."'

Angie's face showed her surprise. 'Now, that's interesting. Did you reply?'

'Uh-huh. I went with one of the blandly enigmatic phrases we discussed. I tweeted BE JUST.'

Angie fell silent.

Chips gave her time. He was used to her drifting off. Thinking things through.

Finally, she explained. 'I'm trying to work out how strong this Judge and Jury connection really is. There's a danger we're getting hung up on something that might not matter.'

'Or that we discount the obvious,' countered Chips. 'Perhaps it *is* all about justice. Today's attack was outside the Justice Department. He came dressed as a costume character who used to fight for justice. And all that comes on top of him having left an anagram at the mall that translates to Judge and Jury.'

'I know, I know. It looks like a golden thread to me as well, but at the same time it all feels a little obvious. Maybe a red herring.'

'Since when have serial killers been subtle? All our studies show they stay cryptically on theme, even when they stray off victim.'

'Or they use themes to throw investigators off course – and if our UNSUB is as clever as you think he is, then that's highly possible. Back at Quantico, I was taught to forget the themes. Remember KYV/KYO?'

Chips did. 'Know your victim and you know your offender.'

'Right. Well, there's a link between the victims, Chips. I can't see what it is, but I know it's there.'

He drained the last of his cranberry and took the glass to the dishwasher. 'I ran all the vic names again today. All the dead and all the wounded. There are some connections but they're tenuous.'

'How tenuous? Six degrees of separation tenuous?'

'More like sixty degrees.'

'Go on.'

'One of the teachers at the Strawberry Fields massacre went to the same church as a woman from the mall shooting who lived around the corner from the restaurant that was hit. That kind of tenuous.'

Angie still had hope. 'I asked Ruis to check out links between Evelyn Richards and Tanya Murison.'

'Why?'

'Because despite the other killings the UNSUB shot them first. We know he took stuff from Tanya's trash, that's how he made the effigy – and I suspect he got the date for the party from Evelyn's trash.'

'The trash I can believe but why would he want to kill the party crowd? There's no connection to the mall, Angie, believe me. I spoke to Agent Costas just before I came over because I wanted to check addresses on some victims. Tanya and Evelyn had never met. They were generations and lifestyles apart. One was a white soccer mom from the burbs, the other a black grandmother from the hard part of town. They couldn't be more diverse if they had been chosen to be.'

Angie frowned at him. 'What did you say?'

'I said, 'They couldn't be *more* diverse.'

She added the missing words, '. . . if they had been chosen to be.' Her synapses were crackling. 'What if they'd been chosen for exactly that reason?'

'What reason?'

'Who chooses diverse people?'

He thought, then shrugged. 'Market surveyors?'

'Maybe. I was thinking something more connected to justice.'

Now he got it. 'A jury?'

'Starts to fit, doesn't it? All this Judge and Justice stuff. Imagine a jury of twelve people – twelve people who wrongly convicted our UNSUB of something and ruined his life.'

Chapter 149

Shooter spent most of his shift thinking about women. Two to be precise. He hadn't met either of them but knew both would figure large in his life.

The first was Elysia.

Judge Elysia to use her full *nom de plume*.

Her past blogs and posts fascinated him. They spat fire. Venom. Hot vitriol. She dropped rage bombs on bankers, storekeepers, big companies, cops, and even the government. She exposed them as the self-serving, greedy, lazy and ignorant good-for-nothings that they truly were. Elysia cried out for a modern-day Jesus to 'sort their shit out', 'clean up the unholy mess' and 'right the wrongs'.

He was that messiah. To her and, he suspected, many others.

Elysia tore into newspaper, television and radio journalists for abandoning their posts, failing in their responsibilities as guardians of freedom, gatekeepers of truth, watchmen for injustice. No one escaped her wrath.

She spoke with his voice.

From what she'd declared on her multiple profiles, Shooter believed she lived alone, wasn't in a relationship, had no pets and followed no one.

She was like him.

He liked that. Liked it so much he couldn't help but take a company E Wagon and roll past her house.

It was almost two a.m. when he parked up near the trees where not so long ago he'd flopped out and played the role of drunken bum. The street was deserted but he still made sure the Ford's doors were locked. This was the kind of hood where you could get jumped any time of day.

Shooter cranked his seat back so he wasn't visible from the street. If any cops cruised by he'd just pretend to be swinging the lead, grabbing a little shut-eye because his boss was such a ballbreaker. They'd understand.

He watched for more than an hour. A light came on in a front room. It glowed for a while behind drawn curtains then flickered out. Another light came on. Deeper in the house. It was barely visible. A slit of brightness through what was probably an open door. Shooter guessed this was her bedroom. It also burned for only a few minutes then went off. Maybe she'd got up to use the bathroom or run a glass of water. Either way she was now in her bedroom and he couldn't help but picture her. Elysia would have long, dark hair and be lying naked on top of white sheets. Her breasts were small but firm, her legs long and thin. A tattoo of some kind was on her hip. He could see it now. It was beautiful. Unique. A butterfly with the head of a dragon, the teeth of a vampire bat and a long tongue that wound its way down her left leg, all the way to her little toe. Elysia's skin would look milky in the moonlight, but her eyes smoldered darkly with centers that glowed like cracked green emeralds. He imagined them open and staring upward at the ceiling while she daydreamed.

About him.

She was ready to fall asleep and take him into her dreams.

A bang on the back doors made his heart leap.

Someone was at the rear of the vehicle. They were trying to break in. The Ford's big wing mirrors showed two youths in muscle vests trying to crowbar the doors open.

Shooter started the engine. The cough of exhaust and roar of the engine startled them.

He floored the gas pedal. Left strips of burned rubber on the blacktop. In the rearview he saw the two figures standing bemused in the middle of the road.

Shooter turned the corner and headed back to work. He had to get Elysia out of his head. He needed to concentrate on the other woman.

The one who had to die.

Chapter 150

Douglas Park, Santa Monica, LA

LA's morning skyline was shrouded in smog when Angie and Chips left her apartment and drove in to the office together. They split at the FBI garage so he could get decent coffee and something for breakfast – another reminder that her kitchen cupboards had been near empty and she needed to go grocery shopping.

Angie edged behind her desk, put her phone on charge and powered up the computer. She felt fat, tired and even slower than her computer's painfully languid start-up. She'd worked late and slept little. Her energy tanks were near empty and she knew the drain on them would continue relentlessly. The baby, the unvented grief, the long hours and the lack of progress on the inquiry, they all took their toll.

Her spirits lifted when Chips returned with coffee, fresh fruit salads and butter croissants still warm from the oven.

While they ate, they worked on finding court trial links to Tanya Murison and Evelyn Richards. They concentrated mainly on juries that they might have served on together, or criminal investigations they might have given witness statements to.

By eleven a.m. they'd contacted all the departments and public records offices that could help and simply had to wait for files to be searched and calls returned. Chips entered both women's names into the archives of all local newspapers in the Greater Los Angeles area to see if they'd been named in association with famous cases.

Nothing came up.

Angie's phone rang repeatedly. But not with the answers she awaited. McDonald wanted to see her. Ruis informed her that there would be a joint case conference with the LAPD in the afternoon to review all the recent Spree cases. Crawford asked her to swing by late afternoon 'for a personal chat'. Suzie Janner called and expressed her surprise and worry that she was back at work so soon and fixed to 'meet for a professional chat' the following morning.

Angie had guessed today was going to be a confrontational one with her boss, so she'd dressed in a no-nonsense navy skirt and jacket with burned orange blouse.

She rapped twice on McDonald's door.

'Come in,' came an unwelcoming voice.

The assistant director met Angie's presence with a forced smile. A bony hand ushered her to a seat. 'I'll start with the obvious question, because you'll only think me a callous bitch if I don't: how you holding up?'

Angie tucked her seat in close to the desk. 'I'm focused and I'm fit to see this through.'

McDonald put down her pen and removed her reading glasses. 'I didn't ask that, Angela. Believe it or not, I'm concerned about you *as a person* as well as a professional and the quality of the job you do.'

'My bad. I'm glad to be back at work. And thank you for agreeing to let me do that.'

The AD folded her hands and placed them on the desk in front of her. A simple gesture, but it was designed to cut the space between the two women, build a psychological bridge. 'I'm going to tell you something personal, something not to be repeated outside this room.' Her face softened and for a second she had to take a slow breath before continuing. 'Twenty years ago the man I loved was killed. Not by a bullet, but by a hole in his heart. He'd had the defect since birth and we'd thought he'd outgrown any risks from it. That wasn't the case. When he collapsed in agony one day and ER surgery failed, well, my life imploded.'

'I'm sorry.'

'Like you, I was determined to work through the grief. I figured I had to be tough. Get my shit together. Get on with things. Anything sound familiar?'

'Yes, of course it does.'

'Well, let me tell you, I lost so much of myself during the first three months after his death, I never got it back. None of it. Those feelings of openness, trust, love and kindness that blossom in a relationship – they all withered and died because of how I responded. And I really don't want the same things to happen to you.'

Angie sat in shock. This was a side of McDonald she'd never seen. One that showed her just how alike they were, rather than how different. 'Thank you for sharing that with me. Truth is, I don't know how else to deal with it. Finding Jake's killer is the only rock I'm clinging to and I'm damned well scared to death of letting go of it and drowning in depression and self-pity.' She had to stop herself opening up too much. 'Let's face it, we both know there's no alternative but to tough it out, is there?'

'In some ways, there is.' McDonald's eyes showed her years of pain. 'Don't link all your hate and anger to this UNSUB – because if we don't find him, then all your rage and pain will still be alive. Some killers go uncaught.'

'That's not an option for me. This bastard is getting caught.'

'Nor is it an option for me, Angie. This UNSUB is on my watch. But we don't always succeed; no matter how hard we try. The Green River Killer went twenty years before his luck ran out. You can't go through two decades of hate and anger.'

Angie knew she was right. 'So what do I do?'

'You open up. We're your family – even me. We'll get you through this, but that means you take advice as well as go your own headstrong way. I want to help you, not fight you, but you're going to have to meet me somewhere in the middle.'

Angie nodded. 'I'm not good at most of those things but I'll try.'

'Good. Trying is at least a start.' McDonald got up and walked her to the door.

Angie stopped on the way out. 'Thank you, I appreciate you taking the time out to talk so confidentially.'

'You're very welcome.' She touched her shoulder reassuringly.

'Tell me one thing?'

'Sure.'

'Honestly, does a day go by without you thinking about that man you lost?'

McDonald's eyes glistened. 'Not even an hour.'

Chapter 151

The morning supervisor had been late arriving. That meant Shooter hadn't gotten away until rush hour. It had been a bad start to the day. There were lots of things to do, places to visit, plans to put into operation. Sitting around waiting had left him frustrated and strangely tired. He wasn't good at doing nothing. He needed to be active. Every moment had to be dedicated to taking a step closer to his goal. To his next kill. To a new photograph on the wall in Death Row. To the fulfillment of his mission.

Maybe it was his imagination, but there seemed to be more police out on the streets today. Extra cruisers in the traffic lanes. Increased cop interviews and appeals on radio and TV. They were talking about new leads, fresh breakthroughs, a surge in help from the public and possible eyewitnesses who'd come forward. He told himself that it was bullshit disinformation. They were churning it out to keep the public off their backs and maybe to spook him as well. They were hoping he would make mistakes.

Well, Shooter didn't make mistakes.

Shooter planned.

Shooter planned and planned and planned.

He didn't make mistakes.

But he was worried.

Edgy.

No matter how many times his mind screamed reassurances, he was becoming stressed. If he was honest with himself, the shooting at JZ's Saloon hadn't gone as he'd intended. He wished he'd had time to wipe down the toilet cubicle and watch the Lone Ranger clothes burn to ashes when he'd torched them behind the billboard. Ideally, he'd have liked to have stuck around to scrape up the charred remains and take them away. But it hadn't worked out like that. Now he had to live with it and move on. Stay on his toes. Keep one step ahead of the FBI. Take no chances.

Inside his sanctuary, he changed and showered. For the first time in more than a week, went straight to bed. His mind numbed by exhaustion and worry. His energy spent.

The dreams that visited him were gruesome ones of being chased and caught. Of the cops killing him in a gun battle, but then bringing him back to life. They kept him tied to a chair in a Death Row cell. Day by day, the barred wall would slide back and one of his victims would come through with a knife and gouge out the bullets from wounds that were doomed to never heal.

A calendar on the prison wall was marked with the day of his execution. It was always today. Beneath it was a typewritten document with the State Governor's seal. Denial of his reprieve.

Shooter woke in a sweat. He went to the bathroom, ran water in the sink, cupped it in his hands and submerged his face.

As he toweled dry he saw the watch on his wrist said it was just after midday. He cursed his decision to lie down and rest. Hours had flown by. Things had slipped. He'd missed a window. A chance to kill.

And yet . . .

His rested mind filled with a new thought. One even more appealing than the last.

Chapter 152

O n the drive to Santa Monica, Angie took a call from Cal O'Brien. She was relieved he didn't open with the usual enquiry about how she was coping.

'I hear you're back at work.'

She put him on the hands-free. 'You hear right.' She exited the freeway and clicked the indicator to turn into 4th Street. 'You got some news for me?'

He admired her directness. 'Maybe. Some of my team and Ruis Costas's squad have been going through video footage from the FBI building. They've blown up a lot of grainy night footage. Long and short of it, we have two interesting leads – people and vehicles that aren't from the regular press pack.'

'You're right, that's interesting.'

'Are you at the joint case conference this afternoon?'

'Planning to be.'

'Then you'll see the footage first hand.' He moved on to more sensitive ground. 'Did you find anything in the letters you took from Jake's place?'

She hesitated. 'Afraid not.' She almost missed the turn onto Pico Boulevard.

O'Brien's tone changed. 'I'm being very open with you, Angie – are you doing the same with me?'

Lamotta's coded message to Jake played in her mind. There was a reason for the secrecy. 'No, no I'm not. But you need to give me a little time to do some private checks. It might just be something personal to Jake and I don't want to regret throwing it into full public scrutiny.'

'Hey, come on!' He sounded short-tempered. 'As lead officer on his homicide, shouldn't I be the judge of that?'

'You're right, you should. I guess I'm asking you to trust me for a little while and then I promise to tell you.'

There was silence.

She knew she was asking for a lot. 'Remember I stepped back for you, Cal – I gave you twenty-four hours of silence on the race angle to the rape-homicide we worked.'

He noticed it was the first time she'd called him Cal. She clearly needed his help. 'Yeah, I remember it.'

'Well, I guess I'm now asking you for the same. You know I won't hold back anything that can catch Jake's killer.'

'I know.' He thought on it. 'Okay, you have the twenty-four, Angie – just don't make me look stupid at the end of it.'

'You've got my word.'

The line went dead and the Pacific rose in her windshield. Shutters loomed up ahead. A rambling, colonial beauty of a building, with white-fenced balconies and luxury rooms and restaurants hanging right out onto the Santa Monica sands.

Angie left her car to valet parking. She slipped off her shades and strolled through the rich dark woods of the cool reception area and the warm, cozy lounge complete with log fire and leather and fabric settees. A few more steps took her into Coast, the hotel's stylish café, where she saw a muscular black man sat at a table overlooking the ocean. He was in a bottle green suit that was fighting a losing battle with his biceps and his eyes were hidden by aviator shades. The table in front of him supported a glass of untouched mineral water and an empty espresso cup.

Joe Lamotta turned and stood as soon as he heard Angie approaching. He took off his glasses and revealed soft brown eyes that contrasted with the shaved head and the rest of his tough guy appearance. 'Glad you could make it.' He shook her hand gently and caught the gaze of a fluttering waitress. 'Another coffee for me, and . . .?'

'Just water,' answered Angie. 'Still, please.'

The waitress disappeared and they sat.

Lamotta looked around to make sure no one was within earshot. 'Jake Mottram saved my ass in the Yemen. I'd been hit by a shot from an al-Qaeda sniper and was lying in the dirt waiting to be finished off. He rattled the living shit out of the guy with an assault rifle and carried me out of harm's way. I can't tell you how sick I felt when I heard he'd been killed.'

Angie could tell his sentiments were heartfelt. 'You said Jake had mentioned me to you.'

'He had. Very warmly.'

'But he never mentioned you to me, why would that be?'

Lamotta smiled. 'I'm not the kind of guy that gets mentioned. I'm in a job that people talk too much about. I know you traced our conversation to Langley, so you get my drift.'

'You're CIA – I'm guessing at Military Affairs.'

'Ex-MA. I'm now with NCS.'

She knew the National Clandestine Service was deep cover and deadly. 'And were Jake's calls to you in relation to your former or current employment?'

He smiled widely. 'The big guy told me you were like this.'

'Like what?'

'Determined. Stubborn. Smart.' His eyes grazed every inch of the café before he continued. 'Jake had me look into something from the past – something military and confidential. I'd advised him that it was best not to do that. From what I found out I was right.'

'What was that?'

'Like I said, it was military related, and with his passing there's really very little point in pursuing the line of inquiry he'd started.'

She knew she was being stonewalled. 'Did it have anything to do with his death?'

'No.'

'You can say that categorically?'

'I can. I can give you my word.'

She searched for a connection. 'Then the messages I heard and saw from you on the covert phone that Jake used must also have related to a case that he was working.'

He tried to cut her off. 'Angie—'

She pushed on. 'It must have been recent information, so that makes it either the Sun Western, the Strawberry Fields UNSUB or . . .' She paused because the penny dropped. '. . . or Corrie Chandler.'

The fact that he blanked the mention of Chandler's name was all the confirmation she needed. 'Chandler was ex-army. Former Tenth Mountain. I'm betting Jake discovered something about Chandler and he wanted you to check it was true.' She saw she'd hit a nerve. 'He wanted you to validate something Chandler had said, didn't he?'

Lamotta turned his eyes to the waitress arriving with their drinks. 'Thank you,' he said, glad of the distraction.

'You're welcome, sir.' She put down the water, coffee and left a ridiculously expensive check for him to settle.

He watched her go then resumed his conversation with Angie. 'I came to see you in order to pass on my personal condolences. And to put your mind at rest as best I could. I realize you are curious, but please believe me, you will do no one any favors by pursuing the line of inquiry that Jake had been going down.'

Angie was not that easily dissuaded. 'You said in one of your cryptic messages that you had what Jake wanted. At least tell me what that was.'

He looked straight through her.

'I need some peace, Mr Lamotta. I'm going out of my mind trying to live with my fiancé's death. You can help a little by not keeping secrets from me.'

He picked up his espresso and bought more time for himself.

Angie watched him take a full hit of the bitter coffee. He blotted his lips with a crisp white napkin and then peeled twenty dollars off a billfold and put them next to the check.

'I'm sorry,' he said, getting to his feet. 'I really think this matter is best laid to rest with Jake. Again my condolences.' He extended his hand.

Angie got up and stared scornfully at him. 'I'll find out what's being hidden. Sooner or later, I'll find it.' She left him hanging and walked out.

Chapter 153

FBI Field Office, LA

The meeting with Joe Lamotta troubled Angie throughout the drive back to the office and into the large meeting room reserved for the case conference.

Inevitably, the excited pre-meeting babble died down as people spotted her and whispered asides.

Ruis Costas broke from a conversation with one of his SKU team and headed over. 'I just wanted to tell you before you heard it in the room – Ballistics have matched gunfire in the restaurant to Jake's homicide.'

The news was hardly a surprise, but it still made her feel like she'd been punched in the stomach.

He read her distress. 'You okay?'

'Yeah, I just wasn't ready for that. My mind had been elsewhere.' She got herself together. 'Witnesses said the UNSUB pulled *two* guns at the restaurant.'

'He did. Both Glock 18s. Only one matched Jake's shooting.'

Other pieces tumbled into place. 'He shot with both hands. So he is ambidextrous, which is what I thought when I first saw the mall footage. And I'm willing to bet the bullet matches were made on Evelyn Richards.' She raised her arm, leveled it and aimed. 'Shots he'd fired into the top left corner of the room, most probably with his left hand.'

Ruis admired her smartness. Even through the fog of grief she saw things sharper than most people were ever able to. 'You could be right.' He raised his left hand like a gun. 'Angle of bullet entry would support your supposition. We took standard 9mm slugs from Mrs Richards and the rifling matched those that had killed Jake.'

Crawford Dixon had taken the room and was politely urging people into their seats. They settled and as he went through the introduction, Angie ticked off the faces in the room: Sandra McDonald, Connor Pryce from the LAPD with Tom Jeffreys from the Bomb Squad and Cal O'Brien from Homicide. Ruis had slid into a seat alongside a redhead she didn't recognize. She was in a black SKU sweat so Angie guessed that because Ruis was now acting up in Jake's job, this was most likely his number two. Ryan Fox from the Media Unit settled alongside a sheepish Danielle Goodman who now had eyes as black as a panda's. Finally there was a young woman from SKU taking notes.

Crawford broke the bad news first. 'In an hour's time, Aaron Bolt will be formally released without charge.'

Groans spread across the room.

'We all may think this young man deserves to stay behind bars, but he's walking free. At least for now. His similarity to the Sun Western UNSUB is uncanny, right down to choice of clothes and weapons, but that's all it is. A similarity.' He shot a disappointed look in Pryce's direction. 'Now, as law enforcement officers, we have to publicly admit we were wrong and apologize for our indecent haste.'

'What about the firearm he posed with?' asked McDonald. 'Surely we can charge him with offences related to that?'

'He claims it was a fake. Says the picture was taken to poke fun at the LAPD after the last murder that they "falsely" linked him to. There'll be a trade-off with his attorney – no charges will be brought and no compensation filed for.' He spoke to the wider audience. 'Okay, folks, the message is simple: forget about Aaron Bolt, he is not our man. Don't, I repeat, *do not*, waste any more time on him.' He waited a beat before he continued, 'There is now a consensus among investigators that the homicides known as the Sun Western slayings, the Jake Mottram killing and the Lone Ranger murders are all down to the same UNSUB. Agent Ruis Costas will walk you through some key points related to this theory.'

Ruis got up and picked a video presentation controller off the table. A monitor on the wall flickered into life and the room's light dimmed. 'Left of screen, you see a freeze frame of the UNSUB from the Sun Western mall, in his all-too-familiar T-shirt, cap, loose shorts and shoulder-slung sports bag.' He clicked a button. 'And on the right you see the so-called Lone Ranger, in his Stetson and cowboy outfit. Note there's another bag at his feet. This was undoubtedly used to conceal his weaponry and a change of clothes. Pieces of that bag were found burned to ash half a block away from the crime scene and Forensics are still pulling together what they can.' He used the controller's laser pointer to guide a red dot over the second image. 'We've run facial recognition software and done photogrammetry on his body size, checking critical points like wrist measurements when he extends and fires the guns, plus shoulder-to-shoulder dimensions and shoulder-to-ankle bone lengths – we're sure it's the same offender.' Ruis gave people a few seconds to study the images on-screen before he added, 'Ballistics have also positively matched the rounds at the JZ Saloon to the ones that killed Special Agent Mottram.' He kept his eyes away from Angie and ran new video on the screen. 'This is night-time footage spliced together from several street cameras outside of our building. In places the quality is truly bad, and the tech team has had to do much more than enhance, color correct and expand this video, which is why we've been delayed with it. The feed marked "Camera One" shows Jake's Lancer leaving its parking bay and heading onto the street. Camera Two is clear enough, it covers the front of our building and you can make out some photojournalists stood there smoking. Camera Three is not so good; it's a very high and wide shot of Wilshire Boulevard and you can just see, at the far right of frame, two parked vehicles. One is a large white works vehicle and the other a station wagon. The picture here is too grainy to pick out plates but we can see both these sets of wheels are behind Jake's car soon after he exits the parking lot.' Ruis changed frames. 'Some of the following shots are even worse, they are from a street camera two blocks away.' He played the red laser over the screen. 'Here is Jake's Lancer again. A car back is the station wagon, a Mercedes by the look of it, and twenty yards behind that is a big white box on wheels that Traffic identified as a Ford E Wagon.' He switched slides again. 'A block later the Mercedes has gone and we're left with only the Ford and Jake.' He turned to the room. 'We're out of footage at that point.'

'Was there nothing on the plates?' asked Crawford.

'Next to nothing. Techies blew up the various pieces of footage and we got a couple of digits off each vehicle. It was enough for us to make up a pool of potential vehicles. We drained it down to ten Mercs and thirty Fords. An hour ago we reduced it to one Merc and one Ford.' He nodded to the redhead from his unit. 'Tess, tell us what you've got.'

She cleared her throat and read from a notebook. 'The old Mercedes belongs to an Anthony Joseph Cheetham. He has convictions for unlicensed taxi driving. Cheetham is twenty-three years old and lives alone in Hancock Park. Neither he nor the Merc have been seen since Special Agent Mottram's death. We've got an APB running on both Cheetham and the car.' She turned a page in the book. 'The other vehicle is a one-year-old Ford E Wagon and it's registered to Cleereroads Inc., a county-wide company that removes road kill and debris from freeways, interstates and main thoroughfares. Before someone asks, yes they work throughout the night, in fact that's when they do most of their clearing.'

Angie caught her eye. 'I'm just wondering, were any vehicles similar to these seen near the mall incidents or the restaurant killings?'

'None were flagged,' answered Ruis. 'Connor, Tom, did any of your teams tag a Merc or E Wagon?'

'We had a suspect Merc,' answered Pryce, 'but it was traced and eliminated. The owner had a disabled wife and he'd taken her to a friend's and parked illegally.'

'Bomb Squad had a long list of suspect cars,' added Tom Jeffreys. 'I'll double check when we're done here, but I don't recall a fit to either of the two vehicles you described.'

Ruis picked up. 'In the next hour we'll approach Dominic Cleere, the CEO of Cleereroads, and make attempts to trace and interview the driver. We'll need to move fast because if we come face to face with the UNSUB it may well be during tonight's shift, and I'd rather catch this particular individual by surprise instead of when he's armed and ready for us.'

Angie's phone was set to silent. It vibrated on the table. She grabbed it to stop the rumble and read the message. It was from Chips: NEWS FROM RECORDS OFFICE – NEED 2 CU URGENTLY.

Chapter 154

A ngie found Chips in their office, pacing anxiously in front of a
whiteboard, a black marker pen stuck like a cigar between his fingers.

'What's so important?' She put her purse on his desk.

'I got news from the records offices. None of the victims gave
witness statements concerning the same crime or served on the same
juries, but get this – some of their loved ones did.'

'Loved ones?'

'Yep, husbands, wives, civil partners and siblings; in short the jurors'
closest relations.'

Angie took it in. 'So you're saying we've been looking in the
wrong place – it's not the victims he's targeting, but those closest
to them?'

'Seems that way. Make them suffer more by enduring a sense of
loss.'

'I can relate to that.'

'I'm sorry.'

'Don't be. You're just being professional.' She looked at the start of
the list he'd scrawled in big black capitals. They were arranged under
two columns.

VICTIM	JUROR/RELATION
TANYA MURISON	HARLAN MURISON
EVELYN RICHARDS	MIKE RICHARDS

'So Tanya Murison was killed because her husband Harlan had served on a jury?'

'That's right.' Chips stubbed his pen on the name under it. 'And Harlan served with Mike Richards, husband of Evelyn, the mom who fixed the party at JZ's.'

Angie's eyes slid down the board to where another two names had been added:

SEAN THORNTON   MARY THORNTON

'Thornton?' She turned to him. 'I've heard the name but can't place it.'

'He's the moneyman, banker-type shot in the john at the Olympic. His wife was the foreman of the jury.'

Another piece of the mystery fell in place. 'I remember now.' She studied another eighteen names. 'And this is the rest of the jury and their partners?'

'You got it.'

MARCELLO YOUNG	CARRIE YOUNG
JORDAN ARIAS	KATHY ARIAS
ALLEN SCHULMAN	CHRIS SCHULMAN
BRITNEY HOPE	CLAYTON HOPE
ROBYN PAYNE	NATE PAYNE
MAGGIE LOPEZ	HERNANDES LOPEZ
LEANNE COSTELLO	CHUCK COSTELLO
NASRA BENGHAZI	CHAHAL BENGHAZI
TRACY REDFERN	MARK REDFERN

Angie turned from the board. 'So there are twenty-four names in total; please tell me they all lead to one special trial and one specific asshole's address.'

'I think they do.' There was nervous excitement in Chips's voice. 'The twelve names on the right were all jurors in the trial of a man called Winston Hendry. He was convicted of First Degree homicide eight years ago and executed twelve months ago. The anniversary of his death came the day after the Strawberry Fields massacre – the day of the Mall shootings. All those people on the right served on the jury that convicted him.'

Angie's eyes roamed the board. She fitted names with crime scenes and morgue pictures. Began to imagine the thoughts of the man who killed them. 'And the names on the left are their partners or children?'

'Or brothers. Allen and Chris Schulman are brothers.'

She stepped closer to the board, as though the nearness somehow helped her memory. 'Am I right in saying none of the vics come from the Strawberry Fields shooting?'

'You are.' Chips looked a little deflated. 'It looks like a flaw, but maybe it's not. For now let's put up with the anomaly and see if later on we can make sense of the fruit field killings.'

'Okay. Then what if the UNSUB has been making the jurors suffer by killing someone who mattered to them? Maybe he was close to Hendry and missed him. Wanted them to endure the same fate. So we're looking for parents, children, brothers, lovers.'

Chips was already ahead of her. 'I know where you're going. Winston Hendry has no surviving parents, children or named wife. But he does have a younger brother. Warren. Twenty-six. No known abode.'

She glanced at the clock over the door. 'Hell, we need to share this with the inquiry team and share it fast.' She made to go.

'Hang on, boss. There's stuff you should know before you let the dogs loose. Neither Warren nor Winston is black.'

She stopped in her tracks. 'What? Our guy is black, all the security pictures show that.'

He pressed his point. 'They grew up in a black hood. But they're both white. I've seen a driver's license shot of Warren on my computer – I promise you he's as Caucasian as you and me.'

She crinkled her brow then looked around. 'Have you printed it off?'

'No, not yet. I only found it just before you walked in.'

'Show me.'

They walked to his computer. He reopened the file from the records office and leaned away from the screen so she could see.

Angie stared at the young-looking white man. 'Jeez. Are you sure that's him?'

'I'll double check that there's not been a screw-up in records, but if you look at the mugshot of his brother you'll see resemblances.' He shrunk the screen so it only filled the left of the frame then opened the file of the other man.

Angie saw that they had the same brown eyes and nose shape. While Warren's face was rounder than Winston's, you could see they were family. 'I get that they are brothers. *White* brothers. But do you think he looks enough like our mall UNSUB?'

Chips punched more keys and opened a JPEG of the pic they'd issued to the press.

Angie looked at the photos side by side. 'Doesn't pop right at you because of the cap and the hair, but yeah, I see that it's him.'

Chips tapped the screen. 'The Lakers cap is the most important part of the disguise. It throws shadows all over the face, distorts nose length, cheek shape and makes ID much harder.'

Angie pondered the image and made a fresh connection between kills. 'And the cap helps fake the hair type, the color and length – just like a Stetson does. The hair we found in the restroom at JZ's had come loose, not because it snagged somehow, but because he hadn't glued it in as well as he thought.'

Chips was filling in blanks as well. 'So we've pretty much been asking the public to look for the wrong guy?'

'Seems we did.' She stepped away from the back of Chips's chair and paced while she gathered her thoughts. Things were coming together but there were also a lot of unanswered questions. Motive being the big one. 'What's big brother's rap sheet say?'

'That I *have* printed out.' He fished for it on his desk and handed it over. 'He was in and out of Juvie. Assault. Wounding. Firearm offences. Gangs Unit will know him. He went to Death Row for shooting a rival gang member. Sprayed so many bullets at his vic he also caught a mother and child across the street. His attorney argued self-defense for capping the other crook and Second Degree for the civilians. The DA and judge wouldn't buy it.'

'Good for them.'

'They were under a White House directive to clamp down on street gangs and shootings so there was no room for a deal.'

'Hence Warren's festering resentment about his brother's judicial treatment. Whose colors did Winston wear?'

Chips searched for clippings on his desk. 'Press reports I pulled on the trail say South Side Crips. Ran with the Pirus gang. I've not had time to check further with Anti-Gangs or LAPD uniforms.'

'Pirus – that's the same outfit as Aaron Bolt.' Angie remembered the picture she'd seen on the TV of Bolt posing with a MAC-10, dressed in clothes identical to the ones the UNSUB had worn during the Sun Western slayings. 'I'm wondering if he and Aaron Bolt knew each other, whether Warren was the guy behind the camera when the scumbag we're about to let go free posed for that picture with the gun.'

'You mean he copied his disguise from Bolt?'

A knock on the door turned their heads.

Cal O'Brien stood there. His eyes were already fixed on the white-board. 'Is there something you guys want to tell me?'

Chapter 155

Time speeds up once a case gets a break. It was a lesson Angie learned long ago. As soon as she'd finished apprising O'Brien of the breakthrough, events happened lightning fast.

First off, the lieutenant rushed to the precinct to question Aaron Bolt about Warren Hendry, before he was very publicly released and an apology was issued.

She and Ruis then briefed the joint FBI LAPD inquiry team. Finding Warren Hendry was now a priority, as he was most likely to be the driver of the van registered to Cheetham.

Crawford left to discuss the Hendry execution with the Anti-Gangs Unit. Connor Pryce headed back to the LAPD HQ to do the same with the police squads.

Chips and two female members of Ruis's team started to focus on the remaining jury members and their families, tracing where they were and detailing covert cover to ensure their safety.

'There's a certain irony in all this,' said Ruis, as he and Angie drove to the HQ of Cleereroads Inc.

'In what way?'

'Well, if you're right and Warren Hendry either took that picture of Bolt with the MAC-10, or he'd at least seen it, then essentially he's fitted Bolt up for a crime he didn't commit, using a photograph that was taken to celebrate Bolt getting away with a crime he did do. And Warren's done all that in vengeance for what he sees as the wrongful execution of his dead brother.'

'Twisted minds always find justification,' said Angie. 'I'm kicking myself now for not seeing the significance of the Judge and Jury anagram he left at the mall.'

'And the memorial attacks? Why did he do that?'

Angie searched for a motive. 'If someone goes to the chair, then they just get buried in an unmarked grave. There's nothing for the family of the deceased to hang on to. Their shame is all that is memorialized. I guess our UNSUB saw the public service for the mall victims as an insult to his own injury, so he lashed out.'

The sign to the Cleereroads building loomed. Ruis indicated and pulled into a scrappy front lot. The blacktop was broken by weeds and crawled around a single-story industrial unit. Four identical E Wagons were parked over the far side.

Angie felt her stomach turn as she walked past them. She imagined Jake's killer sat behind the wheel of one of the road kill clearance vehicles, following him to his apartment.

Ruis showed his badge in the cheap reception area. A plump girl behind a skinny desk called the CEO on her desk phone. 'Mr Cleere, the agents from the FBI are here.'

She put the phone down and smiled nervously. 'I'll walk you through.'

Beyond reception, the building was open plan, noisy and as busy as a train station. A narrow aisle ran past rows of admin clerks cooped behind cubicle screens, garage mechanics hanging up keys of serviced vehicles, and wannabe managers in cheap shirts and skirts passing paper.

The receptionist stopped at a door marked CEO, knocked and opened it. The man behind the title got up from behind a black, leather-topped desk. He was tall, broad and blond, with gelled hair and an expensive brown suit that made him look older than his twenty-eight years.

'Dominic Cleere, please come in.' He waved them to matching leather sofas. A thin, small brunette drifted in, dressed in a matronly blue skirt and jacket.

'This is my attorney, Annabella Weir.'

She offered a weak and bony shake. 'Pleased to meet you.'

'We're here in connection with a homicide,' said Angie. 'And we need certain information from you.'

'We'll do whatever we can.' Cleere sat tall and crossed a spindly leg. 'What do you want to know?'

Ruis produced a photo of the white E Wagon. 'This is one of your vehicles. You'll see we've blown up the license plate, that's how we traced it to your company.'

Cleere looked and passed it to his lawyer. 'We have almost a hundred vehicles spread across five hundred square miles of Greater Los Angeles.'

'And each of them will have been fitted with a tracker system,' added Angie, 'so a smart guy like you is able to know that everyone is hard at work and not moonlighting with your vehicles. Plus, you get a discount on your fleet insurance for fitting the bug.'

Her intuition made him smile. 'What *exactly* do you want?'

Ruis gave him the answer. 'We need the full minute-by-minute movements of that vehicle for the past two weeks, plus the names of every person who drove it matched to those minutes.'

The attorney started up, 'We're not *obliged* to give you that information. Perhaps it's best if you obtain—'

'I *can* oblige you,' snapped the SKU man. 'I can get a warrant and have every computer in here seized and taken away while we find what we want. You never know, you might even get them back within a month or six.'

'Have it done right away, Annabella.' Cleere uncrossed his legs and leaned forwards. 'Is there anything else?'

'There is.' Ruis dipped into his jacket pocket and produced a copy of a photograph. 'Does this man work for you? His name is Warren Hendry.'

Cleere took the photo. 'I don't know. He may do.' He stood up and straightened his suit. 'Give me a moment and I'll ask one of my management team.' He walked out, followed by his lightweight lawyer.

Angie was about to talk when Ruis's phone jangled. He stood up to take it and her eyes drifted to Cleere's desk. There was a photo of him and a brunette, cheek-to-cheek with a holiday sun beaming almost as brightly as they were. It sparked a painful reminder of losing Jake. Vacations were their precious times. Moments when they could sit back and mock the horrors of their work.

'Good news.' Ruis returned the phone to his pocket. 'Labs rushed

MICHAEL MORLEY

a profile on the hair from the restroom at JZ's. There's a familial DNA match with Winston Hendry.'

'That is good news. I wonder if our killer senses us closing on him?' Angie's tone was reflective rather than triumphal. 'If he does, then there's a risk he'll unravel and turn Spree.'

'Kill the rest of the names on his list?'

'It's possible. His whole life is currently dedicated to completing that list.'

Cleere re-entered the room with documents in his hand. Just behind him trailed two suited men, one young and one old. He motioned to each in turn. 'These are my executives, Gary Hawkins and John Taylor. John is my EVP of operations and Gary his VP. John, please tell them about Mr Hendry.'

Taylor ran a finger nervously under his nose. 'Warren Hendry works at our Downtown depot. He's been standing in as supervisor since the usual manager, Januk Dudek, failed to turn up for work. Gary, here, went to see both Dudek and Hendry.'

The young VP filled in the gaps. 'The super wasn't home. Neighbors said they hadn't seen him for days. I went to the depot and informed Hendry of the termination of Mr Dudek's position and offered him the post on a trial basis. To our surprise, he turned it down. Said he wasn't interested in the responsibility.'

'What's he like?' asked Angie. 'I mean professionally, not physically?'

Hawkins shrugged. 'Smart, I suppose. Calm and controlled.' He nodded to his line manager. 'Hendry had volunteered to step in when Dudek disappeared, so Mr Taylor thought he had initiative, ambition.'

'He seemed very confident and assured,' added the EVP. 'He called us when the supervisor failed to show and took charge.' Curiosity got the better of him. 'Can I ask, what's he supposed to have done?'

'You can ask, but for now I can't tell you. The confidentiality is important.' Ruis looked towards the men's boss. 'I need all Hendry's personal details – and Dudek's.'

Cleere took a final look at the papers in his hands then passed them over. 'These are Hendry's employment particulars, his home address and contact numbers, et cetera, along with staff appraisals over the last two years.'

Ruis glanced at the print-outs. 'It says he works nine *p.m.* to five *a.m.*, is that right?'

Taylor nodded. 'Yes, it is. Most of our depots do permanent lates.'

'Why's that?'

Cleere answered. 'The police and state carry out emergency daytime road clearance, we do the night work and a little daytime support when they're stretched. We shift everything – dogs, cats, birds . . . even deer and cattle. You know, around a million animals a year are killed on our roads; it takes a while to scrape up that kind of carnage.'

Angie was not interested. It was after six and she didn't want to learn about the road-kill business. Right now, Jake's killer might be eating his dinner, or coming home to get ready for work.

Ruis was ahead of her. 'Mr Cleere, we're going to have to pay Hendry a visit, and Dudek too. It's vital no one from your company calls either of them or attempts any contact without our okaying it. Do you understand?'

'I do.' He grimaced. 'Is this going to end in bad publicity for my company? Only I don't want my business damaged by your investigation.'

Angie felt her blood boil. She got to her feet and launched a parting shot. 'Just make sure your employees comply, Mr Cleere, or I'll personally make sure you have no business left to damage.'

Chapter 156

C hips kept a close check on Judge Elysia's social media pages. To his disappointment, there had been nothing from Minos. No matter. He was still buzzing with the excitement of a breakthrough, of spotting the links between their case victims, the Winston Hendry jurors, and their loved ones. Angie had pinned down the area in which to look, but he'd been the one to join up the dots and it felt good.

He was still savoring the success when Elysia finally got a tweet. His eyes locked on the monitor and he could see there was a link embedded.

Chips clicked.

It was video of a street. There were trees right of frame, blacktop left, cars zipping by in both directions. There was sound too, the chirrup of birds in nearby trees and the zoom and fade of passing traffic.

The young profiler had already checked his own IP masking apps were running but he checked again. This tricky mother might just have been rattling the system somehow, trying to interrogate Elysia's digital credentials with a program he'd written.

Chips's software said he was safe.

Nevertheless, he dialed the Cyber Squad and spoke to his contact, Sally Brotherson. 'Sal, can you access my computer and take a look at what I'm seeing.'

'Give me a second.' She clacked on her keyboard with painted nails that matched her red hair. 'Yeah, I've got you. Wassup? This an incoming feed from your UNSUB?'

'Yeah, I think so. I just clicked a link from Twitter. Can you tell if he's running some freaky-techie diagnostics on us?'

She engaged her own search and lock programs. 'Can't say. It's masked like the other stuff you showed me. Could be. Feed looks live. You should rest easy; our firewalls are so good nothing will get through.'

'Hang on, it's moving.' Chips watched the camera jerk forward. It was being carried down the street, waist high, and the lens view was wide angle.

The sun hovered directly behind whoever was filming. A shadow fell on the sidewalk – it was of a capped man carrying a box. There were clunks on the video sound and short breaths as though the box was heavy to shift.

Chips felt his heart tighten. 'Sal, do you have any idea where this is coming from?'

She was glued to the screen as well. 'No. I've tried running lock and trace but like I said, it's shielded.'

'Shit.' He grabbed his cellphone and dialed Angie.

The shadow man disappeared as the camera swung right. A small gate came into view. It floated open. The sun was to the right side. Shadow man reappeared on the grass to the left. An oak front door filled the frame. There was the ding of a bell.

'Hello,' shouted Angie down the phone.

Chips ignored her.

The door on camera opened. An inquisitive male face peered out. 'Can I help you?'

'Delivery for Mrs Payne – Mrs Robyn Payne.'

Chips recognized the name. Realized what was happening. This was the home of juror Nate Payne. 'Oh God, where are the cops?' He grabbed the phone. 'Angie, the UNSUB's at the Paynes' and there's no protection there.'

'I'm her husband,' said the man at the door. He stretched out his hands to the box. 'I'll take it.'

'I'm afraid she has to sign.'

Nate Payne frowned. '*I* can sign.'

'I'm sorry, it has to be her.'

Payne turned and shouted as he walked into the blackness of the house. 'Robyn, delivery for you. Apparently, only you can sign for it.'

'I'm coming.' Unseen feet thundered down carpeted stairs.

Angie shouted down the line, 'Chips, I'm onto Ruis. We'll get a chopper up ASAP.'

A blonde in her late forties appeared on-screen. Red spectacles dangled in a hand. 'Hello.' She sounded pleased to see the parcel. Put her glasses on and smiled. 'Where do I sign?'

The gun held beneath the box was silenced and made only a dull *phut* noise.

Mrs Payne made no noise at all.

Her mouth opened and she blew out air, like she'd been winded.

The second *phut* spun her sideward.

A third hit her in the face and spattered blood across the door and inner walls of the house.

Her husband Nate came into view. Horror filled his eyes.

A bullet tore a hole in his shoulder. A second fractured his right ankle.

'Oh God, he's shot them. They're both dead,' Chips mouthed into the phone, his eyes held by what he saw on the screen.

The camera went into the house. It panned over the spattered walls and dipped as the box was put down. It swung up and showed a landline phone cable being ripped out of a socket. A cellphone was plucked from Nate Payne's pocket.

The next shot was a pan over the bodies on the floor. Nate Payne groaned and moved. 'The husband's alive,' relayed Chips. 'He's bleeding from a shoulder and ankle. Looks bad.' In a long wall mirror came the briefest glimpse of a black man in a chocolate brown UPS shirt and cap. The lens swung onto Robyn Payne's exploded head. It lingered. Zoomed in. Then out.

A gloved hand appeared to be mopping the remains of her brow. The camera tilted to the wall above her. The hand wrote two words in the dead woman's blood.

BE JUST.

Chapter 157

Trinity Park, LA

S hooter cut the video feed.
  He'd been running it through his server on a five-minute delay. Should anyone be sat across the transmission then those three hundred seconds might prove precious. So too should the decoy he'd thrown out – a glimpse of the replica UPS uniform he'd created. With any luck, it would make the cops assume he'd parked a parcel van nearby.

He stripped in the hallway and revealed a plain grey tracksuit, which he also removed. He put the UPS uniform minus the cap back on and covered it with the tracksuit. He stuffed the cap down his briefs and opened the large box he'd carried in.

It had been more than just a ruse to bring Robyn Payne to the door. Inside was a black cloth sack containing his means of escape. He pulled it out and then positioned the empty box upside down, so it appeared still unopened. He restarted the camera and fixed it on the now empty box and the bodies.

While the feed was still stuttering into life, Shooter left by the back door.

He knew the garden well. The couple had tended it lovingly and the overhanging trees near the potting shed gave excellent cover to hide behind as he climbed the rear fence and dropped into the alley at the back.

Shooter stood up on a pile of old wood and checked the coast was clear. The sack he'd taken from the box was heavy but he was strong enough to lift it and lower it over before completing the journey himself.

Once on the other side, he walked to the corner so he could see the end of the entry to the road. Off in the not-too-distant streets he heard police sirens. It meant someone had alerted the cops to the footage. Shooter pulled a knife and cut the string on the sack. Inside was a folded bicycle and a box of baby wipes. Within a minute he'd cleaned off his colored make-up, opened up the bike, locked it rigid, pulled up the seat, twisted the handlebars into position and ridden away.

Once he rounded the corner, he pedaled lazily into the flow of busy street traffic. He knew not to rush, not to draw attention to himself. The sun shone high and hot. The sky unfurled cloudlessly as Shooter glided through the streams of cars and buses.

He came to a stop at a red light and leaned against the side of a city-bound bus. A noise tilted his head skyward and he smiled as an FBI helicopter flew right over him.

Chapter 158

Comms chatter from the copter spilled through the radio on the dash of Ruis Costas's Jeep. 'Red Leader this is Eyeball One – we have no sighting of assailant. Repeat, no sighting of a black man in brown delivery clothing. Over.'

The SKU man punched the steering wheel of the SUV. 'Eyeball One, keep in observation formation until otherwise instructed.'

Angie was next to him, her cellphone pressed to her ear. Chips relayed off-screen commentary to her and she passed it on to Ruis. 'The husband has just moved. He's bleeding out near the box but he's moving.'

Ruis knew what she was thinking. 'I can't let paramedics in, Angie, not until we're sure the UNSUB is not still in there and we're certain what's in that box. Jeffreys is on the way with the Bomb Squad; they can get a robot in to snoop, then we'll know.'

'He's gone, Ruis,' she argued. 'He's just buying time with this box. Believe me, there's nothing dangerous in it.'

'I can't take the risk. We got a good description of him from that video grab Chips sent through. It's on the screen in the copter and the flight crew say he's not out on the street. That means he could still be in the house.'

She still wasn't satisfied. 'We're a block away. You and I can take this creep if he's in there.'

He shook his head. 'No one's going through that door until I know the killer is out of there and there's no risk of a bomb going off.'

'It's not a bomb.' Angie sounded frustrated. 'If he wanted to blow people up, he'd have hidden it, like he did at the mall memorial.'

They were still arguing when they turned the corner to enter the tree-lined street where the Paynes lived. Black and white cruisers blocked the way. Ruis rolled the Jeep to one side and they got out.

The FBI helicopter circled low and loud as he and Angie badged their way through the cordon. They passed an ambulance with the back doors hinged open. Paramedics stood in the sun, waiting alongside two roller stretchers laden with emergency equipment.

Angie put on shades. She could see clearer. Two hundred yards away, a number of houses were still being evacuated, reluctant residents forced out at the far end where two more police cruisers were closing access. The scene gave her flashbacks of the blast at the mall. The dead. The wounded. The shocked. She'd sat with them all. And with those who'd lost loved ones. That night, Jake had held her in bed and kept the tears and demons away. Without him she would have struggled.

'Twelve Sixty-Two.' Ruis pointed fifty yards ahead on the right. His finger sighted a modest wood-fronted home with an open gate, patch of well-cut lawn and bending blossom trees. 'That's the Paynes'.'

'Where the hell were the protection officers?' asked Angie.

'That's a question for later. Probably the usual excuses – they went to an old address – no one was available – the detail wasn't marked urgent.'

She turned her wrist and looked at her watch. 'I really don't want to be here. I want to be with the crew kicking Hendry's door in.'

'I know. Me too.' Ruis checked his own timepiece. 'It's almost seven. He doesn't start work until nine. I've got covert units heading to both his home and place of work.'

'And the supervisor – Dudek?'

'On the list as well. Everything's in hand, Angie. You don't need to be second guessing me.'

'Sorry.'

They stood in the shade and she called Chips again. 'How's Nate Payne doing?'

He was glued to the monitor. 'He's dragged himself alongside his wife and is holding on to what's left of her.' The young profiler tried not to choke. 'It's awful. He's cradling her face and it's such a mess. He knows she's dead. Knows it. But he just keeps holding her and talking to her.'

Angie remembered the operating theater. Kneeling in Jake's blood, refusing to believe he was dead. Kissing him. Believing in God, in magic, Mother Nature, anything that could bring him back.

'I can see his blood everywhere,' said Chips, sounding more distressed. 'It's like he's ready to die with her.'

'We won't let that happen, Chips.' She turned the phone off and started walking.

The street was silent but for the thwack of the copter overhead and the crackle of comms radios from nearby uniforms. Her heart quickened as she broke into a jog. She slipped her hand beneath her jacket and unholstered her weapon.

'Angie!' Ruis shouted.

She glanced back.

He was racing towards her.

She checked the safety was off on her gun and started sprinting. Her eyes were focused on the house. The Paynes and the package were in the hall. She was going in through the front window. If the motherfucker was still in there and wanted a gunfight, so be it. And if today was the day she got blown up, then so be that too. What she wasn't prepared for was standing around while a wounded man died.

She slowed and turned in the gate.

The window was ten yards away. Six strides and a jump. She'd take it good shoulder first, head turned away from the glass.

Ruis grabbed her. Caught her round the waist and pulled her down onto the grass.

'No!' Angie tried to fight him off. 'Let me go.'

He kept her pressed to the turf. Climbed over her. Smothered her body with his while his eyes and gun stayed on the door. 'We can't do this, Angie. We have to wait.'

She stopped struggling. He was bigger, heavier and stronger. 'Okay, get the fuck off me, you're pressing on my bad arm.'

He eased off. Shifted warily, still not convinced she wouldn't try again. 'Come on, let's get to a safe distance.'

She got up and trudged with him. Walked silently back in shame towards the waiting ambulance and idling cruisers.

He looked her over. 'I'm sorry if I hurt you, but that was crazy, Angie.'

She was annoyed he didn't share her point of view. 'I can't stay here, Ruis, and watch someone else die. I'll fall apart if that happens. Give me your keys, I'll go back to the office and help Chips.'

'You sure?'

She nodded.

He dug in his pocket. 'Are you okay to drive?'

'I'm fine.' She rotated her injured shoulder a little to prove the point. 'Will you call me; keep me updated on the raids? Let me know if and when you find this bastard?'

'I will.' He handed over the Jeep keys then carefully hugged her. 'We'll get him, Angie. I promise you that.'

Chapter 159

Trinity Park, LA

An orchestra of police sirens filled the smoggy evening air. Two-tone horns rose and fell, near and far, as Shooter cycled steadily through traffic.

There were cops everywhere.

A cruiser had just blocked off a brown delivery van and LAPD's finest were pointing weapons into the cab and screaming their lungs out.

It was all too close for comfort.

Shooter had a handgun and UPS cap stuffed down his briefs. If they did a stop and search he was going to have to blast his way out.

He doglegged right, then across the dusty forecourt of a Mexican fast food joint before taking a left to get himself back on the route home. It was longer this way but safer. The sooner he got out of sight, the better.

Shooter thought of the kill as he rode the last stretch. Robyn Payne had always been next on his list. He'd been working through the order in which jurors had been chosen and she was the wife of the fourth. Had he not overslept, he'd have killed her earlier in the day, right after her shift at a charity shop when she stopped to buy freshly baked bread on the way home. It was an indulgence betrayed by the multiplicity of bakers' receipts in her trash, complete with amount, date and time. Despite missing his window of opportunity, he'd adapted to his mistake and done something daring. Something for Elysia as well as his brother.

The 'live' camera he'd left in the house was simply a tech adaptation to an iPhone he'd bought from a second-hand retailer.

Now he was keen to know what she thought of it – and to work out how the cops had closed in on him so quickly. Perhaps that geek Snowden was right; maybe the Feds were constantly monitoring everyone and everything online.

He cycled the alleyways towards his old factory unit, got off at the corner of the block and scrabbled the padlock keys out of his pocket.

'Yo!'

The shout was from across the road. He carried on opening up.

'Hey, dude, hold up.'

The voice was so close he had to turn.

At first he didn't recognize the big guy in blue jeans and brown bomber jacket jogging his way. Then he realized who it was.

Mike Hanrahan.

The stick-his-nose-in-where-it's-not-wanted cop.

'What you doin', man?' He grabbed the handlebars of Shooter's folded cycle. 'You *really* ride this joke?' He swung a leg over it and laughed.

'Yeah, it gets me around.' He looked him over. 'What's with you?'

Hanrahan ran hands down his sides. 'Day off. It's good to be out of the blues.'

He put his right foot on a pedal, held the back brake and pulled the cycle up into a pretend wheelie. 'Man, you should not go into any kickass hood riding this junk, they'll eat you alive.' He looked him over. 'Or come to think of it, dressed like that.' He passed the cycle back and put a big hand on the young man's shoulder. 'You got a beer for your new friend? I've got a little business to talk to you about.'

Shooter slowly moved away. Hanrahan was much bigger and stronger than him. He'd be no easy fall like Dudek. 'I don't want to sound un-friendly, but now's not good. I've gotta get ready for my night job.'

'There's never a good time with you, is there, buddy?' His tone had changed. 'I'm starting to feel that you've got stuff in there that you don't want me to see – that you don't want no police to see.'

'It's just bad right now, that's all.'

Shooter looked fazed.

The cop read his face. 'Pretty soon I'm going to become a *de-tec-teev*, so don't think you can go hiding shit from me.' He slapped him on the back. 'Now, how about you let me in to your Aladdin's Cave over there and we sort out some business *a-rrange-ment* on those computers you mentioned?'

'Do I have a choice?'

He flashed his pearly whites as he laughed. 'Course you do. There's always a choice, man. You can fuck me off now and regret it for the rest of your life, or you can play the game and stay cool.'

Shooter knew what he had to do. 'Cool it is then. Come on in.'

Chapter 160

Angie drove the Jeep around the corner. She went half a mile then pulled over and sat with the engine off and her head in her hands.

If she was going to cry she sure as hell wasn't going to do it in front of the FBI and LAPD.

Ruis had played things by the book. He'd done nothing wrong. First lesson of being a law enforcement professional was thinking about personal safety. Endanger yourself and you endanger others. If she'd gone through the window then she may have been blown up and so might he. But by doing nothing, they'd practically ended Nate Payne's life. There was every chance he'd bleed out before the medics got to him.

Angie sat up straight behind the wheel and tried to stop a hundred thoughts banging into each other. She needed some clarity. Nothing had ever been what it seemed with this offender. He'd gone out of his way to trick and deceive them. The Spree-like killings to distract from the focus on specific victims, the different weapons he'd used, the switch from guns to a bomb and back again, the changes of clothes – and if she and Chips were right, even changes of his skin color.

She remembered the sports bag in the mall. The canvas bag in JZ's Saloon. It followed that the cardboard box left at the Paynes' house was simply a variation on the bag. He'd probably had a change of clothes in there as well. Then she remembered the video frame Chips had pulled and the alert that had gone out for a man in a brown UPS uniform.

It was obvious now that the UNSUB had played them.

He'd known they'd grasp at straws, and that flash frame in the hallway mirror had given them a handful of false hope to clutch hold of.

She called Ruis.

It tripped to his answerphone. 'It's Angie. I had a thought. I think Hendry played us. My bet is that he had a change of clothes in that box and we're wasting our time looking for a delivery guy in a brown uniform. He'll be dressed down, casual, messy even, certainly not in a uniform. And remember: he might be black or white, or even dressed female as he was at the mall. He looked black in the video grab so one thing's for sure – he probably cleaned off the make-up as soon as he could.'

She hung up and called Chips. 'Hi there. I'm just checking to see how you're holding up.'

'I'm okay.' His voice said he wasn't. It was full of emotional strain. 'SKU are getting a monitor team up and running to watch the feed at the Paynes'. I won't have to focus like I did.'

'That's good. We'll talk things through when I get back. Meanwhile, can you do some things for me?'

'Yeah, I think so.'

'You sure you're okay?'

He dug deep. 'If you can be okay, then so can I. What do you want me to do?'

'We need to respond on Twitter to the video Hendry fed us, get a coded message into his Minos account.'

'What do you want to say?'

'Let's work it through. Hendry either sees Elysia as a fan, or is just feeling desperately isolated and in his madness needs some kind of contact. I guess he's an emotional mess right now.'

Chips followed her train of thought. 'He's going to be elated and anxious at the same time. The kill today will have had his adrenaline pumping like crazy and now he'll be coming down after the rush.'

'You're right. We need to manipulate those emotions, reflect his own mood.' Angie paused, then added, 'Just write "OMG! AMAZING! RU OK?"'

'I've got it.'

'And I need you to dig, Chips. Spade up whatever you can on

495

Warren and Winston Hendry. I know they have no other siblings or living relatives, but I want a friend, an ex-girlfriend, anyone who can give me a lead on him.'

'I'd already started trawls. I'll go back over them.'

'Make it quick. Feed me texts on the cellphone. There's no time for reports. I want to know Warren's schooling, employment, anything that tells me where this mastery of disguise came from.'

'I'm on it.'

'Thanks.' She hung up and dialed Cal O'Brien. 'Lieutenant, it's Angie Holmes. Can you talk?'

'I called your cell.' He sounded annoyed. 'Twice.'

She hadn't noticed the missed calls. 'Sorry, our UNSUB struck again.'

'I just heard.'

'Did Bolt give anything up on Hendry?'

'Just a punk ass smile. Said – I quote –"I ain't no snitchin' nigger."'

'Even though Warren Hendry set him up for a Murder One jab in the arm, he still wouldn't turn on him?'

'Not a degree. Best I could get was that he knew him. Knew his brother too. I called a contact in Anti-Gangs and he says Winston was a gun dealer. He was the guy to go to for an untraceable weapon, or to dispose of a hot one.'

'And brother Warren?'

'No gang profile. He was an outsider.'

Angie started to form a picture of the fraternal relationship. Two brothers growing up in gangland LA without parents. It was a common enough story. One went bad but tried to keep the other good. He became the parent. Took the falls. Winston would have brought in the money, put food on the table, tried to push the kid brother to get properly schooled and make something of himself. Warren would have felt a need to show his gratitude, prove himself. But not physically. He'd have done it with technology. He'd have hacked accounts, unlocked phones and ripped off credit cards to show his gang worth. Still Winston would have kept him away.

Angie was sure the big twist of fate, the fatal step towards today's terrors, would have come when Winston got busted. Big brother would have elicited undertakings from the rest of the gang to keep Warren straight. Only that just built up steam in the kid. He would have felt an acute loss of brotherly love at having to watch his only role model rot away inside.

Winston would no doubt have spun some shit about being innocent of the murders, about him being made an example of and how the government had fixed the jury. He'd probably thought he'd spend decades on Death Row, but the elections had come rolling in and the lack of executions had turned into a political issue.

Angie noted that Hendry had gone to the chair just two months before the state had gone to the polls.

The voters returned the hard line, hang 'em high governor. In the process, they'd unwittingly created a new breed of serial killer. The Hybrid.

Chapter 161

Skid Row, LA

'What do you drive when you're off duty?' Shooter shut the gates behind the cop and walked him towards the doors of the sanctuary.

'What do I *drive*?' Mike Hanrahan laughed and kicked stones as he pulled level with him. 'Why d'you wanna know? You selling stolen cars as well as computers?'

'Just asking.' He stopped and used his smartphone to disarm the outer alarms.

'Okay, I'll tell ya. I've got a late model Dodge Charger.' The cop picked up a chunk of broken brick and threw it wide of an old oilcan some twenty yards away. 'I got it cheap, friends in the trade, you know what I mean?' He dusted his hands and eyed the smartphone. 'That's a snazzy piece of kit. Did you just disable the security system with that?'

Shooter passed him the phone. 'Yeah. It's easy to rig. I can fix an app for your phone if you want to do it for your garage or home systems.'

The cop slid his finger back and forth along the glass and pressed an icon or two. 'I know diddly squat about tech like this, but it's cool.' He handed it back.

Shooter took it and pulled open the door. He knew this was the point of no return. Once the guy crossed the threshold, there was no way he could let him come out again.

Hanrahan stepped into the cool inner shade. 'Neat place. If you're a rabbit and like living in the dark.'

'Sorry, the bulb blew. I meant to get a replacement while I was out.'

The rookie put a hand against a wall to guide himself. 'How much you paying to rent this?'

'Got a startup grant. It's virtually free for the first year.' Shooter shut the door and now the place was as black as an unlit coal mine.

'Hey, you keep your freakin' hands to yourself,' joked Hanrahan. 'Vice Squad warned me about guys like you.'

'You should be so lucky. Just stay close and follow me. I'll guide us to the kitchen.'

The cop put an arm on Shooter's shoulder and tagged behind.

Shooter passed the converted washrooms and turned left. If the policeman pushed a door round here he could walk into Death Row. That couldn't happen.

Or could it?

He stopped and waited.

Hanrahan stumbled around the narrow corner.

'You want to see something that will blow your mind?'

'My mind was born to be blown, buddy. But I doubt you have anything in here that could do the job.'

Shooter stepped away from the touching hand, slipped his fingers beneath his tracksuit and drew the weapon he'd used to shoot the Paynes. 'Here we go.' He clicked open the door to Death Row and then concealed the weapon as he switched on the light.

Hanrahan blinked from the sudden glare. 'Fuck!' Instinctively he stepped into the room.

Shooter could see him now. There'd be no mistake. He had room and time for a perfect shot. He held his fire. Watched the cop stare at the different groups of photographs on the wall and the flickering electric candle on the shelf that eerily illuminated them. His head turned right and he saw another picture. It was of a face Hanrahan would have recognized sooner if a prison number had run across the bottom.

Winston Hendry.

He turned around. 'What the fuck is this?'

'It's where I keep the dead.' Shooter lifted the Glock and shot him in the head. 'There you go,' he said calmly, 'I told you I'd blow your mind.'

Chapter 162

Trinity Park, LA

T wo Bomb Squad officers stood sweltering in astronaut-style blast suits. The kit was state-of-the-art, lightweight ballistic armor, but it was still hot as hell inside the foam-cushioned helmets and full-face visors.

The NATO standard military suits were fitted with articulated spine protectors, groin guards, neoprene-coated Kevlar knee and elbow pads. The helmets had full comms packs and were linked to the support truck that had been set up behind a series of blast shields.

Ruis Costas sat in the vehicle alongside the unit's head, Tom Jeffreys. On a bank of small monitors they watched the men move slowly towards the Paynes' home. They entered the garden and set up their equipment. A telescopic arm, so they could bore a hole through the front door, insert a remote camera and see what lay beyond the wood and brick. They also deployed an extending robotic claw, the type used to dismantle IEDs, and a laser-guided water jet disrupter, powerful enough to destroy many explosive devices.

Ruis felt the minutes tick slowly by as they manipulated the equipment. A second monitor in the truck fizzed into life. The microbore probe had gone through the door. The extended camera showed a man and woman lying unconscious. Pools of blood glistened. A large yellow box gleamed in the half-light. One of the men outside pushed the camera further. It advanced slowly, iron bar straight, into the cold hallway, above the bodies and over the box.

Jeffreys gave instructions to lower it.

Everyone watching held their breath.

The camera wire slackened and the lens dipped.

Ruis could now see the middle seam of the box, where panels folded together. The lens slowly made its way towards the cardboard.

It touched.

There was no explosion.

An emboldened operative manipulated the extended wire.

The lens head dipped inside the box and rotated.

'Nothing.' Ruis stood from his seat. 'It's empty.'

'Put the door in,' Jeffreys told his men. 'Put it in, then stand back.'

Ruis was already out of the truck. He spoke into his radio. 'We have a go. Repeat – go, go, go.'

Three armed men in SKU blacks hurried from behind the blast shield.

A Bomb Squad suit popped the front door with a sledgehammer.

Ruis waved the waiting paramedics into action. He prayed to God that he hadn't left things too late, that Nate Payne was still alive.

Chapter 163

Skid Row, LA

He'd killed a cop.

The lifeless corpse confirmed Shooter's membership of what he knew was an elite club. Cop Killers Anonymous. A group that topped the FBI and LAPD's Most Wanted lists.

He figured Hanrahan had been off duty and wouldn't be missed until tomorrow. At best the day after. But he *would* be missed. Then his friends in blue would start tracing his last steps. Triangulating his cellphone. Looking for his car. Searching street camera footage.

Shooter knew he had to cover his tracks. Shift the body out of there. Get everything cleaned up.

He'd done it with Dudek. He could do it again. It was messy. Sickening. But it could be done.

At least that's what he told himself as he went for the sheeting and the cutting tools.

But he couldn't.

The horrors of sawing and chopping through Dudek's flesh and bones jarred in his mind. The severed limbs, the coils of intestines and puddled fluids. He couldn't go through all that again.

Shooter looked at the wall above Hanrahan's body. Blood and brains were spattered across the photographs he had so carefully fixed there. Even that was enough to turn his stomach. He put his hand to his mouth and almost heaved. Cold sweat prickled the back of his neck. It was a sign that things were getting to him. He couldn't let that happen. But everything was mounting up. It was all so relentless. Endlessly stressful.

Shooter left the room. Leaned against the wall in the kitchen galley. Took deep breaths. He had to get his head together. Stay focused. Before he tackled the disposal of the corpse, he needed to clean up. He filled a bucket with hot water and detergent, grabbed cloths and towels and returned to the body.

He started with the walls. Wiped down pieces of brain and bone. Rinsed his cloth and watched the fleshy detritus float in the bucket. He mopped the wall until the paper peeled, red rain fell and dark puddles hogged the corners of the floor.

Shooter glanced at his brother's picture and sensed disappointment burning in his eyes. A thousand times he'd heard the words, *'You just stay out of it, Warren, you'll only fuck things up and fuck yourself up.'*

'It's not fucked up! It's not.' He banged the bucket down. Watery blood slopped and splashed.

Damn the cop!

He kicked the pulp that remained of Hanrahan's head.

Winston laughed at him. *'You're losing it, bro. Get your shit together.'*

Shooter covered his ears.

'You're useless, bro. Useless.'

Things weren't going to plan. It was his fault. He shouldn't have improvised.

'You ain't cut out for this.'

If he'd stuck to what he'd researched, what he'd intended, then none of this would have happened.

'Warren, I told you – stay out of things. Now look what you done.'

He sank to his knees and pleaded with his brother's picture. 'I just wanted to do right for you. Make them all pay for what they did.' Shooter sat back on his heels and sobbed.

Down the corridor his computer dinged.

He didn't move.

It was her.

Elysia.

He got to his feet and stepped over the corpse. Stood in puddled blood. Walked it into the corridor. All his efforts at forensic cleanliness were falling apart. Bloody footprints followed him to the computer room and the incoming message.

Chapter 164

A ngie was still in the Jeep when a text message beeped. It was from Chips. NEW TWEET. CALL ME. C.

She pulled over and dialed straight away. 'Hi, what've you got?'

The young profiler was sat at his desk, impotently running search programs to nail the elusive IP address. 'What I've not got is a fix on Minos's whereabouts. But he has just tweeted back to our message. He said, "Am not okay."'

Angie was disappointed. 'Is that all?'

'It is. Only he wrote it as just seven capital letters and no spaces –"AMNOTOK".'

She thought on it. 'Sounds like his ego is waning. A loss of self. Maybe even some doubt creeping in.'

'How do I reply?'

'In the same way he wrote. Mirror his language. In his own pathetic way, he's looking for Elysia to engage more closely and offer her support. Be blunt. Just type back, "WHY?"'

Chips hit the four keystrokes and return. 'Done it.'

'He'll be watching his screen.' Angie imagined him hunched over a laptop, waiting for some connection through the darkness of cyberspace.

'Incoming,' announced Chips as his computer pinged.

'What's he say?'

'Not much. "IHURT", that's all.'

'Good.' Angie imagined how she'd really like to hurt him.

506

'Again, there's no separation of the words,' continued Chips. 'What's that lack of spacing about?'

'He's really pressured,' explained Angie. 'Uptight. Condensed. Closed down. All writing betrays behavioral clues, even impersonal computer caps. It's bringing out the fact that he's feeling things are pushing in on him. Write back, "HOw". First two letters in caps, lower case, no question mark though, make it look sloppy, more sincere, as though rushed and eager.'

Chips entered: HOw

Again the reply was quick.

'He's virtually instant messaging,' said Chips. 'He replied "HEADANDHEART", again all caps.'

Angie understood. 'He's stuck in the mood for now. Depressed. The word "Head" suggests he's worrying. Perhaps we were closer to catching him today than we thought. "Heart" is a reference to his brother.' She stopped for a second and pushed herself to think like the killer, to imagine his isolation and his fear. 'I think he's being torn apart by natural grief on one side and some sworn unnatural promise to avenge his brother's death on the other.'

Chips was taking notes as well as replying. 'Shall I write anything back, or just leave it?'

'No. He has to be the one to cut our communication bond. Say, "I feel your pain. You are brave."'

'Brave?' Chips felt a wave of revulsion. 'Are you sure you want to write that, Angie?'

'No, it's the last thing I want to write. I want to say to him, "You are the scum of the earth, go and put a gun in your mouth and save us all a lot of trouble," but I can't. This is psychological fishing, nothing is certain. Mix the cases and spaces and do it quickly, Chips, we can't let him sense any hesitation.'

He clacked out the characters: IFEELyurPAIN–ITHINK ur BRAVE

Thirty seconds passed.

Nothing came back.

The young profiler's fingers hovered either side of his keyboard. 'I'm refreshing the feed.'

Another minute slugged by. Angie grew impatient. 'Anything?'

'No.'

'Damn.' She knew Hendry would be walking an emotional tightrope and wondered if they'd overplayed their hand and opened up to him too soon. Or annoyed him by answering too slowly.

'He's replied.' Chips sounded relieved. 'All in caps again. It says, "THNX. WHERE RU?"'

Angie allowed herself some renewed optimism. 'He's certainly trying to engage – and if you're right about him tracing our address, maybe he's also calling our bluff. Just write the word "home", all lower case, make it seem mundane and unexciting.'

Chips fired off the tweet.

Another heavy silence fell.

This time it seemed to last forever. Chips refreshed the browser again.

Minutes passed.

He cracked first. 'There's no response, Angie.'

'Then we just have to wait. He's trying to locate Elysia. Wants to be absolutely sure she's where he thinks she is before he does anything. If this were a chess board, Chips, he'd be moving in for checkmate, worrying all the while that he's about to make a fatal mistake. Let's hope he does.'

Chapter 165

The ambulance sped away. Sirens busted eardrums. Ruis watched it disappear into a haze of heat at the end of the street. Robyn Payne was long dead and Nate, her husband of fifteen years, was only a fading heartbeat away from joining her.

The acting head of the FBI's Spree Killer Unit felt like his soul had been hollowed out.

He rarely prayed but right then he made the sign of the cross and begged God not to let him die. At the back of his mind were Angie's words, her warning that there was no bomb – just a trick to slow them down. Her desperate urgency to get in there and save Payne before he bled out. If Ruis had gone with her instincts, the husband's life wouldn't be so precariously in the balance.

The world seemed a lonely place as he walked past the Bomb Squad officers, now stripped from their blast suits and cooling down. Ruis was finding making decisions a whole culture shock away from simply following orders. He couldn't help but wonder what Jake would have done.

It didn't take much thinking about.

The big guy would have gone tearing in, much like Angie had wanted to. It was in both their natures. But Ruis wasn't Jake, and he wasn't going to run SKU or his life the way his former boss had done.

The first crocodile of curious residents passed through the now broken blockade. Homeowners gossiped and pointed up the street to where CSIs were already engrossed in forensic searches.

The FBI helicopter was little more than a dot in the distance. It was circling wide and using high-powered cameras to scour the sidewalks for anyone looking remotely like the video grab Chips had given them. Ruis had told them of Angie's warning that the delivery uniform might be a ploy. That he might look black – or white – male or female. It had gotten to the point where they were damned near looking at everyone who was on their own.

The coroner's van turned heads. Parents hurried kids inside as the vehicle with blacked out windows slid by.

At the bottom of the street, Ruis saw the depressed faces of his team. Being one step behind this particular UNSUB had clearly started to take its toll on their spirits. There'd never been one moment when they'd seen him, let alone been able to chase, open fire or capture him.

Ruis dismissed most of them. Told them not to take the job home. Reminded them that family was a priority now. Their duties lay in reading stories, drinking wine and making love. It was a speech Jake had given him several times.

Ruis held back only two units. The ones he needed to target the addresses of Januk Dudek and Warren Hendry.

Chapter 166

Skid Row, LA

Shooter stared at the keyboard and the last tweet from Elysia. He felt incapable of answering. Unable to do anything. His brain was fried.

There seemed no moment to rest. No escape. No peace.

The young cop's body was only a room away, threatening his sanity with its dead flesh.

He couldn't dismember another corpse. All that rage that had fueled him and sustained him through the early kills was spent. Now he didn't even have the strength to dispose of the last victim. Not the physical reserve, nor the mental fortitude.

He was burned out. Wasted.

The Internet was abuzz with his murders. This had been what he'd wanted. The surge of outrage – a preparation for his announcement of the injustice that had been committed. But it was costing him too much. He couldn't sleep. There was no switching off. And his list was only half completed.

'. . . you'll only fuck things up and fuck yourself up . . .'

Shooter covered his ears and tried to block out his brother's voice. 'Waaa—rrr—ee—n . . .'

He ignored Winston's call and stepped away from the computer. He told himself to keep his shit together. He could still see this through.

Focus. That's all he had to do. Stop thinking about how difficult things were and just do them.

Shooter returned to the body. He couldn't just leave it there. The room lacked air-con and the corpse would soon decompose.

Hanrahan was a big guy but nowhere near as large or heavy as Dudek. He opened the door and dragged him by the feet. It was tough but he could move him.

The cop's head bumped over the doorway and spilled red goo as Shooter heaved his way into the washrooms.

It was cooler in there.

He stood panting and dripping sweat. His gaze drifted to the mutilated man. He felt nothing for him, nothing except the fear of being caught. He let go of the ankles and dropped the heavy-as-lead legs. Dizziness whooshed into his brain. A lack of sleep, food and calm caught up with him. He sat down and for a second shut his eyes.

Winston was stood in the blackness of his mind, staring at him, bigger, stronger, all muscle and strength, the man he wanted to be. Shooter tried to banish him. Send him away. But even the thought made him feel guilty. He was betraying his brother's memory.

It was like killing him again.

Winston's mouth was open. He was speaking but no words were coming out.

Warren had silenced him.

Shut him up.

Lost him.

Big brother was dying and disappearing, silent and helpless like a space-walking astronaut who's had his line cut and is drifting away.

Little brother Warren felt left alone again.

Abandoned. Deserted. Desperate.

Chapter 167

Tess Holderbach, mother of two and leader of Team One, banged on the front door of the grubby apartment in Mid City that belonged to Januk Dudek. It was on 3rd Avenue, off West Adams Boulevard, just down from the local Polish church, Our Lady of the Bright Mount.

If there was anyone on the other side of the paint-peeled wood, peering out at her through the dirt-encrusted spy hole, they'd have seen a round-faced redhead dressed in jeans and a baggy red sweatshirt. What they wouldn't have seen was that she was wearing a Kevlar vest, and round the back of her jeans was a loaded Glock 23.

Either side of her stood two more plain clothes SKU officers. One slid a Remington 870 shotgun out of his black carry bag; the other lifted a door sledge into the strike position. Normally, such weaponry would be unnecessary for a call to check out a missing person, but given his connection to Hendry, Ruis had insisted no one took any chances.

Tess gave courtesy one last chance. She knocked again, this time with a balled fist, and shouted, 'FBI, Mr Dudek. Please open up.'

The request was loud enough for a white-haired woman two doors away to open her door and crane her neck into the hall.

'Get back inside, lady.' Tess pulled the Glock and stepped to one side.

The man with the sledge hit the woodwork. Splinters flew. The door bounced back on its hinges. Remington man kicked it wide and swung through the open space. Tess and her Glock followed.

The apartment was a squalid rectangle filled by a moth-eaten sofa and an old box of a TV. A waterfall of fast food cartons overflowed from a stuffed kitchen bin onto a linoleum floor and across to the wall. Flies buzzed the trash and languished on a stack of unwashed plates. Tess could see that food scraps were all but soldered to the top plates. She guessed it was days since anything had been added to the stack.

Remington man shouted from the doorway of a bathroom the size of a single closet. 'All clear.'

'Any soap in there?'

He looked. 'Yeah, small bar.'

'It wet or dry?'

He looked again. 'Hard and cracked.'

'Thought so.' Tess investigated a pile of bills near the moldy crockery. They were addressed to a Mr J. Dudek. This was his place, no doubt about it.

She walked to the bedroom and cringed. It stank to high heaven. She picked up hits of sweat, dust, cigarettes and stale male air. The floor of the tiny room was covered in abandoned newspapers and porn. All the material was in Polish.

Tess hitched a radio from her hip and called Ruis to give him the bad news. 'Dudek's gone. All that's left are his unpaid bills and bad habits. Best have CSIs turn the place – tell them they'll need gas masks and double gloves.'

Chapter 168

South Los Angeles

The Jeep felt like a prison to Angie.

She cracked the window open, not for air but to make a connection to the outside world.

Warren Hendry was close.

It wasn't that she felt it in some inspired cop-instinct way.

She knew it.

He worked and lived locally and had unfinished business. He'd gone to ground and not been discovered. Each time he surfaced he got away with a new murder and they were all local.

Local was his comfort zone.

No doubt about it, Warren Hendry was still close.

Angie wasn't going to wait for Ruis but she was torn between heading out to the home address Dominic Cleere had given them, or waiting a while and driving to his workplace, the road kill clearance depot. The latter was most likely to pay dividends. Her suspicions were that the home address would be bogus.

One thing for sure – she wasn't going back to the office.

Chips interrupted her thinking with a call. She picked it up, guessing there'd been another tweet. 'Hi there, what's the latest?'

'Nothing,' answered the young profiler. 'We haven't received anything from the UNSUB since our last message.'

Angie swore to herself.

'I do have the background you asked me for, though.'

She closed her eyes and tried to clear space in her brain to process it. 'Okay, fire away.'

'It turns out that Winston and his brother were orphaned. Stayed together through care homes and some fostering. Records have gaps but it looks like Warren went to school and did okay. Not so with Winston. He was absent pretty much from the day he got his first curriculum. Some of it, of course, due to his spell in Juvie. Seems that last time he got out of pokey he made some serious money. Anti-Gangs Unit says this was around the time they got rumors he was into dealing guns. Also a spell when he took little brother away from the kids' home and brought him up on his own in Florence-Graham.'

Angie took it all in. 'How old would Winston have been then?'

'Seventeen.'

'That's too young to care for a minor. Anyway, with his record, he would never have got custody.'

'I don't think Winston Hendry was the type who ever asked permission. He'd have just grabbed the kid and vanished. Social workers would have looked for a day, maybe two, then given up. You know the shit they have to deal with out in South Central.'

'Same shit as ours, just earlier in the chain. Tell me more about Warren as a youngster.'

Chips checked his notes. 'Well, he was no school genius. His grades were all average or less, except in drama and computer studies, where he was up there with the best of them.'

Angie smiled at the irony. 'Well, he's certainly put both of those to good use, as we know to our cost. Computers would have been his escape from reality, and I'm pretty sure there was no shortage of drama in his parentless upbringing.'

'I'm sure you're right. The drama training almost gave him a big break – Hollywood style. He won a scholarship to LACHSA, the performing arts school. Dropped out in year three of a four-year course. I spoke to the Dean and he says up to then Hendry was one of the stars of their Tech Track program.'

'What's Tech Track?'

'It's a course all performers have to do. Behind the scenes stuff

– special effects, costumes, scenery, lighting and videography. Our guy really shone at this.'

'Course he did. Explains all the damned costumes and skin color changes.'

'What now?'

'I have to let all of this sink in, then work out how he's likely to behave. Dramatic types tend to be highly strung but organized. They rehearse, they plan, they learn their lines and then they perform.'

'That's certainly our UNSUB.'

'It is.' A theory was beginning to form in Angie's mind. 'What's really interesting, though, is that it was always *Winston* who was in the limelight; *he* was the star of the street and Warren just kind of played a cameo part in life out there. Only when older brother went to the pen did his sibling feel compelled to step up and perform.'

Chips knew she was heading to something. 'You think that date of arrest is significant?'

'Might be. Go back to Gangs. Get me more on Winston's criminality. Where and when he was first and last arrested, any crime scene locations named in his charge sheet, courts he was tried at, station houses he got held in. See if there are any previous fits to JZ's Saloon, Sun Western or the Strawberry Fields massacres.'

Chips typed notes. 'I'm on it.' He glanced at a Post-it he'd written on. 'By the way, McDonald's been down looking for you.'

'Damn.'

'Actually, she was really nice. She was asking how you were. Said she just wanted to touch base when you have a moment.'

'You sure that was McDonald?'

'Yep, I'm sure. She still scolded me for how I was dressed.'

Chapter 169

Ruis took two phone calls as he was driven in an SKU van over to East 87th Street, the last known address of Warren Alexander Hendry.

The first told him that a street patrol had found Januk Dudek's car parked at a West Side hotel after a bellboy noticed one of its tires was blown and they tried to trace the owner among their guests. From what Tess had said, Dudek wasn't the kind of guy who could afford to stay at joints like that.

The second was more serious.

Nathan Payne was dead.

He'd died on the way to hospital.

Ruis thought about calling Angie straight away and then realized he was just being selfish. His motive was solely to get it over with. On reflection, he decided to let her get through today if possible, then break the news in the morning.

He was still in a daze when he got out of the vehicle a block away from Hendry's building – the address Dominic Cleere had given him.

SKU officer Todd Garcetti met him at the curb. 'The guys are all plotted out, boss. They're ready to go when you are.'

Ruis walked to the back of an obs van. He checked the monitor. Garcetti's team was deployed around the doorways, stairwells, fire exits and main entrance. No way was this sonofabitch getting out. 'Okay,' he said to his colleague, 'do it.'

Garcetti bent over the mobile comms box and called Hendry's landline.

It rang for a long time then a male voice answered the withheld number with a hint of suspicion in his tone. 'Hello?'

'Hi,' said the SKU man breezily. 'We're from the State Lottery, we're looking for a Mr Warren Hendry.'

The caller hung up.

Garcetti looked towards Ruis who'd been listening on an earwig. 'You want me to re-call?'

'No. We can't afford the time delay.' He clicked his radio. 'Team Two, go. Go. Go.'

Seconds later, a sledgehammer hit the front door.

The big slab of wood held.

The hammer man hit it again.

It still held.

'Fucker's reinforced,' he announced, red-faced.

'Step away.' Another SKU man leveled his shotgun at the lock and blasted it twice.

It booted in.

Three black-clad operatives burst through the opening.

A man turned and ran, in terror.

'FBI! Stop or we'll shoot.'

He ducked around the corner.

They followed.

A teenager was at the sink, frantically trying to flush a bag of dope. His hollow-eyed girlfriend was cowering in the corner, face buried beneath her hands and pulled-up knees.

Ruis watched it all on a monitor in the truck. He turned away in despair. There was only one more place for them to hit.

Warren Hendry's work depot.

Chapter 170

South Los Angeles

The list Chips sent Angie was a long one.

Fortunately, most of the locations were within a short distance of each other.

She started in Watts, an unimpressive poverty-blighted settlement overshadowed by the extraordinary, Gaudíesque Watts Towers. Even though she'd seen the giant, weirdly Gothic spires thousands of times, she still couldn't help but stare up at them. They'd been built by a local artist back in the early to mid-twentieth century and rose almost a hundred feet. The twisting metal girders were encrusted with broken bottles, tiles, metal and stones that had been found discarded on neighborhood streets.

It was also the spot where Winston Hendry first got arrested as a juvenile.

He and his buddies had clashed with a Latino gang and as a result a Hispanic boy ended up hospitalized with stab wounds.

Watts was certainly a tough hood.

During the day it was filled with locals working hard to make a living. At night, the place crackled with tension. Race. Poverty. Gang grudges. They were all incendiary ingredients that got banged together far too hard and far too frequently.

Beneath the shadows of the defiant towers stood a well-frequented arts center, a place Angie was certain Hendry junior would have whiled away time in.

She spent almost half an hour asking around and drawing blanks. Angie drove away feeling she'd missed something.

Her next stops were schools in Florence-Graham that the Hendry boys had attended. She spent another thirty minutes walking the sprawling blacktopped grounds where they'd played and visiting the worn outbuildings of 96th Street Elementary School where Winston had attended the odd lesson and Warren had shown flashes of promise.

Again no one was saying anything of value. The name Hendry seemed to pull down a curtain of silence.

Angie checked the long strips of nearby wasteland that contained the power pylons and dense trees that ran along the ironically named Success Avenue. She found boltholes for the homeless but nothing sophisticated enough to meet the high-tech needs of the man she was hunting.

Close to exhaustion, she bought a bottle of water and a bar of candy from a shop off Firestone Boulevard. It came as no surprise that the storekeeper knew nothing about Warren or Winston.

Her cellphone showed two missed calls from Sandra McDonald. When she dialed back she was relieved to hear a no-nonsense voice message. 'This is McDonald, leave a message, thanks.'

'Hi, this is Angie Holmes. Really sorry I missed your calls. I'm still out of the office. I guess you're at dinner so I won't disturb you by calling again. Hopefully I'll catch you in the morning. Bye.'

She took a final swig of water and set off to finish her list.

It was creeping towards half-past eight and she knew Warren Hendry was due to start his shift at Cleereroads in just over thirty minutes' time.

Angie looked up at the sky. The light was fading fast and with it her hopes.

Chapter 171

The local Cleereroads depot lay near the cross of the Santa Monica Harbor and Rosa Parks freeways. Ruis Costas checked his watch as he walked through the gates of the local depot.

He passed a sign marked INCINERATOR and a row of E Wagons that would soon be filling up with road kill from LA's highways and byways. Alongside him was Tess Holderbach, the redhead who'd turned over Januk Dudek's apartment. Her squad members and others from Team Two were slipping into covert positions around the outside of the unit.

As he entered the building, Ruis spotted a cleaner in a blue apron pushing a mop kart. He shouted to her, 'Hey, we're looking for the supervisor's office.'

The young Polish woman turned and fingered back a fall of black hair that had escaped from a slide. 'You police?'

'It doesn't matter who we are,' answered Tess. 'Where's your boss?'

The woman swayed a little. 'Have you found that *niechlug*?'

Ruis frowned. 'What?'

'*Pee-eg.* Swine.' Her face flushed and she breathed alcohol fumes all over them. '*Pan Dudek, jest matkojebca – jest dupek, jest—*'

'In English,' demanded Tess.

The cleaner put her hands on her hips and pushed her face forward to make a point. 'He is a *motherfucker*. An asshole. A dork. A cu—'

'Okay, okay.' Ruis cut her off. 'I get the picture. Not Dudek, we're not after him, we want to talk to Mr Hendry.'

She slapped her ass. 'Dudek – he always touching. Always. *Always*. *Swinia. Pokurwiony. Jebak.*'

522

'She's drunk,' said Tess.

'Thank you, *detective*,' quipped Ruis.

The woman swayed again. 'Hendry – Hendry *jest mała mysz.*'

'*English!*' barked Tess.

'*Mouse* – he small mouse.'

A man rounded the corner. His dark eyes fell on the two strangers talking to the cleaner. Then he saw the guns on their belts.

He turned and ran.

Ruis sprinted after him. 'FBI. We're armed agents. Stop or I'll fire.'

The guy speeded up. He pulled over a staff locker as he turned a corner.

Ruis hurdled it.

The man zipped right, through an opening and banged a door shut.

Ruis slid to a halt and twisted the handle.

It was locked.

'Fuck.' He stepped back and heel-kicked a panel near the lock.

The frame shook but the door didn't open.

Tess appeared two yards behind him shouting into her radio.

Ruis hit the locked wood with his shoulder and enough anger to roll a truck.

The door popped.

The guy was halfway through the window.

'Stop the fuck where you are!' Ruis pulled his gun and fired into the wall above the window.

The guy stopped. He froze half in and half out of the small window, covered in brick dust and plaster.

Ruis grabbed him by the seat of his pants and pulled him back into the room.

He flipped him over and knew right away it wasn't Hendry. 'What's your name?'

The man was Hispanic, late thirties and petrified. 'Manuel Fuenta. I am the day supervisor.'

'Of course you fucking well are.' Ruis abandoned his wristlock in dismay. 'What in Christ's name were you running for?'

Fuenta didn't answer.

Back in the day, Tess had worked Immigration and recognized the look of despair on his face. 'How's your paperwork, Manuel? Is it going to get you home tonight, or a one-way ticket across the border?'

His eyes gave her the answer she'd expected.

Ruis put a hand down and hauled the guy upright. 'Tonight's your lucky night, buddy. Sit down and tell me about Warren Hendry, starting with when you expect him to arrive and how you can help us get our hands on him.'

Chapter 172

Skid Row, LA

Shooter hauled Mike Hanrahan's body into the john and left it propped in a corner. It wasn't a long-term answer. Not even a mid-term one. But for now, out of sight constituted out of mind. At least it would have done if he hadn't been almost out of his own mind with anxiety.

Fear – so absent from his early endeavors – had raised its ugly head.

It wasn't just that he was afraid of being caught – though that was palpable enough – it was his fear of failing. Even in his own surmised death, he struggled to live up to what he believed was expected of him.

'You know what I did for you.'

Winston had said those words two days before his execution.

It had been in a visitor's room off Death Row and he'd leaned over the table he'd been manacled to. His stare had bored through Warren's skull. His voice had been so deep and intense it had made his heart rumble.

'What I did, I did for you, bro. Jus' remember, I sacrificed my life for your life.'

The words had chilled him at the time and brought shivers ever since. Winston had gone further. Had told him the real reason he'd shot the other gang member. And once he'd listened, Warren knew it was only right that he avenge his execution.

Shooter felt his world was running at two speeds. His internal clock was painfully slow. It was like being lost on a wild trail without a compass on a hot summer's day. Externally, everything was uncontrollably fast, beyond the speed of his reactions and instincts.

He went back and sat in the room he called Death Row, leaned against the wiped-down wall, and spoke to his brother's photograph. 'I did this for you, bro.' He waved a hand at the still blood-wet photographs of the people he'd killed. 'I gave your jurors life sentences of pain. I executed their loved ones for you, man. Blood for blood.' He squatted on his haunches and dropped sweat between his knees. 'Blood for blood.'

Shooter stared at the floor for what seemed like eternity then looked up and locked eyes on the only human being who had ever loved and supported him.

The puzzle of life and death lay between them. Its pieces scattered by the winds of fortune. He'd thought salvation lay in the pictures of slaughtered victims pinned to the wall. There and in the faces of those he still planned to murder.

Only his plans were coming apart.

He was burned out. The pressure to complete his task, to fulfill his promise, was eating him like a disease, sucking his strength and health.

Shooter stood wearily and walked towards his room full of old clothes. A dozen disguises hung on the rails in front of him. They'd been amassed to facilitate his escape from the homicides. But now the urge was different. He longed to slip on the rags of Old Joe and permanently disappear into the cardboard commune of Skid Row. He could fit in there. Nothing would be asked of him. No expectations. No responsibilities. No worries. He could be Old Joe until the heat had died down. Perhaps forever. It really wasn't such a bad idea.

Through the open doorway an alarm sounded.

Not a security alarm. A mundane clock alert. It was time for him to shower. To get ready for work. To pretend again.

Or not.

Chapter 173

South Los Angeles

Angie was done. Tired out. Desperate to go home.

Chips had kept adding to the list of places that might have had significance for Winston but she was starting to doubt she'd get through them all.

Still to be checked was the now-empty church hall the gangster had hidden in during an escape from Juvie; the old factory building he'd run into during his final shoot-out with the cops, and various lockups in Compton and Florence-Graham where he'd stashed his guns and explosives.

The Anti-Gangs Unit said Winston had been known to have several stashes all over LA and they suspected they'd never found them all. The intel made sense to Angie. She presumed that's where Warren had got his range of weapons.

A glance at the clock in the Jeep told her it was a quarter past the time when Hendry was supposed to have started his shift. She didn't dare call Ruis and pester him. With any luck he might be right in the middle of the arrest.

Instead, she got out and stretched. A walk would keep her awake. Maybe get rid of the heartburn that was developing from sitting too long. Her stomach felt bloated and she worried about how all the physical stress might be affecting the baby. She gently massaged her tummy and gazed at the LA skyline. The old city looked as tired and beat up as she felt. The sun had lost its youthful morning glow and was anemically bowing out for the evening, leaving only shadowy traces of a spent day.

Time ticked slowly on and she decided she had to at least text Ruis. He could always ignore it. The message was simple: ANYTHING YET?

To her surprise, her phone rang almost instantly.

Ruis sounded lower than the sun. 'Hi, how you doing?'

'Okay.'

He got to the point. 'I know you're desperate for an update but we've got nothing here, otherwise I'd have called you.' His voice was monotone. 'We're just sat like dumbasses at Hendry's workplace and a guy who's apparently never late for his shift is – no surprise – late for his shift.'

She grasped at straws. '*Never* late?'

'That's what the jerk of a daytime guy says. Claims Warren's *always* on time.' He took a beat and decided to break the news. 'Angie, I'm real sorry to tell you this – Nate Payne died on the way to hospital.'

For a moment she couldn't talk.

Her mind filled with memories of Ruis stopping her from entering the house and the harrowing calls from Chips, telling her how the husband was bleeding out and couldn't survive much longer.

'Angie, I'm very sorry.'

'I know.' She sounded sad and deadbeat. 'It's not your fault, Ruis. You didn't shoot him, so don't go blaming yourself for this.'

'Yeah, well, I kind of do – and you know why.'

'Then don't. There's no point. You aren't a clairvoyant and you made a tough call.'

'Thanks.' His tone changed. 'We've got movement in the yard. Looks like he's coming.'

The line went dead.

Chapter 174

Angie drove with mixed emotions. Sadness at Payne's death. Elation that Warren had turned up.

She pushed the gate open and looked around the abandoned yard that spread in front of her. Not that there was much to look at. This was one of those patches of earth that progress had left behind. Greens and yellows of thick weeds busted through blacktop that once hosted delivery vehicles and the hurrying feet of workers. Not any more. Windows were shuttered. Roller doors rusted and bolted.

Her phone rang again. She felt a jolt of excitement.

The display said it was Chips, not Ruis. Nevertheless, he sounded excited. 'Where are you?'

She was desperate for news. 'You just talk to Ruis?'

'No. Where are you?'

'Skid Row, the old shoe factory address you gave me.'

'He's there, Angie.'

'What?'

'Cyber Squad finally got a fix on his computer. Warren's online and he's in the factory. You're just yards away from him.'

She felt her heart quicken. Instinctively, her hand reached for her gun. 'You're absolutely certain, Chips?'

'As much as I can be without a visual. He tweeted only a minute ago.'

She walked up close to the side of the dilapidated building so she couldn't be seen. 'What'd it say?'

'Decision Time.'

'That's all?'

'Only those words. Spelled and spaced properly.'

'Sounds like he's refocused.' Angie looked up and around for security cameras. She couldn't see any from where she was but she was damned certain they were there. 'This is what we're going to do. Call for back-up, Chips. Call Ruis. Call Crawford. Call everyone you know with a gun and do it quick.'

He knew what was on her mind. 'Angie, wait – don't do anything crazy. I'll get people to you – fast as I can. Please, just hang off 'til they get there. Okay?'

'No, not okay.' She checked the magazine of her Glock. 'Nate Payne died earlier today because I was made to wait. Not again. No one else dies tonight except the motherfucker who deserves to. It ends now, Chips, and on my terms.'

She hung up before he could reply.

Angie's heart was hammering. She shut her eyes and breathed slowly. It was vital she cleared her mind and focused. A factory unit like this would have several exit points. No way was this bastard going to slip out and vanish like he'd done before.

She was going to have to go in. Take him by surprise. Contain him.

All her FBI combat training rewound in her mind. How to go through an open door, adjust quickly to darkness, sweep the space in front, check behind, take no chances. Kill if necessary.

She took one last pause and began to walk the outer wall.

The roller door was locked. A side door rusted and closed. Cobwebs over the corner said it hadn't been opened for ages. She moved on and accidentally kicked an old Bud bottle. It rolled forever. Sounded as loud as a truck of glass being emptied. Angie took it as a timely reminder to concentrate on her feet as well as the gun in her hands.

The next door had been freshly fitted. It was white metal and clean. Sunk into the wall at shoulder height was a numerical keypad.

Her heart sank.

Ten digits meant there could be a zillion combinations of numbers to enter. Often, it was a sequence of four. She tried zero, zero, zero, zero – the usual factory default. There was no satisfying buzz.

Angie examined the metal edges. A stone had caught in the corner of the doorplate and it hadn't closed properly. She worked her fingertips in and pried open the gap.

Blackness.

Alarm bells rang. Not in the building but in her head.

There was a good chance the door had been left open deliberately. Chips had said Hendry had traced the fake FBI server to the safe house; it followed that he might also have worked out that the Feds were behind Judge Elysia.

She raised her gun and knew she could be about to enter a trap. For a moment, she felt like she was turning into Ruis. Finding textbook reasons not to do her job. Not to stop the murderous piece of shit before he killed again.

Angie counted to three, pulled the door and rolled inside. She kept low to avoid body shots and was relieved when none came. She flattened out on the floor and stared into the black tunnel ahead.

Music ran like a rat towards her.

Distant strains of hard, heavy rock. Somewhere off to the side a TV blared. No, not one. Several. News channels, turned up, different anchors and reporters speaking over one another.

Angie edged forward on knees and elbows, her gun pointing up at what would be gut- or heart-height of anyone stood in the shadows.

The music was now clear enough for her to make out Marilyn Manson singing about being a bullet heading into the heart of God.

A male newsreader reported the shooting of a middle-aged couple.

The door creaked shut behind her. She'd heard nothing outside, meaning the inside had been soundproofed. The space was confined. Tight. The big unit paneled out in a strange way.

Scenery.

Hendry had used his stage skills to create a long, narrow passage with various rooms off.

There was a burst of white light.

Angie edged up to a wall. Swept the gun left then right.

No one was there.

Across the floor glistened swirls and deltas of bloody footprints. Marks of sneakers. A history of going back and forth. And dragging something.

On the wall were four bloody ticks.

One for each victim.

She heard herself breathing. Panting like a dog.

Angie shut her mouth. Drew air in, long and slow. Calmed down like she'd been taught at Quantico.

She stayed low, raised the gun and crept round the corner. Her finger stayed curled around the Glock's trigger. The weapon never more than a hair's weight away from being fired.

There was a door to her left.

She got to her feet, rushed over and pushed it open.

The Glock swept the air as her eyes took in a washroom. Grey. Cold. Old. Three stalls. A shower in the corner. Cracked mirrors over a run of old basins.

In the last silvered glass she spotted the legs of a man. Adrenaline surged.

Hendry.

She swung left and was about to fire.

Then she saw the shattered skull. The matted blood. The lifeless torso. Angie leaned back against the wall while she rode the full shock of seeing the dead young man.

She had no doubt now of where she was. This was the end of the line. The place she might die in. Killed by the same monster that killed Jake.

Anger gripped her hand. Fortified her nerve. Gave her resolve.

If she was going to die here, she wouldn't be the only one.

The coward had caught Jake unawares.

That wasn't going to happen to her.

It took Angie less than twenty seconds to settle her breathing. She opened the washroom door and slowly and silently slid back into the passageway.

Five feet of corridor led to another door. Seeped around the foot of the jamb was blood-colored water. It shimmered. Wet and fresh from where someone had cleaned. She figured it was linked to the corpse she'd seen in the washroom. There had been too little mess in the john for him to have been capped in there.

Her breathing shortened again. More panting. No time to gain control.

Angie saw a hand-made sign dangling in front of her. It said: DEATH ROW.

She pushed the door open.

Everything registered at once.

There was no body. But there had been a shooting in here. The walls had been wiped down and were stained pink. She saw candles on a shelf, throwing cheap light onto nearby photographs. Pictures of men, women and children. Grouped, not alone. Faces familiar. Now she recognized them. The poor souls slaughtered at the mall and in the Strawberry Fields. The dead banker.

Jake.

Angie struggled to breathe.

Jake.

She froze.

Her love. The father of her unborn child. Her future.

She turned. Saw another face. Familiar. Dead.

Winston Hendry.

The music stopped. The TVs stopped. All sound was muted.

The lights went out.

Complete darkness.

Angie moved on her toes. Facts sunk in. Awful truths. She'd walked into a trap and now it *was* sprung. As she'd guessed, the front door hadn't been left unlocked accidentally. The Cyber Squad hadn't got lucky and broken Hendry's IP mask; he'd removed the shield so they could trace him.

He'd wanted this confrontation.

He'd made it happen.

Then so be it. She was more than ready to face him.

She turned the corner of the corridor and glimpsed a shower of red spotlight. It came from up ahead, its source hidden around yet another doglegged corridor.

As Angie edged along the black paneling, she made out white-painted theater signs: STALLS – CIRCLES – ACTORS ONLY – QUIET PLEASE.

The boards ended.

Her fate lay inches away.

Angie clung to the last vestige of cover that separated her from the intense red light glowing in what she guessed was an open area at the center of the old factory.

Laughter tumbled from hidden speakers, then faded into a hiss of static before a male voice announced, 'Come on. Come on. I'm waiting for you.'

Angie didn't move.

'You're on camera.' He sounded bored now. 'Have been since you did that fancy entrance through my front door. Now come on round and don't be shy.'

Angie stepped out, the gun held in a two-handed firing stance. Light was in her eyes but she could see the floor was boarded black and the walls painted green. On a raised platform three feet high was a high-backed throne chair upholstered in red leather with brass studs.

Sitting on it, bathed in the bloodlight of an overhead spot, was Warren Hendry.

His legs were spread wide and he slouched in an open white shirt, baggy blue jeans but no shoes and socks. Beside his bare feet was an empty half-bottle of vodka and a freshly opened replacement. America's most wanted man was half-cut and sat before her unarmed.

'Cool gun,' he said, picking something from his lap. 'My brother did good business with those.' He lifted his right hand and showed her a cellphone. 'But we live in an age when the phone is mightier than the bullet.' He waggled it. 'No really, it is. Take another step closer and I'll use it to blow us both up. As I'm pretty sure you've guessed, I don't really care about living any longer.'

Angie's eyes fixed on the cellphone. The guy had blown up a memorial service and outwitted Chips. She had every reason to believe he could do what he said.

He studied her curiously, moistened his drunk-dried mouth with a swallow and asked, 'Tell me – are *you* Elysia, or just one of her lackeys?'

'I'm an FBI profiler –' she inched closer – 'so yeah, I'm Elysia, but I'm a fuck of a lot more than that.' She had to stop her finger pulling the trigger. 'The agent you killed was to be my husband.'

Hendry's eyes flickered with amusement. 'My, how terrible. Still, these things do happen.'

She edged forward.

'Stop!' He raised the phone again.

Angie stayed her ground. 'He was the father of my unborn child.'

There was no reply, no concern, just a look of curiosity.

'Did you hear me?'

Hendry nodded. 'Yes, I heard you. It makes what's going to happen all the more interesting.' He turned the phone round and examined the screen. 'You can also make calls with this, disarm the security and play songs and films.' He looked at her with disappointment. 'You're nothing like I imagined. Nothing.' He reached down for the vodka bottle without his eyes leaving her, raised it to his mouth and took a long swig.

She waited for him to cough from the heat of the alcohol but he didn't.

Hendry wiped his mouth with the back of a hand and added, 'At first, I thought you were real, Elysia, that you *actually* understood me. Then I saw your so-called home in Watts and I knew. Those cheap lights on timer switches, coming on in the dead of night to make it look like someone was at home. Stupid!'

'As stupid as all this?' She rolled her head to take in his stage and lights. 'Was that tragic drama you acted out really necessary? You're bright and smart – why couldn't you have vocalized your anger over your brother's execution, attacked the politicians and the system verbally instead of with violence?'

He waved down her argument. 'Lots of reasons.'

'Tell me one.' Angie was happy to listen. It burned time. Increased the chance of back-up arriving before the situation got any worse.

'What you won't understand is that he did it all for me.'

'Did what for you?'

'There was this piece of gang shit who tried to kidnap me.' He fell silent. Looked pained. Reflective. 'Winston . . .' He dried up on saying his brother's name. 'He'd refused to supply them with guns and they said they'd teach him a lesson for dissing them. They even told him what they were going to do. Said he'd then have to give them what they wanted. Only they fucked up. I saw them coming on some webcams I'd rigged at the place we lived and I got out. Later, when I showed Winston the footage, he just went crazy.'

'And this was when he gunned down a mother and child as well.'

'Collateral damage.' He shrugged. 'Like the kids and teachers I shot in the strawberry fields, like the little dirtbag I sent to the memorial service with the explosives.'

Angie feigned interest. 'What was with that? More innocents killed – why? To match Winston's sins?'

'You really want to know?'

'Yeah, I do. It's my job to understand these things.'

'With the fruit pickers, I just needed the practice.' He raised the phone like a gun and pretended to shoot her with it. 'I wanted to see if I could hit people when they were moving. Whether I could keep my nerve when I went for the real target in the mall.'

'That's all?' Angie felt maternal outrage. 'You killed a child and teachers because you needed shooting practice?'

'Yeah, that's about it. And before you ask, the street kid with the bomb was just gang scum, from the same trash Winston wasted. He had no future. I just stopped him growing older and fucking up other people's lives.'

'You're empty. Just a shell. There's not even a shred of humanity left inside you.'

Hendry laughed. 'You're right, Mrs FBI lady, absolutely right. Garbage guys emptied my soul out years ago. I thought if I made all of those jurors suffer for the injustice of the system, then I'd find some peace. The more I killed, the more my debt to my brother would be paid.'

Angie sneaked a glance at her watch. Almost fifteen minutes had passed since she'd spoken to Chips. Since he'd promised back-up. Now she had no option but to keep talking. 'Bad debts owed to bad people never get settled. But I guess you know that. And the booze you are hitting says you're off track – behind with your payments, so to speak.'

'I wouldn't be,' he snapped. 'But for the grunt you've been screwing. If he hadn't intervened, with his boy soldier ignorance and his fuckbrain speechifying, I'd have stuck to my plan – to my list.'

'Be smart, Warren, and shut up now.'

He could tell he'd touched a nerve. 'Do you want to see lover-boy again? I can show you him.' He raised an eyebrow and smiled. 'I can show you him like you've never seen before.' He swiped a finger across the screen of the phone and the recessed speakers hissed with static.

Angie's nerves prickled.

The green-screened walls all around her filled with projected moving pictures.

Angie put her hand to her mouth.

Jake was everywhere. All around her. Staring at her and walking towards her.

She felt dizzy.

He was outside his apartment. Half a smile on his face as he peered into a light and tried to make out who was behind it.

Angie could hear his footsteps in high-volume surround sound. Then, even louder, deathly clumps of the man behind the camera, about to kill him.

Angie felt the last of her resolve crack. 'Stop this fucking tape.' She thrust her Glock towards him. 'Or so help me, I will fucking shoot you.'

Giant Jakes crowded in on her. The hand that so often had held hers loomed large in frame as he shielded his eyes and shouted towards the light. 'Hey, buddy, enough's enough.' Angie watched in horror as Jake stepped forwards.

A burst of gunfire dropped the father of her unborn child to his knees.

Angie let out a primordial noise, an unearthly sound somewhere between a high scream and a deep cry.

A second burst of bullets erupted in the speakers.

Tears ran down Angie's face. 'You motherfucking bastard.'

On the screens the camera tilted. A voice behind the lens said, 'Dead or alive, Mr Grunt?' There was a beat of silence before it added, 'I choose *dead*.'

Angie felt the gun in her hand shift up and jerk suddenly.

One shot. Two shots.

Blood spurted from Hendry's skull. His eyes said his brain hadn't yet registered what had happened.

Angie saw his hands twitch.

There was a sudden boom.

Even before everything went black, before the debris flew and the pain raced through her nervous system, she knew what had happened.

He'd triggered the bombs.

Chapter 175

Skid Row, LA

A succession of blasts ripped apart the old shoe factory.
The sequence of explosions cleaved a moat into the surrounding
yard. It blew away the flimsy metal and plasterboard walls. Left a
swirling wall of fire and smoke.

Ruis Costas and his team were a block away when the quiet of the
evening was broken by thunderclaps and the sky filled with rising
clouds of smoke and debris.

He jumped from Tess Holderbach's ops truck before she'd even
braked it. Raced across the road and clambered into the treacle pit of
smoldering blacktop. Bomb-felled trees were on fire. Dozens of shocked
car alarms screeched like alien birds as he scaled the slipping rubble
and shouted, 'Angie! Angie!'

Ruis knew all about the risk of exploding gas pipes, fuel containers,
maybe further booby-traps as he pulled away timbers and steel
supports. But the caution he'd shown at Nate Payne's house had gone
now.

The blasts had turned the old unit into a charred Jenga. Wooden beams,
wallboards, joists, planks and sheets of metal were piled precariously
on top of each other.

'Angie!'

This was survivable. That's the lie he told himself as he shifted
splintered wood and rummaged through layers of broken glass, tile
and stone.

An FBI helicopter appeared out of the darkness, a searing white searchlight crossed back and forth as it neared the blast crater. Across the debris Ruis saw Tess hauling an emergency medi-kit from the truck.

Black smoke rising into the darkening sky was batted away by the blades of the copter. Across the backstreets sirens of fire trucks drowned out the car alarms.

Through the ground dust and spread of rubble Ruis saw a flutter of pink fingers rise like stalks of exotic flowers on barren wasteland.

'Angie!'

The trembling stems curled in a deathly stoop.

Ruis scrambled over the blasted building. Pulled aside a mass of boards weighed down by dirt and asphalt.

He saw her face now. Hair matted with dust and blood. Eyes shut. There was no sign of life.

Chapter 176

A ngie had dragged the conscious world into the unconscious.
The feel of her finger flattening against the trigger guard. The
hole in Hendry's skull. Jake's falling body on the giant green screens.
All of those actions and emotions had tumbled surreally into the vortex
caused by the explosion.

She'd covered her belly, not her face. Wood had thumped her back.
Dust filled her mouth and nose. Then the blackness had swallowed her.

Unconsciousness was like an anesthetic. The chemical onslaught in
Angie's brain left her imagining she was lying on her stomach on a
towel at the beach. Jake had been astride her, bare-chested, with those
tree trunk legs of his threatening to burst his shorts. He'd been rubbing
oil on her shoulders and himself against her. She'd felt him move her
hair and kiss her ear and her neck. His hands had strayed a little too
far – just a little – before she'd grabbed his arm and pulled him down
to the sand alongside her. Their eyes had locked and their mouths
found each other. Her head swam with the dizziness of his touch.

She struggled for breath.

He was kissing her too hard. Too long. She had to break free.

'Angie.'

She coughed dust.

Fingers touched her face.

Ruis Costas wiped dirt from her eyes. Unseen hands pulled rubble
and boards off her body.

'Are you okay?' Ruis dragged things away. Blood dripped from his
grazed knuckles. 'Are you all right?'

She didn't know. She was half in one world and half in another.

Angie put a hand to her stomach. It felt wet. She pulled it away and looked at her fingers.

Red.

Blood red.

Her eyes widened in horror.

The baby.

Her thoughts were only of her and Jake's child.

People around her pulled off the last of the boards.

Then she saw it.

Parts of Warren Hendry's blasted torso lay against her. She got to her feet and scraped his remains from the front of her clothes.

Ruis and Tess supported her as she wobbled. She felt queasy. Her brain ran mental checks. She remembered it all now. Hendry. Her shots. His phone. The blast.

Now she did the physical checks. Fingers touched skin and bone, tested vital areas with gentle pressure, moved tentatively over her body like a scan. Her lip was busted. Her cheek cut.

But her stomach was unhurt.

The baby was okay.

Angie managed a smile. 'I'm fine. *We* are fine. Now get me the hell out of here.'

Chapter 177

One Week Later

Arlington National Cemetery, Virginia

A ngie had dressed in funereal blacks. A new mid-length skirt and matching jacket constituted an outfit she'd vowed she'd never wear. Her hair was pinned up, beneath a modest black hat with lace veil, and, for good measure, dark shades.

In the end, she'd agreed that respects had to be paid. Traditions observed. The Marines, the FBI brass and even the members of his own unit had all wanted Jake honored at Arlington, the vast six-hundred-acre cemetery that was the final resting place for thousands of veterans, astronauts, presidents and even fighters in the Civil War.

It was, they all said, the only place a hero should be.

Chips was similarly suited. He wore a white shirt and black tie for the first time in his life and stayed glued to Angie's side. Her arm looped through his, both of them supporting each other in equal measure.

The sky was cloudless and the sun shone hot and high above the canopies of the centuries-old trees that shared the green rolling hills of the cemetery with tens of thousands of white, cream and black tombstones.

Ruis, Crawford Dixon and even McDonald had all been sympathetic to Angie's wishes, and in the end they'd gone along with the unorthodox accommodation that she'd asked for. Dixon had fixed it with the committee at Arlington that Jake could be cremated privately in Los Angeles, and then a full military service with honors held at the national cemetery, complete with gun carriages and salute.

Angie had personally brought his ashes over on the flight with her and surrendered them to cemetery staff. They had then been placed in a special container that fitted inside what looked like a normal body-sized casket, covered with the American flag. It was a regular practice, and sadly one used by many veterans blown up in war zones.

Joe Lamotta was one of the eight Marines who marched crisply alongside the wooden-wheeled caisson as it trundled across the cemetery blacktop led by six white horses. Whatever secret Lamotta was keeping from her didn't matter today. Nothing mattered except Jake's memory.

A bugle sounded. The Marines moved as one and took their corners.

The casket rose from the carriage and Angie's heart sank.

More than a hundred people from the FBI had flown over to show their respects and most of them were fighting back tears. The President and the Vice President had sent wreaths and private messages of sympathy that Angie hadn't even opened.

A full military band struck up. The soldiers took a synchronized step forwards. The final slow journey to the Columbarium had begun. Chips tightened his link on Angie's arm and she gratefully hung on to the only man left in the world that she could truly say she loved.

With every step, her heart beat as deeply as the military drum booming bass across the hillsides.

Everything became blurred.

The music, the prayers, the dour-faced military chaplain, the staring crowd. They were all smeared across the moment in Technicolor numbness.

The bearers reached the niche wall and lowered the casket onto a waiting plinth.

Angie's eyes roamed the vast slab of grey fieldstone. It ran for almost half a mile and contained more than five thousand plaque-fronted recesses where the urns of veterans, and later their spouses, were deposited. Pigeon holes in symbolic eternity.

This wasn't what Jake had wanted.

She knew it now more than ever.

Crawford Dixon stepped forward and slid open the end of the casket. The other men moved back in unison and saluted.

The section chief began to fold the flag.

Angie let go of Chips's arm. This was her time. There was no shake of her hands, no hint of uncertainty as she lifted the fine china urn that magnetized everyone's eyes. She turned and slowly placed it in the tight space of the niche.

A single bugle sounded 'Taps'. The traditional end to US military funerals. A haunting, fading note floated into the cornflower blue sky and slowly disappeared like a dematerializing spirit.

Then came a heartbreaking silence.

Angie had asked that no final words were said. She wanted only total quiet. Sixty seconds of peace for people to remember Jake in their own private way.

The minute and collective memories of his life ticked by.

Smack on sixty seconds, a volley of shots burst from the seven-strong funereal firing party.

Three times their fire filled the sky.

Angie closed her eyes and felt them fill with tears. There was no more hanging on. The sound of gunfire was too acute a reminder of how he'd died.

Chips gripped her arm.

Crawford finished folding the flag and handed it to her.

It was almost over.

Soon she'd be in private and able to cry her eyes out.

Chapter 178

A small reception was held after the inurnment. The type of somber event where people instantly split into small groups and, wine glass in hand, shared respectful reminiscences. No one laughed too loud or drank too much. Angie observed the restrained behavior as she bravely did the rounds, thanking people for coming.

Sandra McDonald broke away from a cluster of FBI directors and caught her attention. 'I just wanted to congratulate you. I thought you handled the ceremony with great grace and dignity.'

Angie was touched. She and her boss had certainly had their differences but recently the AD had shown herself to be hugely supportive. 'Thank you.'

'You're very welcome.' McDonald took her hand and squeezed it reassuringly. 'People remember these kinds of ceremonies. It helps them have a sense of closure. I know for you it will take a lot longer, but you *will* find it.'

'I hope so.'

She let go of her hand. 'When you've rested and had some private time, come and see me. You made some big calls on the Hendry case and got them right when others, including myself, didn't. That's impressive. I'm hoping your future plans include staying with the unit after the baby.'

'I haven't thought that far.'

'You don't have to. Not for now. I just want you to know I value you and the special skills you have.'

'That's appreciated.'

'Good.' McDonald gave her a respectful nod as she prepared to depart. 'And I hope today's "other arrangements" go well.'

Angie stiffened.

McDonald smiled knowingly. 'Crawford told me. He had to. And don't worry, you have my tacit approval as well as his.' She drifted back to the group.

Chips had been hovering anxiously. Now he stepped forward with some urgency. 'The car's waiting – we really need to go.'

'I'm ready.' She put down the glass of water she'd been drinking and headed to the coat room. Their exit came as no surprise. They'd been saying goodbyes for twenty minutes and everyone knew they were catching an evening flight back to LA. Most people understood that a lonely hotel room in a strange town was no place to spend the night after you've buried a loved one.

Outside, a cool breeze blew in off the Potomac and shook the leaves on the trees on Memorial Drive. A spotless, black Crown Vic idled by the curb. A uniformed driver got out to open the back doors for them.

'Angie.' The call came from Ruis.

She turned and was glad to see him. 'I looked to say goodbye but couldn't find you.'

'Call of nature,' he explained. 'Even at military funerals they happen.'

She smiled. 'Thanks again for making all the arrangements. For helping me see things through. I couldn't have done it without you.'

'I'll always be there for you.' He leaned forwards and kissed her cheek.

'I know you will.' She held him and hugged gratefully.

'Before you go –' his tone changed – 'you need to speak to someone. He's been waiting until now.' Ruis motioned to a man standing back in the doorway.

From the shadows, Joe Lamotta walked forward.

'Doctor Holmes.' He sounded apologetic. 'I'm sorry to come to you today but I just need one minute alone, please.'

Ruis backed off. 'Call me tomorrow?'

'I will.' She looked from the SKU man to Lamotta. 'A minute is all I have. I'm heading for a plane.'

'I know.'

Chips shouted from the other side of the waiting vehicle, 'Angie, we have to go!'

'I'll be right with you.' She walked towards Jake's former brother-in-arms, fearing another helping of platitudes. 'So, what is it that you want, Mr Lamotta?'

He turned his back to the car, reached inside his jacket and produced an envelope that had been folded in half. 'This is what Jake asked me about.' His voice was hushed but firm. 'In here are copies of official documents that confirm a war crime Corrie Chandler witnessed had been covered up.' He put them in her hand. 'Look at them, or don't look at them. The choice is yours. You know how to contact me if you want to take this further.'

She turned the envelope in her hands. 'This is what you and Jake spoke about?'

'It is. Chandler told him about the incident after he was arrested at the observatory. Jake believed it might have caused post-traumatic stress and –' he hesitated –'might have been contributory to Chandler's homicidal actions.'

She slipped the envelope beneath her jacket. 'Thank you.' She added, 'For giving me this, and for being here today for Jake.'

'It was my privilege.' He nodded and started to go.

'One thing,' she asked. 'What made you change your mind?'

He paused and blew breath. 'I got to thinking how Corrie Chandler had murdered his wife, a neighbor and had almost killed Jake. Fella like Chandler doesn't rate high on my scale of concerns. But then, I'm not like Jake. He'd clearly felt compelled to right an injustice – regardless of whom it involved or what the consequences to his own career might have been. And that *does* rate high with me. Highest of the high. Fact is, I would have dishonored the memory of a fine friend and a great man, if I hadn't given you those papers.'

'Thank you.'

He looked to Chips, peering anxiously from the car. 'Now I think you really do have to go.'

'I do.'

They managed half-smiles before they both turned and headed in opposite directions.

Angie stopped at the car and shouted back to him, 'Mr Lamotta!'
He slowed and wheeled round.

'Next time you're in LA, please call me. I'd like to know more about Jake and your years together.'

'That would be my pleasure, ma'am. My real pleasure.'

Chapter 179

Dulles Airport, Washington

The wind gusting in from the Potomac River heralded the start of a storm. The sky blackened ominously as the Boeing 757 rose from the runway and began its five-and-a-half hour, two-thousand-mile flight to LAX.

Chips and Angie had changed out of their black suits at the airport and were so exhausted they'd fallen asleep almost as soon as the big plane had leveled out.

Not for them the distractions of pre-dinner drinks, movies, snacks and enforced reading. They just wanted to shut out the world and get home.

The flight touched down fifteen minutes early.

Still tired and weary, the young researcher drove Angie's Toyota from LAX. Not back to her place. But half an hour south, to Pelican Cove and the ocean.

In the trunk were Jake's real ashes and the special candle lanterns that he'd had made in Chinatown.

Thanks to Crawford and Ruis – and latterly McDonald – Angie was about to give him the goodbye he'd dreamed of as a young soldier. Once she'd explained the letter he'd written, her senior colleagues conspired to dupe the cemetery and afford Jake a full military funeral as well as the private goodbye and send-off Angie was sure he really wanted.

Chips parked and got out.

From the trunk he carefully handed her a wicker basket that contained the lanterns, Jake's ashes, a gas lighter, flashlight and tissues. He hoped he'd thought of everything. 'Are you sure you don't want me to come?'

'I'll be fine on my own.'

Chips took his cellphone out and checked it. 'I've got a good signal here, so call if you want me to walk down and be with you. Otherwise, I'll just sit here and say my own goodbye.'

'Thanks.' Angie hugged him, flicked on the flashlight and began her final walk with Jake.

The sky was ink black and myriad stars shone like scattered white diamonds. The moon was waning but remained bright enough to cast silvery sparkles way out on breaking waves.

Angie couldn't yet see the ocean, but she could hear it down the hillside in front of her. The rhythmic crashing of waves seemed to pull her closer, as though unseen hands had taken hers and were guiding her to exactly the right spot. The noise of the tide was soothing and peaceful and with each step she increasingly felt this was a fitting place for a brave Marine to find a final resting place.

Angie knew she was approaching the junction of her past and her future. Jake had once said that every end was just a new beginning and right now those words made more sense than they had ever done.

At the foot of the hill, near the water's edge, she sat on rocks and carefully arranged the ashes in the scooped cradles of the four lanterns that would carry Jake's soul to the four corners of the compass.

Angie lit the wick of the first candle and let the strong paper sphere fill with hot air. It came alive in her hands and tussled to break free. She wasn't yet ready to let it go. Each lantern deserved its own farewell message. The young soldier that had dreamed of such an end to his existence on earth deserved the most eloquent send-off she could manage. Angie held the impatient lantern between both hands and looked at it as though it were the face of the man she loved. 'Jake, my darling, my rock, my everything, I will never forget you, not for one minute of one day. I'll always remember how you transformed my life and taught me to feel and love without fear, to grow and be the person I'd been frightened to be before I knew you. Goodbye, my darling, I will forever love you.'

Angie kissed the curve of the lantern, lifted it and let go.

It rose in the dark sky, a ball of burnished white and gold floating to the heavens.

She lit the second quickly and set it free to chase the first. 'Fly high, my sweetheart. Go to the places we never managed to get to. Look down on the mountains and the seas we would have climbed and sailed. Find the forest paths we would have walked and those quiet, hidden places we'd have sat and loved and laughed together in. Find them, my darling. Find them for us and make them our own, for when we are together again.'

The third was soon in her hands. But it was shaking. Emotion was pounding in her chest and she feared she'd fall apart before she completed this most private of rituals. Angie took a slow breath and kissed the hovering orb as it filled with warmth. 'This, my love, is to say sorry.' She struggled to go on. 'Oh, my precious man, I am *so, so* sorry that I ever doubted you, criticized you, or got angry with you. What a stupid woman I am. If I'd known how little time we'd had, then I'd have made you so much happier. Forgive me, sweetheart, that I hadn't loved you more, and learned to love you sooner.' Tears broke and she sobbed. Only the sight of the other two lanterns burning in the dark sky, hovering, seemingly waiting, gave her the strength to continue. 'Oh Jake, my darling, darling Jake, I'm so sorry for *that* night – for keeping you away from me – for being so selfish . . .' She couldn't speak now, couldn't fight the sobs as she opened her arms and let him go.

One more lantern.

She was emotionally exhausted but determined to hold it together. A look to the distant sky told her to light it quickly so it could catch the others.

Angie fumbled with the lighter. Her fingers were wet from wiping tears. It took her several desperate clicks to produce a flame.

The candle's wick was reluctant to burn. The lantern refused to fill with warm air.

It was as though the last of Jake refused to leave her.

Angie bent close to the cradle of ashes and whispered, 'This is for our baby, darling. It is our child's goodbye to you.'

Slowly the wick glowed. The lantern proudly swelled in her

trembling hands. It grew to fullness but didn't fight. There was no breeze around her. Nothing to help it rise.

Not until she kissed it. Not until her heart thumped so hard she felt she'd burst.

Then it soared.

Streaked upwards, right towards the waning moon. It stayed soldier straight. Proud and true. Just like the son she was certain she was carrying would grow up to be.

The child she would call Jake Junior.